THE NIGHT COUNTER

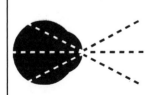

This Large Print Book carries the
Seal of Approval of N.A.V.H.

THE NIGHT COUNTER

ALIA YUNIS

THORNDIKE PRESS
A part of Gale, Cengage Learning

Detroit • New York • San Francisco • New Haven, Conn • Waterville, Maine • London

GALE
CENGAGE Learning

Thorndike Press® Large Print Basic.
The text of this Large Print edition is unabridged.
Other aspects of the book may vary from the original edition.
Set in 16 pt. Plantin.
Printed on permanent paper.

LIBRARY OF CONGRESS CATALOGING-IN-PUBLICATION DATA

Yunis, Alia.
    The night counter / by Alia Yunis.
        p. cm. — (Thorndike Press large print basic)
    ISBN-13: 978-1-4104-2260-6 (alk. paper)
    ISBN-10: 1-4104-2260-7 (alk. paper)
    1. Arab American families—Fiction. 2. Scheherazade (Legendary character)—Fiction. 3. Families—Fiction. 4. Parent and child—Fiction. 5. Mothers—Fiction. 6. Large type books. I. Title.
PS3625.U55N54 2010
813'.6—dc22   2009039681

Published in 2010 by arrangement with Shaye Areheart Books, an imprint of the Crown Publishing Group, a division of Random House, Inc.

Printed in the United States of America
1 2 3 4 5 6 7 14 13 12 11 10

To my family, especially my parents and my brother.

The Abdullah Family

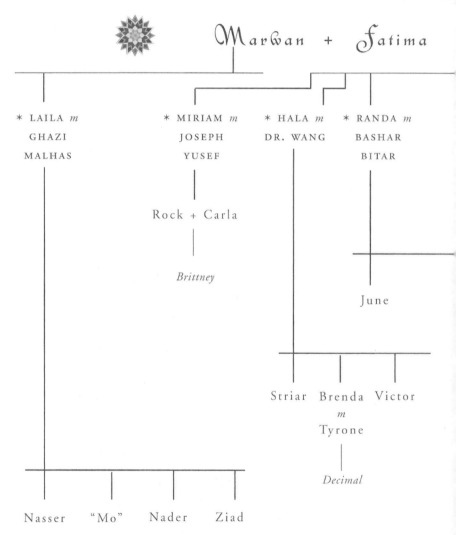

Marwan + Fatima

* LAILA *m*
GHAZI
MALHAS

* MIRIAM *m*
JOSEPH
YUSEF

* HALA *m*
DR. WANG

* RANDA *m*
BASHAR
BITAR

Rock + Carla

Brittney

June

Striar   Brenda   Victor
          m
        Tyrone

        Decimal

Nasser   "Mo"   Nader   Ziad

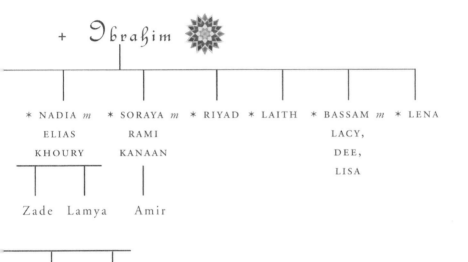

+ *Ibrahim*

* NADIA *m*   * SORAYA *m*   * RIYAD   * LAITH   * BASSAM *m*   * LENA
ELIAS   RAMI   LACY,
KHOURY   KANAAN   DEE,
                                              LISA

Zade   Lamya   Amir

Loretta   Dina

■ ■ ■ ■

THE 992ND NIGHT

■ ■ ■ ■

FATIMA

Selma Haddad's funeral had lasted much longer than Fatima had expected, longer than the two funerals she had attended the previous week. She could only hope that when it was time for her own burial in ten days, her guests would not leave so exhausted. Her other wish for her impending goodbye was that her children would not bring Ibrahim with them. An ex-husband should be spared having to walk in his former wife's funeral.

Despite her memorial service fatigue, Fatima managed to let her dentures smile at the bus driver when he stopped for her.

"Hasta mañana, sí?" he said as Fatima got into the bus with her cane.

"Sí." Fatima nodded and adjusted the waistband on her black skirt. *Sí* was the only word of Spanish she had acquired since arriving in Los Angeles from Detroit 992 nights ago at the age of eighty-two, and

11

everybody on the bus seemed to expect her to use it — so she did. If she had known that she would be alive and well in Los Angeles this long, she would have tried to learn more Spanish.

On her hundredth night in Los Angeles she had asked her grandson Amir, in whose arms she planned to die, why everyone on the bus ended everything he or she said to her with a questioning *see.* She took pride in how she could make her frailties — including her sight — come and go as needed, with the help of two different eyeglass prescriptions, a cane, and a hearing aid.

"*Sí* is 'yes' in Spanish," Amir had explained.

"Do I look like I speak Spanish or something?" Fatima asked. Before Amir could confirm that except for the size of her nose, she did look Mexican, Fatima interrupted him, as she usually did.

"Well, of course Mexicans look like me. The Arabs were in Spain for eight hundred years, and then we left Spain and went to Mexico. Appearances travel across oceans, you know. If only we'd made the Spaniards learn Arabic, then they would have made the Mexicans speak Arabic instead of Spanish, and my conversations on the bus

12

wouldn't be so boring."

Amir's answer had been to look at both his watch and the chrome clock above her dresser.

"There is still plenty of time for you to get married before I die," Fatima said, looking away from the clock.

"Jesus Christ, when that day comes, Tayta, I'm still going to be ga—" Amir started to tell her before Fatima put up a hand to prevent him from finishing.

Today, 894 days later, Amir still was not married and still was using that awful word.

Fatima waved goodbye to the bus driver and walked home down Santa Monica Boulevard. West Hollywood, according to Amir, was a fashionable neighborhood, but Fatima mostly saw the homeless men and women with their shopping carts piled with plastic bags and bottles. Some days they waved, but mostly they ignored her, and so she didn't have a chance to ask why they didn't go back to their families. She especially wanted to ask the homeless young man with the dimple on his chin, just like the dimple her son in Las Vegas had. Instead, she glared at him the hardest, and sometimes he smiled back, just like her son.

Fatima walked up the steps to Amir's duplex and let herself in. Her head hurt

instantly. All the loud chrome Amir decorated with never allowed her to relax.

She went straight up to her bedroom.
When she had moved in, she had made
Amir remove all the chrome from that
room. The only chrome he had insisted on
her keeping was the clock on the wall to
remind her when to eat; her appetite had
gone too long ago to serve as a guide.

The chrome clock said 5 P.M., but time
was marching even faster. Nine days left on
this earth. She redid the math on her
fingers, just as she used to add up the price
of the groceries in case the cashier hadn't
been properly trained on his machine. Yep,
nine days. Her math was never wrong.

Fatima already had had 992 days to
prepare for death, but the two most important things still had not been done. It was
not that she was a procrastinator. No one
who had raised ten children could be a
procrastinator. However, in dying, Fatima
had been given something she had never
had at her disposal before as she prepared
for an event: time. She did not know how to
manage such a luxury, and so she had
languished in it. Now she no longer could
afford to do that any more than she could
have when her children were children.

In the last 992 days she had attended

14

enough condolences to know exactly how she wanted her funeral to go. She would leave those instructions with Amir. More importantly, she could no longer put off finding him a wife, preferably before she had to give him the funeral instructions. Equally seriously, she had yet to choose a child to inherit her home in Lebanon, a home she had not seen in seven decades. For years she had been haunted by these two vital matters. She absolutely had to take care of them in the next nine days if she wanted to rest in peace, which she did.

Her children, all somehow having ended up with their own thoughts and ideas, did not make easy heirs. Still, she would have liked to have seen them — and the house — one more time. Alas, life was now too short. She was sound in mind and body at the moment, but a debilitating disease could strike her down at any moment and incapacitate her for her remaining days. One never knew. After all, everyone had a cause of death.

Fatima took off her black skirt and black sweater and pressed out the creases with her hands. She left her bra on, although it did nothing to hold up her shrunken breasts. She noticed an olive oil stain on the skirt from the tabbouleh served at the condolences. Dry cleaning was very expensive in this Los Angeles of Amir's, but perhaps she would not need it again before her own funeral.

Fatima had purchased the skirt when her third daughter had graduated from medical school in 1972, and it still looked brand new. She had bought the bra at the same shop on the same day because there was a storewide 70 percent clearance.

"A good bargain never goes out of fashion," Fatima said to the skirt as she tossed it into the laundry basket.

The skirt she could leave to any one of her daughters, although they were all American size, bigger than she was. But which one of them was most worthy of the one thing of value she possessed? All across the vanity were framed photos, some black and white, some full color, covering many long-gone days. No one seemed to grow up much in those photos, grown up to be the adults who troubled her, adults who might not be responsible enough for such a precious gift as her house in Lebanon.

Fatima put on her baby pink robe, sat down in front of the mirror, undid her thick purple hair, and watched it cascade down her back.

I might have to color my hair one last

time, she thought as she brushed it out. She had been coloring it four times a year for thirty-nine years, since the February after the birth of her youngest child, when her hair had looked too much like the Detroit snow out her living room window, gray with dirt and age. She didn't know exactly when her hair had stopped being black. Ibrahim had never said anything about the change. Politeness had been the foundation of their marriage.

Fatima picked up a strand of her hair and began twirling it. She forced herself to let it go, shaking her head to release the worry, a feeling she often got when she remembered Ibrahim. If only I could relax, she told the photos of her children. Maybe if I took up smoking. But cigarettes were smelly. Expensive, too.

No, nothing she hadn't had a chance to do in this lifetime in America still interested her, not even eating cookie dough right out of the tube as her American neighbor in Detroit, Millie, used to do while she watched *The Guiding Light*. Fatima used to watch both Millie and her soap from her kitchen window while she peeled garlic, chopped onions, or washed diapers. At first, she thought Millie was disgusting for eating raw eggs mixed with God only knew what.

17

Then she started to notice how every crease in Millie's face would iron out and how her shoulders collapsed more and more with each bite, as if she had found paradise after a long journey. Like being in love with the person you're having sex with — that was how Millie had explained it. Fatima had blushed then, but today she missed the filthy jokes Millie told in hush-hush whispers. They were funny, she admitted now, and with less than two weeks to live, who cared if she had acquired Millie's dirty mind. At her age, Fatima found that most people didn't care a whole lot about anything she had to say.

"Even though I'm always right about everything," she said to the children in the photos. "I can't help it."

Her hairbrush caught on the tattered sleeve of her robe. She plucked away an unruly thread. The robe was still in pretty good condition considering that she had worn it for thirty-one years. When her children still had a sense of humor around her, they used to laugh at her frugality. But how else did they think she and Ibrahim had paid for their college — or rehab and bail, as the case may have been?

She lifted the robe closer around her drooping shoulders. It was still stylish enough to die in, right? She would ask Scheherazade. That woman had been going to funerals far longer than she had. For hundreds of years, in fact.

Fatima looked at the chrome clock and turned on the television to catch the baseball highlights. Watching sports was a habit she'd acquired during her first marriage, when she was searching for things to talk about with Marwan, her first husband.

An hour later there was a knock on the door, and Fatima sat up straight and turned off ESPN. A smile worked its way across her face as the door squeaked open, and she got her first look of the day at her favorite grandson, a face not in any way her own but more breathtaking than any mother could hope to look upon. She put on her bifocals — or nearby glasses as she called them — so that she could catch the dancing hazel sparkles in his eyes better.

"It sure was a beautiful day outside, Tayta," Amir said. "After the fog lifted, that is."

Fatima ignored Amir's weather report, just as he had ignored her years of sage marriage advice. But there would be no gentle wisdom from her today. Instead, she was prepared with a one-two punch. In Las Vegas, where her son Bassam had spent too many years, people got married in less than twenty-four hours, as Bassam had himself — several times. Surely, she, Fatima Abdul Aziz Abdullah, the granddaughter of one of Lebanon's greatest matchmakers, could marry off Amir in nine days. Once married, he would not be able to use that terrible word, and therefore he would be respectable enough to inherit the house in Lebanon. Kill two birds with one stone, as Millie used to say when she had a cigarette with her sandwich.

Amir placed a pill tray on her lap. There were so many to take. She didn't need them anymore, but she didn't want to alarm Amir, and so she swallowed them dutifully.

"I just found out today I'm doing Shakespeare in the park this summer," he announced. "You're going to have a front row seat."

She couldn't tell him she wouldn't be there in July. "Shakespeare was really an Arab," she said instead. "Sheikh Sabeer. A British man stole all the great Arab plays — *Qais wa Laila, Abla wa Antar* — and took his name."

"Many say the reason Shakespeare liked men in tights so much was that he liked men period," Amir replied. "Just like me, Arab and —"

Fatima held up her hand. "Trying to be a comedian now? Acting isn't a ridiculous enough hobby? A natural-born engineer just wasting away time. *Haram.* Sacrilege. Neda Namour's granddaughter is visiting from Detroit. Nice girl. I saw her today at the funeral of Selma Haddad, *Allah yerhamha,* God rest her soul. The girl is not much to look at, but she is honest. Listen to God, son."

She pointed to the mother-of-pearl-inlaid and leather-bound Koran on her nightstand. Amir pointed back at it.

"Tayta, there's nothing in the Koran about it being a sin to be gay," he said, getting the word out before she could prevent it.

"First of all, I'm sure you've never read the Koran," Fatima retorted. She lifted her hand to stop him from saying what she knew was coming next. He would say that she had never read it, either. However, she had good reasons. He didn't. He wasn't illiterate.

Although Fatima was sure that awful word was a sin, she could not ask anyone, not even Ibrahim, to find a Koranic passage banning it because she rarely acknowledged in any language that she couldn't read for herself — nor would she want anyone questioning why someone as virtuous as

21

herself was asking about such a topic.

Amir handed her two pills and waited for her to swallow them. "Stop this nonsense and it will be the last thing I'll ever ask you to do," she vowed, hand to her heart.

"You've been making me that promise since I was seven years old and I had to read you the instructions on the box of the new L'Oreal semipermanent Midnight Black," he reminded her.

"This time I really mean it," she said, and began twirling a strand of purple hair around her index finger as he helped her with the bedcovers. She let him think that she was going to go to sleep because that was what she always let him think at this time of night, ever since she had moved in with him two years and 255 days ago.

"I'll call Neda tomorrow, *inshallah,* God willing," she said. "She and her granddaughter can come over, and you can make them some glassy mole. You make it so delicious."

"It's guacamole, Tayta," Amir said.

"Yes, I always tell the ladies on the bus how tasty your glassy mole is." Fatima beamed, and then she went for her one-two punch. "Listen to me, Amir. If you get married in the next few days, I can leave you my house in Deir Zeitoon when I die."

For the house, Fatima was sure Amir would fall in love with Neda Namour's granddaughter tomorrow and forget that dreadful word, a word she had never heard in Arabic, as such dreadful nonsense did not exist in Lebanon.

"Jesus Christ, what would I do with a house in Lebanon?" Amir said.

"*Shoo malik?* What's wrong with you?" she shouted, louder than either one of them was expecting. "It's not just any house in Lebanon. It's our house in Deir Zeitoon. The house where I was born, where my mother was born, where my grandmother did her best matchmaking, *Allah yerhamhum.*"

Amir jumped up when the microwave beeped downstairs.

"Excuse me, Tayta," he said. "My quiche is done nuking."

"What?" she asked. This was not one of the secret recipes she had taught him.

"It's a gay pie," he answered.

Fatima teared up. It was her fault Amir was such a good cook. She would not have him make glassy mole for tomorrow. "Let me fix you something," she said, reaching for her cane. "You'll have plenty of time to cook for yourself when I'm dead."

"Tayta, it was a joke." Amir laughed. "I'm just heating up the *majedera* you made. And

I hope you ate something at the condolences."

He was gone so quickly that she could not tell him that at Selma Haddad's condolences she had eaten the best *ma'amoul* she'd had since leaving Detroit. And he had left before she could tell him about climbing the house in Lebanon's cobblestone steps, from which one could look down at the entire valley, where shepherds tended flocks of sheep and goats and farmers tilled brown wheat and red poppy fields.

He really was going to like the house, but she would tell him no chrome allowed. If not Amir, the choice of whom to give the house to would be impossible to make with so few days left, especially when her children barely spoke to her.

Fatima assumed that most women who had ten children and fourteen grandchildren spoke to all of them every day. Only half of her children called daily. The others telephoned just once or twice a week. But how good they all were with weather reports. *Mashallah,* Fatima knew the weather in half the cities in the country through her children's phone calls. Today Detroit was steamy, Washington, D.C., rainy, and New York foggy; New Castle was having an early summer.

She was still reviewing the weather map of America when the rattle of an armful of delicate gold bracelets brought her back to the room. *Alhamdulilah,* God be praised. It was time for the night to begin. Fatima looked up, and there she was. Scheherazade. A few minutes early this evening, perched on the windowsill, seductively shaking her bangles for attention.

Tonight she wore a chocolate-brown *thowb* of Damascene silk and Persian gossamer that touched the tops of her delicate feet and was trimmed in red embroidery. Fatima recognized the embroidery as a circular Baghdadi pattern. Her hair flowed like Fatima's, but Scheherazade's was still as crystal black as when King Shahrayar had fallen in love with her eleven centuries ago. Her thick lashes were almost as long as Amir's, and she batted them at Fatima.

"It was 101 degrees in Houston today," Fatima told her.

Scheherazade sighed, showing no more interest in Houston's impressive heat than Fatima had in Amir's fog update. In fact, Scheherazade's mood seemed as bothered as her own this evening. "My dear lady, *inshallah* yes or *inshallah* no, it will either rain or turn fine tomorrow," she said in a lilting voice that made her words come together like a little song regardless of her mood. "If it is fine tomorrow, I'll finish plowing, and if it rains, I'll finish weaving. . . . As long as your children know how to deal with the weather, all is well, *ya seiti.* Tonight we can skip your review of the temperatures of your children's gardens so that we can get to my story for the evening more quickly."

Fatima picked up a strand of her hair and began twisting it. She had been a little troubled the first night Scheherazade, with her jiggling belts and breasts, had awakened her from sleep. That had been 992 nights ago, the night Fatima had moved in with Amir to keep him company. Scheherazade had returned every evening since, asking Fatima each night for some story from her past.

"What if I don't tell you a story?" Fatima had asked on the third night.

"To know you have 1001 nights to tell your stories is a gift and a curse," Scheherazade had replied. "But when our tales are over, so are our lives. Do you understand what I mean?"

Fatima was no *hamara,* no stupid donkey. That was how she came to understand that she, Fatima Abdul Aziz Abdullah, would die in Los Angeles, California, USA, when Scheherazade visited her for the 1001st time. Maybe she'd never read the *The Arabian Nights* — again, not her fault — but she knew the stories by heart. This woman, Scheherazade, of whom *rawis* — bards in villages from Iran to India — had spun tales since the time of the Caliph Rashid Al-Harun, was herself the greatest storyteller of all time. For 1001 nights Scheherazade had saved herself from beheading by pausing at the most climactic point in one of her tall tales. She would promise King Shahrayar that she would finish the story just for him the next day. Thus, her life was spared each night, unlike the hundreds of women before her. By the time Scheherazade had nearly run out of stories, King Shahrayar loved her too much to do anything but marry her and have three children with her.

Fatima twirled a strand of purple hair, angry that her nightly visitor had not let her ease into her stories with the usual weather report. Maybe she, too, has been counting the days, Fatima thought, and has realized time is almost over for me.

"Come on," Scheherazade coached. "Tell me a tale of your more recent husband."

Fatima continued to twirl the purple strand by way of answer.

"We have memories so that we can share them." Scheherazade sighed for the second time that night. "Otherwise God wouldn't have given us the ability to remember."

"No one was ever kinder to me," Fatima murmured; that was all she ever said about Ibrahim, and kindness never sounded sadder. Then she let go of the strand of hair and smiled. "But I do have a good one for you."

Fatima then began yet another story about the house in Deir Zeitoon. It took her until the middle of the night to finish the tale, which was about the chicken farmer's wife who hid out in the Abdul Aziz house until her hens forgave her for accidentally feeding them leftover omelet and then were able to lay eggs again. Fatima did not notice Scheherazade's yawns, and she did not mention Ibrahim once.

■ ■ ■ ■

THE 993RD NIGHT

■ ■ ■ ■

IBRAHIM

Three days after Ibrahim had stopped driving his Ford Mercury for good, he recalled that he once had read in the *Detroit Free Press* that Japan had a better public transportation system than the United States. He would never believe Japan's cars were better, but he was convinced Japanese bus schedules had to be.

Whether the Middlebelt stop was slicked with ice or was Ford engine–hot — as it was on this humid, blossomy evening — SMART Bus #285 always arrived at exactly 6:17 P.M. That was eleven precious minutes behind schedule, according to the DDOT timetable Ibrahim had memorized and adjusted for reality. Ibrahim let his cane guide his weary legs up the bus steps. This was the third and last bus he would board today for the seventy-eight-minute trip from his house in Dearborn to the Detroit Metropolitan Airport, now only nineteen minutes away.

The bus driver, Dwayne, stood up and gave Ibrahim a hand. "How you doin', Mr. Ibrahim, sir?" he said, as he did every Wednesday and Friday at 6:17 P.M. Dwayne spoke just as paternally to Ibrahim as he did to the six-year-old girl with pigtails who had hopped on the bus right before him.

Ibrahim could pass, as he had all his life, for a much younger man. He looked no more than eighty-two years old, which was not bad for a ninety-six-year-old man. But even eighty-two was up there, and so Ibrahim had gotten used to everyone talking to him as if he were a child, a practice that had increased annually since he had started wearing a hearing aid on his seventy-ninth birthday.

"Traffic sure is movin' slow today," Dwayne said, as if it were news.

"What we goin' do, buddy?" Ibrahim said, and shrugged, unaware that he still spoke broken English, that people could tell that he was not only old but foreign, too.

The whiteness of Dwayne's teeth stood out against the blackness of his skin, blacker than any skin Ibrahim had seen in his eighty years in America, so black that it reminded Ibrahim of the Sudanese peanut sellers who

32

used to travel with their carts through the streets of Lebanon. But Ibrahim had given in very little to senility, and so he was aware that today was very far away from his boyhood, when he used to skip up Lebanon's mountains with his sisters in search of fresh figs for his mother's jam.

Ibrahim took his place three seats in back of Dwayne, avoiding eye contact with the young lady with the pierced belly button. She had stood up to give him the handicap seat, exposing her peace sign tattoo. It was situated right in a place Ibrahim thought only mothers and husbands should ever see. In looking away from the tattoo, Ibrahim found himself facing the six-year-old girl with pigtails.

"You dropped this," she shouted at his hearing aid, and handed him a letter addressed to Fatima in Los Angeles. Every Wednesday and Friday he mailed Fatima a check. She had not asked for alimony, but he felt obligated to provide it. Today's letter was different, though.

"Thank you," he said. The girl took her mother's hand and stared at Ibrahim's full white mustache as he twirled it.

Ibrahim turned to the window. Dwayne's bus stopped more than it moved in certain spots. That was when Ibrahim could see into the windows of the houses of people who didn't seem to change much between Wednesdays and Fridays.

With the lights turned on early because of cloudy skies, Ibrahim could view his regulars more clearly this evening. He could even see the dirty movie the fat man at Dwayne's third stop was watching in his town house. No matter what the wild girls were doing on the TV, they stirred Ibrahim's heart rather than the regions of his body they once might have. The TV girls made him think of Dalal, the girl in his village he was supposed to marry, the one with the two long thick black braids. She had always remained fifteen years old to Ibrahim, even eighty years later. In the only memory of her that had accompanied him to Detroit, she was looking at herself in her bedroom mirror, quietly crying, unraveling her braids just minutes after he had told her father that he couldn't marry her. She would never know he had been standing outside her house staring up at her, her voluptuousness tempered by her virginity.

"I must go to America to build cars," he had said to her and her father, patting a mustache that was no thicker than the fuzz on those mountain figs near his mother's house. "I will make enough money to build us the biggest house in the village, and then *inshallah,* I will come back worthy of marrying you."

That promise quietly, almost imperceptibly, faded away, lost to reality for years, until his own heartache brought Dalal's tears back to him. He had arrived in Detroit in 1924, one of the last Arabs let in before new quotas restricted the influx of immigrants, particularly "yellow people," as Arabs often were classified then. It wouldn't have been easy to bring Dalal to America then. At least that was how he explained to himself never having written to her.

Traffic inched forward, and the bus reached the house of the peroxide blonde, who was sitting on her front steps in her usual orange sweat suit, rolling a joint discreetly inside a newspaper. Ibrahim recognized that action from his son, who had fooled him for many years. The peroxide blonde was just forty-three or so, he guessed, about the same age as his son. With her football player chest and toothpick legs, she looked like the second and only other woman he had abandoned. Betsy was her name, the waitress who had taken him in when he'd first moved here without a job and with a three-word vocabulary — *yes, sir,* and *no.* He'd married her and then left her sixty-nine years ago when he had seen his best friend, Marwan, come back from his mother's funeral in Lebanon with a beautiful bride from their village named Fatima.

"There comes a time when you don't want to live with a stranger anymore," he had told his devoted first wife after ten years of a fairly pleasant marriage.

Ibrahim wished that Betsy had yelled at him or clawed him instead of staring at him through a stream of silent tears. At the time he had thought that he had gotten off easy, but today he knew there was no redemption in shattering someone's faith in you. For the last three years, he often jolted awake at night desperate to apologize to Betsy. But when dawn came, he never tried to find her, as he assumed she was dead, as were more than 99 percent of people his age. He hoped at some point she had realized how lucky she was to have lived the rest of her life, however long that had been, without him.

Ibrahim looked away from the world outside and managed a slow smile at the little girl. It felt good. He wanted to tell her not to live as long as he had so that she wouldn't have so many memories. If he had died thirty years ago, there were terrible things he would not have lived long enough to know. Nor would he have had the time to remember all the wrong he had done.

An airplane flew over the traffic, distracting the little girl from Ibrahim's mustache. Another plane followed in the wake of the first. The planes reminded him of his ten children, all but one of whom had fled Detroit forever. If he had known that in old age in America having children was the same as not having them at all, he never would have had so many.

Ibrahim didn't expect his children to come back, even to visit. He would accept occasional telephone calls from them that mostly consisted of weather reports, with long silences afterward as the person on the other end tried to think of something that wouldn't raise Ibrahim's rage. But he no longer had any rage, just loneliness, an aching for them that overwhelmed him during his nearly nightly bouts with insomnia.

Maybe it wasn't America that had ruined his children, but rather their mother. If Fatima had disciplined them more, maybe they would have been afraid to leave. Someone was to blame for their absence. America and his wife seemed like the most logical scapegoats. But for all his complaining about America and Fatima, Ibrahim had not left either one.

"Inshallah," Fatima had answered when he had asked for her hand in marriage sixty-five years ago. Not yes and not no. *Inshallah.* God willing. He had been in America long enough by then to need more precise responses. But now, even as a man who hadn't been friendly with God for many years, he knew *inshallah* to be the only true response to anything. Will you marry me? Is the fig tree bearing fruit? Do you think the Tigers are going to win the World Series? Your son is going to do great things, don't you think? *Inshallah.* While there were sometimes definite no's, nothing in life was as simple as yes.

"*Inshallah,* you will smile again without me in your life," Fatima had said when she had surprised him with the divorce three years ago.

In the divorce, she had split everything between them fifty-fifty, down to the penny. Each got one of their 1983 Ford Mercurys, although neither one of them had any business driving anymore. She had given him exactly half the money in the bank account and exactly half of their forty-two family photos. She took the garlic press, and so she left him the coffeepot. She kept one of her grandfather's canes and gave him the other, as her grandfather had intended one for her husband in her dowry in case they both should live to be old. She had left the apple tree but uprooted the fig tree so that it could go with her. She had insisted that he take the house in Detroit. He had told her it was hers, but she had said that she had her house in Lebanon, and so she did not need a house in Detroit as much as he did.

What he wished she had left him was her hair. He had no doubt her purple hair — she never knew how to dye it, either rinsing the dye off too quickly or leaving it on too long — still flowed to her knees, just as it had when they first married. He missed the purple in his life.

The bus finally reached the exit to the airport, and the little girl bounced her knees in excitement. Here Ibrahim would wait for KLM Flight 6470 from Amsterdam, as he did every Wednesday and Friday. He'd wait for the passengers to come out of customs. Most of them would be Arabs, coming from Lebanon and Jordan and connecting through Amsterdam. They weren't his relatives, but as they wept and embraced their waiting entourages, he would hear the sound of his childhood dinners in their hyperbolic greetings. He would smell his mother's evening gatherings in the heavy perfume of the overly made up grandmothers and in the sweat of the young men who somehow didn't believe in deodorant but eagerly indulged in Western things such as Marlboros and druggie music with no meaning. In the travelers' bulging suitcases, tied together with ropes so that they wouldn't burst open, Ibrahim would picture the gifts of baklava carefully inserted between the sweaters and coats they would make much use of here.

Ibrahim didn't need his earring aid, as he called it, to hear his bones creak as he pulled the cord for the bus to stop. If he was lucky, he would inhale jasmine with the arrivals, it being in bloom in Lebanon now. No, it was September when they bloomed, right? Wasn't May the honeysuckle's time?

Dwayne winked at him, as he always did every Wednesday and Friday when he helped Ibrahim get down the bus steps. Ibrahim checked his pocket to make sure Fatima's letter was still with him.

"*Salam-alakum,* Brother," Dwayne said slowly and paternally.

"*Wa-alakum-a-salam,* Son," Ibrahim answered. He did not wish to disturb Dwayne's customary respect by telling him that it was much easier to just say "bye-bye."

"Rock on, dude," Ibrahim added. He tried to stay "white groovin'," as Dwayne called it. That way, if any of his children or their children came to visit, he would be able to speak the same "lingo," as his son used to wish.

As Dwayne drove away, Ibrahim looked at his watch. It was six forty-five. Six minutes late. He was sure things like this didn't happen in Japan. Well, perhaps the plane was delayed, too. *Inshallah.*

He opened his usual mailbox with the hook of his cane and let the letter drop from his hands into the slot. Ibrahim had not argued about the divorce. He always had given Fatima what she wanted, even though she did not know that because she did not know all the things he had kept from her. He always avoided telling her anything she did not want to hear, but he knew in this letter he was doing just that. For that, if nothing else, he was glad that they were divorced and someone other than he would have to read the letter to her.

Ibrahim hobbled to the terminal. He knew it was the American in him that was in a hurry. The Arab in him wondered why he was hurrying. After all, as Fatima's Koran said, everything is already written, so no need to rush, no need to worry whether his

41

children had bought Japanese — or Swedish or German — cars. No need to regret the past. He could not have changed it even before it started.

AMIR

Amir scooped up the last of the *majedera* with piece of pita bread. He burped, enjoying it for the second night in a row. He was sure the lentils and fried onions would come back to haunt him that night and make him momentarily grateful that he slept alone. Arabic food was what Fatima had raised him on, but he knew for certain that it wasn't the best food for dating. He burped one more time, which mercifully drowned out Fatima talking to herself upstairs, a cacophony that unsettled him every night.

"I finalized my divorce, and I'm coming to California," Fatima had said to him on the phone 994 days ago. "Northwest Airlines Flight 435, in case you're interested in knowing."

She had never been west of the Mississippi, and she hadn't even specified to Amir where in California she would be landing. However, in the seven hours it took her to fly to Los Angeles via Salt Lake City, Amir had figured out her flight details, changed

42

the sheets in the spare bedroom, and broken up with his boyfriend, who was also his next-door neighbor. Amir had come out to Fatima long ago, although she wasn't listening, but her arrival worked as a good excuse to end a really mediocre relationship that had gone on for four months, about three months too long.

The boyfriend had wanted to fight for their coupledom, but when he had trudged back across the street with his bags to his own duplex, he had found a message waiting for him. "I'm the new Dr. Grayson," he informed Amir from his cell phone, giving him the finger from his front yard. Dr. Grayson was the lead role on a fairly popular daytime soap opera. Amir was relieved and somewhat disappointed that his latest ex would not have time to mourn his loss. He was also jealous about Dr. Grayson.

But he tabled his jealousy and was at the airport to meet Fatima with a smile on his face. When they got home, the new soap star waved from his driveway, where he was polishing a new Chevy Tahoe he'd been eyeing at the dealership for the duration of their relationship. "Very handsome neighbor," Fatima had remarked, and then pointed at Amir's beat-up Honda Civic. "You should drive an American car, like him."

The next day was September 11, 2001. If Fatima had finalized her divorce one day later, she probably never would have come to L.A., and he certainly wouldn't have asked her to stay. When the planes hit the towers, she screamed for her daughter Lena, who lived in New York. When she found out the next day that Lena was okay, she started praying for those who might still be alive in the wreckage while asking God somehow not to make it Arabs who had done this terrible thing. As the TV continued to relive the moment on screen every few minutes and the news did not change, she got angry. "These animals have turned my Islam into a death trap," Fatima said, and motioned for the mother-of-pearl Koran neither of them could read.

About the time she began to worry about what revenge the United States would wreak on the Middle East, Amir decided he didn't want her living alone. Fatima had always taken the news from the Middle East personally, in the same way she personalized the funerals of those people in Los Angeles she barely knew. That was not what worried him. It was everyone else's reaction. In the remaining weeks of that September and well into October, his neighbors, coworkers, and friends, people who had never internalized any news but box office and Botox disasters, reacted as though they knew someone who had been in the towers, as though they had someone in their family who was about to be sent off to Afghanistan, as though their apartments had been surrounded by smoke and death. Just as Fatima's steps were now more weighed down, so, too, were theirs. His grandmother had passed on to him her sensitivity to Middle East news, and many times he had been burdened by suicide bombings over there, but in his West Hollywood bubble a car bomb was a drunkfest cocktail: a shot of whiskey dropped into a glass of beer and chugged frat boy style. He had been more comfortable then, when the Middle East was his alone, when a good audition or a nice ass passing by could make him forget it. But if Los Angeles suddenly was talking and walking in black and white, evil and good, couldn't the citizens of the rest of the nation — say, in Detroit — see an old lady from Lebanon as a danger to society? It was like the way he'd been told people in Lebanon thought most of the Americans in their country worked for the CIA. No, she would live with him, he decided. Ibrahim couldn't protect her. As for Ibrahim needing protection, Amir couldn't imagine it.

When he told Fatima to stay, she nodded, not mentioning 9/11 but rather his grandfather. "Now that we're divorced, there is no need for us to live in the same city," she decided. Then she told him to write a check from her account to one of the 9/11 charities. "*Zaka,* giving alms, is one of the true pillars of Islam. You don't hear CNN talking about that."

A few months later, she told him everything on CNN was a lie. The whole thing was a setup, and Osama bin Laden was a U.S. agent giving the United States an excuse to occupy Iraq. That was what everyone was saying at Rashida Khaldoon's condolences. The next day, he took the TV out of her room and agreed to bring it back only when she promised to watch sports and nothing else.

"You need to get out," he told her. "Going to funerals is not getting out."

"I've lived most of my life indoors," she said. "You don't raise ten children going to tea parties. Do I look like Marilyn Monroe or something?"

It was now halfway through 2004, and like anyone else on the planet, Amir didn't revel in having his grandmother still living with him during one of the busiest decades of his life. However, years of acting lessons made it possible for him to hide his agony from her. She had, after all, insisted on paying for those acting lessons, even though she would not have done so if she had known what they were for.

"I want to study the stars," he had told her when he was looking for an acting coach. He let her believe that the stars were in the sky rather than in Hollywood and he was working on becoming a "freelance physicist," which was how his mother, Soraya, had explained it to her.

Fatima had raised both him and his mother in the same house in Detroit, albeit at different times. Soraya had been around so rarely for his childhood that it was Fatima who had held Amir close to her bosom when he awoke in the middle of the night asking about his father.

"Shush, *noor hayati,* light of my life," Fatima would say while his grandfather stood at the doorway, neither denying his tears nor responding to them. "Your father was no silly ordinary man. You will understand one day. Right, Ibrahim?" With the only light in the room coming from the street, Ibrahim's small shrug was barely visible.

Years later, Amir still had not met his father and had become Fatima's comfort instead. Most of the time.

"My grandson thinks he's a filthier word than anything Millie, *Allah yerhamha,* God rest her soul, ever uttered," Fatima shouted to herself from upstairs, banging her cane on the floor.

Jesus Christ. He let out a final burp of *majedera* and stepped outside to water his front lawn and garden. He knew it was not very gay, not very Arab, and not very Californian to weed and water his own garden when he could hire someone to do it for practically nothing. It was the Midwest in him, summers spent in Fatima's garden. Since she had come to live with him, this garden was most importantly his escape from her conversations with herself. Luckily, unlike Detroit, here he could keep the garden going all year, and so he always had an excuse to leave the house.

In the front yard, Amir had planted roses, jasmine, and *aautra,* as Fatima had done in Detroit. The eucalyptus tree had come with the house, but next to it was the small fig tree Fatima had brought with her. Amir was trying hard to nourish it, as he had watched his grandmother nourish it for as long as he could remember.

While Amir watered the fig tree, he noticed that a new SUV was parked in front

48

of the house of his summer fling soap star, a GMC Yukon. Jesus Christ, the jerk had bought a new SUV without even needing to sell the old one, which still was parked on his side of the street and still ten years newer than Amir's Honda Civic.

"Asshole," Amir shouted at the soap star's house, as if he had been dumped by the soap star rather than the other way around. He got his mail, slammed the mailbox shut, and went back inside, where Fatima still was talking to herself.

The first piece of mail he saw was a tattered envelope from Detroit. From Ibrahim, of course. There would be a check in it, what Amir called hush money, a ten-dollar check that was supposed to make up for his stone-cold silence during most of Amir's twenty-nine years. Still, days were better when Fatima used to talk to his grandfather rather than herself. There was no Ibrahim in the picture these days. Literally. On the credenza by Amir's computer was a photo of Fatima in her wedding dress — with no groom.

There were also a couple of checks from a couple of aunts. Good. Fatima was expensive some months. Her children loved her, he assumed, but this didn't naturally lead to the desire to cohabitate. That was why in taking her in as a roommate he had become a saint of sorts — unquestioned, funded, and never criticized, at least to his face.

Amir reread the e-mail he had drafted the previous night.

Dear Fatima relations,
    I hope this 141st weekly update finds you all well. The weather in Los Angeles began foggy today, but ended sunny and bright. Those of you who sent in, thank you for your checks. I used the money to buy Tayta a pair of new "far-away" glasses, as she calls them. Her "nearby" glasses are fine. So is she. She continues to plug herself into the Arab funeral circuit in L.A., and seems to get out at least once or twice a week to pay condolences to someone. She still talks to herself every night, going on about villages in Lebanon and sultans and kings of Persia. I get to hear your weather reports in Arabic every night☺.
                    Peace out, Amir

He hit "send" on his computer, delivering yet another perky message to twenty-three relatives he would have had no contact with if it weren't for Fatima. Prior to her moving in, he hadn't even thought to put most of them on his Christmas card list, and he loved any chance to show off his holiday cards. Each year, the cards featured a photo of him from the set of the biggest movie he had gotten a bit part in since the last Christmas card.

When the phone rang, Amir fully tuned out Fatima.

"You have an audition at CBS tomorrow. Nine A.M.," Darcy Dagrout, his agent, shouted on the line. "Wear the extra-long beard to this one. No mustache."

"Jesus Christ, I'm tired of auditioning for every terrorist role," Amir said.

"Don't flatter yourself, Osama" — she continued shouting — "because there are a lot of terrorist auditions that don't ask for you. And dude, it's an audition to be a New York cabbie. So stop stereotyping Holly-wood. Don't wear anything with chenille. If they think you're gay, they'll never let you audition for the terrorist parts."

"Well, don't you think Osama and all those men hiding out in caves is kind of gay, anyway?" Amir asked.

"Are you being profound? Don't do that tomorrow," Darcy cautioned. "You're a cab driver, and there's nothing profound about that."

He was getting a headache from Fatima's cane tapping on the floor above. "Darcy, I'd make a great doctor," he suggested, thinking that even if he had stayed with his ex, he never would have let him help take care of Fatima, especially after he'd seen what an unconvincing doctor he was on TV. "The soaps are always looking for handsome doctors. And what about Omar Sharif? I heard Warner Bros. is casting his biopic. He played a doctor once."

But Darcy had hung up.

THE SUV PEOPLE

When Amir had gone back inside, two people dressed in black from head to toe looked out the tinted windows of the GMC Yukon. Neither one of them had the soap star qualities of Amir's former lover, and the SUV was loaded with camera equipment, including a wide selection of lenses.

"You see how he just called out 'asshole' to the world like that?" the man in black noted.

"Haven't you ever had a bad day?" the

woman in black sighed.

"Hey, you're the one that's been high for years to use our paparazzi skills to a more noble purpose."

"I'm not sure being a vigilante qualifies," the woman in black said. "I was more thinking along the lines that we could go on a safari and get never-before-seen close-ups of lions doing it or something like that. That at least might have been romantic."

" 'Vigilante' is an unpleasant word choice," he replied, ignoring her hint at romance. "Look, we have a tip, and we have to follow up every tip. That's what the FBI does."

"We're not the FBI," she reminded him. "And some tip — a soap star who didn't want us following him around so he turned us on to his neighbor."

"Which he wouldn't have done if you hadn't told him you wished you had something better to do with your life than follow him around," he replied.

"What was I supposed to say?" she whined. "He was about to break my camera."

"Look, we're just helping the FBI, hanging out waiting for probable cause. And if we don't get anything on him, maybe we'll make a few bucks from the *Enquirer* for catching the soap star with a newly adopted child or a boyfriend — because our tip on that was pretty solid."

The woman in black sighed again. "All right, if this Amir terrorizes as well as he gardens, we'll have saved the day."

"That'd be sweet revenge on all those people who diss our work," the man in black agreed.

FATIMA

Scheherazade was wearing even more gold tonight, more than last night, when Fatima had revealed the story of her cousin Samira, who at six years old lost her sight but not her hearing when she looked at an old woman with a missing ear, and more than the night before, when Fatima had told her of the chicken farmer's wife in Deir Zeitoon.

The jewelry's glitter strained Fatima's eyesight with or without either pair of her glasses: ruby and diamond rings on nearly every finger, dangling hoops from her ears, and gold and emerald bangles up to her elbows.

"You have on more jewelry than a Bedouin bride on her wedding day," Fatima complained.

"*Ibad e sher,* keep the devil away, one mar-

54

riage was enough for me," Scheherazade said. "How about you with the two husbands?"

"Tell me how I'm going to die," Fatima replied. "Will I stay fit until the 1001st night? You can tell me, whatever it is. It's too late for it to be long and crippling. I just want to know if they will all be healthy days that I can focus on finding Amir a wife and someone to take my house in Lebanon."

"Just let your children solve it for themselves," Scheherazade suggested.

"Are you saying that I will not have all healthy days?" Fatima countered.

"Tell me a good story for once, and I just might tell you." Scheherazade winked.

"Fine," Fatima said. "I know. . . . Did I ever tell you about the time me and *awlad aami,* all my cousins, tried to paint the house with pomegranate juice?"

"Yes, yes, pomegranate, my favorite fruit of God." Scheherazade yawned and stretched. "The stains did not wash away even after a winter of nonstop torrents of rain."

Fatima had told Scheherazade 993 stories of that house: the time her cousin Najwa got stung by twenty bees from her father's hives and became sweeter than honey; the day a peddler from Damascus came to the door, fell in love with her aunt, and persuaded her to marry him in exchange for all the perfumes on his cart; the year her uncle drove up the mountain with the village's first motorcar and everyone looked out from the wheat fields to see where the horse or donkey was hidden; the year her grandmother arranged seven marriages in one hot July, all of which produced firstborn sons. Those events had occurred in Fatima's first seventeen years of life, which was the last time she had seen Lebanon and that house.

Scheherazade jumped down from the windowsill and cuddled up to Fatima on the bed. "*Ya seit el beit,* oh, lady of the house," she begged. "*Wahayat deen el-nebi,* in the name of the prophet's religion, you've had ten children and two husbands. Surely something must have happened in the last sixty-eight years. Chicken pox?"

"I never told you about the week my grandfather's autumn grapevines trapped five bandit farmers up to no good," Fatima offered.

Scheherazade sighed and ran a finger across her full lips. "You have told me stories of love in Deir Zeitoon, unrequited, forbidden, fated, but you have not told me your own."

"I do not have a love story." Fatima

56

shrugged.

"Yes, you do," Scheherazade argued. "No one could live so many years as you without a love story to sustain them. Maybe it lasted but a moment or maybe it still lives, but love, memory or living, must nourish our heart to keep it beating."

Fatima twirled a strand of hair.

"For example, how was the lovemaking with Ibrahim?" Scheherazade asked. "Did it get better or worse with time?"

Fatima slapped Scheherazade hard enough to shake the bells on her belt. *"Ya bint al-sharaa,"* she shouted. "Nothing but a common street girl."

"How dare you," Scheherazade said, and slapped Fatima back. "When did mortals become so uptight? In the chambers of my palaces, lovemaking flourished proudly and —"

Fatima turned her back to Scheherazade so that she would stop talking.

"I swear on my own mother's heart, once you start remembering love, the passion for its stories comes back, if not the love," Scheherazade vowed. "I will commence with the line from one of my own stories, and then you go on. . . . *Yallah,* let us begin. . . . *I shall wed the only man who can tell me a story whose beginning is impossible*

57

and whose end is untrue. . . . Yallah, proceed."

Fatima twirled a strand of purple hair again.

"I'm still waiting," Scheherazade cooed.

"Could I have a cigarette?" Fatima asked.

"Smoking prematurely ages you."

Fatima ran her palm across the cratered map of wrinkles on her face. "I'm eighty-four," she said. "Premature was a long time ago."

"But look at me — 1,128 years old and not even a dent," Scheherazade bragged.

"You're immortal," Fatima said. "That's different."

"And you're eighty-five."

Fatima rearranged her pout, which seemed to satisfy Scheherazade. "My story, please," she demanded.

"What if Amir does not marry and does not take the house?" Fatima fretted. "Then who?"

"The answer will not come if you only picture long-dead people in it," Scheherazade countered. "God knows and sees best what lies hidden in the old accounts of bygone peoples and times, not us. Let us look at the past that is still growing. That is where the answer to the fate of your house lies. Before there were the children, there was the father. So let us begin there."

Fatima continued to twirl her hair for thirty seconds according to the chrome clock. Then she let go of the strand of hair and readjusted the shoulders on her pink robe. "Help me up. I want to show you something."

"As long as it comes with a story."

"Haven't I spent the last 993 nights telling my stories?" Fatima said.

"I mean one that will make me swoon. A sexy, passionate, juicy one."

Fatima pretended not to have heard those adjectives, but they were disturbingly embedded in her mind now. She motioned for the cane. Scheherazade picked it up and accidentally smacked it against the bed.

"Hey, watch it," Fatima admonished. "My grandfather made that. He was the best —"

"Cane maker in all of Lebanon. Yes, yes, you already told me that one. Come on, *ya ikhtiyara,* old woman."

Scheherazade handed her the cane.

"Be nice to me," Fatima insisted. "I'm missing the sports update on Channel 11 for this. They're making their predictions about the NFL draft this week. I'd like to know who's going to be playing at the Lions' new stadium before I get to heaven."

"You are certainly most confident of your

destination beyond this world," Scheherazade said, and hooked her arm in Fatima's. The two made their way down the hallway silently, aside from the tapping of the cane, until Fatima stopped in front of a door and motioned for Scheherazade to open it. Scheherazade gasped at what greeted them on the other side. "What kind of guest would want to stay in such accommodations?" she exclaimed.

Fatima sighed. All Amir's chrome and glass, never mind how distasteful, always glistened. But nothing in this room shined.

Scheherazade stubbed a perfectly polished red toenail on one of several boxes and yelped. "Your Amir is such a triumph in the way that many perpetual bachelors are often neater than any person they could have married," she remarked. "But this . . . I once told stories to a sultan's son who had banished all his servants and yet had a palace more tidy than this."

"These are my boxes from Detroit. The mess is not Amir's fault," Fatima insisted. "I told him not to touch anything in here."

Scheherazade picked up a large wooden stick. "I said don't touch!" Fatima shouted in a voice so loud that a surprised Scheherazade dropped the baseball bat. It rolled along until it hit a stack of badly aligned boxes, tipping over the top one, a tattered Oster sixteen-speed blender box. Out of it spilled many small white tubes. Scheherazade bent down and randomly opened a few, finding them filled with cracked and ill purples and pinks.

"Those are my samples from when I used to sell Avon," Fatima explained. "I've kept them for forty-two years in case I needed extra cash. But I haven't had to go out and sell them again. God be praised, *al-hamdulilah,* Amir and I have enough money."

Fatima gently eased her knees down to the floor and knelt in front of a wooden chest. She inhaled the cedar.

"This is it." She smiled. She reached into her pink robe but discovered she had forgotten to bring both her nearby and her faraway glasses. *Ya Allah.* "Come, come," she beckoned Scheherazade. "Is the wood still the color of black honey?"

Fatima's hands gently massaged and stroked the chest, and she laid her head on the cool wood, letting her purple hair nearly cover its length.

"Is your story for tonight in there?"

"My grandfather built this from the cedars back home. . . . He was the best carpenter —"

"In all of Lebanon," Scheherazade concluded.

"I was not going to talk about him," Fatima said. "So don't complain." Her weak eyes focused on a world left behind long ago as she opened the chest, swatting Scheherazade's hand away when she tried to help her with its weight.

"I closed it myself, and I'll open myself," she declared, and slowly, carefully raised the lid until it stood upright and enveloped her in the powerful aroma of cedar and time.

Lying on top was a white damask gown with just a hint of yellowing on the lace. Fatima tried to pull it out, but she was overwhelmed by its weight and the smells of her mother's house — the cardamom her aunt stirred into the Turkish coffee as she boiled it not once but twice, the garlic and lemon juice that permanently stained her mother's fingertips, the sweetness of the hibiscus and gardenia petals from the veranda — all still sewn into the fabric, along with the cold, muddy aroma of fresh figs.

Scheherazade took the gown from her just before its many layers of lace toppled her. She examined its embroidery and then let the train glide behind her as she twirled with it and then held it up to Fatima's body. In the sixty-eight years since Fatima last had worn the dress, she had become too short for it.

"I got married the first time in the early summer," she reminisced. "The year the Palestinians started to rise up against the British, and in Deir Zeitoon, everyone was already talking about getting the French to leave Lebanon."

"That was 1936, *habibti*. Or 1355 in the year of the *hijira*."

"We didn't have calendars in my house." Fatima shrugged.

"You left Lebanon just in time. Another great war was around the corner, and you would have never gotten out then," Scheherazade said. "Did you like him, this first husband?"

"Marwan? Sure, why not? He was very nice." Fatima nodded. "He was working at the Ford River Rouge plant and came back home to Deir Zeitoon to attend his mother's funeral. She had refused to go to America with her husband, so he took Marwan with him and she kept the older boy with her. Marwan's older brother and my father had been best friends before my father died, so I went to pay my respects. That was my first funeral. Two days later, Marwan came to the house and asked Mama and my uncle for my hand. Mama was so excited."

"With a dress like this, you must have been, too," Scheherazade marveled as she spun around with it.

"I told Mama that Marwan was the same age as her, so why didn't she marry him? She slapped me three times. She told me that Marwan made six dollars a day working for Mr. Ford. Mama was sure that in America I would have a better life. Both she and Marwan were born when Lebanon was starving because Britain and France had blockaded our harbors to defeat the Turks."

Fatima touched her wedding dress, letting go when she noticed that even Scheherazade was weighed down with its stories. "Marwan and his father left Deir Zeitoon right before the blockade, when he was just a child, only eight," she continued. "So he barely spoke Arabic anymore. His Arabic was so hard to understand some days, and I had no English."

"Love has no words," Scheherazade gushed.

"Your King Shahrayar fell in love with you because of your words," Fatima reminded her. "But I did like Marwan because I was getting older and I didn't have a father and I wasn't so good-looking. And my grandmother, the greatest matchmaker of all, died two years before, just when I turned fifteen and hit the prime marriage age. Mama had begun to worry that I would have to work like an animal like she had, with no man or sons to help me plow the fields."

"She only worried because she loved you more than the moon," Scheherazade said.

"Mama had no one else to love," Fatima replied. "I was born eight months after my father died; the Turks killed him for refusing to be conscripted in their army. Mama always said not to feel bad about him deciding to become a martyr because the Turks would have put him on the front line, as they did most of the Arabs, and he would have probably been killed anyway. Then, a month before I was born, the influenza took her two other children. I explained all of that to Marwan when the officer at Ellis Island asked when I was born. Marwan wrote down 1919."

"You were blessed you came after that influenza," Scheherazade remarked. "It killed three times as many people as the Great War going on then across our lands and beyond."

"That was what Mama always told me when I felt cursed having to work with her instead of going to school like the other girls," Fatima said. "Mama promised me she'd teach me to read one day, but that time never came."

Scheherazade fondled the white trim of the dress.

"Try it on for me," Fatima requested. "For you are still beautiful."

"If that is your command," Scheherazade said with a nonchalance that did not match the care with which she slipped the gown over her head.

Fatima clasped her hands in delight. "You look like an angel worthy of heaven seven times over," she gushed. Scheherazade cupped her hands around breasts that had remained very full for eleven centuries and pushed them up. Fatima forced Scheherazade's hands down.

"You have no idea how many times Mama had Bedia — that was the village's seamstress — come over to adjust the hem," Fatima said. "Bedia's eyesight was going, the old goat."

Using long-buried memory, Fatima moved her hand over to a spot with a reddish-pink stain. "Is it still there?"

"Is it from your wedding night?" Scheherazade cringed.

"I was eating a fig, and Bedia pinned me instead of the dress, and I dropped the fig." Fatima giggled. "I can still hear Mama barking at Bedia with her scratchy voice as she grabbed the fig and juggled it as if it were a grenade."

"It must have been an explosive wedding." Scheherazade batted her eyes.

Fatima stopped giggling. "It was the last time I ever saw Mama — and our house," she said. "When I left with Marwan, Mama gave me a key. She told me that if Marwan ever did anything bad to me, I should come home. Even if for some reason she was not there, I would still have the key to go inside. Then she kissed me twelve times. The morning after the wedding ceremony, Marwan's family came to inspect the bedsheets; they saw blood and were satisfied I had been a virgin, and so we went to Beirut that afternoon and sailed to America the next day." She stopped, too worn out by memory to continue.

"It was a good story, *ya qalbi,*" Scheherazade said. "And we've got you on a boat away from Deir Zeitoon."

"It wasn't just a story," Fatima said, mustering the powers of all the djinni to close the lid. "I thought you might think this dress would be nicer to die in than this robe. But it's too heavy to wait for death in. It'd kill me first. I'm not going to die from an overweight dress. Right? Come on, *yal-*

67

lah, I've told you a story of a husband; now you tell me how I will die."

"Is there no more passion to this story, more details of the wedding night?" Scheherazade asked by way of an answer.

"No," Fatima said, and crossed her arms.

"So now you will leave this dress and its stories to Amir's bride?"

Fatima uncrossed her arms. "No, I cannot give it to a grandchild when I still have a daughter that is not married," she lamented, not realizing she was opening the storybook on her children

"An unmarried daughter? You are eighty-five," Scheherazade said. "How could you have a daughter not yet married?"

"I had Lena late in life." Fatima sighed, thoughts of her death easily made subservient to her daughter's marital failings. "She is choosing marriage late in life."

"Choosing?" Scheherazade said.

"This is what she tells me," Fatima said, and began twirling her purple hair. "But my children do not often tell me the truth about anything but the weather. And when the weather is very bad, they do not even tell me that."

"Only one unmarried daughter," Scheherazade said. "That is not so bad. You must give her the dress."

Fatima shook her head. "She will turn forty in ninety-seven days," she said.

"Every woman has her time," Scheherazade offered. "Marriage later is better than sooner. How many years can you really spend with one man? I'm going on 1,108 years with the same one. Even with all the help of astrologists, magicians, and alchemists, it has not been easy to keep it alive in my stories. And look at you. Your marriage lasted only sixty-five years."

"True, but I did not have a matchmaker," Fatima said. "How good my family used to be at marriage. It was not for nothing that my grandmother, *Allah yerhamha,* was the greatest matchmaker in all of Lebanon."

"How bad could your marriage have been if you made ten babies?" Scheherazade said, seductively running her hands up her body and licking her lips.

Fatima covered her ears with her hair to shut out Scheherazade. She wanted only to spend time with her boxes.

SCHEHERAZADE

Alas, Fatima had not been enticed to speak of her nuptials. However, talk of this daughter with no groom was the farthest the old lady had traveled away from Deir Zeitoon in a story. Perhaps a little more provocation was required.

"It is possible that if you had been a more vigilant mother, your daughter would not be a spinster," Scheherazade goaded. "She would instead be a wife."

"My daughter is too beautiful to be a spinster," Fatima snapped back, and her eyes squinted in anger. "And you cannot blame me. I was more vigilant with my children than any quarterback guarding his ball."

Scheherazade was not familiar with the duties of a quarterback, but her shrug implied that the old lady's words hadn't altered her beliefs in any way.

"For your information, my family may soon reclaim its success with marriage," Fatima added. "Through my grandson Zade. He is my fifth daughter Nadia's son. He runs a matchmaking service for Arabs."

"*Smallah, smallah,* your daughter sounds like she has raised a son more amazing than the logicians, geographers, and philosophers of the Abbasids," marveled Scheherazade, who knew that nothing endeared her to people more than excessively complimenting their children.

"He has his own coffee shop in Washington where young people can meet each other even without these computer things," Fatima boasted. "Did you know Nadia can speak Arabic?"

"Don't all your children speak Arabic?" Scheherazade asked.

Fatima bowed her head. "No, only Nadia." She sighed. "Ibrahim and I would speak to them all in Arabic, but they would answer us in English. Then one day Nadia told us she had gotten a scholarship. Oh, our joy. We thought for sure it would be in accounting. She was always helping me write the bills. But it was a scholarship to study Arabic. *Subhan Allah,* God is mysterious, she went to a university to learn the only thing her parents could have taught her at home. Here she was happy to learn Arabic from strangers when Ibrahim is an excellent reader and writer of Arabic, and as you can hear, I speak very eloquently."

Scheherazade could not tell Fatima that her Arabic was fossilized, as her own use of the language was even more dated.

"Nadia and her husband, Elias, are both professors, *mashallah,*" Fatima continued. "They used to teach Arab things to mostly Arab kids who also could have just listened to their parents. But since September 11, there are many people who want to learn Middle East things, and her classes are very full. Now, help me back to the room for my glasses."

She stood up, and they walked down the hallway arm in arm.

"Elias is a Christian name," Scheherazade said, prying.

Fatima picked up a strand of hair and began twirling it. "So you wish to reprimand me on how I let my daughter marry a Christian, just like the women in the Arab Ladies Society did in Detroit. Both the Christian and Muslim ladies accused me of being a lenient mother."

"Did those ladies dance at the wedding?" Scheherazade asked her.

"Oh, how everyone danced," Fatima recalled, and let go of the strand of hair.

Scheherazade shrugged. "If people could still dance at the wedding, how bad could it be?"

"It was the last wedding where people danced for my children," Fatima said.

Scheherazade was sure Fatima no longer was talking about religion or even Nadia, but before she could pursue this, the old lady put on her nearby glasses and picked up a picture from the vanity of a young man and woman smiling at the camera, arms around each other.

"This is Zade and his Giselle," Fatima

said. *"Aladdin and Jasmine, Inc. We guarantee it won't take 1001 nights of bad dates to find love — or your money back"* was written across the bottom of the photo. She put the photo back on the vanity. "The writing is their engagement vows, I believe. Probably some new fashion for romance. . . . Oh, how I would like to make sure my children are all okay before I go," Fatima said. "*Ya Allah,* I wonder if Mama had so much to do before dying. Of course, she had given me the key to the house in Deir Zeitoon long before she died. It is in one of the boxes in the attic. I must find it for Amir."

She motioned for her cane and fell silent when they reentered the guest room. She used her faraway glasses to get to a certain section and then put on her nearby glasses to inspect the boxes more closely, twirling her hair all the while.

"Why do you not give the house to this Arabic-speaking daughter?" Scheherazade wondered.

"No, someone might kill her there," Fatima said.

"Kill her?" Scheherazade perched herself on the windowsill, ready for more, but Fatima was lost in her boxes. The rustle of the eucalyptus tree turned her attention outside. Two people in black clothing were

73

descending from the large petrol caravan.

"How about instead of calling the FBI tip line, we contact the bureau in Washington directly," the man in black whispered. "When we've got enough, that is."

"And who is waiting for our call in Washington?" the woman in black whispered back. "Washington, my ass."

Hmm, Washington, indeed, Scheherazade thought. *Bejouz.* Maybe. She had never seen the capital of this nation that was born more than seven hundred years after her own birth. Fatima had told her a story finally that was not about Deir Zeitoon, but it was not complete.

She would go see for herself this astounding matchmaker and Arabic-speaking daughter whom people wanted to kill. After all this time with Fatima, she was curious to see what kind of people the old lady would leave behind in this world. And she would find out if this child was in fact in danger, for as much as she provoked the old woman, it bothered her to see her so burdened by worry and fear.

Scheherazade pulled out a gilded silver compact and looked at herself. Even though no mortal but Fatima could see her, it was important to her to live up to her timeless beauty, especially as she was visiting Fatima's family for the first time. She adjusted her kohl and then she slid off the perch and flew out the window past the fig tree.

She traveled on her flying carpet, which was much in need of a good beating by Omar the Carpet Cleaner to rid it of the dust it had accumulated in the 993 days since she had followed an American soldier home to see what the world looked liked from this side of it. The boy had returned from Iraq to Los Angeles for his father's funeral, and it was at the cemetery that she had been drawn to the prayers mumbled in Arabic at a nearby grave site. Fatima, too, had just arrived in Los Angeles and stood watching the Arabic mourners, an impatient Amir carrying her suitcase and trying to lead her back to his car. But it wasn't Amir's frustration that held her attention. It was Fatima's hair. Purple had been the color of Scheherazade's sister Dunyazad's hair, which Scheherazade used to braid every night as they planned their future. Dunyazad had been part of the past for centuries, and she had never lived to Fatima's age. Still, Scheherazade had understood that this old lady was the mortal with whom she was fated to spend the next 1001 nights. The trill of Dunyazad's laughter had danced in her head as she followed Fatima's purple hair home.

As she had on that first day in America, Scheherazade flew, albeit in the opposing direction, across the Rocky Mountains and over lakes and rivers and plains and another greener, smoother mountain range until she arrived at a river from which parkways of the most verdant trees she had ever seen were laced through geometrically pleasing gardens and monuments, many of which reminded Scheherazade of old Athens and Rome when she and her husband had summered away from Baghdad. Everything here was much newer, whiter, and brighter than Athens or Rome, even brighter than she imagined Athens had been in its glory, long before scholars in Baghdad would commit its history to paper.

Scheherazade had left the great white monuments and statues of long-gone men in the distance by the time she came upon a place alive with shops and cafés. She began to look for Zade's coffee house among them, but it was Zade she spotted first. She recognized Fatima's bumpy nose on him and the rest of him, from his khakis to his dimple, from the framed photo on Fatima's vanity.

He was on the escalator at Georgetown Park. Scheherazade had never seen so many

76

things for sale, not even in the souks of Damascus. But this place was so much cooler and more spacious than those souks. America had a great deal of room. It was easy to avoid bumping into people, especially as most of the people seemed to move around alone rather than in clumps the way they did back home.

She readjusted her hair and veil with her hands in a wall mirror. So many of the women didn't even wear kohl on their eyes, just as Fatima didn't. Femininity was a lost art in America, Scheherazade thought. Yet she had never seen a land with so many places to look at oneself. She posed for all the mall mirrors until Zade reached the exit.

Zade walked the length of two streets before he stopped in front of a place with beautiful mosaic calligraphy welcoming everyone. The place was called Scheherazade's Diwan Café. Under the words was a drawing of a half-naked belly dancer. Who is that supposed to be? Surely not me, she thought. ALADDIN AND JASMINE, INC. MAGICAL DATING FOR ALL was written underneath. She was not happy to see her stories — and herself — so cheapened by commerce, even if it was in the name of love.

ZADE

It took Zade a few seconds every night when he entered the café to realize he didn't have to wait to be seated in this crowded, cologne-infested capitalistic enterprise. He owned it. In those few seconds, Zade's eyes would rest uncomfortably on a large poster bragging of Aladdin and Jasmine, Inc.'s, matchmaking powers.

Despite Scheherazade's Diwan Café's romantic darkness — carefully orchestrated by Giselle with the haze of smoke from the water pipes, the red velvet couches, and the dim chandelier lighting — no one could miss the poster. It hung over a tiny stage where the Ali Baba Band-Its were covering a Raghib Alami song. In it, Zade and Giselle's lips nearly touched, the Washington Monument rising between their heads. The girls in the café giggled when they recognized Zade from it. He had no energy to go welcome them, although he knew any other sane male would have taken full advantage of his café star status.

"Zade, we need to order more apple tobacco for the hookahs," his almond-eyed hostess said. Her hair was wrapped in a coin-trimmed scarf supplied by Giselle. He tried to put on a dimpled smile as he forced his eyes away from the poster, but then he remembered he was the boss and didn't have to be all that nice.

"I'll order some more tomorrow," he told her. "Any other problems?"

"My boyfriend's a dickhead, but other than that, it's going pretty good." She smiled.

"What?" he said. He hoped she wasn't flirting with him.

"Just kidding, boss." She laughed. He had told all his employees during the first interview that they had to keep their personal problems to themselves. It was enough that he had to listen to the customers'. He had been raised to disdain the majority of his clientele: the Arab elite's children, rich through business or family name, shallower, his father once remarked, than the plates of hummus the café served.

As usual, Zade went straight to the office with the ESCORTED GUESTS ONLY sign on the door. An escorted guest was already seated, mesmerized by a poster of Zade and Giselle as they waved to the camera from the Key Bridge. "There are more than 1001 stories of love — the possibilities are infinite" was written above their heads. It was the only decor in the office.

Zade and Giselle had parted 142 days

short of having reached 1001 days together, but no one knew that aside from himself — and his mother, Nadia, who was now in charge of the business part of the business even though she opposed profiting from other people's loneliness. She was opposed to profiting in general.

His wasn't an enterprise in which he could display his heartache to his clients, and so he politely nodded at the Qatari business-man sitting across from him. His job barely had begun for the night, and he was already set for it to be over. The Qatari was smok-ing the hookah with one hand and sipping cardamom coffee with the other. He tight-ened his diamond cuff links and pointed to the poster with his right hand while placing his left hand on his heart.

"I want that," the Qatari said, marveling. *"Love is my law and remedy, whether hidden or revealed. Blessed my eyes that gazed on you, oh, treasured revelation."*

Zade knew that this was poetry from *The Arabian Nights,* but he did not let on. Although he spoke perfect Arabic, in busi-ness he chose English because Arabs always thought they were getting a better deal in English. Inferiority complex, his socialist parents used to say.

"You both fear and wish to be your oppressor," Elias once had explained to the delegates gathered at an Arab American Institute convention at which Zade passed out the bibliography of his father's speech.

"The girl is as beautiful as you are handsome," the Qatari continued as Nadia walked in, her tailored suit as sharp and crisp as her makeup and polished pumps. Zade believed his parents were the best-dressed far lefties he had ever met. He saw his mother's mouth start to open, a process that sadly never seemed to stop once it started.

"If I were the kind of mother who interfered in her son's business," Nadia began as the Qatari exhaled smoke and gave her his full attention, "I'd tell Zade's clients that some people are only truly lovable when they are in well-designed posters."

Nadia said this in classical Arabic, the kind studied in school but not actually spoken by real people.

"Your mother is not Arab?" the Qatari asked Zade.

This always silenced Nadia. It shamed her that she was a widely quoted expert on Middle Eastern languages yet was much more convincing as an American.

"An American wife." The Qatari nodded. "Your father was wise. The girls back home want too much. They want you to be rich, handsome, from a good family, generous, worldly, and ambitious."

"Dude, you are all those things," Zade proclaimed while his mother pursed her lips and left for the back room. He soon heard her banging on the computer as she prepared his 2003 tax returns, for which he'd filed for an extension. These were the business matters he used to count on Giselle for, as she, like his mother, had more of a thing for work than he did.

"In return for being all that I am, I want my bride to be nice to me," the Qatari continued. "Americans — aside from their government — are so nice, *quayseen khallas*. That is why I want my second wife to be American. Yes, Arab for our children's sake, but yes, nice American for my sake."

"Like my mother," Zade offered in case she was eavesdropping. "My friend, have you divorced your first wife first?"

"Why should I do her any favors?" the Qatari asked.

This was Zade's first client who was already married. "Huh . . . there is the possibility that your first wife and the second wife might end up liking each other more than they like you and gang up on you," he cautioned.

"My wife has given me five daughters and no sons," the Qatari countered.

"Well, perhaps one should remind oneself of secondary school biology," Nadia called out in classical Arabic from the back room, "during which most good students learned a man's sadly perceived biological misfortunes are his own doing, not his wife's."

"I really don't understand your mother's accent," the Qatari whispered loudly.

Nadia banged on the computer harder, making Zade's dimpled smile appear as he reviewed the Qatari's questionnaire.

"So basically, sir, you want a nice Arab-American bilingual highly educated virgin not opposed to wearing the *abaya* and conversant in French cuisine," Zade read.

"Yes." The Qatari beamed. "I am a simple man looking for a simple woman. But she should be nice."

"Of course," Zade agreed. "Any woman in my database who's not nice, I will not even put in the potential *habibti* section of your profile. Now, what kind of plan would you like?"

"I'd like her ready by Monday," the Qatari said.

"I was referring to the payment plan. We have the six-months-for-the-price-of-five or the month-by-month plan."

"Monday is still this month," the Qatari answered. "So I guess we're on the month-by-month plan."

"There's the American part of the word *Arab-American,*" Zade reminded him. "Marriage is one of the few things Americans do at a slower pace than Arabs. I recommend that you go with the six-month plan. *Affendi,* you know our girls. They're a little shy about this service. That's why I don't do the on-line thing. But if you want the very best, I would go with the six-months-for-the-price-of-five-months plan. We prefer MasterCard or Visa. By the way, is your visa in order? That's very important."

"Fine." The Qatari sighed. He pointed at the poster. "Just get me that."

"My mother arranged my meeting with Giselle," Zade said, shocked that all it took to make him persistent in a sale — for once — was the thrill of knowing it was devastating his mom. "That's the way our family does it. And now you're part of our family."

"Is that your mother when she wed?" the Qatari said, pointing to the black-and-white photo of Fatima in her wedding dress, which Zade kept on the desk for ambience. Nadia banged extra loudly on the computer keys. "Actually, that's my tayta, married sixty-five years," Zade said. He did not mention his grandparents' divorce. But if his Tayta Fatima and Jiddo Ibrahim had died in their seventies, like Giselle's grandparents, they wouldn't have lived long enough to get divorced. Perhaps he and Giselle would not live as long as his grandparents.

"*Mashallah,* God be praised," the Qatari said, looking at Fatima's photo with a squint, as if she might reveal the secret of love if he looked harder. "I will be patient."

"Yes, yes." Zade nodded.

"I bought a little vacation farm in Jordan two summers ago," the Qatari continued. "It has many olive trees. One day, I asked the gardener why he was letting the olives fall off the tree. Why not make them into olive oil? He told me that these ones on the ground were not worthy of becoming olive oil, that we had to wait for the others still on the tree to blossom and they would one day make wonderful oil. He promised, and he was right. On the day he brought the olives back from the press, we sopped up that crystal-green liquid with bread for dinner, and it was the finest meal I ever ate. These women of yours are also fine olives; they cannot be pressed until they are ready. Along with the $29.99 for this month's service, I'm going to throw in another thousand to help our less fortunate brothers and sisters in America who want more than just an olive that falls on the ground early."

He stood up and left with an impassioned handshake. Just when Zade had been ready to dismiss the Qatari as what his father called another sad product of the Gulf social welfare system for millionaires, the man had to go do something kind — odd in its poetry, but still . . . How much work would it really take to give him a chance at Aladdin and Jasmine, Inc. love?

He looked at the check, opened his computer file, and added to his questionnaire: "How do you feel about being a second wife? (a) abhorrent (b) mildly abhorrent (c) acceptable if there is no other option and I still want to get married."

Zade looked over the first part of the list one more time:

- Name:
- Age:
- Family Name:
- Paternal Grandfather's Name:
- Maternal Grandfather's Name:
- How would you best describe your family roots (a) peasant (b) city (c) Bedouin?
- On a scale of 5 to 10, how

important is that he/she is from a "good family"?

- Education: (a) Ph.D. (b) M.A. (c) less than an M.A.
- Would you like children? (a) Yes, but I'm physically unable to do so (b) Yes, less than five (c) Yes, more than five.
- Are you (a) Arab-born (b) American-born (c) other (please specify country of birth)
- What type of Arab do you prefer to date (circle all that apply)? (a) Mediterranean (b) Egyptian (c) Persian Gulf (d) North African (e) East African
- What religious constraints work for you (check all that apply)? (a) Arab Muslim (b) Arab Christian (c) non-Arab Muslim (If also seeking non-Arab Christians, please see Match.com or eHarmony, which will allow you a selection far beyond the reach of our core clientele.)
- How much Arab blood does the

person have to have? a) 100%
(b) 50% (c) less than 25% (d)
irrelevant as long as she/he
wants to be with me for
reasons other than money or
a green card.

- Muslim Women Only: Do you
wear a hijab? (If you need a
translation of hijab as "head
scarf," the answer is no.)
- Muslim Men Only: Indicate
whether you prefer a woman
who (a) only uses sunscreen
as extra coverage (b) wears
a hijab (c) wears an abaya
(d) covers her face (e) covers her hands
- Do you have your parents'
permission to date or will
this be in secret? (All
clients, regardless of age,
must answer this if parents
are still living.)
- Approximately how many relatives and family friends do
you expect to attend your
wedding? (a) 500 (b) 1,000–
2,000 (c) over 2,000
- If a U.S. citizen, do you
exercise your right to vote?

(a) yes (b) no (c) why bother as it is all run by the Israeli lobby? (d) I would if someone would tell me how.
- Do you support the war in Iraq? (a) kind of (b) no way

Zade felt his mother in back of him. "So much for Arab unity," he said with a shrug as she looked over the questionnaire on the screen.

Nadia didn't laugh. Arab unity had been the point of his father's existence, his true passion, aside from Nadia and, consequently, Zade and his sister. His father now was spending a semester as a visiting scholar at the American University in the emirate of Sharjah. The money couldn't be turned down, not that his parents would ever admit that a lifetime of roving academia and near-communist politics in the Reagan era had left them unprepared for impending old age. Nor would they admit that their son was doing well enough to take care of them, although Nadia had the numbers in front of her every evening. Nadia's own teaching commitments had not allowed her to go with Elias, and Zade consequently had inherited her evenings. She had chosen to handle Zade's taxes rather than stay home alone. Being alone reminded her of the six months she had lived in Lebanon while trying to secure Elias's freedom from those who had kidnapped him off the Beirut University College campus when her children were small. She felt lucky that Zade had no interest in doing his own taxes.

"What was that man saying about purchasing a farm in Jordan?" Nadia asked, and looked away from the computer. "Nothing to do with their money except buy, buy, buy."

"Actually he was complimenting Tayta and Giselle . . . and you," Zade said.

She ignored him and looked at the poster. "Nadia, how could you have not known Giselle was so filled with capitalist greed?" she demanded out loud, using the third person as a diplomatic cushion; she'd developed that habit while negotiating with Elias's kidnappers.

What mother wouldn't have set them up? Hell, what dating service wouldn't have? Giselle was the daughter of a fellow professor of Middle Eastern studies at the University of Chicago. Just like Zade, her mother was Arab American, her father Arab. She was also half Christian, half Muslim. Both had fathers who had sat on panels with great scholars such as Edward Said, Kamal

Salibi, and Hanan Ashrawi, and both had fathers who had been hostages in Lebanon. Four years ago, when Zade and Giselle were both twenty-five, their mothers were moderating a panel on "Cross-Cultural and Middle East Education in the U.S. Secondary School Classroom" at an Arab American University Graduates conference.

Zade, Giselle, and their mothers all sat at the same table during the chicken Kiev luncheon. "Zade loves *kusa bi laban*," Nadia announced to the air. "I wish someone could go with him on the days it's the special at Mama Aisha's."

"I love it, too." Giselle smiled. "I love it most when I can't get it. When I'm hanging out in the Middle East, I kind of forget about it and start missing pizza that isn't an oil spill."

Zade laughed. "Yeah, but I don't miss passable Pizza Hut as much as I miss organized waiting lines."

"Dude, so true. To stop myself from going all Red Brigades at the post office here, I just remind myself that the line is nowhere near as long as the checkpoints over there," Giselle explained. "Fascist paper tiger regimes."

And that was it. That was the moment when both Nadia and Zade fell in love with

Giselle: Nadia for Giselle's astute politics, Zade for the way her raspy voice and wild hand gestures made checkpoints — and even post offices — sound steamy. But there are a lot of things people can have in common that can't make up for all that they don't share. Zade did not tell his clients this.

Nadia's love for Giselle ended a few months after the two started dating, when Zade announced that he and Giselle were coming over for dinner. Nadia made grape leaves, the only Middle Eastern dish she knew how to make, having been as uninterested in learning cooking from Fatima as she had been in learning Arabic from her.

"Your mother said that if she were the kind of wife who told her husband what to wear, she would have told me to wear a tie tonight," Elias said that evening. "So I did." That was when Zade knew that his parents were expecting him to reveal that Giselle and he were getting engaged, and so he took her hand. Giselle gave it a squeeze and beamed first at him and then at his parents, eyes shining with the bright future she had planned for them.

"We're going to open a hookah bar," Giselle blurted out.

"You're going to give people lung cancer?" his parents said in unison. "Shame. *Aabe.*

Hasn't Philip Morris done enough to destroy the world?"

"The water pipe uses all-natural tobacco," Giselle countered.

Nadia and Elias turned away from her. "Zade, what about completing your Fulbright proposal to research the influence of progressive nonsectarian Islamic politics on post–civil war reconstruction in southern Lebanon?" Elias asked.

"We will be promoting the revival of Arab culture," Zade replied, not mentioning that he hadn't downloaded the application. "The hookah is a four-hundred-year-old tradition. There are thousands of Arab students in D.C. who miss back home. Commerce isn't a dirty word. It's perceiving a need and meeting it."

His parents' shoulders slumped. "It's like you never read Noam Chomsky or Gore Vidal," Nadia said. "My mother has never read anyone's words, and she wouldn't open a hookah bar, especially after my sisters used to call her and her friends backward when they used to smoke the *argileh.* That's the actual real word — you're not even using proper Arabic."

"Just like your mother and her friends were then, these students are a new generation of immigrants hungry for a place to come together," Giselle explained.

"Arabs are always together," Elias argued. "They don't know how to be alone. The point is to bring them together to talk about something more important than their neighbors' affairs."

"But we're catching a trend," Zade said.

Catching a trend was exactly how Giselle had pitched to it to him the night before, when she had also defined commerce for him. They were walking home from an Arab-American Anti-Discrimination Committee gala dinner at which both Nadia and Elias were speakers.

On the Key Bridge, Giselle took his hand. "I want to ask you something," she said. "Something big."

"Me, too." Zade smiled. "You first."

It was a beautiful full-moon night with a perfect view of the Capitol and the Washington Monument. In a setting like that, Zade was sure she was going to suggest that he move in with her, and so he asked a passerby to take their picture for posterity. The picture, it turned out, was poster-quality, and today hung above the Ali Baba Band-Its.

"Would you like to go into business with me?" she asked. "I know a trend we can catch, a need we can meet. If we open at

94

Christmas, we'll capitalize on all the kids having nowhere to go at break."

Their relationship by that point was balanced enough that the question had been perfunctory. So while Giselle borrowed money from her brother, who had a booming engineering business in Saudi Arabia, Zade borrowed money from his twin sister's husband, a wealthy Qatari she had met while working at Al Jazeera TV as a reporter. Nadia and Elias had been so proud of Lamya until her pretty face destined her to doing fluffy celebrity interviews.

And now Zade had disappointed them, but he didn't want to be without Giselle. Others — say, his parents — hadn't heard the smart-ass comments she whispered to him during movies through a mouthful of popcorn, hadn't felt the smallness of her waist when she reached up to kiss him, and couldn't see that her face was always as luminescent as the moon on its fourteenth day, something his grandfather Ibrahim had murmured about his grandmother at her seventieth birthday party, an event Nadia had insisted on celebrating when she had taken Zade and his sister to Detroit years ago, with his grandmother protesting the whole time. Zade had heard Ibrahim's words right after everyone sang "Happy

Birthday." He wished other people had been listening because no one, least of all Nadia, believed him when he quoted Ibrahim. It was only when he met Giselle that he knew there were women worthy of such a description. He sprang the moon thing on Giselle the day their business became profitable, and she had gotten uncustomarily flustered, the way he always was in her presence. She was the first person, place, or thing that had ever motivated him to finish something he'd started. His family's passions had had the opposite effect on him, making him shrink away from accomplishment, as if without their noble goals he couldn't hold his own, so why even bother? He couldn't equal Giselle, either, but just the scent of her inspired him to try, at least occasionally.

A week after Zade and Giselle signed the café lease, taking over a doughnut shop that had become passé, the World Trade Center was hit. Zade then assumed that the planet was doomed — and that he and Giselle had a bad idea on their hands. But Giselle hired a security guard, and they opened to a packed house a few months later. Scheherazade's Diwan Café was the envy of bar owners from Georgetown to Adams Morgan, and it didn't even serve alcohol.

September 11 had left Zade's parents

decidedly grayer and sadder. Perhaps that was why the success of Scheherazade's Diwan Café touched them, and for a while, if not for the hookah smoke, they would have been almost proud of how Zade was fostering Arab understanding.

One night, as the crowd began straggling home, Giselle grabbed Zade in a hug and they swayed to the Ali Baba Band-Its' version of Fairuz's *"Habetuk bi Seif."*

"I want people to be as happy as we are," she whispered.

"Me, too," Zade said.

"I was thinking about our future," she hinted.

"So was I," he said. He already had the ring in his pocket. But before he could get on his knees, she took his hand and looked deep in his eyes.

"I want to ask you something," she said.

"Me, too." He smiled. "You first."

"Let's let the world see our love."

"Just what I was thinking."

"Really?" She blushed. "Oh, *habibi,* I should have known. Your mother told me that your grandmother always brags about your great-great-grandmother's matchmaking skills. Guess what? I bet with my help, you'll find out it's genetic. We're going to have one hell of a matchmaking service."

Zade let go of the ring in his pocket. They both borrowed more money from their siblings and started Aladdin and Jasmine, Inc.

"How could you possibly know your clients are going to be a good match if they don't sit down and hash it out first?" Elias asked.

"Arguing about Middle East politics over dinner without actually listening to each other isn't love for everyone," Zade said, summing up the spice in his parents' marriage.

Within five months, Aladdin and Jasmine, Inc., had over a thousand people signed up. It was a ratio of four males for every female, but it was working. It went national within a year. Elias almost boasted that Zade was the owner when a student in his contemporary Middle Eastern politics seminar said that Arabs' devotion to their heritage could be manifested in the popularity of Aladdin and Jasmine, Inc. "Love is very important in maintaining a culture," Elias told his students. "Cultures without love die."

At the wedding reception for the first couple to meet and marry through Aladdin and Jasmine, Inc., Giselle sniffled and Zade took her hand.

"Look at this beautiful thing we've created," she gushed.

"Sit down, Giselle," he said. "I want to ask you something."

She sat down, big eyes aglow with tears. "We've had several successful engagements since we opened," he began.

"Twenty," she confirmed. "We're probably doing far better than Match.com and eHarmony, speaking per capita."

"Yes," Zade said. "So I was thinking —"

"So was I," she interjected.

"Okay, me first," Zade said, drying off his palms on his suit jacket. "What if we took ourselves to the next level."

He pulled the ring out of his pocket.

"So you want to go global, too?" she said, looking in his eyes and not seeing what was in his hand. "Think of all the Arab immigrants in Brazil, West Africa, and Canada and all the Lebanese, Egyptian, Iraqi, and Moroccan guest workers living in the Persian Gulf, all looking for true love. We can bring that to them, sweetie."

He put the ring back in his pocket. "Expansion is expensive," he said. "We don't even have people on the ground in those places."

"We can do it," Giselle countered. "We'll spend a month in each place. Hire a good part-time person to be in charge, work out the initial marketing. We'll start in London. Guess what? There's a restaurant there that makes the best *kusa bi laban* outside of Lebanon."

"What about here?" he pointed out. "This is where love cashes the checks."

"You're right," she conceded, momentarily as defeated as he was. "No, we have no choice. I'll be the one that goes. You stay. Your mom would go all loco alone, with your dad away for the next two semesters."

"And you won't go loco without me?"

"I'll be fine," she answered too quickly. "And so will the business. Your mom can handle that end. She already does, even though she won't admit it."

"You know who won't be fine?" he said. "Remember me?"

"You can live without me for a couple of months." She grinned. "We've got the rest of our lives. And we'll talk on the phone every day."

"If you go, Giselle, then we're over," Zade decided aloud. He felt the pores on his underarms release significant amounts of sweat, as using ultimatums on her — or anyone — was not something he had ever tried before.

"Why are you talking to me that way?" she said, taking a step back.

"We know from our own website that three in four of our long-distance matches end in failure," he said, pressing his feet into the ground to help keep his shoulders lifted.

"What if I come back at least once a month?" she offered, but did not step forward.

"Don't bother," Zade said with no threat implied this time. He let his gaze leave her moonlike face, focusing on the ground instead. "I don't want to spend my whole life trying to make you happy by becoming the greatest entrepreneur love has ever known."

"God, you sound like our parents," she said.

He had no response to that. Giselle crossed her arms.

"I love you," she said. "But I don't want to stand in the way of your happiness. If you want to find someone more socialist, then I won't deprive you of that. We'll just stay business partners."

It was not the answer he was hoping for, but it was the one he should have expected.

"I might become a member of Aladdin and Jasmine, Inc., myself," he declared.

Giselle teared up but did not protest. She hugged him tight. "Bye, baby," she whispered, and walked out right past their poster.

It had been four months since they had decided to expand their business and break up. He had not seen her since. Nor had he joined Aladdin and Jasmine, Inc. He hadn't even filled out the questionnaire. But he had added to it: "Please note that there is a 20% surcharge for clients in Latin America, West Africa, and Canada."

He looked at the clock. He still talked to Giselle every day, mostly about the sales figures Nadia put together. Today he couldn't wait to tell her about the Qatari who had just left.

The phone rang, as it did every night at eight-thirty. A nine-hour time difference necessitated planned, rather than off-the-cuff, communication. As a result, business was at a peak, and he often wondered what heights their personal relationship would have reached with more scheduled talking.

"Hi, sweet . . . I mean Zade," Giselle said from Dubai. "I signed up twenty new clients at a mixer we cohosted with a local radio station at the Jumeirah Beach Club. I wish you could have seen the crowd. It rocked."

"That's great," Zade said. "But check this out: Today a Qatari guy came in looking for an American second wife. He's some business associate of my sister's husband, so I had to listen to him talk about olives in Jordan."

"Hey, we should get your sister to find him some American woman working in Qatar," she screamed over the buzz on the line. It was not the outrage or laughter he had sought. "I'm flying to Qatar tomorrow, anyway. Your sister's going to interview me about the business on TV. Cool, huh?"

"Okay, then I should give the Qatari dude the five stages of love the next time I see him," he said.

"Attraction, uncertainty, exclusivity, intimacy, and engagement," she responded, quoting one of the dating tips she, with his help, had spent a day acquiring from the back covers of relationship books. Then she got quiet. "Oh, and guess what. I met the most amazing guy today."

He had practiced various reactions to this inevitability many times. "Hey, cool," he began, forgetting all the more sophisticated words he had planned for this moment.

"This guy is handsome, rich, and talented, and guess what?"

"What?" he answered, starting to sweat.

"He so wants to meet your gay actor cousin," Giselle shouted from Dubai. "Maybe if your Tayta Fatima saw how hand-

103

some this guy was — and an Arab guy, no less — she'd accept the whole gay thing. Or at least your mom wouldn't be so angry at me for going all global because I'm doing her mom a good one."

"Huh," he responded. It wasn't his mom who was truly angry. But just as with the Qatari and his money, just when he was hoping he could learn to despise Giselle, she was reminding him of why he couldn't help loving her.

"And I think I found someone for your Aunt Lena," she went on. "He's divorced, but I think divorced is better for her than never married. At her age, it's better to be with a guy who has some experience with the long run."

It wasn't easy to stop loving someone who still loved you, even if it wasn't the way you'd like to be loved. Suddenly, he wanted to compliment her on how good she was with other people's relationships, and that made him laugh uncontrollably. Nadia walked out of the back room just as Zade's laughter climaxed.

"Giselle, I got to go," he said. "My mom's here."

He hung up, and Nadia crossed her arms.

"You know what they say in Middle East negotiations when no happy solution can be found?" Nadia said. She pointed to the Aladdin and Jasmine, Inc., poster and pantomimed ripping it off the wall. "They say let's tear down those old maps and look at the world anew."

"Giselle found an Arab guy for Amir," he announced, and waited while she thought up a diplomatic response to Giselle's overture.

"What the hell is wrong with Giselle?" Nadia screamed instead. "We're only pretending to look for someone. For my mother's happiness, not his. And we're pretending to look for a woman. If Giselle loved your family, she'd find someone for Lena, not Amir."

"She did," he said, glowering. "Without us even asking her to."

But Nadia had no gratitude. "Then why don't you let her help you? She has signed up at least thirty-eight new women you could date since she left. Perhaps, just perhaps, you could stop being so lazy and make an effort to date some of them."

"Dating is a numbers game, Mom," Zade said, quoting from Aladdin and Jasmine, Inc.'s, online dating tips. "Love is not."

"Then why does your business — Giselle's business — avow that there are infinite opportunities?" she said. "Take one of them."

105

"Giselle's going to see Lamya tomorrow," he answered. "Lamya's going to interview her on Al Jazeera."

He wasn't sure if Nadia's sigh was out of longing for his twin sister or from disapproval of Giselle being in the same room with her other child.

She placed Aladdin and Jasmine, Inc.'s tax returns in front of him. "I'm done. If I were a greedy corporate monster, I would say that Giselle's expansion idea has made sense," she admitted. "During her travels, she has increased membership 50 percent, and the costs of running the business in Europe and South America have not even come close to the contingency figure."

"See?" Zade said.

"See what?" she asked. "Perhaps it would be advisable to not confuse her commitment to the business with — well, anything else. We all have different things we can commit to. Love isn't one of them for her."

"I'm the one that broke up with her," Zade said.

"Then act like it," his mother snapped. "I filled out the questionnaire for you and added your profile to the database. We'll find a good match for you. I'm going home to call your dad and find out how his lecture on Middle East civil disobedience in the

British and French colonial era went. And before I forget, there's a girl waiting outside to see you."

Nadia said the last part as if it were an afterthought, which it most certainly wasn't.

"Remember who introduced me to Giselle," he warned.

"I don't know this girl," Nadia said rather convincingly. "See you tomorrow."

Zade was sure she would tell his father how she wanted to drown Giselle in the Qatari's Jordanian olive oil. Elias would calm her down, as he always did. His mother and father certainly could be on a poster for Aladdin and Jasmine, Inc.

When the girl walked in, Zade didn't recognize her from the database, but he didn't pay as much attention to the photos as his mother did. She shook his hand. There was a slight awkwardness to her confidence, as if it had come with much practice rather than naturally. But his mother did have a good eye. "Cute with kick," he might have written for her profile. The girl sat down on the ottoman. Her skin was very white and was framed by very black hair that fell down her back in thick, straight strands.

"Hi, I'm Mina Parstabar," she said.

"I'm sorry to put you through this, but

107

I'm not looking for anyone right now," he apologized.

"How do you know that if you don't know what I have to offer?" she replied. "Offer you exclusively."

He sat up straighter, almost rising out of his lethargy. She was bold.

"So, Mina, what are you offering?" he said, and arched an eyebrow. "Exclusively."

She returned his gesture with an eyebrow raise of her own. "What do you think?" she said. "A partnership."

"Like I advise my clients, let's start slow," he said. "Partnership is a big word."

"Do you think I'm going to let you run the show?" she said. "Fifty-fifty. I already get more marriage proposals than you."

"Oh, yeah?" Zade said. He leaned in without meaning to. "What's your secret?"

She leaned back and pulled out a photo album. "I can claim to have nearly 1001 marriages under my belt," she announced, and handed him her card. Then she flipped through the brides and grooms, photo after photo. She was not the bride in any of them.

Zade looked at her card: "The First 1001 Nights to Forever. Iranian singles no more. Mina Parstabar, CEO."

"Look, I know you already have a partner," she continued, and pointed at the poster. "You guys got your little Arab-on-Arab business going, like I got my Iranian thing going. But I'm thinking bigger. Big Middle East and Muslim lovers plan. I've already been to see an Afghani matchmaker and another one well entrenched in the South Asian community in New York. I've also been in touch with the Black Muslim Alliance. I'm going to see a Turkish dating service based in New York tomorrow and a Bosnian one later this week. I got a lot of people that come to me that aren't necessarily Iranian but are looking for a Muslim. I also got a lot of Armenians. Word has it you've got a few Lebanese and Syrian Armenians signed up. We combine databases and there will be no end to what we can do."

He couldn't help being a little turned on by her enthusiasm. Like Giselle's, it had the energy of the social revolutions of the 1960s his parents spoke of so often. Perhaps Giselle had set him up to be attracted to overambitious hotties. Maybe, like the clients in his database, he had a type; that meant that there was more than one girl in the world to fulfill his needs. That would be a relief. He cleared his throat, which he thought gave him a businessman's demeanor. "We're committed to expanding to include as many people as we can," he confirmed. "Just today I added, 'How do you feel about being a second wife?' to our questionnaire. Put that in after a Qatari came in here describing women like ripe olives."

"I already have that," Mina said, and handed him a copy of her client questionnaire.

"I see you don't have anything on alcohol," he read. "I got that and pork covered under numbers forty and forty-one." Zade handed her his list.

"Do you eat pork or drink alcohol? (a) yes (b) no (c) no, except for pepperoni on pizza yes (d) yes, but don't tell anyone," Mina read. "Good, but I don't see you've got any mention of in-laws. Check out my number six and number seven."

"Would you be willing to take in your spouse's mother, brother, and sisters should they decide to immigrate here? How about cousins?" Zade read.

He looked for something else on his questionnaire that she had missed. He couldn't find anything.

"Talk it over with your partner and get back to me," Mina offered.

"You don't have a partner?" Zade asked.

"Nope," she said.

"Then what inspired you to get into this business?"

"My grandmother was always telling me stories about how her grandmother was the greatest matchmaker in all of Abadan," Mina said. "She always said matchmaking was an art, not a donkey race."

"That's how I got into it, too," he lied. "My grandmother told me the same stories about her grandmother. Say, why don't we discuss our grandmothers over dinner."

"Don't you want to talk to your partner first?" Mina said. "I don't want to go into business with someone who doesn't communicate well with his partner."

"We communicate every day," Zade said.

"Good." Mina nodded. "Tell her this could be just the beginning. Maybe we'll take on all of Asia America next."

"Yeah, we could call it the International Dateline," he said. "Sometimes these ideas just come to me. The entrepreneur in me, I guess." Zade smiled, showing off his dimple.

Mina got up in her awkward yet confident way and shook his hand. He was willing to bet she had never used her database for herself, either. She was a lot like Giselle. Then she turned around and cracked a big smile. "How exactly did your Qatari say a woman is like a ripe olive?" she asked.

She had given him the reaction he had thought Giselle would. Mina and Giselle were not types. "Have a seat and I'll tell you," he said, and despite his exhaustion, he winked, something he'd never tried before. He'd gotten a lot done today: talked to a customer, contemplated growing the business, signed the tax returns his mother finally had completed, and, to top off the night, made the decision to explain to a girl who perhaps might offer infinite possibilities the connection between women and really good olive oil. He felt for the ring in his pocket. It was still there, still made his heart skip. But Mina also had a face that just possibly resembled the moon on its fourteenth day.

■ ■ ■ ■

THE 994TH NIGHT

■ ■ ■ ■

SCHEHERAZADE

Upon returning to Los Angeles, Scheherazade's carpet landed among several dust-covered homeless men on Santa Monica Boulevard. It had been a smooth ride back from Washington. The West had embellished her with many qualities she did not like — including the half-naked way she was portrayed at Zade's café — but every now and then it had endowed her with a good idea, such as the flying carpet.

Outside Amir's house, Scheherazade saw that the new petrol caravan had not moved. She heard with little strain the two people in black talking inside.

"Check it out," the man in black said. "This Amir Abdullah's blogged about a cousin who runs an Arab dating service. You know what kind of information these folks could be exchanging on these so-called dates. The dude's café is all over Google."

"So are most of the photos we've taken,

and for worse things than being a love doctor," the woman in black replied.

"Do you know anyone trustworthy who could hack into this guy's e-mail account?" the man in black suggested.

"No way," she warned him. "My dad was with the bureau his whole life. He died bringing down a drug cartel. And you want me to hack into a two-bit actor's e-mail?"

"Yeah, we shouldn't be doing illegal stuff trying to get in good with the feds," the man in black agreed.

"I should have taken that full-time job with the *Enquirer*," the woman in black lamented. "My dad was right. I'm not agent material. Busting eating and drug binges; that I get. Counterterrorism? Not so much."

"Hey, admit it, we're having fun." He grinned. She turned red and dropped the camera lens she was cleaning.

Scheherazade shut her ears to the people in black and climbed up the eucalyptus tree that shaded the fig tree.

"Just one more minute, I'm sure," Scheherazade heard Fatima croak from downstairs.

Fatima sat on a black leather couch trimmed in polished chrome to match the chrome table. Two women sat on either side of her: Neda Namour, with hair hennaed so red that it paled the rosacea on her blanched skin, and Rana, her twenty-three-year-old granddaughter with a pierced nose. Rana looked everywhere but at Fatima and Neda. Fatima was still in her pink robe, but she had placed a sparkling bobby pin in her purple hair to dress herself up a bit.

"I'm sure when you get married, Amir will never be late," Fatima said, patting Rana's leg with her sinewy hand, hoping to stop the girl's focus from shifting all over the place.

"Suheir Lababidi had another stroke yesterday," Neda announced. "It's quite possible she won't make it this time."

"Within the next eight days?" Fatima inquired. Neda nodded, and Fatima thought that she would have to dry-clean her black skirt one more time, after all. Suheir Lababidi had been the one who had told her which mosque to have Amir contact for her burial, a very helpful woman.

"Can we go now?" Rana grunted, eyes still moving around the room.

The eye shifting was making Fatima dizzy. She took off her faraway glasses and put on her nearby glasses.

"What color are your eyes, Rana?" Fatima said, and began twirling her hair.

Rana moved her eyes from the mirrored ceiling to the chrome fruit basket on the chrome dining room table. "Black," she said, but did not let Fatima see for herself.

"They get brown when she is happy," Neda explained.

The girl's very black eyes shifted to the doorknob, which was turning, and Amir sauntered in wearing Baluchi pants and tunic and a beard that ran to his knees. Fatima forced her lips to slide over her dentures into a smile. She hoped it hid her anger.

Her knees snapped unappreciatively when she stood up, followed by Neda and Rana, who needed a slight nudge from her grandmother.

"Amir, this is Rana," Fatima said. "You remember her grandmother, Madame Neda."

"Sure, we met when I picked Tayta up from Ghada Bilal's condolences," Amir said.

Amir shook hands, everyone politely smiled uncomfortably, and Fatima motioned for Amir to sit between the two guests on the couch. As he did, the ends of his beard rested on both women's laps. They flinched.

"Take that disguise off," Fatima demanded.

"We call it wardrobe, not disguise," Amir corrected her, making no effort to remove it. "I just got back from my second audition for Middle Eastern Cab Driver #2."

"He is an actor?" Neda grimaced.

"No, no, *aauthu billah,* God forbid, just a hobby," Fatima said.

With another snap of her knees, Fatima leaned forward, grabbed the beard, and yanked it. Amir pulled away, but Fatima's grip was tighter than either one of them expected. She yanked harder, and he pulled away harder. This time the beard did not follow him but stayed in Fatima's hands. The recoil was worse than the quail-hunting guns Fatima's uncle had taught her to use as a child, and she stumbled back onto the couch. The beard flew out of her hands and landed on the hummus in the chrome platter on the chrome coffee table.

The four of them stared at the beard in the hummus in silence.

"I don't think there will be a wedding between these two," Neda decided. She motioned for Rana to stand up.

Fatima grabbed hold of Neda's arm. "Wait, wait, ladies," she pleaded. "I wasn't going to tell you, but he makes the best glassy mole."

Neda walked toward the door, and Rana followed her, eyes growing browner.

"Now I get to pierce my tongue tomorrow, Tayta," Rana said to Neda. "We had a deal, and I did my part by meeting this dude."

At the doorway, Rana gently took Amir's arm and leaned in, giving Fatima hope again. "If you really want to get a chick, the Al Qaeda thing just isn't going to work for you," she whispered. "Living with your grandma and decorating gay isn't helping much, either."

"How dare you use that word," Fatima shouted. "You don't deserve to be buried next to him one day as his wife."

The girl showed her brown eyes and smiled. Fatima found the strength to push her out the door and slam it shut. Then every wrinkle on her face was used to give Amir a full scowl.

"Come on, Tayta." Amir smiled. "The beard is clean. We can still eat the hummus for dinner. I'm starving."

Fatima refused to loosen her scowl. "What you have just done could be the death of me," she swore. She reached into her bra and pulled out an envelope. She threw it at him. It just missed the hummus plate before landing on the edge of the chrome table. "So you better take this now — the instructions for my funeral. I had Mr. Kim the dry cleaner write them up for me so that you wouldn't get depressed writing them. Pick them up now. And if we don't speak again, I ask that unlike Selma Haddad's daughter the other day, you remember to start the condolences on time."

SCHEHERAZADE

Scheherazade beat Fatima back to her room and fluffed the old lady's embroidered pillows for her. Then she perched on the windowsill and waited.

When Fatima entered, she pointed her cane at Scheherazade. "At least the beard wasn't real," she vented. "Like the girl's mustache was."

"That reminds me of something I've been meaning to do for the last 994 nights," Scheherazade said. She reached into the band of her head scarf and pulled out a pair of tweezers. She lifted up Fatima's chin and plucked out a dangling thick black hair.

"Even preparing for death is no excuse to

let yourself go," Scheherazade asserted. "Why do you think Ali Baba could not give up his obsession with the thieves' gold? Because it never lost its shine, *ya oukhti,* my sister. Perhaps you should have let Ibrahim see you could still shine."

"I left him, *ya mejooni,*" Fatima retorted. She put the covers over her head. "Curses on your house, Scheherazade — is this how you wish me to die? A whole night I spent looking for that key for Amir, and see the thanks I get. And I didn't even find the key. Bring me water."

Fatima motioned to Scheherazade to hand her a glass on the table.

Scheherazade sniffed the glass and then quickly pulled away. "It doesn't have any rosewater." She grimaced. "At least some orange blossom."

"It has fluoride," Fatima said, and chugged it down.

"I've got something better." Scheherazade winked. She reached into her headband again. "Smell."

She swung a handmade cigarette under Fatima's nose, but Fatima brushed it away. "I thought you didn't smoke."

"Only on special occasions," Scheherazade said.

"What, my death?" Fatima whispered. "Is

Amir's behavior really what will kill me?"

"I rolled it myself in 1875," Scheherazade bragged. "In Lebanon." Fatima looked at the cigarette and forgot about death and Amir. "This was just a few years after the opening of the Suez Canal, so I was able to get the last of Lebanon's fine silks at the same time."

Scheherazade lit the cigarette and took a deep first inhale before handing it to Fatima. "But, I've never actually . . ." Fatima protested.

Scheherazade put her finger to Fatima's mouth. "Shush," she murmured. "Just breathe it in. Or are you a chicken, cat, and mouse all rolled together?"

Fatima sucked it lightly and coughed for more than twenty seconds on the exhale, according to the chrome clock. "But it tastes worse than anything from Lebanon could," she finally rasped.

"It will taste better soon, *inshallah,*" Scheherazade vowed.

"One of my uncles used to smoke a smell like this, but never in front of Mama." Fatima inhaled again, more delicately, and sighed on the exhale. "*Ya Allah,* none of my kids ever saw Mama. I was going to go back and visit her finally, and then I got pregnant with Lena and couldn't. In my seventh

123

month with Lena, Ibrahim read me a letter from my uncle that said she had died. Of all the girls I had, it never occurred to me to name one for her until Lena came. Mama never knew that I had a daughter with her name. But I have taken good care of our house, and she would like that, *al-hamdulilah.*"

Fatima got up, a little dizzy, and picked out a picture of a limestone and *carmede* house that looked exactly the way she described it every night.

"*Mashallah,* how have you managed to maintain it from here?" Scheherazade asked, trying to sound interested in the house.

"Ibrahim did go back to Lebanon after . . ." Fatima started. "After . . ."

"After what?"

Fatima shook her head. Then she took her deepest inhale yet. "Ibrahim went back to Lebanon many years ago and fixed up the house. Then he hired someone from the Mansour family to clean it once a month. A couple of times I asked Ibrahim for the Mansour woman's number so I could remind her to pick the grapes in fall before the mice got to them; she was just rude, perhaps because she never met me. In any case, she likes Ibrahim more than me, which doesn't happen very often, so I even asked

124

Ibrahim to keep dealing with her after the divorce."

"It was that way with my servants and my king," Scheherazade recalled. "They liked him more because it was not he who told them to scrub the grout between the mosaic tiles."

The two women passed the cigarette between them. Slowly, very slowly, the wrinkles on Fatima's face started to flatten out. She giggled and pursed her lips, motioning for Scheherazade to look at her. Then she blew out a perfect smoke ring.

"Why, a djinn defying Solomon doesn't rise out of the sea with such precision," Scheherazade marveled.

"Millie used to do that with her Virginia Slims," Fatima said. She fell silent when she gazed again at the photo of the house, which was still in her hand.

"It's like the house in Deir Zeitoon was built for your Arabic-speaking Nadia," Scheherazade suggested. "The dress to Lena, the house to Nadia, *khallas,* finished."

"Nadia was terrified when Elias was kidnapped," Fatima said. "My only child to ever go to Lebanon could not go back."

"I saw her yesterday," Scheherazade casually threw in. "She will be fine anywhere when you are gone."

Fatima felt a creeping wooziness taking over her head. "What do you mean you saw her?"

Scheherazade did not want Fatima sensing that she had visited Nadia to give her peace of mind, knowing that she would be too proud to accept such a gift. "You weren't paying any attention to me," she said instead. "Watching you dig through those boxes was even more boring than listening to another story of Deir Zeitoon."

"Why didn't you take me with you?" Fatima demanded. "She's my daughter, not yours."

"You were busy with your boxes," Scheherazade reminded her. "Besides, mortals can't travel on my carpet. That is not how my story was written."

"Are you sure she's fine?" Fatima said, and clasped Scheherazade's hand. "The kidnappers never told Elias who they were, and they always spoke to him in classical Arabic so he could not tell where they were from. They could still be out there."

"It was the 1980s," Scheherazade said with a dismissive wave. "Professors were always being kidnapped. Whoever they were, they've surely moved on to new games. No one stays in the same one in Lebanon for that long."

She put the cigarette to Fatima's lips, but Fatima pulled it out to speak. "One day Millie saw Nadia on the six o'clock news at an anti-Vietnam rally," she began. "She came running over from next door, curlers in her hair — she hardly ever remembered to take them off — saying Nadia was a commie. President Nixon and Millie didn't like communists. Millie loved Nadia, so I know she didn't mean to be afraid of her after that, but she was."

Fatima inhaled again, almost burning her fingers. "Ibrahim wasn't happy, either," she continued. "He was so silent when she said she was going to study Arabic instead of accounting things. He told me to ask her what kind of job she could get with Arabic at the university if, God forbid, she did not marry well and had to work. Nadia went to Ibrahim and told him that perhaps, just perhaps, money was a noose around mankind. Then Ibrahim told her that life was a noose, not a vacation like her life in Detroit, and she had to do real work. He could only speak from his knowledge of life, which he did not share with the children. But I know in Lebanon, Ibrahim was responsible for his mother and his sisters from the age of eleven, when yellow fever took his father. He would tend the sheep herd, fetch the water from the hills, trade his mother's chicken eggs for cheese and bread — and go to school. He even arranged the marriage of his oldest sister to another sheepherder when she was eighteen so she would not die an old maid."

"Alas, what's done by the next generation cannot be forced undone," Scheherazade remarked.

"So unfortunate," Fatima agreed. "But it was fate, too. The day Nadia graduated from high school was the second day of the Six-Day War, and many of the Arab parents in the audience were crying. Grief, sorrow, humiliation, anger, worry, fear — none are the right word alone to describe the parents. Nadia became interested in back home then. She could have become a hippie like Hikmat Kanaan's daughter did, but *al hamdulilah,* instead she joined the Peace Corps and went to Algeria. She thought she could use her Arabic there."

"But that was just after the revolution of one million martyrs against the French," Scheherazade recalled. "Algerians barely had their Arabic back yet."

"So she found out." Fatima nodded. "She was trying to help farmers with her school Arabic, and they didn't understand anything. Then, *subhan Allah,* Elias arrived with the Red Crescent and helped translate her

Arabic into French . . . then he saw how good she was at helping him put together the North Africa budget for the Red Crescent."

"So he married her," Scheherazade concluded. "At least Nadia would be able to read the deed to the house, unlike your others."

Fatima shook her head and motioned for the cigarette. She inhaled one last time, and hope rose inside her as quickly as the smoke she exhaled rose to the ceiling. "You know, I still have something I can leave her as dear as the house," she realized. "When I am gone, at least one of my children will still be able to read Mama's letters. I will leave Nadia Mama's letters. That is safe and good for both Nadia and Mama."

Fatima got up, still holding the cigarette, and went to her dresser. She pulled out the letters, which were wrapped carefully in embroidered silk ribbons from Damascus. The letters peeked out of fading blue envelopes, covered to the very edges in carefully drawn Arabic letters scrunched together in lines with no breathing room, as if the writer had not wanted to waste any space. Fatima untied the ribbons, so lost in the words that Ibrahim used to read her that she didn't hear the footsteps.

"Your grandson is coming up the stairs," Scheherazade hissed. She grabbed the cigarette out of Fatima's hand.

"Hey," Fatima protested, and tried to reach for the cigarette. But Scheherazade flew out the window.

AMIR

Amir stepped into Fatima's room and recoiled from the funk and haze of smoke over his grandmother. He went to the window and leaned out.

"Screw you, asshole," Amir yelled at his soap opera star neighbor's house. "Smoke whatever the hell you want in your bedroom but close the windows so you don't kill my grandma." He didn't completely recognize the smell. The jerk must have upgraded from low-rent weed with his fat new SAG checks.

"Sorry about the stink, Tayta," Amir said. Her pale green eyes were oddly bright this night, and she didn't seem quite as pissed at him as before.

"That's all the sorry I get?" Fatima pouted and started twirling her hair on her finger.

"Jesus Christ, give me a second," Amir said. "I came up to say I was sorry about tonight's engagement dinner."

"You should have been wearing your orange shirt," Fatima replied. "Tighter shirts to show that you have a body that can work a good day and provide for a family. Your name means 'prince,' and you should dress like one. No more queen stuff."

Queen stuff? Fatima often surprised him with her unexpected knowledge of certain words.

"And what is this for?" Amir asked. He handed her the envelope with her funeral instructions.

"Marrying that girl tonight was the last thing I was ever going to ask you to do," she said. "Now this is."

"Take it back. I won't need it for a long time."

"Not if you keep doing what you did to me tonight," Fatima answered.

"Never again," Amir promised. "Take back the envelope."

Fatima held up her hand. "We'll just have to start all over on Wednesday with Tiffany."

Jesus Christ, no, Amir thought.

"She's an American, but we don't have time to be picky. She's a wedding photographer I met at the Iranian Jew's store — he's the only one that sells *jeranic,* green plums, and good pistachios."

Fatima always justified the store owner to

Amir, as if Amir might accuse her of supporting Israel's occupation because of her shopping practices. She had discovered the store on her way back from a memorial service in Westwood, at the same cemetery where Marilyn Monroe was buried. Now she managed to make a side trip there after any funeral, regardless of location, to buy Amir "real food."

"I was very subtle with this Tiffany," Fatima continued. "I did not mention marriage. I have convinced her to take your picture for your acting hobby. She agreed in exchange for dinner. Either the two of you will fall in love tomorrow or we will send the photos to Zade's computer lovemaking business."

"Matchmaking, Tayta. Matchmaking, not lovemaking." Seventy years in this country and it was amazing what words she didn't know. "I'll be nice to Tiffany, and you keep this." He tossed the envelope onto the bed, and it rested atop the bundle of Fatima's mother's letters. The letters were more faded than the last time he had seen them, but he remembered all the times Fatima used to flip through them in Detroit when she was sad, as if she could read them.

"They're for Nadia when I'm gone," Fatima explained.

"You'll outlive us all."

"Don't say such wicked things," she admonished.

"I'm sorry again, Tayta."

He kissed her hand and held it for a few minutes. Then he went downstairs without taking back the envelope. In the kitchen, he rinsed the hummus out of his beard and hung it up to dry. He would make a point of not wearing the beard for Tiffany. He had always hoped that he would not fall in love until Fatima was gone, as she would not like his taste in a partner. However, he wasn't in a hurry to be in love or for her to die.

In fact, in the last couple of days he had learned a lot from Fatima's conversations with herself. He could picture Nadia in her diplomatic speech pleading for Elias's release. But he couldn't see Lena in any wedding dress. It would be hard for a guy to get close to someone who never told anyone what she was really thinking. Amir, unlike his cousins and most of his aunts and uncles, had lived with Lena for many years, as they both had been raised in Fatima's house at the same time, the favorite grandson and the youngest child. Lena had been Amir's baby-sitter, had taken him to *Star Wars* movies the very day they came out,

133

and had bought him anything he wanted with the money she made at McDonald's during high school.

Fatima needed her kids, and he could use the break. Lena was his best bet because she never said no. Even on the days when Fatima would say that she herself would drive Amir to school, Lena never said no. Fatima would drive the whole way, telling him that if the cops stopped them and asked for her license, he had to pretend that his appendix was bursting and they needed to get to the hospital. Fatima couldn't admit to anyone, not even the Department of Motor Vehicles, that she couldn't read, and so she had never taken a driver's exam. Still, Fatima's driving beat going to school with Ibrahim, who never said a word.

Amir sat down in front of the computer.

Dear Lena,
    I hope this e-mail finds you well. I am fine. Tayta is fine, and the weather is a beautiful 75 degrees here today. Foggy though. They call it June Gloom. Tayta talked a lot today to herself, but that could be because I upset her.

Why would Lena do him a favor? The last time he had even bothered to befriend her had been when he was looking for an agent.

```
 Did I ever tell you that
Darcy, the friend of your
friend, turned out to be a
doll? She's really putting my
career on the map, and I'm out
on auditions for all kinds of
parts. I just wanted to thank
you for that. Please come
visit. We miss you!
                    xoxo, Amir
```

He picked up a mustache and stuck it onto his face. He looked at his reflection on the computer screen and then at the picture of Fatima on his desk.

"By the name of Allah, woman, I will cut off your balls and feed them to the goats," he declared. "My camels will curse you from hell."

He reached down for a script and checked the line. Yeah, he was ready for his audition tomorrow. Saddam Hussein as a young man. Jesus Christ, he needed a better agent. Or a better heritage. Or the Omar Sharif audition.

FATIMA

If Amir had been looking out his window instead of at himself, he would have seen Fatima under the fruitless fig tree, her pink robe now tucked into sweatpants, bobby pin readjusted to hold up her purple hair. Scheherazade's special cigarette had left her awake — and hungry.

"Psst," Scheherazade whispered from atop the neighboring eucalyptus tree. "Where are you going in this desert wind? My midriff is shivering, and I'm not even making love."

"I just received a call that Suheir Lababidi has passed," Fatima whispered, holding up her black skirt. "And the dry cleaner has free doughnuts."

Scheherazade hummed a Samarqand folk tune as she climbed down from the eucalyptus tree. "I'm hungry, too," she decided. "I was looking for a fig on the fig tree."

"Be careful, *dyiri balik,* don't break any of its branches," Fatima pleaded. "I brought that tree all the way from Lebanon."

"Lebanon?"

"Well, Detroit," Fatima clarified. "Ibrahim planted it in our backyard in Detroit with seeds from Mama. I had my oldest girl ship it from Detroit and replanted it here. Amir had to take down a persimmon tree for it."

136

"Why aren't there any figs on it for me to eat?" Scheherazade complained.

"I could never make it fruit." Fatima sighed. "But Detroit's soil was very hospitable to the *fe'oos* and *baeli* that I grew."

"Why leave Detroit, then?" Scheherazade asked. "Nations have been destroyed for valuable soil."

"After the divorce, I didn't want to buy another house in Detroit, when I had a perfectly good one in Lebanon," Fatima explained. "I thought I'd just spend a couple of weeks with Amir and then move back home to Lebanon. Then September 11 happened, and I didn't want Amir to be alone in such terrible times."

"But of course," Scheherazade said, nodding as if she believed her. She sniffed the air. "Do I smell cucumbers?"

"They're in Amir's back garden," Fatima said. "Let me use your arm, and I'll take you back there. I don't want my grandfather's cane to get muddy."

"You know you can make it without your cane or my arm," Scheherazade said.

"You wouldn't be saying that if you'd carried ten children on your hip for so long that it wore your bones out."

"Fine, use my arm," Scheherazade said. "*Yallah,* I'm very hungry."

137

Fatima held on tightly as they approached the patch of vegetation in which she took so much pride. She had spent too much time in that room with Scheherazade, as if it were the only place stories could be told. There was no reason not to come to the garden at night, when Los Angeles's cool breezes let its fragrances waft.

"*Kusa,* eggplant, mint for salad, tomatoes," Scheherazade marveled, delicately walking through the garden. "Everything to make the summer dishes."

Scheherazade plucked a young cucumber and bit into it.

"*Zaatar* for the *labneh,*" Fatima added, holding up a sprig of thyme to Scheherazade's nose. "When I came here, Amir already had the garden. He said he had designed it with seeds from our garden in Detroit. A good boy. A boy who should have a wife."

Fatima had created her garden in Detroit with the seeds of her mother's garden in Lebanon, seeds that her mother had tucked into the cedar chest for her on the day of her first wedding. Somehow Fatima had made the garden flourish, but she had had a harder time re-creating Lebanon in Detroit than Amir had had re-creating her Detroit garden in Los Angeles. Both he and the vegetables were in their natural environment in West Hollywood, but Fatima didn't permit that thought to take hold in her mind.

"Amir even added a lemon tree, which we did not have in Detroit," Fatima boasted. "The house in Lebanon has three lemon trees in the back. Come on, the bus will be here in five minutes."

They walked arm in arm with the only sound between them the growling of Fatima's stomach. At the MTA #4 bus stop, the homeless man with the dimple looked up from his smoke. "Out late tonight," he noted.

Fatima frowned at him before boarding the bus. She let go of Scheherazade's arm to show the driver her senior citizen card. The short ladies holding bulky tote bags on their laps rattled a variety of Spanish niceties to Fatima. *"Sí,"* Fatima responded. They were as young as her daughters but too old to be cleaning houses, which was what Amir told her they did when she asked why so many of them got picked up at houses so much bigger than his.

She sat far away from two teenage boys with nose rings conversing in a language that required only two words — *dude* and *cool* — and the gesticulating of their hands and heads in a pattern that resembled wild animals more than people.

She didn't want to appear even crazier than they, yet there was so little time to waste. She could sit and fret about Amir and the house. Or she could tell Scheherazade more about her two husbands so that Scheherazade could reveal her method of death and therefore let her know how much time she actually had left to fret. Everyone on the bus would think she was talking to herself, but what was wrong with her being just one more crazy person on the bus? It was not like she'd be riding it many more days, anyway. And there were no Arab ladies onboard to gossip about her tomorrow at Suheir Lababidi's funeral. She turned to Scheherazade to begin the story of the man who brought her to America. "This Los Angeles does not even have a football team, so Marwan would not have liked it," she started. "They try to be beautiful with their beach, but this is no Detroit."

"As my father the *wazir,* the minister of state, used to say, the people of Mecca know their streets best." Scheherazade nodded.

"Detroit's streets are not mine, but still it is the best city in America," Fatima continued. "When I arrived in New York with Marwan, it wasn't paved with gold, like

140

Mama had heard it would be. But I had never seen buildings so tall, so tall that I thought they might have touched God when their tops disappeared into the clouds. I was sure humans could not live so high up in the sky. I thought something so far up could not stand by itself for so long, and I kept covering my head, anticipating one to fall. When I finally opened my eyes and looked ahead instead of up, people stood in long lines for bread that was hard and thick, and shop clerks chased kids in rags for stealing apples. Big, big signs with lights advertised things I'd never heard of, and the streets were filled with hundreds of motorcars, not just one like Deir Zeitoon, and women wore funny hats, and so did the men, even Marwan, who said it was what gentlemen did."

Fatima did not know that in telling this story of America she had reverted to English. The black and white people on the bus listened to Fatima as she told a story they should have gotten from their own grandparents. Whether the Mexican lady — who, to the passengers, seemed like the direct recipient of Fatima's words — understood her or just pitied her solitude, she took Fatima's hand and patted it comfortingly in her lap.

"It takes time to love a place, just as it

takes time to love a man," Scheherazade said. "Did you learn to love Marwan by the time you got to New York?"

Fatima shook her head, and the Mexican lady patted her hand again. "We stayed only one day in New York — with a cousin of Marwan's and his six kids," she continued. "The cousin didn't have a job. He had lost his job at a Syrian silk factory that made Japanese robes for Japan. All the factories were closed because Marwan said the country was depressed. The entire way on the train to Detroit it was depressed. But then in Detroit there was life, smoke pouring out of buildings so big and long that I thought they could reach Deir Zeitoon. And everyone had jobs."

"Just like Marwan." Scheherazade smiled.

"Almost." Fatima sighed. "On the boat, Marwan told me that because of the depressing times, Mr. Ford had let him go when he went to Lebanon because so many other people needed his job. But when we arrived at the train station in Detroit, the first thing Ibrahim told Marwan was that General Motors was hiring again to build machines for the war in Europe, and *inshallah,* his friend there could get Marwan a job."

The MTA #4 bus came to a stop, and

Fatima motioned to Scheherazade to help her up. Several passengers took it as a signal for them, and the two boys with nose rings quit bobbing their heads to silent music and assisted her down the steps. Others clapped as she left, as if thanking her for the story.

"*Sí,*" Fatima said, and waved goodbye. She took Scheherazade's arm, and a smile folded up her face until it took up half of it.

"What's so funny?" Scheherazade wondered.

"I was just remembering how Ibrahim met us at the station holding two blocks of melting ice," Fatima said. "It was the hottest summer Detroit had ever had, and I was wearing a big wool coat, as Mama had heard that in America sometimes people actually froze solid. The ice felt so nice even though it was melting all over my coat. Ibrahim asked after everyone in Deir Zeitoon in Arabic much better than Marwan's. It felt good to be able to really talk. Betsy, Ibrahim's wife before me, was there, too. Marwan said that Betsy and I would be great friends. She hugged me when she saw me, but I couldn't speak English. The longer we stayed with them, the less friendly she got. Marwan said it was my imagination, as did Ibrahim later. I think that she was probably in love with someone else and worried that,

143

being a woman, it wouldn't take me long to figure it out. I think she thought I would tell Ibrahim if I knew. I don't know to this day if she ever did tell him before she left him. I never asked him about her."

By the time Fatima finished telling Scheherazade about the first time she had laid eyes on Ibrahim, they had reached the dry cleaners. Fatima handed the balding owner her skirt. "Mr. Kim, I have condolences tomorrow, so I'll wait."

"No problem, Mrs. Abdullah," Mr. Kim said. "Anything you would like me to add to your funeral instructions?"

"No, thank you," Fatima said. "I've got other things to get to now."

He nodded and pushed a box of doughnuts over to Fatima. She took two powdered sugars.

She led Scheherazade to a secluded veranda table at the café next door. Fatima plunged into her doughnut, letting the powdered sugar coat her mouth and nose. She offered Scheherazade a bite, but Scheherazade was drawn to the café's young male patrons' physiques. Fatima snapped her fingers.

"Aren't you the one that wanted a story about *my* men?" Fatima reminded her.

"Right. So while his wife daydreamed of

someone else, Ibrahim helped Marwan get a job to give his new bride — you — a good life," Scheherazade said, and attempted to wipe Fatima's face clean of powdered sugar.

"It was Marwan who got Ibrahim his job with Mr. Ford and took care of him when he first came to America," Fatima explained through another mouthful of doughnut. "So Ibrahim got Marwan the job at GM soon after we arrived, but then later Ibrahim felt even more obligated to Marwan."

"You mean Marwan then got Ibrahim a better job at the GM plant?" Scheherazade asked.

"No, no, that job was terrible enough for Marwan," Fatima remembered. "Poor man. He had already bought the house in Dearborn because Mr. Ford had told his men before the depressing times that they would work at River Rouge forever. But Marwan drove all the way to GM in Flint every Sunday night — seventy-five miles away, and cars weren't what they are now and no radio in it for distraction — and for only twenty dollars a week instead of thirty dollars like before. He would come back late Friday nights and just stare at the walls, maybe listen to the baseball game. Which is what I did all the nights he stayed at his cousin's house in Flint — ten men from

145

Deir Zeitoon lived in that house during the week. He told me that at the factory he would do the same thing over and over for hours and hours, always bent over as his back ached him if he stood straight. Sometimes he came home with really big cuts all over. I thought he was clumsy at first. But once when Ibrahim stopped by to read a letter from Mama, he told me that Marwan worked with very dangerous machines."

"So then Ibrahim felt guilty about getting Marwan a bad job," Scheherazade interrupted.

"No, no, *hamara*, Ibrahim showed me then that he had cuts like that, too. More than half the men had lost their jobs in the last seven years, so they were all happy to have income again," Fatima said, and bit into her second doughnut. "But Marwan knew it was wrong to treat workers that way. So he joined the union. It was a new organization to protect the workers and make sure they got fair money. After I had been in America just five months, the men said they refused to work until things got better. Marwan was never home even on weekends after that, always out organizing."

"You must have missed Deir Zeitoon the most then," Scheherazade said.

Fatima nodded. "Millie would invite me

146

for coffee with the other wives, but I didn't feel comfortable with no English — except around Millie alone," she said. "None of them knew how to make real coffee anyway except for the Greek lady two houses down. The only time I laughed in those days was when Ibrahim would come by to read a letter from Mama and tell me some new joke he had heard at the Syrian grocery. One day, Ibrahim came to my house and didn't smile as usual. He told me that Marwan was in the hospital. The police had shot at the strikers with something called buckshot because the workers were throwing iron nuts, bolts, and milk bottles at them and squirting them with water. And Marwan's arm was cut so deep, it was a miracle they were able to sew it together again."

"So sad," Scheherazade said.

"But it was because of men like Marwan that GM and Mr. Ford had to give the workers fair money and good treatment," Fatima said, and licked the last of the powdered sugar from her fingers. "Marwan's courage proved that we didn't just care about sending money back home, which is what most people thought about Arabs. I know because that's what Millie told me her husband told her. He told her we'd just take off back to 'garlic eater land' as soon as we made enough money. Marwan went back to working for Mr. Ford when I got pregnant with my oldest so he could be nearer to me. Even though his left arm was always weak after that strike, he was starting to get Ibrahim and the others to talk about unionizing Ford. One day, Ibrahim came to tell me that Marwan was in the hospital again. This time he died, Allah *yerhamu*. He was barely thirty-nine years old and had a heart attack. He was putting a door on one of Mr. Ford's new model Tudors. I have never ridden in a Tudor in my life. I can't."

"So you did love him," Scheherazade said.

"If he had lived longer, I probably would have loved him more," Fatima admitted. "I think God was willing me to love him a little. But it took a while. That's why it took a while to make a baby. And he was always tired or gone."

Mr. Kim came out with the black skirt, which had been pressed perfectly. He cleared his throat, pretending not to have heard the tail end of her story. "Will you be able to carry it by yourself?" he asked.

"Of course," Fatima said. "I'm not dead yet."

She took the carefully hung skirt and waited for Scheherazade to take her arm, but she was too busy looking at a man whose muscles rippled under his tight T-shirt. "Men's body parts sure have grown since I was mortal," she gushed, ignoring Fatima's proffered arm.

Fatima walked off in a huff but did not get far. After eleven steps, her cane caught on the edge of the plastic bag covering the skirt. As she made her way to the unquestionably harsh concrete of the sidewalk, she began to form the thought that she probably would die in six days of complications from a broken hip. But before the thought had enough seconds to crystallize, Fatima found herself caught by firm yet comforting arms.

"I got you, ma'am," a voice said, and she looked up into the turquoise eyes of the handsome neighbor boy.

Fatima attempted to recompose her dignity as Scheherazade ogled his beauty. She glared at Scheherazade. "Act like a lady," she scolded.

"I'm sorry, ma'am," the handsome boy said, standing her upright. "My grandmother used to always tell me the opposite. How about I give you a lift home? I'm your neighbor."

"Yes, with the nice big cars." Fatima blushed, completely embarrassed by her helplessness. "I was just smoking something special today. First time. I didn't know it could make me so dizzy."

"Right on. It mostly makes me hungry." He shrugged. "Got to watch the body, you know, so I don't do it anymore. And I'm not saying anything about the white powder around your nose."

"The dry cleaner has free doughnuts," she whispered.

"Yes, ma'am," he said in the same irritating tone Amir used when she told him she was inviting a potential wife to dinner.

He helped Fatima into his SUV. Scheherazade climbed in the backseat, taking her first ride in one of the petrol caravans.

"Smoother than a camel indeed," Scheherazade said to Fatima.

"Chevy." Fatima nodded. "You're a good boy. Patriotic. I like that. Look at these cars on this street — Mercedes, BMW, Lexus. You wouldn't see such behavior in Detroit. These boys here with their Japanese and German cars have no loyalty and respect for their grandfathers' toil. During the war, my husbands and the others were all making war vehicles to defeat the Germans and Japanese, and now their factories make more cars for their grandkids than Ford."

"Yes, ma'am," the handsome boy said

again. He stopped in back of the other SUV parked in front of his house and helped Fatima out.

"You should meet my grandson," Fatima said. "You could teach him a thing or two about loyalty. Look at his Honda."

"I'd love to show him my next new car if it would make you happy." He smiled. Then he got out and helped Fatima, who was still a little shaky from her near fall, down. "Everything good?"

"Sí," she said. "Thank you." Scheherazade stood next to her as she watched the handsome boy park in his driveway. Nice boy. If she had more time, she'd find him a wife, too.

"Al-hamdulilah, we're home," Fatima said. "I was so worried if I fell, I would be bedridden for the rest of my days, and I don't have that kind of time with the house and Amir still left to settle. *Ya oukhti,* my sister, I'm tired."

"But you accomplished much in the last two days," Scheherazade pointed out. "You left your mama's letters to Nadia, let your grandson know that the funeral papers are ready, and bequeathed to your unmarried daughter the dress you married her father in."

"I did not marry both husbands in that

dress," Fatima corrected. "Ibrahim and I do not have wedding pictures. I was in mourning and pregnant. There was no celebration. My only wedding pictures are alone or with Marwan. I told Laila, who is Marwan's only child, that she could wear the dress for her wedding, but she said it would be an insult to Ibrahim, who had been her father since she was born."

"It was very normal for her to believe that," Scheherazade concurred.

"Laila is like that," Fatima boasted. "Normal. She married an Arab boy, of course. Egyptian. Everyone came to the wedding, all the children. His mother came from Egypt for it, and even though she was from a good family, I was grateful that she would live far away from Laila. Do you know what Laila makes at Thanksgiving?"

"Thanksgiving?"

"It's an American holiday where they sacrifice a turkey," Fatima explained. "So do you know what she makes at Thanksgiving?"

Scheherazade licked her lips. "Does it have pistachios and cinnamon?"

"She makes turkey," Fatima boasted. "*Subhan Allah.* Normal, see. Do you know how I know this? Because she would invite Ibrahim and me every year, like a normal

152

daughter does. . . . You could go see for yourself."

"You should rest for Suheir's funeral tomorrow," Scheherazade advised.

But Fatima did not leave, did not even slouch, despite the ache in her hip. The two women regarded each other under the streetlight until Fatima nodded good night. "I should rest. It's going to be a very big funeral," she said, and hobbled into the house.

When Fatima was out of sight, Scheherazade clapped her hands for her carpet. It was not her duty to visit this daughter, but the way Fatima had talked about Detroit's glory, it made her wonder. Scheherazade had seen many of the world's most beautiful sites: Mount Ararat at sunset, the Oracle of Delphi at dawn, the Nile channeled by the Aswan Dam in the spring. Why not pay this daughter in Detroit a visit?

She departed just as the handsome neighbor boy stepped back out and tapped on a window of the petrol caravan under the eucalyptus tree. She heard him say to the man and woman in black, "I got a scoop for you," as the wind swept her toward Detroit.

The next afternoon, following storm clouds that were moving in that direction, Scheherazade found Fatima's normal daughter in a place with more food than an army marching through the Sahara needed. She recognized Fatima's nose on Laila's face.

■ ■ ■ ■

THE 995TH NIGHT

■ ■ ■ ■

LAILA

Laila stared at a slab of pork at the super-market and calculated the cost of a nervous breakdown: $150 an hour for the shrink, $200 a month for pills not covered by insurance, another $200 for a homeopathic doctor and nutritionist, at least $500 for a lawyer to write up her will in case she became suicidal, and $850 for a self-actualization yoga retreat in California. Throw in another $600 for a couple of colonics and a massage. Expensive.

The one thing Laila had inherited from Fatima, besides the nose, was the ability to do math and shop at the same time. A nervous breakdown, along with all her other medical expenses, was not in the family budget. She would have to settle for prayer, her husband's response to everything these days. Or she just might get as much satisfaction from purchasing pork.

It was so cold in the meat aisle that Laila

found herself readjusting her wig as if it were a ski cap. She shivered and reached for the pinkish-gray pork. Her hand jerked back. How did people touch this stuff? She watched a frazzled woman with three kids grab a large armful of packages — it was a pretty good pork sale. One of the kid's suckers popped out of his mouth and landed where Laila used to have 36D breasts.

"I'm sorry, ma'am," the woman apologized, reaching to pull off the Jolly Rancher.

Laila brushed the woman's hand away. "It's okay. My boys were always doing things like that," she said, and then plucked the sucker off her sweater and handed it to the mother, who handed it back to the kid. This woman isn't the germophobe I was with my boys, Laila thought. The woman's two other kids were tossing one of the pork packages to each other as if it were a football.

"What do you do with this stuff?" Laila asked, pointing at the flying meat.

"The pork chops?"

"Yes, the pork."

"Well, you can broil them and then cover them in barbecue sauce," the woman recommended. "That's what they do in the South."

She pointed to a row of barbecue sauce

bottles lined up above the pork section. Laila thanked her as she and her kids rolled away with their cart, which was overflowing with cereal boxes redeemable via the coupons the youngest child was waving around. Laila grabbed a bottle of barbecue sauce and saw the price: $4.99 a bottle. It was a good thing she'd never eaten pork. She could get two bottles of ketchup for that price, and that would take care of at least fifty hamburgers. She bought a couple of cans of tomato sauce instead. It was not as if Ghazi had ever eaten pork. He wouldn't know how it was supposed to be served.

As she put her groceries in the car, Laila almost slipped on a greasy rain puddle made the previous night during the first thunderstorm of summer. She could smell more rain on the way. She and Ghazi used to talk about moving to Florida when the kids grew up. In truth, she had flown on an airplane only once in her life, she'd never lived anywhere but Detroit, all her doctors were here, and her relationship with Ghazi wasn't such that either relaxed at the thought of living in a place where the only people they would know would be each other. And Ghazi's mosque was here. She slammed the trunk hard.

When Laila had discovered her cancer,

Ghazi had discovered Islam. Until then they had been the kind of Muslims who fulfilled their duties by giving to the poor and not eating pork. They knew when the Muslim holidays were only when Ghazi's mother called from Cairo to say *Eid Mubarak.* Now Ghazi was the kind of Muslim who went to the mosque five times a day, didn't drink, and gave all the money he used to spend on his fancy gym membership to the new mosque, as if trading in fat for prayer would make his family healthy again.

Laila drove by the new mosque as she headed to Dearborn for what her mother called real food. She couldn't serve just tomato-sauced pork for dinner, any more than she could miss the mosque's minarets from the freeway. Michigan's Muslims bragged that the mosque was the largest one in North America.

At Greenland Supermarket, she bought *halloumi* cheese, a bag of pumpkin seeds, and a five-liter bottle of olive oil from Lebanon, which she noted didn't cost half as much as the pork, despite the sale. She usually got the ingredients to make *foul* for Ghazi, but today, for the first time in her marriage, she wasn't in the mood. Amani, Ghazi's mother, could make it for him later in the week. After all, she had come here from Cairo to help, as Ghazi described the purpose of her chaotic arrival.

The store was packed, as usual, and Laila waited in a very long line with women in head scarves, black *abayas,* or tight rayon tops with glitter designs. It all fit in here, but Laila remembered that when she was a girl, it was very rare to see a head scarf, let alone an *abaya,* in Dearborn. The Arabs of her childhood had been blenders; they just mixed into the rest of the country. She didn't know where those Arabs were now, all those popular girls from high school.

The shoppers at Greenland, mostly women, checked one another out as usual, either in judgment or out of curiosity. Laila used to think that gave the *hijabis* the advantage because she couldn't see the secrets under their scarves. However, with the wig, she felt that they were on even ground, and she stared right back. It turned out that after all these years, she was a better starer than anyone else. A few minutes later, no one would look at her.

She turned her attention to the collage of posters at the exit behind the cashiers. Most featured big-eyed children in rags, lone figures among rubble — with one sign asking its readers in both English and Arabic to sponsor a child in the refugee camps, which Laila did; another asking them to give money to the schools in southern Lebanon, which Laila did; and another asking for contributions to restore Egypt's classic black-and-white films, which Laila also did.

There were posters asking for money to rebuild Iraq. This Laila did not give to. Many of her neighbors had kids in the military, and Laila felt sad for them every day, but she did not agree with the destruction of Iraq, and so she could not bring herself to give to its reconstruction. This was also how she had responded to the loss of her breasts. Ghazi had said that reconstructive surgery would make her feel like a woman again, but she still felt like a woman, even if he couldn't see that anymore. Laila had found her cancer 430 days ago, the same day the United States invaded Iraq.

The bagger, Ahmad, asked her how she was doing. Everyone in Dearborn knew her "situation," as they called the cancer in whispers, because of Ghazi's generous contributions to the mosque. Ahmad was a sweet kid, twenty-four, about the same age as Zaid, her youngest. Ahmad had been in the United States only fourteen months, and he always said how lucky her boys were to have her so close. He missed his mom. Laila definitely would have had a nervous breakdown if her sons had talked about missing her. But on the days when the boys took her to radiation instead of Ghazi, she smelled their fear through their clothes, which she still ironed for them. If her boys were married, they would not miss her so much if the cancer came back. When she had told them that if she died, they would want someone to lean on, they had told her that the cancer would not come back. They did not mention any girlfriends.

"Allahu akbar," Ahmad grunted as he heaved the five liters of olive oil into the trunk. The pork bag tipped over.

"That's funny-looking chicken, Auntie," he said.

Laila stepped between him and the pork. "It was on sale," she explained. "Fifty cents a pound. What can you expect for that, you know?"

Ahmad was impressed. Dearborn's stores, like ethnic markets everywhere, sold meat and produce at rock-bottom prices, but fifty cents a pound?

"You shop well, Auntie," he said. There were ten people on this planet who could call her "Auntie" by blood, but she had hardly ever seen them. Most of them, un-like her sons, had gotten married long ago. Maybe she and Ghazi should have left

Detroit, as her siblings had.

Laila drove home along Warren Avenue, where she had grown up but had not lived since her marriage. Then it had been Arabs mixed in with Slavs and Irish. She passed the messy Arabic calligraphy on mom-and-pop groceries and boutiques, the syncopating Iraqi pop music seeping out of Lincolns and Buicks, and the McDonald's bragging in red letters, WE PROUDLY SERVE *HALAL* McNUGGETS.

Maybe there were fewer women willing to marry a guy with an Arab name nowadays. Even so, her sons should have been married long before 9/11. Laila feared that the boys now jinxed each other. The younger boys' girlfriends would be turned off, she was sure, by the fact that their much older brothers hadn't married yet. She would have thought it weird if all of Ghazi's older brothers had been single when she married him.

Laila was so anxious to think of reasons for her sons' singleness that she almost hit an old man coming out of Masri Sweets. She skidded to a stop just in time. It was the old man's cane she noticed first: the cedar carvings of her great-grandfather.

She had called her father last week, but when was the last time she had seen him?

She got out of the car, the humid summer

164

breeze causing her head to hurt as it whipped through her wig.

"Hi, Baba," she said. Like all her siblings, Laila answered Ibrahim in English even when he used Arabic, but she was the only one who called him Baba instead of Dad.

Ibrahim looked up. "Fatima?"

"No, it's me," she said. "Laila."

Laila read the thought on his face: How could this old woman be my daughter?

"I've been a little sick," she explained. "That's why I look like this."

Laila expected him to turn away before admonishing her for never exercising or for eating bad food, as he always used to, but he stared her right in the face. Actually looked. And kept looking. She couldn't remember him ever looking at any of his daughters without turning away the minute they caught him. He reached for her cheek, and she remembered the last time he had touched her. He had held her hand on her wedding day.

"Why aren't you fat no more?" Ibrahim whispered.

The trembling in his fingers quietly drummed her face. She did not know if it was from age or from seeing her. Whatever the reason, that was when Laila gave in to her nervous breakdown, whatever the cost,

165

right in front of Masri Sweets, amid the scent of fried dough and rosewater. Her father's kindness was the last surprise she could handle. She kept on crying, right in the middle of the sidewalk, as women covered in black stepped around her in the summer heat, their emotions displayed in their heavy walk rather than in their impenetrable faces.

Laila was sixty-five years old now, too old to lean on her father, and he was too small now to hold her. Ibrahim still didn't look away. Neither did the people in Masri Sweets, who were watching her from the safety of air-conditioning.

The *Ithan* went off, calling all believers to the nearby mosque. The a cappella chant of the *Ithan* had always moved Laila in the way "Ave Maria" did when she attended Catholic weddings and "Amazing Grace" did at Presbyterian funerals. They all made her feel God, even though He really annoyed her of late. God had tested her much more than she was capable of handling. His recent tests were made for stronger people.

Ibrahim took out a handkerchief embroidered by Fatima. He shook it out and handed it to Laila.

"Would you like to come to dinner tonight?" Laila asked, and looked up at him.

"I'm making grape leaves."

His eyes floated in as many tears as hers. "It's just dinner," she said, and lowered her eyes again.

He nodded. Then Laila remembered the pork. It stopped her tears.

"Or better yet, I'll tell Ghazi to pick you up on his way home from work tomorrow," Laila suggested. "That way you could rest today. You probably want to rest today."

"No, I'll come with you now," Ibrahim said. "I taught your mother how to roll grape leaves, you know. She couldn't cook nothing before we got married."

Laila assumed that was a joke. He so rarely tried to make her laugh; she could not take back the invitation now.

She motioned him to the car. "Maybe we're going to stop at the pharmacy for my pressure blood medication?" he asked.

"Sure, I'll get my pills, too," she replied. It had taken old age and disease to give them something they could do together.

They drove to the pharmacy and home in silence, which was how they were most comfortable with each other.

In her house, Laila quickly shoved the pork in the refrigerator while her father was in the bathroom. Then she washed her hands very, very well and prepared tea with sugar, or "sugar with a little tea," as Laila referred to the way her parents liked it. Ibrahim came back to the kitchen with *Al-Ahram,* one of Ghazi's Egyptian newspapers, which he had acquired along with God at the mosque.

Laila let Ibrahim read and sip his tea as she rinsed and cut stems off the grape leaves. Amani had picked them from the garden that morning before going to English class. Laila did not tell Ibrahim that her mother-in-law lived with her. She would not mention her at all. Amani undoubtedly would play cards after class with her Arab mother-in-law classmates and not come home until Ibrahim was gone.

"Do you want to help me?" she asked.

Ibrahim put down the paper. "I'm sorry, it feels good to sometimes read Arabic. I haven't read no Arabic since I used to read your mother her mother's letters." He smiled and pointed at the paper. "The world has all different news in Arabic."

Laila did not ask him what the paper said. She didn't want to know. She put a plate of grape leaves in front of him and one in front of herself. She placed a bowl of rice and ground beef stuffing between them and put on her bifocals and began rolling. Ibrahim pulled out his bifocals, and his eyes followed her hands. Then she put a leaf in front of him, and he awkwardly tried to straighten it out.

"I didn't teach your mama nothing about no grape leaves," Ibrahim finally said. "No, her mama taught her in Lebanon so she could cook good for your real dad when they came here. Marwan was a great man."

That was what Ibrahim always said when he mentioned Marwan. Fatima had told Laila many times how Ibrahim had asked to marry her after Marwan died — just because she was pregnant with Laila. It was a great act of kindness, and so Laila felt disloyal talking about Marwan with him.

She laid a leaf on her plate, taking out every crease. "Follow me," Laila said.

Laila took a little bit of the rice and meat and placed it in the center and then began folding the leaf in. He tried to do the same thing.

"What a mess, right," Ibrahim groaned.

Laila stood in back of him and took his hands to guide them over the leaves.

"No, it hurts," he pleaded. "It's the arthritis. I can't do no folding now."

She looked at his hands, a map of purple and red veins. She set them down.

"Would you like to take a nap while I finish?" she offered. "The sheets in the guest room are clean."

"I'm not sleepy," he answered. "Maybe it's okay if I'm just going to sit here?"

"I guess," Laila said. How was she was going to make the pork with him watching her all the time?

"Maybe Nasser and Mo could come for dinner tonight," he said. "Zaid and Nader, too. Four boys, *mashallah*."

It was strange to hear her sons' names come out of Ibrahim's mouth, especially since Ghazi never said "Mo" anymore. He had told her last month that Mohammad was not a name to minimize.

"We should have named a child for you," Laila apologized.

"That is a son's job, not yours," Ibrahim said. But none of your sons will name a son for you, Laila thought to herself.

"I had four boys to name. I could have called one Ibrahim."

"If anything, you should have named one Marwan," Ibrahim told her. "Me, I was the man who didn't let you do nothing but homework."

"You raised me when you didn't have to," Laila said. Conversation with him, let alone conversation about something that mattered, was more foreign than his accent. "You didn't have to marry my mother."

170

"Yes, I did," Ibrahim replied. "I wouldn't have had no nine other children with her if I did not want to marry her."

Laila stopped rolling grape leaves. She could feel goose bumps under her wig. "It wasn't for me?"

"Well, for you I would have married her anyway," Ibrahim said. "I owed your father that much. But I didn't owe him loving his wife from the moment I saw her."

More goose bumps rose under her wig.

"Oh, you should have seen her hair. But it wasn't just about no hair," Ibrahim went on. "When your mama talked, she laughed a laugh — she brought Lebanon back to me. It wasn't just that, but that's what I told to my first wife — Betsy — who knew the minute Fatima got off the train that she had never really been loved by me like she do deserve. Then I left Betsy."

"That's terrible," Laila said. Ibrahim nodded. She could not quite see the old man in front of her as someone capable of being love-struck. He had always been more of symbol to her — a father symbol — rather than a man with a life of stories, including some about love.

"Your mama to this day thinks Betsy left me like that for another man," Ibrahim continued. "Your mama doesn't know no

171

different because she wouldn't never have forgiven me the pain I caused Betsy. I myself cannot do no forgiving me for coveting my best friend's wife. A union hero, too."

Laila couldn't envision what anything would have been like if Marwan had lived. It was not just that all her siblings wouldn't have existed. She couldn't picture how Ibrahim or Fatima could have managed all those years without each other. That was why their divorce had baffled her as much as her sons' collective inability to get married did. She couldn't imagine how Ibrahim lived without Fatima these days, especially now that she knew that the marriage had not simply been his duty to an old friend. He had always treated Laila slightly better than her sisters. She had assumed he was overcompensating for her not being his blood, but now she understood that it had been guilt.

"Maybe I could invite Mama for Thanksgiving, like I used to when she lived here, and you could come, too, like before," she offered. "I'll make a big turkey. Just like before."

Ibrahim waved away her idea. "Before is over," he said, and once again he stared straight into her eyes until she finally had to turn away.

"That's a new hair color you got," he noticed. "I liked your real color better. It was the color of your father's hair. Not so black black, like mine."

"I liked it, too," she admitted. "But sometimes change . . ."

"You girls was always not wanting no curly hair," he remembered. Then he reached to touch a lock, and she pushed the chair back.

"Don't touch me," she said, worried that he would feel its fakeness.

"I understand. I'm no good man. I'll leave."

"No, Baba, stay," Laila said.

"I can take the bus home," Ibrahim said. "You keep rolling."

"No, no," she insisted. "How about you take a nap for a little while instead?"

It was a lot of time they'd spent together today, more time than Laila ever remembered being alone with him.

"I should go," he said.

"No, no, please don't go," she said. "Just a nap. No leaving."

Ibrahim picked up his cane. "I can take a nap at home."

Laila took the cane from him and gave him her arm. "No, Baba, please," she said. "Just a nap."

After a few moments, he took her arm.

"Okay, a nap," he agreed. "A nap."

"Good; you know where the guest room is."

"No," he said. "I have never slept in your house."

It was not a judgment, just a fact.

She took him to the room and helped him into the bed. "Do you want me to get you the paper?" she asked.

Ibrahim shook his head. She heard the creaks in his body as he lay down. "Baba, it's okay that all you let me do was home-work," she said. "That wasn't so bad. Ghazi is much harder on our boys than you ever were."

"That's because he was educated enough to do checking homework," Ibrahim reasoned. "I could only make you do it. I couldn't tell you if it was wrong."

"My boys used to shake as soon as they heard his car in the driveway," Laila told him. "They would run to their homework."

"So they got no confidence." Ibrahim nodded. "*Inshallah,* grown up on their own, they're going to get enough confidence. It takes confidence to love a woman. Then when they love a woman, they can marry her."

In one sentence, her father had given her the only explanation for her sons' singleness that could be true. She had let her husband take a hard line with the boys, and so she could not blame him alone, as she wished she could.

Laila did not stay in the guest room when Ibrahim looked at the family photos on the dresser: Laila and her boys, Laila and Ghazi, Laila and her brothers and sisters, Fatima alone in her wedding dress. There were no photos of him. It wasn't intentional, but she couldn't tell from his face whether he knew that.

Laila went back to folding grape leaves, working faster on her own, hoping the speed would eliminate the disturbing thoughts of her sons' cowering in front of Ghazi and of her parents' unfamiliar love story. Did her mother-in-law have a love story, too? Laila would not ask Amani when she came home. Too much melodrama would be involved. There always was with Amani, from the day Ghazi had introduced her as his bride and Amani had cried that she already had picked out someone else for him, with the implication that her someone was better. Had she and Ghazi really had a love story of their own once? Maybe if her boys thought she and Ghazi had a love story, they would have more confidence and get married. No, she didn't know her parents had a love story when she married Ghazi. She looked at the clock. She needed to start making the pork.

She pulled the meat out of the refrigerator. She stared at it for a while, as if it might have something it was waiting to tell her. The she turned on the oven to five hundred degrees. She yanked the chops out of the packaging, grabbing them quickly and flinging them into the broiler pan, holding her nose, looking away as they landed, minimizing contact with them with all her senses. She did that with twelve pieces. A heck of a lot of pork. Too much pork. The pork chops were starting to land on top of one another. They weren't all going to fit in one pan, and she did not want leftovers. She closed her eyes, grabbed the extra chops by their edges, and forced them down the garbage disposal. She'd dig them out and throw them away later, when it was dark and the neighbors wouldn't see. In the meantime, no one would think to look in the garbage disposal for pork.

Laila understood that the Koran referred to pig meat as rife with disease, not sin, and that American industry had wiped out all worms and microbes. Yet she looked away again as she dumped the cans of tomato sauce over the meat. She opened the oven door with her foot so that her pork-stained fingers wouldn't touch the handle. Then she washed her hands with tub and tile cleanser, a smell that was an unpleasant reminder of the hospital but preferable to porky hands.

She looked through the oven window. Yes, a lot of pork. She called Ghazi.

"Why don't you bring some of your friends from the mosque over for dinner," she suggested. "I was in the mood to cook today. I made grape leaves and a few other things."

"Are you sure?" Ghazi asked.

"Oh, yes," she said. "Very sure."

Laila used to invite people over for dinner, but that had stopped with Mo's car accident, which had come six weeks before her cancer. Mo's back wasn't good anymore. Harder to get married with back problems, especially at thirty-nine. She then had told her second son, Nasser, who was already thirty-seven, as well as her younger sons, to watch their backs. It was one thing for a woman to marry someone who later got sick; it was another to find someone willing to marry someone who was already sick. Just two weeks later, Nasser lost his job during another Ford layoff. Who would marry an unemployed son? Then came her cancer, which was almost as unfortunate for her

177

sons as it was for her. As a sick mother-in-law, she would put another burden on a new bride. Laila thought about how much Amani weighed on her nerves even long after she had stopped being a new bride, and Amani hadn't been sick a day in her life.

Laila looked in on the pork and turned the oven down to 350 degrees. She checked on the grape leaves. Perfect.

By the time Ghazi and his three friends arrived, just after the *aasyer* prayers, she had made hummus and salad; laid out the table; garnished it with oval plates of olives, pickles, and radishes; and filled wineglasses with apricot juice. Her father would be impressed to see how she could set a table. Still, she was happy to hear a faint snore from his room.

"Hi, hello," Laila tossed out as she led the men right to the dining table. No wasting time with appetizers in the living room tonight. Ghazi once had viewed himself as quite pharaonic but was now more Santa Claus, with a big belly and a very full white beard. The three men, mechanical engineers like Ghazi, could be described the same way, except that their accents were much stronger than his. They hadn't been in the United States as long as Ghazi and didn't speak English at home as he did. Laila and the boys could understand a lot of Arabic, but unlike these men's families, they didn't converse in it.

She motioned for the men to sit down. They stayed standing. *"Salam Ala kum,"* they said to her, slightly bowing their heads in unison. In her rush to get dinner started, she had forgotten to greet her guests properly.

"Wa ala kum al salam," she responded.

"It was very kind of you to invite us to dinner," one of them said as they sat down. Laila tried to keep their names straight. The one with the curliest hair was Abdul Kareem, the one with an accent so thick that he had never pronounced the letter *p* in his life was Abdul Latif, and the one with a baldness equal to her own was Abdul Wahab. Abdul Kareem, Abdul Latif, and Abdul Wahab. Their parents had named them servants to three of the ninety-nine names of God. They were practically named after God. She decided to bring out the pork a little later.

Ghazi started filling the men's plates for them, and she joined him.

"The meat in the grape leaves is *halal,* of course," Ghazi said, as if he actually had cooked something once. The beef in the grape leaves was indeed *halal,* meat from cows slaughtered under Islamic laws that showed as much mercy to the animal as possible. Laila was sure that if Muslims ate pork, it would be *halal.*

The men looked at Laila and waited for her to sit down so that they could eat. When she did, she picked at some hummus with her pita bread while they took seconds to swallow the grape leaves she had spent hours rolling.

"These are delicious," said Abdul Kareem. "Like my mother's, *Allah yerhamha.*"

The others repeated the blessing to his deceased mother. Then they dug in for seconds.

"Looks like it might storm tonight," Abdul Latif remarked.

"Thunder and lightening," Abdul Wahab added.

"Maybe even a tornado," Abdul Kareem threw in.

Laila didn't like talking about the weather, especially tornadoes. "How are your wives?" she asked. Their wives had visited her in the hospital more than once, even though she had never met them before her illness. She could have invited the women to dinner tonight, but they were very nice, and so she had spared them.

"Sanaa sends her greetings," said Abdul

Wahab. "Did my daughter visit to thank you for the dress you sent her?"

"Yes, she brought me a Koran from Mecca," Laila said. "From your family's pilgrimage there last year." Abdul Wahab's daughter had turned eighteen the previous month and had been inspired to put on a beige head scarf. Ghazi had told Laila that it would be polite to give the girl a gift to congratulate her on her decision. Laila bought the girl a long nightgown, which somehow she and her mother took as a dress to go with the *hijab,* although the girl still seemed confined to a wardrobe of jeans and Gap shirts. Laila couldn't bring herself to correct them, these two strangers who had brought her flowers while she was in the hospital — twice.

"How is Mohammad's back doing?" Abdul Latif asked as he dipped a grape leaf in yogurt. "It was great to see your other sons with Ghazi at Friday prayers this week."

Laila looked at her husband, but he turned away and poked at the grape leaves on his plate. Ghazi had not made any mention of the boys going to the mosque with him. She had noticed that Nasser was growing a beard but had thought it might be fashion, as he was the most stylish of her sons.

"I made a meat dish, too," Laila said. "Let

me go get it."

"Mohammad will join his brothers at the mosque soon, *inshallah,*" Abdul Wahab said.

"*Inshallah,*" everyone but Laila said.

"He gave up alcohol last week," Ghazi noted.

"*Al-hamdulilah,*" everyone but Laila echoed.

What woman was Mo ever going to meet at the mosque? It wasn't like a church where he could end up sitting next to a nice girl.

Laila stood up to get the pork. "Mo is not named for the prophet, peace be upon him, you know," Laila told them. It was important to her that these men know that. "He's named for Ghazi's father."

She went to the kitchen and hesitated for just a moment before she pulled the pork out of the oven. She tipped the pan so that the tomato sauce would slide over the meat and then slipped the meat onto a platter without touching it. She cut off a sprig of parsley and put it in the center. Who knew pork could look so pretty? She went back out and laid the tray down with flourish. The men salivated.

"What is a meal for guests without meat?" Laila announced. "It's with tomato sauce, like they make in the South."

"We do not make veal with tomato sauce in the south," Abdul Latif said, helping himself to a piece. Abdul Latif was from Lebanon. Although he had been in the United States for nearly twenty years, the south still meant to him — and half of Dearborn — the part of Lebanon that bordered Israel, not Alabama and Tennessee.

Laila handed a serving fork to Ghazi. She said nothing as he served the others. Abdul Kareem lifted his plate up to his nose and sniffed it.

"Great," he said. He took a bite at the same time as the others. They stopped in midchew. She held the serving fork in midair, waiting for the damnation. Then they began chewing again.

"Too much sauce?" Laila suggested, grabbing for a culinary diversion.

"No, no, very interesting veal," Abdul Wahab said. "Very chewy."

"Yes, *chewy* is a good word," Abdul Kareem agreed.

"Perhaps that is because it isn't *halal,*" Laila confessed. She felt she had to be at least a little honest before she went to hell. And she had never said the word *veal.* They had.

Ghazi furrowed his brows at her not because the meat wasn't *halal* but because she had told them it wasn't.

"Back home we could not afford veal in my family," Abdul Wahab recalled. "Life is bountiful here. Everything and lots of it, *al-hamdulilah.*"

Too late to take it away now.

"*Wallah, Seit* Laila, my littlest daughter would disown me now," Abdul Latif said. "She told me no eating veal for it is not compassionate killing. She showed me pictures. Most cruel. But for you I will. For you, *maalesh,* no problem."

For you with the cancer, Laila thought. Abdul Latif took a big bite, and the others kept chewing. "It is delicious," Abdul Kareem reassured her. "Forgetting that we only eat *halal* meat is no big deal. *Suhtain,* bon appetit."

They each took another bite and smiled. Their humanity gave birth to many more goose bumps.

"When your youngest finishes medical school, Madame Laila, he might want to spend a year working for the Red Crescent, helping our brothers and sisters back home," Abdul Kareem said. The other men nodded as they kept chewing.

Laila wanted to scream that no son of hers was going to be dead. She calmed herself by watching them chew the pork.

"My daughter spent a year helping doctors in the camps in Afghanistan and Pakistan," Abdul Wahab said. "She's in medical school now."

"Oh, is she married?" Laila asked, thinking a doctor for a daughter-in-law wouldn't be so bad.

"Of course — she's already twenty-five," Abdul Wahab said. "It was a huge wedding. Our relatives flew from across the country to be here, and they all got through airport security in time to make the reception."

Laila was the only one who did not laugh. She did not fear God, she did not fear her religion, but she was terrified of other people's fear of it.

"You shouldn't laugh about the airports," Laila said.

"Yes, but our people's paranoia is also blown out of proportion a hundred times over," Abdul Kareem said. "This country allows freedom of religion, true faith. They're just worried about the crazies. They'll see soon enough that the crazies aren't in Dearborn. We won't allow that kind of sacrilege."

Not only were they pious, they were naive. Naive about the government. Naive about meat. Laila was not. She looked at Ghazi to back her up.

"Allah karem," was all he said. "God is kind."

Laila never raised her voice, even when her chemo was unbearable, because she did not like to cause a scene. However, these men needed a wake-up call about how easy it would be to put them in a compromising position. She had meant the pork as her secret revenge on her God-fearing husband, but she grabbed his plate and held it up.

"What you are eating is —" Laila stopped as she saw her father, disheveled from his nap, come out of the guest room.

Ghazi leaped up upon recognizing Ibrahim, and the others followed him. Ghazi shook hands with the man he barely had seen since getting his blessing to marry Laila, which Ibrahim gave even though he was not from Deir Zeitoon, which Ibrahim believed Marwan would have preferred. But Ibrahim had taken comfort in the fact that Ghazi had met Laila at a wedding for a couple from Deir Zeitoon, where they had spent the whole night dancing to the Who and the Rolling Stones. That dancing Laila had died long before any cancer could get her. Ghazi used to say he missed the old Laila when all they did was watch TV on Friday nights. Now Ghazi told her that he considered their quiet life God's will and wisdom. He spent most Friday nights these days at the mosque praying to God to keep her with him for as long as he could, leaving her at home to watch TV alone.

"You forgot to wake me up," Ibrahim said to Laila, looking away from her as he admonished her in a way that had been familiar to her all her life.

"Welcome, *Amo,*" said Ghazi, guiding Ibrahim to a chair. The men all shook Ibrahim's hand as Ghazi introduced him. "Sit, sit, *Amo;* let me make you a plate."

Abdul Wahab helped guide Ibrahim into this chair, Abdul Kareem spread out his napkin for him, and Abdul Latif poured him a glass of apricot juice. Laila stood frozen, still holding Ghazi's plate.

"He helped me with the grape leaves," Laila told Ghazi. "Give him lots of those."

Ghazi put grape leaves on the plate and then a little yogurt.

"Veal, *Amo?*" Ghazi said, and placed the largest pork chop on Ibrahim's plate.

"Who says he wants any meat?" Laila snapped. She stabbed the pork chop with the serving fork and put it back on the platter. The guests stopped chewing, exchanging words with facial expressions that she knew said they thought the cancer was acting up.

"No, I like veal," Ibrahim reassured her.

"Eat the grape leaves," Laila almost ordered. "You helped me make them, after all."

"My father-in-law — your father — should get the best piece of meat," Ghazi said to her as she glared at him.

"Save the meat for your boys," Ibrahim said. "I don't need no meat at my age. You don't go waste no luxury on me."

Oh, God, she thought, I've hurt him so many times today trying to protect him. "No, no, go ahead," she said.

"No," Ibrahim said.

"I insist," Laila said.

Ghazi put the pork chop back on Ibrahim's plate. Ibrahim looked at Ghazi and the guests.

"Laila is a good cook, no?" Ibrahim said. They all nodded a little too enthusiastically.

"Sorry I overreacted, Baba. You were supposed to stay asleep," Laila apologized. "I mean, I wanted you to get enough rest."

"It was nice, thank you." Ibrahim nodded. He cut into the meat and started to raise it to his mouth. Laila watched as if his fork had been suspended in slow motion like the baseball replays her mother always watched. When Ibrahim's mouth began to open, Laila leaped up and yanked the fork and plate from him. Ibrahim bowed his head.

"Laila!" Ghazi yelled.

The men stopped chewing again.

"It's okay," Ibrahim whispered.

"I want you to eat the grape leaves," Laila said. "Eat the grape leaves. They're my specialty."

Everyone stopped in midchew. "I'm sorry, *Amo,*" Ghazi said. "It's the can—"

Laila yanked Ghazi's plate from him to jolt him into remembering that her father did not know she had been ill.

Ibrahim looked down at his plate for what seemed like his long life over and then slowly lifted his head. "Oh, Laila," he murmured, and in his voice she knew he had not figured out the cancer but rather the pork.

"Maybe we should go," Abdul Wahab said.

Ghazi nodded. Then Ibrahim pounded the table with his fork. "No, sit," he said. "She's so crazy like her mama. We will all only eat grape leaves. So my daughter will be happy. Laila, take everyone's meat away."

"Yes, Baba," Laila said. "Everyone sit, and I will bring new plates just for the grape leaves."

The guests were nearly back in their seats when a ferocious growl from the kitchen jolted them all upright again.

189

"Bullshit," they all heard come out of the kitchen.

Laila ran into the kitchen and found Amani, Ghazi's mother, head-scarfed and overweight, staring down at the garbage disposal. Laila turned off the disposal, which chugged to a stop. The smell of burning rubber came out of it, as did another odor, unpleasant but unidentifiable to Amani.

Amani had come to live with them two years earlier, and Laila often wondered if it was possible to revoke an F-1 visa, the student visa that meant Amani had to go to English as a second language classes every evening in order to stay with them.

"Bullshit," Amani repeated, staring down at the malfunctioning garbage disposal. "Curses on Americans who think they can build anything. And is this the way that our dear God repays me for trying to help my son's wife keep a clean house?"

Bullshit was the only English word Amani seemed to have learned at school, and she wouldn't believe anyone who told her it was a bad expression. "If it was so, so bad, not everyone would use it all the time," she told her son. Other than *bullshit,* Amani said most of her words in Arabic, although she could understand about 30 percent of the

English she heard, which had proved to be a good thing and a bad thing.

"Why did you leave cards early?" Laila asked, trying to move her mother-in-law away from the garbage disposal. She should have risked having the neighbors see her take out the pork. How did one unstick pork? Damn her mother-in-law for being helpful. It always resulted in trouble. Who comes home and starts doing dishes right away, anyway?

"Bullshit game," Amani said.

"Would you like me to make you a plate, some grape leaves . . . and meat," Laila responded, and lifted up the pan holding the remaining cooked pork chops. Amani sniffed and examined the meat long enough for Laila's heart to race.

"No, thank you," Amani finally said, grimacing. "Too much tomato sauce."

"Sorry, *Khalto,*" Laila said, relieved for once rather than irked by Amani's insults. "We have company."

"No?" said Amani. "Bullshit."

Amani waddled out to the dining room, and the men all stood up for her. Even Ibrahim made his way back up.

"Who are you?" Ibrahim asked as he shook her hand.

"I'm Ghazi's mother," said Amani, all

191

pride. "Who are you?"

"I'm Laila's father," Ibrahim answered.

"Bullshit," Amani replied. "You were already so old at their wedding, I thought you had died already. Where have you been? Never even visit to say 'Happy Eid.' "

"Your mother-in-law lives with you?" Ibrahim said to Laila.

"It was either that, Baba, or we'd have to go to Egypt every year to visit her, and you know how much that can cost," Laila said a little too desperately. "We would have never been able to buy a winter home in Florida."

"You don't have no winter home in Florida," Ibrahim said.

"That's because we've given all our extra money to the mosque," Laila explained. "Ghazi and the boys go to the mosque every day now."

She waited for her father to be surprised, and he was. "Religion can go this way or that way for you," Ibrahim told Ghazi. "Just pray it goes the right way."

"Inshallah," Ghazi said.

"Inshallah," the guests repeated.

Then Amani's 30 percent English comprehension kicked in. "What money extra? Where money?"

"I want to go home," Ibrahim announced.

"Please, *Amo,* you can live with us, too,"

Ghazi offered.

"I don't need no taking care of," Ibrahim replied.

"Like I do?" Amani fumed. "It's your daughter who does."

Ibrahim looked at Laila, confused. In that instant, Amani understood that Laila couldn't tell her own father she was ill.

"Laila is on a special diet," Amani said. "It takes a lot of work. I came all the way from Egypt — twenty hours on the airplane — to help with her diet. I cut vegetables all day, but I do not eat them myself."

Amani patted her belly as proof and took Laila's hand. Amani was protecting her secret as if she mattered. What next? This was a day to give anyone a breakdown.

"Bullshit," said Ibrahim, having always understood the word perfectly. "Since when have any of Laila's diets been so important? I want to go home."

The guests shuffled and mumbled about how they had to get going to the mosque. Their religion's schedule was proving to be an especially convenient excuse today, even for her; she could not clean up the pork mess in front of Ibrahim.

"I'll give you a ride, *Amo*," Ghazi said. "Let's get you home before this storm comes in."

"Let me pack some grape leaves for you," Laila said.

Ibrahim shook his head. "But perhaps I will stop by on my way to the airport tomorrow; that is when one of the KLM flights comes in."

Laila didn't know anything about the airport schedules, but she was relieved he wanted to visit again.

"This diet is making you too crazy to be left alone with this woman," Ibrahim warned, pointing to Amani.

"*Amo,* take the paper with you," Ghazi offered, and held out *Al-Ahram* to Ibrahim. "Maybe it will keep you company on the way to the airport tomorrow."

"No, *ibni,* my son, I don't want to scare no people on the bus reading Arabic," Ibrahim said. "It's plenty scary that I am old."

Laila took the paper from Ghazi, and he held the door open for Ibrahim. The others followed them out. Ibrahim turned around and patted her cheek one more time.

Laila was left alone with Amani and the pork

"You did not tell your father you might die?" Amani said.

"The doctor said it is gone, *Khalto,*" Laila replied, glad that Amani's usual melodrama could not tip her over the edge tonight as she already had tipped over.

"Inshallah," Amani replied.

"Thank you for not telling him."

"I got to help you. I'm the only mother you got in Detroit." Amani shrugged. "But your father should know. I would want to know if something, *Allah yustur,* happened to Ghazi."

"Fine, then I promise to tell you," Laila said. "But not my father."

"Why not, in the name of God, the most merciful?" Amani said, gesticulating in all directions. "May He protect us from all evils."

"Khalto, do you mind not making our life one of your Egyptian soap operas?" Laila asked.

"Egyptian soap opera?" Amani fumed. "At least in an Egyptian soap opera my grand-sons would be married by now. I said take them to Egypt, we'll find them brides from good families, but did anyone listen to me? No. Bullshit. I must go to sleep now or faint. Save some veal for me to eat later." Cleopatra had never made such a dramatic exit to her chambers as Amani did in storming off to her tiny room.

Laila took the platter of pork and dumped it in the garbage, careful not to touch it. She scrubbed her hands and looked at the disposal. She got out the bleach and put on a pair of kitchen gloves. Two hours later, she had destroyed three pairs of rubber gloves and her gardening mittens and scraped her hands twice getting the meat out of the disposal. Then she took the garbage out and put the meat at the bottom of the trash bin. Good thing the garbage-men were coming tomorrow.

She was watching news coverage of the storm when Ghazi came home, swept through the door by a rush of wind. She did not lower the volume on the TV. He kissed her on the cheek.

"Thank you for inviting my friends over," he said. "The veal was delicious. I just told your father it was terrible so he wouldn't feel bad about not eating it."

"So Mo joined you tonight at the mosque?" Laila said.

"Maybe Mohammed will pray next to a man who has a single sister," Ghazi suggested. He assumed that his sons would marry Arabs, whereas Laila had assumed years ago only that they would marry. She wanted to tell him about having the boys become part of her nephew Zade's marriage service, but he would consider such public airing degrading.

"I'm sorry I made a scene in front of your

Muslim friends," Laila said. "They are always very nice."

"Your father can live with us any time you want," said Ghazi.

"I know."

"I was glad to see your father," Ghazi said. "He looked well."

"He looked about as well as I do," Laila said.

"You look fine."

Ghazi had adopted the worst clichéd American husband responses to everything.

"I'm not getting fake boobs," Laila said.

"Then don't," Ghazi said. "I mean, I don't know why you wouldn't. . . ."

"I would only get them to not offend you," Laila said.

"You do not offend me," Ghazi said, and took her hand.

"Really?" Laila said. She started to unbutton her blouse. He turned away. She buttoned it back up.

"I'm glad you don't miss them," she said, and turned back to the TV.

"I do care so much for you," Ghazi whispered. That was not easy for a man from Egypt, an engineer no less, to say. Maybe it wasn't easy for any man. Laila had no experience with any other man. One day, Ghazi might even try "I love you," although she knew he would never be American enough to throw it around like "hello" and "goodbye" the way her regular American friends' husbands did. He had said the three words to her when he had asked her to marry him, and that had been enough for both of them through the years.

He took her face in his hands. With her shirt buttoned, Ghazi was able to put his arms around Laila and hold her, something she understood as proof of his love. They stayed that way for some time.

"Has Laila wooed you with longing? Departing amidst her tribe," Ghazi recited from an old Arabian poem he had courted her with, a poem she had not heard since several years before she lost her breasts. *"Yes indeed the tears come flooding in streams over my breast."*

Ghazi's lips bent down to kiss hers. Laila pushed him away.

"You should brush your teeth first," she said. "There might be veal stuck in them." She hadn't meant to push him away. It just happened. The way he had loved her these last few months had left her more alone than she had ever felt since meeting him. Yet she could not tell him that. It would make her cry, which would result in him forming tears he would try to hide, which would take her nervous breakdown to the point of no return.

Ghazi ran his tongue along his teeth. "You are right," he said. He went up to the bathroom and flossed and brushed and waited for Laila to come up after her television show was over.

Many hours later, after Ghazi was sound asleep, Laila got up. She took off her wig, washed her hands and feet in the bathtub, and pulled Ghazi's prayer rug out of the linen closet. She faced the direction in which Ghazi said Mecca lay. Then she did the only the thing she knew to be true and right.

"Authu bilah min el-Shetan," she began. She clasped her hands together and went through the *rikkahs,* rhythmically bending and repeating phrases asking for mercy and wisdom by rote, as she had heard her husband do so many times over the last year and three months, as she had heard Fatima do since she was a child. Finally, she knelt. "Dear God," she prayed quietly, eyes closed, ignoring the wind beating outside. "I am sorry for the pork tonight. I was angry for the way things couldn't be anymore. God, as my sons turn to you, protect them from the dangers their love for you could bring them. Also God, I don't want anyone or

anything — not the Red Crescent, not the CIA, not you — no one but a marriageable woman to take my sons away from me. I hope you understand.

"Do you know what I wished in the supermarket right before I bought the pork? I wished that just once I had worn one of those fancy silky bras with all the lace and padding that make a lady's breasts spill over. Just once. I should go to sleep now before Ghazi sees me. I don't want him to know how much I talk to you, although I am lucky to have a good man, which is hard to find in any religion. I want to also thank you for bringing my father to me. Grant me more patience for Amani and her bullshit. And God, I promise to go to California and bring Baba with me. And then Mama and he can be normal again. I will look for cheap airfares tomorrow. And I will get a better wig for the visit. Amen."

Laila stood and rolled up the carpet. For the first night since this time of war and cancer, she felt at peace.

■ ■ ■ ■

THE 996TH NIGHT

■ ■ ■ ■

SCHEHERAZADE

When Scheherazade left Laila's home, she was assaulted by a ferocious blast of swirling air reminiscent of the *shamal* winds during winters spent along the Persian Gulf. Unlike those desert winds, the Detroit winds did not threaten to blind one with sweeping golden sand but rather promised to strike one down. When she saw a cloud in the shape of a funnel, she sought refuge for the night in the women's section of Ghazi's mosque. Scheherazade had known earthquakes, floods, sandstorms, mud slides, and other formidable forms of divine intervention. But her homeland, for all its woes, had been spared the tornado. The next morning she was glad when the funnel cloud decided to leave Detroit alone.

The remaining winds were still strong enough that they propelled Scheherazade to Los Angeles far more quickly than she had expected. From her flying carpet, she saw

Fatima getting off the bus, holding her cane in one hand and carrying two plastic bags from the Iranian Jew's store in the other, clean black skirt on and brown scarf tied around her head to prevent the wind from irritating her hearing aid.

Scheherazade checked her makeup in her gilded silver compact and then tapped Fatima on the shoulder.

"Where were you last night?" Fatima demanded.

"I encountered a tornado and had to wait for it to pass."

"Tornado." Fatima shuddered. The old lady had very strong reactions to weather reports sometimes.

"How were Suheir Lababidi's condolences today?" Scheherazade asked.

"They had even better *ma'amoul* than at Selma Haddad's," Fatima reported. She showed Scheherazade a business card for Victory Bakery. "I'm going to ask Amir to add them to my funeral menu — wait, where did you encounter a tornado?"

"I met your Laila yesterday," Scheherazade admitted. But she did not enjoy revealing news of illnesses and so momentarily distracted herself with the half-naked handsome men coming out of Santa Monica Boulevard's exercise palaces, men who politely ignored Fatima talking to herself but could not resist looking at her head scarf with its wisps of protruding purple.

"My Laila is always going on a diet and going to gyms," Fatima said. "Sometimes in Detroit she would pick me up and I would go with her and watch everyone exercise. So how normal was Laila?"

Scheherazade searched for words that didn't involve cancer.

"So how normal was Laila?" Fatima repeated, eyes drilling into hers.

And then Scheherazade knew that Fatima already knew.

"How did you find out?" Scheherazade whispered, as even immortal Arabs spoke of cancer as if it were a contagious scandal they didn't want to spread.

"One day she stopped talking about her diets and stuck to just the weather," Fatima said. "So I asked her why she wasn't on a diet, and she said she had lost plenty of weight and she would send me a picture — as thin as her wedding day, she said. She never sent the picture, and when I ask my other children about her, they start talking about the weather again. Then I knew. Has she stopped losing weight? Like all the other chubby-type people, she never used to lose weight for long. Normal, see."

"The cancer is gone now," Scheherazade confirmed. "She will get fat again, *inshallah*."

"*Inshallah.* I am so far from Laila because she will not talk of it. It's funny; I never felt how far away Mama was until the day Laila was born," Fatima said. "I kept calling out for Mama in the delivery room, but the nurses didn't understand me. My English still wasn't so good. So the nurse told Ibrahim he could come in, but he said it was shameful because he wasn't the child's father. By the time Miriam — my second — was born, I spoke English pretty well, so Ibrahim never had a chance to see any of his children born as they all came before people thought it was okay for fathers to be in the room."

"God forbid, who would want the man there?" Scheherazade asked.

"Times change, *ya oukhti.*" Fatima sighed. "When I first came to this country, I couldn't understand how the women — Millie and those big picture show stars — let men boss them around. And when we got the TV, you should have seen how the women let their husbands talk to them. They'd scheme behind the men's backs and then smile and obey them. Who had time for such nonsense? 'Oh, Ricky,' 'Oh, Ward,'

'Oh, Rob,' they would say. I thought the men were silly, but Millie loved them because they didn't yell and say 'I'm going to kill you' like her old man — that's what she called her husband — 'I'm going to kill you,' he used to shout. In the beginning, I was alone at the house at night because Marwan was in Flint, and I would raise the volume on the baseball game so I couldn't hear him. It was the first sentence I learned in English. When I could say more things in English, I once told her to tell him right back she'd kill him first, but she never did."

"Or at least divorce him," Scheherazade said.

"She said her religion didn't allow that," Fatima said. "Then, about the time we got our second television, in Technicolor, you know, women went marching and yelling in the streets. They called it women's lib, and Millie's husband forbade her from going to the marches and said that you couldn't tell a man from a woman anymore."

"You said it, sister," the homeless man with the dimple piped in from the sidewalk.

"Don't call me 'sister,' boy," Fatima warned him. "I'm old enough to be your mother. Did you look for a job today?"

Scheherazade let Fatima find the homeless man's woes a distraction from Laila's until they reached Amir's home.

FATIMA

Once she was back in her bedroom, Fatima took off her scarf, hung up her black skirt, and put on her pink robe. Scheherazade wrapped herself under the bedcovers, Detroit's violent wind still coursing through her timeless blood.

Fatima sat at the vanity mirror and brushed out her purple hair. She paused, dusted her hands off on her robe, and carefully opened the mother-of-pearl Koran at her bedside.

"This is Mama's Koran. She could read it herself," she said. "My grandfather made a pretty good living with his carpentry, and she was able to go to school until she was fifteen."

"Mashallah," Scheherazade replied. "God be praised."

Fatima took out a tattered sepia photo from inside the Koran. "She died of something the doctor found in her bosom, my uncle told me," she said, and handed Scheherazade the photo, which showed a woman tilling a tobacco field, the sun having given her skin a beating. She wore a long black *thowb.* What little embroidery it had was also in black. The woman looked as if she never had experienced youth.

"I only knew Mama in mourning clothes because someone in her family was always going away and dying," Fatima continued. She twirled a strand of her hair. "The only thing that ever stayed the same was the house."

Scheherazade sat up. "Give the house to Laila. A place to relax and pray with her husband when he retires. Perhaps it will be better than their Florida dream."

"What if the doctors tell her . . . ?" Fatima said. "What if they say it is back for good? Then she will have to give the house away herself. I don't want to trouble her with that decision, especially when all four of her heirs are unmarried. Worry is bad for sickness."

From the vanity, Fatima picked up a black-and-white photo of a girl with two braids running to her knees, standing on tiptoe and struggling to hang up a huge bedsheet on the clothesline.

"So helpful, always," Fatima said to Laila's picture. "Does her hair still curl up at the ends?"

Scheherazade was too slow to respond. "It will come back."

"We never had any time left to even comb

the other girls' hair when I braided Laila's for school. So thick. So strong. Like mine. But not so black like mine. Almost red," Fatima said, and then stopped twirling her hair.

Fatima opened the vanity drawer and handed Scheherazade a pair of scissors. "Cut my hair. Short, short."

Scheherazade leaped out of bed, put the scissors back on the vanity, and stepped away from them. "A woman's hair is her proof of wealth and happiness," she said. "It is her crown."

"Laila is my firstborn." Fatima forced the scissors back into Scheherazade's hands. "The first to suck on my breast, the first to graduate from high school, the first to marry, the first to have children. She did everything the right way in the right order. Normal. I have loved watching her go normally through life's stages. I am blessed I will not live to see her die a normal death. If it comes again, *Allah yustur*, then I want her to not worry about losing her beautiful hair again. She will have mine. Cut it or I'll do it myself."

Fatima's hands were shaking, and so Scheherazade took the scissors, as she did not wish to see any blood. Scheherazade combed out the long hair and then hesitated. But Fatima did not move, and so she lifted the scissors, hesitated once more, and then cut five perfect thick strands of purple. Instinctively, she began braiding them while Fatima watched in silence. She laid them on the vanity just as the door opened.

Amir dropped the pill tray at the sight of Fatima's braids. Scheherazade got out of the human fray and perched herself on the windowsill.

"Jesus Christ, what have you done, Tayta?" he screamed. He touched the spikes of purple on her head. Fatima pushed his hand away and put the braids in the top drawer of her dresser, caressing them as she laid them down.

"When I go one of these days, don't look in this drawer," Fatima ordered. "It has all my underwear. *Aabe,* shame, if people look in my underwear drawer upon my death."

She was still angry with him, but she had no time for anger. She had spent most of the night thinking of Laila, but Scheherazade had assured her of Laila's health. She could focus again on what needed to be done for him before her own death.

"You should see someone professional," Amir said, tentatively coming closer to the purple stubs. "I'm going to call Auntie Hala tomorrow."

211

"She is a doctor and a daughter," Fatima said. "From both directions she will want to find something wrong with me when nothing is wrong with me. It's the nature of children and doctors."

She put her scarf on over her stubs. "See, no one will know," she explained.

"People will think you're Muslim."

"I am Muslim."

"Yeah, but since when are you one of the scarf-wearing ones?" Amir asked.

"My head gets cold on the bus," Fatima said. "The air-conditioning is twenty-one degrees cooler than outside. It will be even colder without my hair."

"Look, it's not so great that you're walking down the street talking to yourself. Luckily, this is L.A., so that's not going to stop traffic, but the scarf," Amir said. "Even in this community we've got punks. You're old and vulnerable, and it's better to pass as Mexican in that condition. Without the scarf, you can pass."

The color drained from Fatima's face. "Now you're insulting our religion," she fumed. "Every day, are you going to tell me things you're going to have to apologize for?"

A car braked in front of the house before he could come up with an answer more sophisticated than "no."

"That'll be the messenger from Warner Bros. with my audition pages," Amir said. "This could be the big one; I had to go behind my agent's back to get it. Omar Sharif, baby."

He looked at her one more time and picked up the scissors. He left with them, humming the score from *Lawrence of Arabia.*

"Lawrence was not a hero but a betrayer," Fatima shouted after him. "We should have stayed with the Turks."

"I was just trying to bring a little music into our lives," he shouted back.

Fatima reached up to twirl her hair, but it was not there. *"Ya Allah,"* she said, and ran her hands through her stubs with fierce energy.

Scheherazade leaped down from the windowsill. "Here, let me try," she offered. She fluffed out Fatima's purple spikes with her more agile fingers. "Better."

But Fatima decided not to risk looking in the mirror. "Do you think I confused him too much about the underwear drawer?"

"Nothing is more transparent than false modesty," Scheherazade replied. "It is the first place he will look."

"He'll open the underwear drawer, and

there will be my gifts to my children." Fatima nodded. "This is where I will also put the key to the house and Mama's letters."

Fatima began taking her underwear out of the drawer and tucking it neatly in the TV credenza. There would be no *aabe,* shame, when Amir opened the drawer, just inheritances. She also would leave Laila her bra. It was still in great shape. It would give her hope that it would hold her breasts whatever they looked like for as long as it had held hers for only $2.99. Laila could always fill it with tissues the way Millie used to do.

Scheherazade was her most gentle as she laid Fatima's purple locks in the drawer, but Fatima pushed her aside and smoothed out the locks with her hands.

"Close the door, please, and tell me a story," Scheherazade said.

"No, you tell me of my death," Fatima demanded just as a car backfired outside, startling her enough to drop one of her braids.

Someone opened and then slammed the car door shut. "Hello, hello, hello," said a laughing voice from downstairs.

"*Ya Allah,* Soraya is here," Fatima told Scheherazade, and swiftly picked up the fallen braid.

"Who?"

"Amir's mother." Fatima grimaced and forced the underwear drawer shut. "Back from spreading good fortune."

"Generosity is the hallmark of noble people," Scheherazade said.

"Generosity should first be revealed at home," Fatima barked. "She's always giving big fancy-word excuses for herself: attention deficit disorder, acute adult-onset paranoia, obsessive-compulsive something or other. Just say you are selfish."

"*Inshallah,* her son is more excited to see her," Scheherazade said.

"*Minshan Allah,* I hope she didn't bring one of her boyfriends with her — fifty-four years old and still using the word *boyfriend,*" Fatima lamented as Soraya let out another loud laugh.

"Excuse me, but I have to sleep so she doesn't talk to me," Fatima explained. "I want to see my children before I go, but God forgive me, I do not have the energy for this one tonight. And she will not wake me if she sees me sleeping."

Fatima took off her nearby glasses and got into bed. Scheherazade pulled the covers up for her.

"You tell me a story for a change so I can sleep," Fatima whispered.

Scheherazade began to tell her of the king who met his death when he obtained by deceitful means a book that contained the secrets of the world. A less greedy but wiser man had dressed each page with poison, and when the king licked his fingers to turn the pages, he learned the secrets, but it was too late for him to make use of them. Soon Fatima dozed, for she had listened to this story as a child nearly as many times as Scheherazade had endured her stories of Deir Zeitoon.

Fatima heard Scheherazade sneak out to see the woman with the laugh so determined to envelop everything. It was a laugh Fatima could still hear in her sleep, a laugh that now prevented her from asking Scheherazade about her own death. This child had always timed her entrances and exits badly.

SORAYA

Soraya laughed bravely as Amir stood in the doorway glaring. She was dressed in a long Paisley dress she had purchased at the Indian store just for the occasion of seeing her son and perhaps her mother. She had accessorized with hoop earrings from the African store and an electric red scarf that revealed the length of her pitch-black hair

216

underneath, hair as long as Fatima's had been just a couple hours earlier. Since her mother had moved into this house, Soraya felt less kumbaya here.

"Hey, baby cakes," she said with an unconscious question mark. Everything she said came with a question mark, even when she was feeling almost confident, which was never the case in front of her family, particularly Amir. Years of reading *A Course in Miracles,* daylong meditations in which she chanted "I am the beloved," and attendance at several uplifting sermons at the Agape Spiritual Center had helped her a little, but not much. "I checked the mail for you. Look who sent you ten dollars."

She laughed more loudly still and handed him the only piece of mail. From Ibrahim, of course, but twice as thick as usual. Maybe cash this time instead of a check. Whatever. He tossed it on the desk as Soraya followed him in. When he turned around, she went in for a hug. Amir pulled away after counting off five seconds and patting her back, which she had told him years before was the minimum level of politeness to maternal figures. At the time, she had been talking about how she treated Fatima.

"Tayta cut off her hair," Amir said when he let go.

"Don't be silly, sweetie," she replied, feeling that she sounded too much like the mother of a small child.

"Go up and see the disaster for yourself."

"Okay, sure, after I buy nuclear weapons stock," she retorted. "Stop saying things just for attention. You have your acting for that."

There. Now she at least sounded like an adult talking to her teenager, if not her adult child. Right?

"Nuclear weapons are not publicly traded," Amir mumbled. "How long are you staying this time?"

"There's a cute guy in the car," she offered.

"Jesus Christ."

"Not for me, but for you, sweetheart," Soraya said. "He's only twenty-seven years old. My cutoff is thirty."

She waited for Amir to join her in laughter, but today he was putting up a tough fight against her humor, the only thing on which they usually agreed.

"Everyone in this family is a freaking matchmaker," he said.

"Then why am I still single?" She laughed. "Anyway, he and I are going to Tijuana to work at the new spa hotel where everyone's going for cheaper cosmetic and dental surgery and other what have you health issues. He's an aromatherapist, so his skills are going to be needed down there as much as my psychic powers."

"My mother wants me to have a relationship with someone who profits off of desperate people as much as she does?" Amir asked.

Soraya ignored the slur on her profession. "You have a fear of commitment, so the distance would allow you to nurture the partnership slowly while you tame the fear demon in you, and maybe taking in Tayta was an excuse to stay out of life," she suggested, trying to sum up the years of their dysfunction in one modified zinger sentence from Dr. Howard, who had been her favorite therapist. Longer explanations forced her to question herself rather than him.

"Are you coming or going, Mom? I'm busy," Amir said. "I'm preparing for an audition. The producer said it's a role to die for, but he wouldn't tell me the details. Word on the street is they're looking for the next Omar Sharif to play Omar Sharif in the Omar Sharif biopic."

"I like Danny Thomas better," Soraya tossed out, unable to think of any other nonthreatening Arab who ever had been on TV.

"Danny Thomas is just about you idolizing fatherhood," Amir said.

"Is not," Soraya said. "I'm perfectly fine with how emotionally absent my father was. So there."

"Whatever. A mother's job is not to pick fights with her kids." Amir shrugged. "It's supposed to be the other way around."

"You're so conventional," she said. "Could I use the bathroom?"

Amir shrugged. "You came all this way to go to the bathroom?"

"No, I forgot my crystal ball here," she replied. "When I was on my way up to the Vajrapani Institute Tibetan Buddhist Retreat Center. Remember? It does help to accessorize one's own fortune-telling skills. I also need to pee."

Amir started up the stairs and then paused. "So did you call the sperm bank again like I asked you to? Maybe they'd release the information to you, since they won't to me."

Oh, Goddess, not this again. Wasn't it enough that no mother had gone to greater lengths to have him, especially at that time? She had been a pioneer in this type of motherhood because she had wanted him so desperately. But she knew even better than he did that she had done nothing in his life to convince him of that. "I'll try

220

again, Son," she promised.

"I'd appreciate that," he said. Then he put his finger to her lips. "Be quiet so we don't wake her up. I don't feel like listening to her tell you how it's your fault I think I'm gay."

"Me, either," she agreed. "Hopefully, she's fallen asleep dreaming of Lebanon: 'Oh, the figs in Deir Zeitoon at this time of year.' "

Amir didn't join her in mimicking Fatima's grandiose talk of Lebanon, which had been a bonding ritual for them over the years.

"Did you tell Tayta about Auntie Laila?" he asked. "She was talking to herself about her tonight."

"What kind of uncentered creature do you think I am that I would subject her to information like that? I only spread good things."

Soraya prided herself on being the keeper of all secrets. Her siblings — and anyone who came to her for a reading — vaguely hoped she really did have psychic powers; that was how they justified telling her things they didn't tell anyone else. But the main reason everyone told her everything was that she never stayed in one place long enough to be bored enough to start gossiping. She was sure she loved her family, and from a distance she felt no pressure from that. When Amir was a child, she would call from whatever state fair or international festival she was working and tell him what the kids there were like. She was great with other people's kids because they weren't expecting maternal instinct — or anything else — from her.

Amir interrupted her thoughts. "Wait until you see what I did with the bathroom," he said.

"I can't imagine any other place I'd rather pee." She sensed her son's expectations, as if her motherhood still held value despite his better sense. She followed him up the stairs, expecting more chrome. Instead, she found herself standing in front of a bathtub surrounded by mosaic tiles, lantern lamps, and dark marble countertops. "It's beautiful, Son," she marveled.

Amir grinned, and she felt slightly vindicated, especially as she was being honest about the bathroom. On the way downstairs, he paused in front of Fatima's room. The door was open, and Fatima was sleeping in her pink robe.

"Let's get going," Soraya whispered. "We'll wake her up."

As she turned back toward the stairs, he shoved her inside.

She tried to go back out, but his arms blocked the doorway. Then he gave her another shove toward Fatima. She looked back, hoping her son would show her some mercy, but he pointed to her to go on. She tiptoed to Fatima's bed to kiss her. Her lips nearly had touched her mother's cheek when she recoiled at the purple stubs. She rushed out of the room, and this time Amir allowed it.

"She's never cut her hair as long as I've been alive," said Soraya. She clung to her son as they went back downstairs. "Maybe I should go talk to her."

Luckily, Amir didn't expect that much from her.

"See you next time, Mom," he said.

"And my crystal ball?" Soraya asked.

"Oh, yeah," Amir said. "I put it in the guest room because it kept reflecting off the chrome."

"What guest room?" Soraya said. "Isn't Tayta staying in the guest room?"

"Tayta in a guest room? No, she would never impose like that," Amir scoffed. "Once she arrived, it became Fatima's room and she started calling my office the guest room."

This time he waited for her to join him in laughing, but she couldn't. Laughter was impossible with the image of her mother's stubs now the prime visual in her cluttered mind.

Amir went back upstairs, and Soraya told herself to "inhale, exhale, inhale," taking in breaths so big that they blew Ibrahim's envelope off Amir's desk. She picked it up and, as if it might hurt her, put it down quickly, leaning it against the old photo of Fatima in her wedding dress, Fatima with her beautiful hair. That photo sat next to Amir's laptop. His Yahoo! account was on the screen.

She was his mother; she could peek at his e-mail, right? As she read the open e-mail, she pulled out a stack of cash from her purse and counted out forty-three hundred-dollar bills. Amir mocked her work, but she got more gigs than he did.

```
Dear Fatima relations,
    I hope you are all doing
well. We are all fine here,
too. Tayta is well. I am well.
Today we had a sunny high of
77 degrees, despite the con-
tinuing June Gloom. Tayta
still insists on wearing her
scarf because she's afraid of
catching a cold. You'd think
```

224

she hadn't spent 60 some years in Detroit. She's had a lot to say lately, not that I've been eavesdropping. When I get a chance, inshallah, I will share much of it with you.

Regards,
Amir

Soraya had put the e-mail list together for Amir. She reread his e-mail. Her eyes then focused on the picture of Fatima in her wedding dress.

"PS," she added, "she cut off all her hair."

The young man in the car honked, and Soraya put the $4,300 in an envelope in front of the envelope from Ibrahim just as Amir came down with the crystal ball.

"So you don't want to come out and meet the guy?" Soraya asked.

Amir shook his head and took off his Polo sweater and handed it to her with the crystal ball. "In case you get cold," he explained.

"Yes, Scheherazade the Magnificent always likes to be warm," Soraya said, using her fortune-telling name.

"Wait a second," Amir said. He opened the overflowing freezer, and several Tupperware containers came crashing down. "She keeps making me food, thinking I'm going to starve when she's gone if I'm not married."

Soraya almost could laugh again, and this time he almost joined her. "Anyway, the stuffed eggplants are veggie, so take them," Amir said, and handed her a Tupperware container. "I'm supposed to serve them at her condolences. It's all in her funeral instructions. But what if she lives for another ten years? Freezer burn."

She held the freezer door open so that he could shove the containers back in. Together they slammed the door shut and laughed.

"Wait a minute. She gave you her funeral instructions?" Soraya asked. She felt sweat form on her upper lip.

"In an envelope bigger than one of your wads of cash," Amir said. "The menu alone could feed most of West Hollywood. The dry cleaner wrote it all out for her. He's Korean, so there are a lot of spelling mistakes, but it's pretty elaborate. A lot of the crap I've been putting up with lately is morbid."

"She's a Pisces," Soraya said, finding that her mother's obsession with death, even at the age of eighty-five, needed a rational explanation. "You just have to tell her things that will make her think she's happy. And happiness is about thinking tomorrow will be good and next week even better."

Soraya first had developed her psychic powers trying to make Fatima happy. Then she had realized it wasn't just her mother but the whole world that wanted to see a perfect vision of the future. Now the daily grind of keeping her mother happy was her son's.

She touched Amir's cheek. "I love you, my gorgeous baby boy." This was the only thing she ever said to him without sounding unsure. She had been sure about having him but ever since his birth had been unsure of everything else. Whenever she quit this Mexico job, she decided, she would come back to the States and really try to find out more about the sperm donor. He deserved that much. And who knew — maybe the sperm donor might want to know what a great guy he'd helped put in this world.

She walked to the car, blowing kisses all the way. The driver opened the door for her. He was cute, and she hoped Amir saw him. She looked up at her mother's bedroom window. An envelope of funeral instructions and purple stubs were not good signs. They bothered her so much that she hadn't even asked Amir if Fatima had listed her in the instructions as one of the people who were to wash her body for burial. She wiped the sweat off her lip. She was glad Amir was going to tell her brother and sisters about her mother's hair. Its beauty was one of the family's few givens.

She waved again as they drove away, leaving behind the boy whose future she always left in someone else's hands — someone who, for all Soraya had mocked her, made a much better mother, at least for Amir. That vision had come to her the moment she and her mother first had laid eyes on her beautiful baby together. It was in Fatima's arms, shrouded under her veil of purple hair, that her son finally had calmed down enough from his long trip out of her womb to fall asleep.

AMIR

In one of his acting classes, Amir had been trained to do improv to get into a new state of mind. Improv worked better with more than one person, but what the hell. "Hey, you ever heard the one about the world's worst mother?" Amir said aloud to himself. "Yeah, she . . ." He struggled for a clever line to throw back at himself, but funny wouldn't come. He was, as usual, sad to see Soraya go. He had grown up in a silent house. Ibrahim and Fatima had only two

228

kids still living at home when he was born, and they were just as quiet as their parents, especially Lena. He had loved — still loved — the sporadic arrivals of Soraya, if only for the commotion, loud clothes, and loud voice she brought with her.

Amir went back to the computer. He knew the envelope with the money would be in front of Fatima's photo. Before he could open it, he saw what Soraya had added to his e-mail: "She cut off all her hair." He looked at it for a while and then deleted it. Why worry them? He was about to hit "send" when he realized Lena had not e-mailed him back about visiting. Fatima looked so much more fragile without her hair. He stopped and rewrote what Soraya had written. Then he added a question mark and an exclamation point: "Tayta cut off all her hair?!"

The phone rang. He hesitated on the e-mail one more time and then hit "send."

He was not expecting Ibrahim on the other line. "Oh, hi, Jiddo," Amir said, and waited a few seconds until his grandfather thought of the next logical piece of the conversation.

"How you doin', Son?" Ibrahim asked.

"Good, Jiddo," Amir answered. "And yourself?"

"Good, Son," Ibrahim said after a while. "You get my letter?"

"I'm going to use the money to buy her new faraway glasses."

"I mean that fat envelope," Ibrahim clarified.

"Right on." Amir remembered seeing it peeking out behind Soraya's cash.

"Did you get someone to read it for her?" Ibrahim said.

"Not yet," Amir said. As he opened it, he saw it was in Arabic. "Maybe you could give her the gist of it over the phone."

"Maybe," Ibrahim said.

But Fatima was pretending to sleep. If he pretended to wake her, she'd whine about Soraya into the middle of the night after she got off the phone with Ibrahim, to whom she would not mention Soraya's visit, at least not the part about her taking off for Mexico.

"So maybe this isn't a good time," Ibrahim got in first on the other end. "Maybe it's better you find someone else to read it."

"Yeah, maybe," Amir agreed. He had his own stuff to worry about, and since Fatima had divorced Ibrahim, he didn't see why Ibrahim should be dragged into the insanity — from the hair chop to the funeral instructions.

"I'll make sure I find someone ASAP," Amir said. "Good?"

Ibrahim was too slow thinking up the next line of conversation. The doorbell rang first.

"You take care, Jiddo," Amir concluded.

"Okay, Son," Ibrahim said. "You both, too."

This time it was the messenger with his audition pages. He opened the envelope and looked at the highlighted part. "Jesus Christ," he groaned. It wasn't the Omar Sharif biopic.

The messenger shrugged an apology, and Amir watched him leave in a Honda as badly in need of detailing as his own. He went outside to water the garden.

THE SUV PEOPLE

The man and woman in black watched Amir as he watered the fig tree.

"Let's admit we're bored and follow up on that Prince William at the Mondrian lead we got," the woman in black said. "You know how much we could get from the *Sun* for those?"

"And you end up feeling dirty again?" the man in black answered. "No, hon. Hey, what if he's drugging the grandmother to get her to do something? Like a mission.

231

Our contact said the old lady admitted to being high when he drove her home. And she was yakking about imminent death."

"Our contact's a soap star," the female in black pointed out. "He's a natural drama queen. And you were so grateful for his tip that you didn't let me take any pictures of the guy from *One Life to Live* that showed up at his door afterward."

"Next time we'll get him," he said. "But for now, we've witnessed enough suspicious activity to call the FBI on this house. Then we can go to the Mondrian and make some bank feeling good about ourselves perhaps saving the country."

"What have we witnessed?" the woman in black demanded to know.

"There's the freaky, loud friend/relative of theirs that just left," the man in black offered.

"We all got those," the woman in black answered.

"And the religious nutcase husband of the daughter in Detroit," he continued. "It's missing all the little clues that caused all the big incidents. Remember how we didn't listen to the guy that told us Britney Spears was on a bender in Vegas, and then she went and got married there. Thousands of dollars down the drain because we ignored something we thought wasn't really newsworthy."

"Okay, okay, let's just call the tip line and get to the Mondrian." The woman in black sighed. "Ugh! Maybe I should move back to Cleveland. Get a job at Olan Mills Portrait Studio taking pictures of people's still innocent babies."

"I'm not going to let that happen to you," the man in black promised. "If this pans out, and it will, I got a lead from the assistant of a certain supermodel about a falafel restaurant owner in Orange County."

SCHEHERAZADE

As Scheherazade came down the eucalyptus tree, Amir sprayed both her and the fig tree, but that was not the reason Scheherazade was highly displeased. She knew that Amir had not meant to water her. He was still far too young to see her immortality.

His mother was a different matter. She — Scheherazade, daughter of the Great Wazir and wife of King Shahrayar, reciter of love stories, religious legends, and the poetry of the magnificent Abu Nawas — was not a charlatan playing out people's fates with devil's cards and fiberglass balls. It was bad enough that the boy Zade had named his café after her, but now a cheap fortune-teller? Did no Abdullah respect her memory? She climbed through the window to enumerate her grievances to Fatima, but the old lady was curled up in a way that begged for sleep as a distraction from life's agonies.

"Go back home where you are loved and come back to America tomorrow," Fatima mumbled in her sleep. Scheherazade did miss her homeland. That was true. But loved? She and her 1001 nights were better remembered in Hollywood. In the Middle East, her stories were no longer the fabric of women's gatherings, as they had been when they used to sew, read each other's fortunes in coffee cups, and tell her stories of caliphs, beggars, and wild fools.

She took Fatima's hearing aid and put it in the underwear drawer with her other precious things. Then she saw her faraway glasses. She picked them up. Without them, Fatima would be annoyed in the morning, much the way Soraya had left her annoyed. She was pleased with this action, only momentarily jolted from it when she saw the strands of purple hair shimmering in the drawer. So lovely; she sighed. She put the glasses atop them and closed the drawer.

She checked her appearance in her silver gilded compact, as she always did before retiring, and found a place to sleep in the eucalyptus tree. She threw a silk veil over her hair to keep it from being messed up during the night. Fatima had sacrificed her beauty in cutting off her crown. But beauty was nothing next to a child's life. Scheherazade had outlived her own by centuries. She had outlived everyone she had ever loved. All that was left was her name.

■ ■ ■ ■

THE 997TH NIGHT

■ ■ ■ ■

FATIMA

The next afternoon, Fatima sat in an uncomfortable high-backed chrome chair in Amir's chrome kitchen, her nearby glasses almost falling off her nose as she formed a paste of ground sirloin and bulgur wheat into fist-size balls. It was the thirtieth kibbe Fatima had made this morning. She took each meat and wheat ball and drilled into it with her index finger, turning the ball around until she formed a perfect hollow oval. She then filled each oval with spiced ground beef and dipped her fingertips in ice water before sealing the oval.

The television played highlights from the previous night's baseball games. The Detroit Tigers were a big strikeout this season. How could they get swept by the Twins, a team playing under a plastic bag on spongy cement? She was glad she would not be there for the Tigers' next game.

The TV was on exceptionally loud because

239

Fatima hadn't known to look for her faraway glasses this morning in her underwear drawer, and without them she couldn't find her hearing aid. Her only sense in full working order today was smell, and the stale aroma of Scheherazade's cigarette filled the house. She pushed her bifocals back up her nose; it was hard to keep them on her head without the volume of her hair.

Fatima's purple spikes had evolved into a psychedelic Afro after a night of tossing and turning over the house in Lebanon, Amir's marriage, and, almost as important, the precise method of her impending death, which Soraya's untimely visit had prevented her from asking Scheherazade about. Soraya's questioning laugh was still grating in her head, a troubled reminder of yet another child to whom she could not leave the home in Deir Zeitoon. Home was a concept Amir's mother had been running from since he was born.

Fatima covered the completed kibbes with a white towel so that they would not dry out. Before the engagement dinner tomorrow with Tiffany from the Iranian Jew's store, she would deep-fry the balls in corn oil, just as Marwan had taught her to do when she first came to America, a place where olive oil was a hard-to-find luxury, even when he started making more than thirty dollars a week. Her troubles without olive oil in the early days of her marriages would be a story she could tell Scheherazade tonight, a story about her life with her husbands. That would more than entitle her to an answer to her own question.

The doorbell rang when Fatima was on her thirty-third kibbe. She went to move her hair from over her ears, as she always did when she doubted her hearing. But her hair was not there. The doorbell rang again before she could find her cane.

She could not make out the time on the chrome clock, but early or late, the doorbell hardly ever rang for good reasons. No one in America just stopped by to say hello except for Millie "popping over for a cup of joe." But Millie was gone. Perhaps it was the prospective bride Tiffany. It wasn't tomorrow yet, but Tiffany was American. Americans with their fear of tardiness. Fatima washed her hands and took off her bifocals, putting them next to Amir's computer, before using her cane to feel her way to the door.

"Fatima Abdullah?" said a woman in a severe blue suit. Even through blurred vision, Fatima had never seen anyone in Los Angeles dress so seriously, not even at Ra-

241

bia Hoss's memorial service last month in Beverly Hills, and she was from one of the best families in Lebanon. In fact, Rabia's granddaughters had looked like they were going dancing in their black dresses afterward, shame on them.

If Fatima had had on her faraway glasses, she would have known that the reason the blurry woman's head kept bobbing up and down was that she was trying not to stare at Fatima's purple orb.

"I'm Sherri Hazad," the woman said, and showed her FBI badge.

It didn't occur to Fatima that the badge was something to read. "I know I look terrible, but you can put that thing away," she said, assuming the badge was Scheherazade's gilded silver compact. "I've seen enough."

"As long as you saw it, ma'am," Sherri Hazad said, and put the badge away. "Can I talk with you for a few minutes?"

Scheherazade had the same black hair as usual, but perhaps immortality allowed her to transform into many human styles. "Why are you here so early — and why are you dressed that way?" Fatima asked.

"Regulations, ma'am," Sherri Hazad said.

"Why didn't you just come in through the window?"

"Regulations, ma'am," Sherri Hazad repeated.

Fatima shrugged and offered her arm. "*Yallah,* let's go. I have to get back to work." The agent hesitated and then turned right. "You act like you've never been here before," Fatima chided. She pointed straight ahead, and Sherri Hazad, with Fatima's nudging, guided her into the kitchen and to her chair in front of the bowl of raw meat and bulgur wheat. Fatima motioned to Sherri Hazad to take a seat opposite her.

"Why are you speaking English today?" Fatima demanded.

"I've been trained in Arabic, if you prefer," Sherri Hazad said in Arabic that lacked several expected letters and sounds, Arabic loud enough to drown out the Tigers on TV. "My grandfather was Lebanese."

"Everyone knows that maybe he was Persian or from Damascus or Baghdad or Samarqand. There's not a drop of Lebanese in you." But she decided to allow this imitation of Americans. After all, Scheherazade had endured Soraya's imitation of her. "Amuse yourself, but we also have to be serious. Remember, we only have four days to settle the house in Lebanon."

"The house in Lebanon?" Sherri Hazad shouted over the TV. "Four days?"

243

"Do you mean I'm going to be incapacitated before then?" Fatima asked.

"What did you say?" Sherri Hazad said. She lowered the volume on the television.

In the absence of the TV noise, Scheherazade sounded even odder. "Wash your hands so you can help me," Fatima said. She picked up the thirty-third ball again and began drilling.

"What's that smell?" Sherri Hazad said as she dried her hands and sniffed the air.

"Either it's that special cigarette smoke or Amir's soap," Fatima said. "He paid ten dollars for soap. Neither of my husbands could afford olive oil when they came here."

"So only recently he's acquired the ability to pay ten dollars for, um, soap?" Sherri Hazad asked.

"Do we look like the Rockefellers?" Fatima sighed. "But lately he does care more about money. Always talking about the handsome neighbor boy and how he'd do anything to have everything he has."

Fatima handed Sherri Hazad a ball of kibbe. But Sherri Hazad, as would have been clear to anyone who hadn't just misplaced her nearby glasses, was no kibbe maker.

"Huh, I've eaten kibbe a couple of times," Sherri Hazad said. "There is a great Lebanese restaurant in Glendale."

"It's Armenian," Fatima corrected. "But so many of them came to live with us after the Turkish massacres that they're practically Arabs now. Two of them — sisters, one of whom never found her children — rented a room from Mama for a while in the house in Deir Zeitoon. Then the sisters moved to Beirut, where their brother had opened a watch repair shop. And then —"

"Before we move on to more relevant matters," Sherri Hazad interrupted, "I must tell you, ma'am, that you do not have to speak to me."

"Fine, you do not want to hear a story of Deir Zeitoon. That is okay. I've thought about it, and talking about my children — and Ibrahim — is the best thing I can do for their sake," Fatima conceded. "I know Deir Zeitoon is a safe house for everyone but Nadia, but still I think Amir would be the best one to go there."

"A safe house, ma'am?" Sherri Hazad inquired.

"Don't keep rolling the kibbe like that," Fatima admonished. "You're going to get the meat tough."

"I'm not much of a cook, ma'am," Sherri Hazad admitted.

"Stop ma'aming me, *ya sitti,* I know you're

245

having fun being American today, but Americans are not as uptight as you're making them seem."

Sherri Hazad took the ball of kibbe she had handed her. Fatima picked up another ball and deftly tunneled into it.

"Even without my glasses, I got kibbe fingers," Fatima said as Sherri Hazad tried to keep up with her graceful speed with the meat and wheat. "Long fingers. Mama always said that kibbe fingers are an asset that will get you a good husband."

Sherri Hazad's finger bore right through the other end of the kibbe ball. "Oops," the agent said, and held it up close enough for Fatima to see right through the tunnel to the blue suit. Fatima took the kibbe from her and molded it back together.

"But I do know how to roll grape leaves," Sherri Hazad offered.

"Ah, so can anyone who has got a drop of blood from Iran to Greece," Fatima said, and handed Sherri Hazad another kibbe ball. "My daughters make them every time someone comes to dinner because they don't know nothing else. But they married well without kibbe fingers. To tell you the truth, I don't think kibbe fingers are why either of my husbands married me. Ibrahim wasn't much of an eater, especially after . . .

Well . . . Marwan would eat anything and say it was *zaki,* delicious, one of the few words he said in Arabic. Marwan was so easy to please. He'd had a childhood of peddling with his father. For weeks they would live off of baked beans, which, by the way, come out of a can and you don't bake them. He told me that sometimes his father's mustache would turn white with snow and ice but they would keep going. He was peddling in Massotwoshits when his father died of the TB."

"Yes, madam, my great-grandfather was a peddler, too," Sherri Hazad chimed in. "Not in Massachusetts. In upstate New York. He told my grandfather how he would go with his cart around his neck from door to door selling soap, sponges, and even toilet brushes."

Fatima glared at the blur of Sherri Hazad's face. "I told you this story about Marwan and his father before, didn't I?" Fatima asked, suspicious. "So is this how you get your stories? Taking other people's history and turning it into your tall tales?"

"It's my job to get to the truth, madam, not make up lies," Sherri Hazad said, and took her kibbe drilling much slower this time. "But I got a lot of stories my grandfather told me. I adored him. I used to love playing with his mustache."

"Millie used to say that Marwan's and Ibrahim's mustaches made them mysterious," Fatima recalled. "She said they were dream ships with their accents and dark eyelashes. To me, they were husbands, not mysteries."

Sherri Hazad proudly held up her first successful kibbe. "Look, madam," she said, beaming.

But Fatima was lost in thought on her thirty-fifth kibbe. "I didn't like making love with Marwan because he smelled unfamiliar as long as I knew him, kind of like what we were smoking yesterday does," she said. Sherri Hazad dropped her kibbe.

Fatima reached for her hand. "*Ya Allah,* I can't imagine having such discussions with anyone but you, although Millie used to have them with me, but I never said anything back."

Sherri Hazad's hand pulled away. She picked up her kibbe and went to the sink to wash her hands. "Don't use the expensive soap," Fatima warned. "It's only for special occasions." It was more than time, Fatima decided, to tell Scheherazade all the things she could possibly ever wish to know about her husbands in exchange for the information she wanted about her death. Scheherazade would have no excuses then. *Inshallah,* things would work out with Tiffany tonight, and she would be able to leave Amir and his new bride the house. Then she could relax in her remaining days, maybe even visit one of her children. But she wanted to know how her death would be, because if she was to be incapacitated at some point, she wanted to be home with Amir by then, where she would feel comfortable dying. For that, it would be worth revealing her deepest secrets.

"With Ibrahim it felt different. When he touched my skin, even by accident, it prickled up." Fatima blushed. "For sixty years, which Millie would have said was impossible. But it's true. But I never would have told him that, especially since he married me just to be nice."

Sherri Hazad scrubbed her hands harder. "I should be honest and say that what I really want to talk about is Amir Abdullah. Really. And that's all."

"But I deserve to be informed," Fatima said. "How will I die?"

"Excuse me?"

"What more do you want me to tell you?" Fatima asked.

"Any information about Amir Abdullah," Sherri Hazad said. "Only."

"Ah, easy stories. Despite everything he does, he is still one of my favorite topics. Did you know Amir has kibbe fingers, too?" Fatima bragged. "He makes perfect kibbe. Should I let you in on a secret?"

"That's why I'm here," Sherri Hazad said. She took out her notebook.

"A dash of cardamom in the filling." Fatima winked. "That's the secret to my kibbe. I've never revealed that to anyone except Amir. He was the only child who asked for the secret. Now you, *ya oukhti,* have it for immortality."

"Okay," Sherri Hazad said. "Thank you for that information. Now . . ."

"He could have been a chef in one of your courts," Fatima bragged.

"Oh, I don't doubt it," Sherri Hazad agreed. "Courthouse food is not that good. How long has he been pursuing acting?"

"That's just a game, I told you," said Fatima. She hoped she had clarified this acting hobby once and for all. She did not want tales told by Scheherazade one day centuries from now that would call her grandson a member of such a low-class profession.

"Haven't you ever wondered how Amir pays for a house like this, decorates it like this, buys the expensive soap on a bit actor's salary?" Sherri Hazad asked.

"Are you kidding? He doesn't pay a penny."

"Oh?" Sherri Hazad said, and moved to the edge of her chair.

Fatima put down her kibbe and motioned for Sherri Hazad to bring her hungry ear closer. This near, Scheherazade's skin today was not as porcelain as the finest china in the world.

"His mother — Soraya — pays for everything," Fatima said, and then leaned back and began forming a new kibbe. "In cash."

"Oh," Sherri Hazad said.

Fatima pointed toward the envelope by the computer, next to her picture in the wedding dress. "That's from Soraya," she said. "I counted it already. It's always in hundred-dollar bills. Four thousand three hundred dollars cash. She left it and then went to Tiajumama just like that."

"You mean Tijuana?" Sherri Hazad said. "Mexico?"

Fatima shrugged. "Always off to help others, but at least she makes money while she does. Cash only, and almost all for Amir."

"What exactly does she do?" Sherri Hazad asked.

"Soraya embraced her heritage as a business opportunity," Fatima explained. "That's how Amir describes it."

"Oh?"

"Some might say shame, *aabe.* But she suffered a lot," Fatima said. "That bastard husband of hers. May he rot in Saudia forever."

"Oh?" Sherri Hazad said again. "He is Saudi?"

"No, Beiruti," Fatima said.

"Oh, really?"

"His mother, Tamara, *yakhrub beitha,* curses on her house, and I started the card club of the Arab Ladies Society together, so he and Soraya knew each other since they were children," Fatima continued. "Then they both went to Wayne State. He started out as a good Lebanese boy born just two days before Soraya in the same hospital."

"Sounds perfect."

"He cheated on her and left with another woman," Fatima said. "*Haram.* Sacrilege. And it was her best friend, no less. Do you know what that lousy *afreet,* devil, did next? Moved to Saudi Arabia and worked for the Aramco company as an engineer and got very rich. Then he moved his no-good mother there with him. *Inshallah,* Tamara drove her son and his floozy to hell because she was loose, too."

"Oh," Sherri Hazad said. "Well, Amir . . ."

"You don't know how many times I would

come home from playing *basra* with the other ladies and find her sitting in the living room with Ibrahim watching the news, crying," Fatima fumed. "Every time a war started back home, she would say she couldn't bear to play cards, like she was the only one upset. But then I'd find her in my home, saying she couldn't bear to be alone with the news. I saw how she was looking at Ibrahim. He wouldn't notice because he was usually so busy telling Nixon or whoever was president on the TV that he was going to kill him."

"Kill him?" Sherri Hazad said, and dropped another kibbe. "Have you heard anything about any current political leaders? Anyone you've heard people saying they'd like to kill? Just out of curiosity."

"Don't get me started on that list," Fatima said. She stood up to get more water for her hands and stepped right into the kibbe Sherri Hazad had dropped. Frustrated, she bent down to clean it up. "Haven't you learned anything from the servants who rule your palaces for you? Or are they just trained puppets?"

It was hard to tell if Fatima was talking about Middle East political regimes or food. Sherri Hazad formed another meat and wheat ball and began drilling.

"Let's go back to Amir and Saudi Arabia for now," she suggested. "So does Amir ever go to see him there?"

"Who?"

"His father."

"What father?" Fatima said.

"Soraya's ex-husband," Sherri Hazad reminded her.

"He's not Amir's father. *Ibaad el-sher.* Keep evil away," said Fatima.

"Oh, sorry," Sherri Hazad said.

"Do you want to know the big secret of Amir?" Fatima hissed. "This is the big one."

"God, I hope so," Sherri Hazad said.

Fatima motioned for her to come closer. "Amir is an immaculate conception," she said, and leaned back, wishing she had on one of her glasses to witness Scheherazade's jealousy that she, Fatima Abdul Aziz Abdullah, had a miracle grandchild.

"Oh?" Sherri Hazad said.

"Oh, nothing," Fatima explained. "Soraya didn't have Amir until thirteen months after she got divorced and the creep was long gone to Saudi. Immaculate, *ya Allah.*"

"Oh . . . well. . . . But what if Soraya was . . ." Sherri Hazad stuttered.

"Soraya what?" Fatima said, lifting up her hand to stop any smirch to her daughter's character by anyone but herself. "All my girls married the first man they kissed. *Khallas,* that's all. After Soraya found out that the other woman was having a baby with her no-good man, she cried and cried, for a child is the one thing everyone should get out of a marriage, no matter how it ends. It was as if God heard her tears and gave her Amir."

"Okay, okay, then," Sherri Hazad said, struggling for words. "So, moving on, um, to the best of your knowledge this daughter is now supporting Amir from money made in a Mexican border town."

"She's been everywhere helping, as she calls avoiding her own family," Fatima said. "Circuses and festivals all over the world. And she makes people think she has mystical powers like you."

"Don't believe all the wild stories you hear about my job," Sherri Hazad advised.

"No need to be modest," Fatima said. "Could you start making the hummus?"

"Umm . . ." Sherri Hazad said.

"*Ya bint el-hara,* weren't you trained to do anything?" Fatima exclaimed. "Look for the can with the picture of chickpeas on it. Just open it and put it in the food processor."

"I can do that." Sherri Hazad sounded relieved.

"So help me, if Amir lets any of his

disguises get in the hummus today," Fatima vented.

"Disguises?" Sherri Hazad asked.

Fatima began dividing the kibbe into smaller batches. She kept out ten to fry for tomorrow. The rest she started bagging to freeze for her condolences.

"I told you what you wanted to hear," she said. "Now you tell me how it's going to happen."

"What's going to happen?" Sherri Hazad asked.

"There's only four days left, so just tell me. Is it going to be big?" Fatima said. "An explosion of drama and emotion?"

"Let me look into that a little more on my end," Sherri Hazad said. She put her notebook in her purse. "Do you mind if I come back later?"

"How much later?" Fatima scolded. "I want to know now. You are not being fair."

"That's a complaint I often get," Sherri Hazad said. "I will come back, I promise. And you'll call me if you know more."

"Ha," Fatima said, wondering what was written on the silly card she had just handed her. "Before you go, at least look at the clock for me."

"It's about four-fifteen, madam," Sherri Hazad said.

"Strange. Randa hasn't called today," Fatima thought aloud. "I wonder if she's heard anything from Gaza."

Sherri Hazad sat back down. "Gaza?"

"If you're going to stay, add the tahini to the hummus," Fatima instructed.

Sherri Hazad looked for the jar that said tahini and began pouring its contents into the food processor. "You were saying about Gaza?" she shouted over the food processor's whir.

"Her daughter Dina should be in Gaza now," Fatima informed her. "Her mother was not so clear on her whereabouts yesterday. She went to Beirut, even southern Lebanon, too, can you imagine? But she has not had a chance to go to Deir Zeitoon yet. Soon, *inshallah.*"

"Inshallah," Sherri Hazad mumbled, still pouring tahini.

"What are you doing?"

"Putting in the tahini," Sherri Hazad responded.

"You should have stopped doing that by now," Fatima said. "Just let the food processor run for three and a half minutes."

Sherri Hazad was good at obeying orders and left the food processor to whir on its own. "Why was Dina in Beirut?"

"I don't know exactly," Fatima said. "She

257

started law school in Los Angeles 188 days after I came here, but she was too busy to come visit, and then all of a sudden she decided to go to Lebanon. That's what Randa says from Texas, but Randa's life is a web of lies. It's hard to keep up with the truth with her. Maybe you can go figure it out."

Sherri Hazad looked at her: no hearing aid, no eyeglasses except reading glasses she couldn't use to read. "This is not how I wanted our meeting to turn out," she said under the din of the food processor.

"What?" Fatima asked.

Sherri Hazad turned off the food processor and saw Fatima's nearby glasses next to the cash envelope. She picked them up and tightened the ends with her hands. "You should put your glasses on. It's safer in these troubled times."

"Was there a time when things were not troubled?" Fatima countered, and put them on her face. "Hey, I think they fit."

When she looked up, Sherri Hazad was gone.

Fatima shrugged. She moved to the food processor. The hummus was very gray. "Who puts half a jar of tahini in?" she said to the food processor.

She went to the chrome fridge to get some

lemons to counter the tahini. Why was she having so much trouble outsmarting a woman who didn't even know how to make hummus into revealing what could be so terrible about her death that she kept avoiding telling her?

SCHEHERAZADE

What Fatima hadn't seen without her glasses was the real Scheherazade, who had awoken to the surprise of daytime chatter in Amir's home. When Scheherazade had found the serious female in the kitchen, she had looked on from the stairwell. She wanted to see Fatima's reaction when she finally figured out this woman was not her. That did not happen.

Scheherazade pulled out the hearing aid and faraway glasses and put them on the vanity for Fatima. No matter how blind she was, how dare Fatima confuse her with a bumbling woman who wore pants — with no embroidery. She wouldn't go see Randa as Fatima probably was taking for granted. But Scheherazade was also hungry, and the aroma in Fatima's kitchen propelled her instead toward Gaza — and the chance to get some good *labneh* and tamarind juice.

It did not take Scheherazade long among

259

the crowds, bullet holes, and collapsed buildings of Gaza to see that she was not likely to find Dina, for nearly no one who had the choice to be somewhere else was there. She continued to fly across the Mediterranean, across lands that smelled of the sweets and spices of Fatima's kitchen. Off the sea, Beirut gleamed with tall buildings and newly engineered cobblestone streets, so many of its pasts gone and rebuilt over, although several craters of war remained. Beirut, the Paris of the Middle East, the Geneva of the Arab world. That was what people had been calling Beirut for nearly sixty years, as if it had to be compared to a great European city to prove its worth. As the afternoon call to prayer began over the sound of honking, Scheherazade spotted Dina. This was a city of women who spared no expense or effort to achieve beauty, but the shiny waves of one girl's flowing locks stood out. The girl did not have the bumpy nose, but she had the vibrantly lush hair Fatima had had that first day she'd met her, although Dina's was perfectly blond.

■ ■ ■

THE 998TH NIGHT

■ ■ ■

DINA

Dina had not made it to Gaza because it wasn't the kind of place to go to when one already had a broken heart. Well, actually two broken hearts. At least in Beirut there were places to escape misery.

Dina's perfect thighs stuck to the vinyl of the taxi's backseat, and she was stuck somewhere between Texas and Gaza and somewhere between pissed off and depressed as hell.

The taxi driver rolled his 1984 Mercedes 190E through another red light along the Corniche, which was crowded with Friday afternoon walkers trying to catch a Mediterranean breeze on a very humid summer afternoon. The driver lit a cigarette, using the cab's NO SMOKING sign as a flint. When she had arrived here, the law student in Dina would have said something, but now she absently waved the smoke aside and closed her eyes. Today both of her boyfriends had broken up with her — via e-mail. Cowards. Losers. Assholes.

Dina had come to Beirut for love and to make up for (a) being so lucky in life, as one of her boyfriends called it in his e-mail, and (b) being oblivious to reality, as the other one had said in his e-mail. But she wasn't feeling lucky or oblivious right now. Nor was she feeling way sweet, way generous, way cool, or way hot — all words written next to smiley faces to describe her in her high school yearbook, right next to a picture of her in the air cheering the Kinross Falcons, one of the most well-funded football teams in one of the most expensive schools in Houston.

A tiny fist clutching a lottery ticket shoved its way through the taxi window. "Auntie, is this your lucky day?" shouted a little Lebanese boy wearing a tattered "New York Jiants" T-shirt. He had patches on his skin that were a mixture of dirt and vitiligo. He fanned the ticket in front of her face. She basked in the fanning for only a moment.

"Get lost, kid," the cab driver said to the boy. His cigarette smoke formed a carbon monoxide blanket in front of Dina's eyes when he turned to her. "Sorry for the intrusion, miss."

The boy, unfazed, stuck his head back in

and gave her an exaggerated frown. She forced herself to turn away.

"I guess it's not your lucky day, Auntie." The boy shrugged, waving the tickets one more time. Dina looked back until the boy had been folded into the strolling masses.

"*Occasion, occasion,* get your lottery tickets here," was the last thing she heard him say.

"You know, before the lottery tickets, before the war, they used to sell Chiclets," the cab driver said as he rolled up the windows of the Mercedes to fend off another boy approaching with more tickets. "This is better. No dentists needed, and there is hope in lottery tickets. What good is there in American chewing gum? No offense, miss."

No one in Beirut saw Dina's Arab features, and she didn't point out the fact that she was not only American but Texan, too.

It was because of Jamal Masri's fine butt that Dina had spent the last month in Beirut. Jamal had sat next to her on the first day of her business law class at UCLA the last winter quarter. He had soft black curls that framed eyes as big and green as those of Fluffy, her mother's cat. He had handed her a flyer with a brown girl in rags sitting on a pile of rubble. It was for an antiwar protest. "I thought you might be interested in joining us," he said with an accent that was there in that barely-there-sexy-foreign-accent way.

"Why?"

"Bitar is a pretty well-known Palestinian family," he said, pointing to the name on her notebook and pronouncing it as only her grandparents did. "So are you of the Nablus Bitars? We're probably related, if that's the case. I'm a Masri. Jamal Masri."

No one had ever identified Dina before by family name or village. It made her uncomfortable. Just being Texan — heck, just being Houstonian — was enough identity, never mind American and Arab. Nor had it ever occurred to her that Arabs could be so hot. She pictured Yasir Arafat, Saddam Hussein, or her grandfather Ibrahim when she heard the words *Arab man,* which she rarely did except when she was watching the latest terror alert on FOX News. Jamal, however, was unmistakably hot. She forced herself to think of Jake.

"I have to study on Saturday." She handed him back the flyer, failing for the first time to give a guy a perky smile. "Sorry about that."

"They're interviewing me on KPFK tomorrow morning," Jamal said to her on the way out of class. "Check it out."

Dina asked Jake later that night what KPFK was. "Oh, Pacifica Radio." Jake laughed. "A bunch of crazy, liberal, Arab-loving, Spanish-speaking Jewish homosexuals." Jake was actually quite open-minded compared with most of the people she'd grown up with, and so she knew that he had laughed without meaning any harm to anyone crazy, liberal, Arab, Spanish-speaking, Jewish, or homosexual. The next day, Jake caught up with her on campus and handed her his iPod. "I downloaded this for you." He smiled. She stuck in the earphones.

"Look, nobody better than the people in Middle East understands what it is to have your land attacked, as we were here on September 11," she heard Jamal's impassioned voice resonate. "But let's look at how President Bush responded. He took an eye for an eye and then went for every other body part — on people who had nothing to do with it."

Jake was making the cuckoo sign. Dina turned away from him and pushed the earphones farther into her ear. Jake pulled out the right earphone.

"That's enough of the kooks, D," he said.

"Give me back my iPod."

She waved Jake aside. The rest of the day Dina was preoccupied with Jamal's voice . . . and butt.

After watching the Lakers game on TV with Jake that night, Dina closed her business law book and ran her finger along her bookshelf several times until she found *A History of the Arab People,* a colorful paperback her Tayta Fatima had sent her on her twentieth birthday. Dina had dutifully replied with a thank-you note and placed the book on the shelf, as she had done with all the other books her grandmother had given her. Tayta Fatima chose books for their color scheme, and Dina found that they added life to her apartment's decor. She sat down and began reading.

Two days later, Dina was looking at Jamal's flyer again when her mother called from her veranda in Houston.

"How's Jake?" Randy asked before Dina could tell her about how she herself was doing.

"He's sleeping off an all-nighter," Dina answered, letting her mom believe she was talking about studying when in fact he was at home puking from Los Angeles tacos and too much tequila at his frat house the night before. "But it works out fine because I can study by myself today without any distraction."

"See, his passing out couldn't have happened at a better time," Randy said. "It's a sign. Soraya says we just have to see the signs. She saw a baby giraffe at the zoo thirty years ago, and that's how she knew she was pregnant with Amir."

Randy's signs were all about Jake. Jake, so blond, so blue-eyed, so tall, so white-toothed, the son of a corporate executive whom Bud, Dina's dad and lawyer to Houston's star crooks, had kept out of jail so far. Jake was a fantasy son-in-law for Randy, who also claimed that it was a sign that both Dina and Jake had been accepted to UCLA law school and that both had immediately felt that the Mexican food there was nowhere near as good as Texas's.

After saying goodbye to Randy, Dina went on eBay to forget her conversation with her mother. She bid on a vintage Pucci dress with her dad's credit card. Then she went to the library.

However, Randy was right. Signs were exactly what Dina witnessed as she looked outside the window of the law library. "No Blood for Oil," "Not in My Name," and "How'd Our Oil Get under Their Sand?" she read as an antiwar protest marched by, giving her a perfect view of Jamal Masri's butt. Holding up one end of a banner saying "Say Can You See My Democracy," Jamal was the march's leader.

Dina guzzled half of her bottle of water to purify her skin, as her mother had taught her. Then she ran a brush through her hair, thinking her dark roots were getting too obvious. After the quarter ended, she'd go see Carlo, maybe let him give her bangs, too. She slapped on some lipstick and checked her teeth for color stains in her window reflection. She closed her books and left the library.

Randy would have killed Soraya if she knew what signs Dina was reading. Beyond snide comments on the spending habits of the rich Arabs shopping at the Galleria, whom no one could really differentiate from the rich Mexicans, the Middle East had kind of faded out of daily conversation in Houston since the 1973 Arab oil embargo. But with September 11, Arabs were back, worse than ever. Dina, who hadn't been alive in 1973, didn't remember Abscam and Munich. Randy had worked hard to make such history irrelevant to all three of her daughters.

She and Bud had moved away from Detroit, away from Om Kalthoum on staticky speakers, talk of tangled global conspiracies, and the odor of frying falafel.

With Bud, Randy had built a life doing all the right things for maximum public viewing: the Junior League, the Humane Society, elite gym membership at the Houstonian. Hell, if she didn't think she'd get caught, she would have tried to join the Daughters of the American Revolution.

She was very glad that Bud was almost pale, not dark like Laila's and Nadia's husbands; didn't have an accent; and had a last name that could pass as anything, even Jewish. Just to make sure they weren't mistaken for Arab or Jewish in Texas, Randy got a nose job to get rid of the bump she'd inherited from Fatima. Then she had given all her girls solid American names: Loretta, June, and Dina. She had named her youngest daughter after Dina Merrill, the pretty heiress to the Post cereal and E.F. Hutton fortunes. She didn't discover until years later that Dina was a far more common name in the Middle East than in the States.

She had even changed her own name — and Bud's — when they arrived in Houston. "Oh, Bud and I just thank y'all for inviting us to your barbecue," she had said with her nasal Midwestern accent to her new Texas friends. That barbecue was where Bashar

271

had learned he had become Bud. His eyes had poked up out of the cowboy hat she'd purchased for him for the occasion. It was one of the few times Bud had questioned his wife, now Randy even to him.

"When's the last time you heard someone say what kind of name is that — oh, Palestinian — oh, yeah, that's what I need, a Palestinian lawyer?" she had whispered to him as he bit into his chiliburger. "A lawyer descended from people who lost their land and haven't been able to win their legal right to return. Oh, yeah, that's the kind of lawyer everyone wants. If anyone asks where you're from, just say our house is in the River Oaks area."

And if anyone asked where his grandparents had sailed from, he asked if they wanted to partake of his membership at the Houston Yacht Club. That usually sealed the deal. Bud's only ambition was to succeed enough to honor his parents adequately for all the hours they had spent doing research at a small university's chemistry lab so that he could go to a bigger university. He knew that was why they both had died of lung cancer so young. Anything else on Randy's agenda, he accepted. He preferred domestic peace to arguing. He did enough arguing at work.

Dina stood on the steps of Royce Hall, forced her eyes away from Jamal's butt, and telephoned Jake like a good girlfriend.

"Hey, babe, I'm going to protest this war," she said. "Come join me, sweetie."

"I got to go blow chunks again," Jake howled. "Montezuma's revenge is back."

Dina put away her cell phone and saw Jamal's eyes locked on her. He waved her over.

"So you came, after all," Jamal said. "There'll probably be camera crews by the time we get to the Federal Building."

"Oh," she said. He hadn't said she looked pretty today, which was usually how guys said hello to her.

A graduate student in a head scarf handed Dina a sign that read "No Blood for Oil."

"Thanks for coming," the girl said, sounding anything but sincere as she looked at Dina's platforms from the Nordstrom Half-Yearly Sale.

"I like the color of your scarf," Dina replied. "It really brings out your eyes."

Jamal laughed. "Come on," he said, chuckling. "Move your ass."

Move yours, she thought, her face turning redder than her Clinique blush.

"I knew deep down you had to care," Jamal said. "After all, how could you not? God, in our families, if we weren't talking about the Middle East at dinner, we probably weren't talking."

Dina pictured Randy and Bud and her sisters gathered around a roast with succotash and twice-whipped potatoes, their faces lit by an elaborate deer antler chandelier, the five of them distant dots on a long table made of Texas Hill Country oak.

Then Dina remembered something. "They flinch and bite their tongues," she said.

"Hey, let's save that for later." Jamal winked. "Whatever it means."

"I mean my parents have started flinching and biting their tongues when they watch the news and it's about the Middle East, especially when others are around," Dina said. "Like at the gym."

He nodded. "My mom bites her nails when Bush comes on TV in a restaurant or something . . . but at home, look out. We got to hold our plates down."

"My mother would never break her china," Dina said. "It's Limoges."

"I can't tell if you're shitting me or not," Jamal said, and gave her a decidedly flirtatious sock in the arm. "But it's sexy. . . .

274

Whoa, look at the turnout."

Jamal was swallowed up by thousands of chanters and hundreds of signs surrounding the Westwood Federal Building: READ BETWEEN THE PIPELINES, ANOTHER PATRIOT FOR PEACE, and RESISTANCE IS FERTILE. Dina couldn't see much more than signs in the swelling crowd. Police maneuvered through the masses, avoiding getting nicked by the signs. Luxury cars drove by and honked approval. Passengers in other cars leaned out and made the peace sign or gave the finger. Dina was swept into a wave of protesters moving to the demonstration's epicenter.

"No democracy in my name," a girl with the kind of brown hair that should never be without highlights — but was — shouted into a megaphone, one of many megaphones with a crowd chanting back to its user. After a few more rallying cries, the girl spotted Dina and gave her a smirk as if to say, "What'd you come here for?"

"Support our troops," the girl chanted into the megaphone, and everyone repeated after her, "Bring them home now."

Dina hesitated only for a moment when the girl looked at her again. She joined in, using her full cheerleader lungs.

Dina was very pretty and very loud, and

so she was used to being watched. But now she wondered whether these badly dressed people were looking at her because they questioned her sincerity. To make sure they — and Jamal — knew she was just as committed to world peace, Dina expelled even deeper from her diaphragm. Miss Sissy, her first and favorite cheerleading coach, had taught her well.

After a few more chants, the girl took a break and stood next to Dina. "You got some set of lungs, sister," she said. "And I can't believe that you got here in those shoes."

"Kinross squad leader senior and junior year." Dina shrugged. "I'm Dina."

"Allison," the girl said. Dina noticed her twang.

They shook hands. "So where are you from?" Dina asked.

"San Diego," Allison answered. "How about you?"

"Houston," Dina said. "But you sound like you're from Dallas."

"I was born there," she replied. "My granddad's in Houston. Harlon's BBQ rocks. Don't get stuck in California forever, like me. When you start jonzing for decent barbecue, you're screwed."

She patted her stomach and handed Dina

the megaphone. "I got to go pee like a pregnant lady, which I most definitely am not — and you got the best pipes around here."

Dina tried to give the megaphone back, but Allison already had gone off in search of a toilet. Dina looked for someone to hand the megaphone to. Instead she found lots of brown faces, as well as several black and white ones, turned to her for guidance.

With no chanting, the home team's crowd could lose its cohesive spirit. Every cheerleader knew that.

"P . . . E . . . A . . . C . . . E," Dina spelled out into the megaphone, hesitating just a fraction on the first two letters. Then she found the groove she knew so well. She started stomping her feet. "How about, how about, a peace shout. Say P . . . say E . . . say A . . . say C . . . say E. How about a peace shout." She clapped to the beat to get the crowd pumped.

"War, hell no, hell no, no hell, hey no war," she chanted, reading off the signs. She almost lost the beat when she saw Jamal looking at her. When he smiled, she was energized far more than she had been by Kinross's overtime games, even when she was dating the quarterback.

Dina made up three new chants for the

277

crowd before a Channel 13 reporter in a really great Armani jacket stuck a microphone in her face.

"You've got quite a following," the reporter said. "What message are you sending to Washington today?"

Jamal was making his way toward her. She didn't want to disappoint him. "Nobody better than the people in Middle East understand what it is to have your land attacked, as we were here on September 11," she said, echoing what Jamal had said on KPFK. "Two and a half years later, let's look at how President Bush —"

Jamal subtly pushed Dina to the side. "What she means is that we don't really care about human rights in Iraq," he told the Channel 13 reporter. "A rebel insurgency in Uganda has killed 300,000 people in the last eighteen years, and 1.2 million people have lost their homes. Darfur in Sudan has refugees starving to death by the thousands. Do we care? No. We're picking our atrocities based on oil."

The crowd around him clapped and roared. Dina heard a lot of "Way to go, Jamal" and "That dude so rocks."

"Anytime you need help with the press, just let me know," Jamal said to Dina. "I would have been here earlier if I had known."

"It was only Channel 13," Dina said, surprised that she was so annoyed with him for coming to her rescue.

"Want to come over for dinner?" Jamal asked. "We can watch ourselves on the news. We got a lot of awesome coverage."

As a general rule she didn't accept going to a guy's place on a first date, but . . . well, he was very committed to human rights. As such, he'd understand her position on sex, she told her better sense.

"Just dinner," Dina stressed. "And I'm serious."

"Did I say anything else?" he asked. " 'Cause if I did, I'm sorry."

"No, no, just me being silly," she apologized, worried that perhaps for once she didn't have the upper hand with a guy. He kept walking and because she didn't want him to get too far ahead, she skipped a step ahead of him and turned around. "Slowpoke." She smiled. He smiled, too, and they kept walking.

Jamal stopped at the 7-Eleven on Wilshire Boulevard.

"You want anything?" he asked.

"Nah."

"Ah, come on, let me get you something."

"Oh, all right, big spender," she said. "I'll

have whatever you're having."

"Right on." Jamal smiled. He went up to the Indian man at the counter. "I'll have two lottery tickets."

When they left the store, he handed her one of the tickets. "Do you know what your chances are of winning?" she asked.

"What the hell," Jamal said. "I'm not going to get rich doing the right thing, so I might as well try and get lucky tonight."

Dina put the ticket in her purse and ignored the double entendre.

The walls of Jamal's apartment were decorated with posters of Malcolm X, Che Guevara, Cesar Chavez, and Zapata. Dina did not know all their names, but she recognized them from T-shirts sold at hipster stores on Melrose Avenue. All the remaining space was dedicated to photos of Jamal protesting something: Iraq, Alaska oil drilling, antiabortion measures, capital punishment. There were also photos of him teaching at an Indian tribal school and working at a soup kitchen.

Jamal put out hummus and bread and olives and smiled — no, grinned — at her. She was starving, and so she wolfed down the food, not inspecting the plasticine plates for caked-on leftovers, as Randy had taught her. Jamal reached over and put more olive oil on her plate.

"Better that way," he explained. "Hey, grab the remote. Let's see who put us on. Try Channel 7. I talked to them for a long time."

As soon as Dina turned on the TV, Jamal grabbed the remote from her and flipped through the channels quickly, past car chases, vitamin scares, and Brad Pitt and Anna Nicole Smith updates until he found coverage of the demonstration. Then he got pissed. "Man, ten seconds is all they gave us," he fumed. "What the hell, they aired a lost puppy story instead. Dogs, man; they care more about dogs than peace."

Dina got lost in his excitement and let him put his arm around her. "Michael Jackson might have had another nose job?" he yelled at the TV. "Where's the humanity, man?"

That night in Houston, Fluffy leaped off Randy's lap when she squeezed him too hard upon seeing her daughter on CNN with "Arab-American peace activist" typed across her chest. Bud pumped his fist in the air after getting over his own initial shock.

"Go peacemakers," Bud chanted. "Go peacemakers."

When Jamal came on, Bud said, "That Palestinian kid next to her has eyes as green as Fluffy's."

"How do you know he's Palestinian?" Randy asked.

"The Masris are a good family. From Nablus," Bud said, sounding more like an Arab than he ever had since they had moved to Houston. "Hey, sweets, we ought to be recording this."

"Give me my cat back, Bud," Randy said, and yanked Fluffy away, ignoring his protesting meow. She turned off the TV.

Dina did not see herself on TV because by the time CNN, FOX, and MSNBC showed her clip, she had dropped the remote and could only feel Jamal's warm hands on her breasts. The guy knew how to kiss a girl. She'd never felt herself losing control of the situation. That was what guys did, not she. Oh, God, she could feel herself getting wetter as his hands went down to her stomach.

A Taco Bell commercial on the TV stopped her. Jake was puking on Mexican food right now while she was making out the way only people in her mother's romance novels did. She pushed Jamal away.

"Watching yourself on TV must really turn you on," Dina joked.

"It wasn't the TV," he said, which was what she had hoped he would say.

282

"I should go home," Dina said.

"Okay, I get it. You're one of those good girl types," Jamal said. "That's what bites about Arab chicks, I got to say. Give me a second to deflate here."

Randy always had attributed Dina's virginity to a righteous Texas upbringing. But Dina knew from every guy she'd ever gone out with that her virginity made her a minority in Texas. Jake even claimed to have "biological and hormonal anxiety disorders" as a result of respecting her virginity. She had had many chances and temptations to lose it, especially with Jake, but she was just as determined to keep her virginity until marriage as she had been to become head cheerleader and Phi Beta Kappa. She did assume her marriage would be to Jake, but still she held on to virginity. It was something she alone could control, not Randy or Jake. She decided to not mention either Jake or her virginity to Jamal.

"I guess it's for the best that we don't get involved," Jamal said. "No regrets, then."

"Regrets?" Dina wondered. "This was just a hookup?"

"No, *habibti,*" Jamal said. "It's just that I'm off to Islamabad next week."

"Pakistan?"

"Yeah, they need some relief volunteers

for the Afghani camps," Jamal said. "I'm part of a volunteer organization affiliated with the UN — 1.5 million refugees over there and growing every day."

Dina wasn't sure it was the heat from Jamal's hands on her stomach, which she still felt even though they were no longer there, or what he was telling her — and she hadn't planned on saying anything — but she said, "Can I come, too?"

"Where?" Jamal said.

"With you."

"And do what?" Jamal asked. "We can connect when I get back, baby."

"I'm sure there is something I could do to help."

"Have your dad write a check."

"I can write you a check without asking him first," she said, sneering.

"I may have underestimated you," he said, and pulled her in for a kiss that it took all her effort to let go of.

"That's right, you're a good Arab girl," he said, and stopped.

She made her way to the door. The lottery ticket fell out of her pocket.

"You almost lost your luck," he said. She took it from him.

"Listen, I'm sorry," he continued. "I think it's great you want to help. But Pakistan is nowhere to start."

"Do you have somewhere less tragic to start?" Dina said. She was being sarcastic. At least she thought so.

"Not less tragic but maybe more familiar to you," Jamal said. "The camps in Lebanon. I'll be there in June with the same organization. Why don't you join me then?"

The next week, Dina registered with the CAMES program at the American University of Beirut, where she told her parents she could do research on Lebanese law. That was the least traumatic explanation she could give them for the trip.

"What about Jake?" Randy fretted on the day Dina was leaving.

Dina didn't worry about that. Jake loved her, and she loved Jake. She wasn't going for Jamal but to do good.

A car honked. "My ride's here," Dina said.

"I'm scared, sweetheart," Randy said. "Your dad did a lot of business with a lot of guys who died in the Trade Towers. And your uncle was kidnapped over there."

"I'm not going to New York," Dina said. "And Elias's kidnapping — Mom, the eighties are so over."

"Just don't let anyone know you're American," Randy said. In all her life she never imagined such a sentence would ever come out of her mouth.

"Just please stop the anxiety thing," Dina said, and picked up her duffel bag and got into Jake's BMW. Randy was starting to spook her.

"Don't drink the water," Randy called out as they drove away.

She looked at the Louis Vuitton suitcase Dina had refused to take with her, a suitcase she had begged for just last Christmas.

On the way to the airport, Jake took his hand off the stick shift and put it on Dina's knee. "I'm going to miss you, D."

They were both so sad that they didn't even laugh, as they usually did, when they passed Bud's billboard on the I-70: BUD BITAR AND ASSOCIATES. IF IT WASN'T A LEGAL HASSLE, WE WOULDN'T LOVE IT.

"It won't be forever," Dina reassured Jake. She hadn't told him about Jamal. There really wasn't anything to tell. Just a few kisses between two people momentarily high on peace. Daily e-mails didn't count as a relationship. Even when Jamal's e-mails left her flushed, she remembered that they were mainly about helping her get the paperwork together for the trip. Besides, it was poor etiquette to not to reply to someone's e-mails. Jake would be busy interning at Bud's office over the summer. He and Dina would be together back in L.A. in the fall.

"So your dad's going to let me assist on the Tucker Chicken case," Jake said. "Did you know they got migrant workers in there working twelve hours a day, seven days a week, no overtime, no days off, not even to have a baby."

"That's so cool." Dina smiled. "I mean that you're working on it."

The Tucker case was a migrant labor lawsuit her dad had taken on pro bono at her request after Jamal had e-mailed her a *New York Times* article about it.

"D, do you think I should keep the Beamer, or should I get a Range Rover?" Jake asked. "Which car says 'I'm not just a lawyer — I win'?"

"A Honda Civic." Dina laughed but saw that Jake wasn't laughing.

"Seriously. If I go with the Rover, I should get it this weekend," he said.

"Well, Bud has a Lexus," Dina suggested.

"Boring," Jake said.

When she saw a 7-Eleven, she told Jake to stop. She went in and bought them each a lottery ticket. At the terminal, she handed Jake his ticket.

"Maybe you'll get lucky this summer,"

Dina said.

"I'll hold you to that when you get back." He smiled.

She blew her official boyfriend kisses until she came to the spot where she legally exited the United States.

On her own, Dina let her nerves take over, nerves she hadn't felt since the cheerleading squad's state championship finals. Without her squad members, Dina's senses took on a darker flavor as she flew from Houston to Paris, where she changed planes to Beirut. The passenger demographics got decidedly louder after Paris: more children, more yelling over her head, more shuffling of bags crammed with electronic gifts.

At the airport, Dina saw Jamal's butt first. When he turned around, so did a tiny person with unremarkable features: Allison from the protest. Jamal's butt was still nice, but he was darker than before, thinner, his eyes bigger and even greener. Dina wasn't sure how she was supposed to greet him. He reached his hand out for a shake. Jerk. Then he leaned in and kissed her on both cheeks. A little better.

"Welcome, Dina," Jamal said. Then he put his arm around Allison. "Allison's been the summer volunteer coordinator with the UN branch that manages the camp, for four years. She'll be your roommate at AUB."

Allison kissed her on both cheeks with lips colder than the iced tea at Harlon's — and with none of the enthusiasm she'd had for Dina as a protester.

Dina sat in the back as they drove away from the airport in Jamal's dented 1987 Peugeot. She tired to ignore the stink from the overflowing ashtrays as she wondered when Allison and Jamal had slept together. She was sure they had, and she was sure they did not anymore. In any case, there was no need for Allison to go hostile on her. It wasn't like she was planning on sleeping with Jamal. Dina remembered her team spirit award from senior year. Surely, Allison could be won over again.

"So, Allison, when did you get here?" Dina asked.

"Two weeks ago," Allison replied without turning to look at her.

"Allison's grandparents were missionaries here way before the war," Jamal added. "Even taught at AUB."

"Jamal didn't tell me what your skills were," Allison said. "You know, so I know how to place you in the volunteer schedule."

"Just being here is a help," Jamal answered for Dina.

Allison gave a grim smile, and the three

fell into silence, allowing Dina to look out at Beirut, which was alive with cars, people, music, women in miniskirts, others in long dresses and head scarves, peddlers selling roasted corn, posters of pop stars right next to Khomeini flyers, and billboards overhead with women in skimpy lingerie hawking everything from toilet bowl cleaners to perfume. Along the crowded beachfront, along streets filled with boutiques, at nearly every intersection, young boys carrying lottery tickets ran up to Jamal's car, pasting their faces against the window. But he would not roll it down.

Jamal looked back in time to catch Dina's disapproval. "I knew you'd be giving me the business," he said, laughing. "But if I bought a ticket from every single boy, I'd have no money to buy my own lunch. In Lebanon, either you are born lucky or you aren't, and not much changes after that."

He drove into an area of lush palm trees, blooming hibiscus vines, perfect rose gardens, and beautiful limestone brick buildings. As he took Dina's suitcase out, Jamal told her for the tenth time how great it was to see her.

"I'll get you in the morning," he promised, and blew a kiss in the general direction of both women. Dina followed Allison into the women's dorm of the American University of Beirut.

"That's your bed," Allison said. She put on shorts and a T-shirt and crawled into her bed. "Good night."

Dina, thrown off by jet lag, barely could sleep that night and was relieved when her bed was covered in hot sunlight. She went to the communal bathroom and felt like she had entered the makeup room for the Miss Texas pageant. The young women looked more like her than her cheerleading squad, only more perfect. She got a little confidence back when she blow-dried her hair because she saw that Carlo had done a particularly good job with the highlights. Allison came in just after Dina had loaded up her mascara wand.

"Jamal's waiting," Allison said. "Let's go."

"I got to finish my face," Dina answered.

Allison stood waiting, wearing no mascara, no lipstick.

Jamal was in the Peugeot, eating the biggest loaf of pita bread Dina had ever seen. He tore it and handed her half. Then he shifted the stick and drove. Dina lost her appetite ten minutes later. The beachfront cafés and hotels gave way to roadside shacks, Fiats puttering down the road with families the size of militias stuffed in them, and mechanic shops working on thirty-year-old Renaults. The sights, smells, and sounds of poverty increased with each meter they went south until they stood before a mass of trash piles, mud puddles, and honking, all enveloped in the stench of summer sewage.

"This is the entrance to Shatila," Jamal told her. "It's one of sixteen refugee camps in Lebanon, but unlike the other camps, less than half the residents are Palestinian. The rest are Syria's and Lebanon's poorest."

Stepping outside of the car into rancid air bogged down with humidity, the three entered a crowded, dusty maze of tiny alleys, vegetable markets spilling over with people and tomatoes, haphazard rows of tin shacks, and faded clothing hanging on rooftop lines. Women in head scarves sat on the floor sorting through lentils. Other women carried jugs of water on their heads. Diesel minitrucks transported wilted produce, kicking out pungent fumes as they swept by. Pepsi and Fanta posters hung on the doorways that led to makeshift one-room homes with only pillows for furniture.

In back of the market, Dina saw a vacant lot with garbage piles higher than any cheerleading pyramid she had ever seen. "Why don't they clean up that garbage and at least build some decent housing?" she asked. "I'll get my dad to pay for it."

"God," Allison said through clamped teeth.

"Dina, under all that garbage is the mass grave of many of the women and children who were victims of the 1982 massacres here," Jamal explained. "There are anywhere between a thousand and two thousand people buried there."

Dina was glad she didn't have more in her stomach than the pita. She had read in the books Fatima had given her about those massacres during the Israeli invasion of Lebanon, an invasion that had left eighteen thousand people dead, in addition to tens of thousands who had died in the civil war raging at the time.

Most of the older boys waved lottery tickets in their faces as they walked through the camp. "Luck, miss, luck day, miss," they sang, surrounding Dina.

Dina smiled and handed a boy with two flies perched on his head a thousand-lira bill, ignoring Allison and Jamal's attempts to stop her. The boy, wearing a school uniform he had outgrown two grades ago, gave her ten tickets.

"No, just one," she told him, handing back

the others. "You try your luck with the others."

"Crazy lady pretty," the boy told Jamal.

"Yes, she is," said Jamal, not seeing Allison's face cloud over. "Get to class, kids. *Yallah, yallah, ya'awlad.*" The kids giggled when he switched to Arabic.

Dina handed Jamal and Allison each a lottery ticket. Allison gave hers back.

"If you are going to insist on giving money, then it should be the right amount of money," Allison said. "They don't want charity. Right, Jamal?"

At the whitewashed building with the UN flag waving overhead, there were several other aid workers, some Lebanese, many European.

"Everyone, I'd like you to meet Dina," Jamal said. He began introducing her around. "Most of these guys are staying in the dorms, so you'll get to know each other pretty well."

"Where are you from?" a French worker asked.

"She's from Texas," Allison replied for her.

"I'll show Dina around today, and we'll see where she fits in best," Jamal offered as a few Europeans mumbled "Texas," disturbed.

He took Dina's hand as they walked back

out to the squalor. She melted without the sun's help and would have mistaken this for paradise for as long as he held her hand if it had not been for an old man hacking an endless cough from the rubble of a former building. Dina saw that there were people living in the rubble, mattresses laid out, and food piled up. From where she stood, the people in the building looked like toy tenants in an old dollhouse kicked over and stomped on by an angry big brother.

She was still looking at the sad dollhouse when Jamal was swarmed by a pack of kids in blue school uniforms who themselves were encircled by a swarm of flies searching their Fanta-encrusted lips. Like the Pied Piper, Jamal led the jubilant kids to a one-floor concrete building covered with student drawings — kids throwing rocks at tanks; a woman in a head scarf shedding tears made of the red, green, and white; and Ariel Sharon in a gorilla suit holding a baby gorilla dressed in a U.S. flag.

The students sat at their desks, crammed together to fit sixty students in a space the size of Dina's bedroom in Houston. She sat down to watch Jamal charm the kids into learning basic English with flash cards of things they did not own in Arabic or English: house, car, computer, air-conditioning. He won the kids over as easily as he had the reporters back in L.A.

"*Filistine* is Palestine," Jamal enunciated, teaching them how to say the name of their lost country in English, using a map of pre-1948 Palestine, old and out of date like everything in the dilapidated classroom aside from the students.

"Ballstein," the kids repeated.

"Palestine," Jamal said very slowly.

"Ballstein," the kids said in unison.

"What do you think, Dina?" Jamal threw up his hands in frustration.

"Sounds German." Dina smiled.

"Oh, fine, you try and teach them," he challenged her.

"I didn't even know there was an Arabic word for Palestine."

He gave her a questioning squint. "Okay, kids, Palestine one more time," he continued.

"Ballstein," they shouted.

"You tell, miss," said the boy with the most flies around him.

Jamal motioned with a big sweep for her to take center stage. She found sixty faces looking at her as though she knew something about Palestine, at least in English.

"Try it again," she encouraged.

"Ballstein," they said.

"P, you guys, *P,"* Dina said, popping her lips. The kids started popping their lips in unison. She developed a popping beat to Palestine. They echoed her. *"p . . . pppp . . . ppp . . . pp . . . pppp,"* they said to different stomps Dina made up.

"Pa . . . le . . . stine. One, two, three, four, five . . . Pal . . . es . . . tine," Dina popped.

"One, two, three, four, five, Pa . . . le . . . stine," the kids replied, joining Dina in clapping.

"Bes, stop," Jamal called out, laughing, just as she got a good cheer going. He had worked up a sweat cheering along with the kids. "No more playtime."

Dina sat down and watched Jamal be a real teacher. She could not understand what Jamal said to the kids in Arabic or recognize the letters in old newspapers he was helping them read. When the kids did raise their hands to speak, she could only make out the words *Iraq, Iran, Gaza,* and *Washington,* places that rolled off their tongues as easily as Paris Hilton or Xbox did at Kinross Prep.

Feeling useless, Dina absentmindedly cut up a leftover newspaper, making a pom-pom the way she used to when she was the same age as these children.

A little girl left her desk and came up to her.

"What this?" the girl asked.

"Just something my friends and I used to make before we became real cheerleaders," Dina said. The girl shrugged, and so Dina showed her a basic pom-pom salute. The girl giggled, and the others gathered around Dina.

"Our pom-poms were a little more fun because our newspaper had color photos," Dina explained. "You know colors?" They continued to stare at her. She turned to Jamal, but he pretended to be confused, too. Dina looked around for help and found only the pictures the kids had drawn. "Yellow, red, blue, black, and white." Dina pointed to those colors on a drawing of a man facing a machine gun, a rainbow overhead in the distance. The kids repeated after her.

"You'll teach them English," Jamal said after the kids could repeat the whole rainbow. "And arts and crafts. And gymnastics. There are volunteers coming from France next month who speak pretty good Arabic, and they can help with the academics."

I'll teach the useless classes, Dina thought, me Miss Phi Beta Kappa. But for the next month, Dina cheered the kids through cartwheels, toe touches, and jumps done to English vocabulary. "It's all in the prep, lift, execution, and landing," she'd tell them.

"Practice, practice, practice."

Escaping the camp in the evening gave her two things: fresh air and a chance to walk with Jamal around campus or to Bliss Street for dinner. Even on the days Allison didn't come with them, he did little more than kiss her.

"I respect your boundaries," he said more than once. "All men should." Jamal's sensitivity heated her up the way she imagined hot flashes would one day, but in a good way. It was merciful that her virginity intimidated him because when the heat finished passing through her body, she would remember Jake, her hidden boundary.

"Come on, we've got time to see the sun set over the sea," Jamal said one evening. As they walked past the McDonald's, he took her hand. "You've become more beautiful here."

"I haven't had a manicure in so long." Dina blushed.

Jamal laughed and swung his hand in hers.

She had forgotten to call Jake back the previous night. Before she could feel guiltier or Jamal could get more romantic, two guys waved Jamal over: AUB students who had helped spearhead a clothes drive for the camps the previous Christmas. He introduced her in English, but the guys couldn't help switching in and out of Arabic as they talked to Jamal about the possibility of getting CNN to come down to Shatila. The conversation continued all the way to the dorms, and only Dina noticed the sun setting over the campus's pristine gardens and the sea.

"They're going down to Solidaire for coffee," Jamal told her. "You want to go?"

"No, make it a boy's night out," Dina said. She had to call Jake.

Jamal casually kissed her goodbye, so quickly that she didn't have enough to time analyze whether his lips had accidentally landed on her lips or if the kiss had been purposely restrained in order not to reveal too much.

"Hey, Dina, what do you think about me going a little shorter with my hair?" Jamal called back as he joined the other guys. "Do you think that'd work better for television?"

Dina giggled only long enough to realize it wasn't a joke.

Back inside the dorm, Dina escaped Allison's scowl and phoned Jake.

Dina expected that the first thing Jake would say was that he missed her, but instead he said, "Your dad's a hard-ass."

"Yep." Dina laughed. "So did you stay

with the Beamer?"

"Yep," Jake said. "These Tucker employees are amazing, D. The primary spokesperson for the migrant workers has been supporting her family since she was twelve because her mom has tuberculosis and her dad lost his leg in a farming accident. If she could go to a bilingual college, there would be a real chance that she could finish. But that wouldn't be likely with a regular community college. After this case, Bud and I are going to look into a case requesting Spanish-language community colleges."

"That's so cool, Jake," Dina said. "I wish you could come see these kids here. They're really amazing, too."

"I got to run," Jake said. "Adios, sweets." Sweets. Jake was even picking up Bud jargon.

The next day, Jamal left Dina on her own at the school to serve as a translator for two human rights observers visiting from Amnesty International. Dina was in the middle of teaching the kids how to cheer to "Eyes, Ears, Nose, and Toes" with their pom-poms when a CNN reporter and his Lebanese cameraman came in with Allison.

"Where's Jamal?" Allison asked. "This is Matt Reynolds. He wants to interview Jamal on changes since 1982."

"Jamal wasn't here in 1982," Dina said.

Dina and Allison looked across the reporter's head at each other.

"Duh, but he can get together some of the people who were," Allison answered.

"Let's start with you and get some B-roll while we wait for Mr. Masri," the reporter suggested to Dina. "Whatever you were doing here looks like fun."

The reporter motioned for the cameraman to start rolling. Allison smirked, but Dina turned to the kids and clapped. "Let's go, team," she hollered. "Woo!"

The kids fell into squad formations. "Eyes, ears, nose, and toes," they chanted for the camera, using hand drills to point out the eyes, ears, nose, and toes on the kid next to them and then the kid in back of them.

"Way to go, team," she cheered. "Let's pick up the pace."

As Dina worked with the kids, the cameraman filmed. "How did you come up with this approach to teaching?" the reporter asked. She shrugged.

"Come on, what's your story?" he pressed on.

"I'm from —"

"I've been working with kids in camps all around the world, and I think Dina's work is genius," Jamal said upon arriving, putting his arm around her.

"I'm glad you got here," Jamal said directly to the camera. "We've been working to get more global attention on this refugee problem. This is just humanity taken to its most wretched."

"He's going to be a while," Allison told Dina. "I'm going to check on the embroidery co-op to see if they need any more supplies."

Dina continued to look at Jamal from his butt to his eyes, but he never motioned for the camera to turn back to her.

"I hope for your sake he's not the only man you're in love with," Allison hissed.

Dina shook both Jake and Jamal out of her head with an absentminded wave of the pom-pom still in her hand. "Can I come with you?" she asked.

Allison was slow to answer. "Yeah," she said. "But be careful what you say around these women. They're into virginity and God big-time."

"I'm from Texas, remember?" Dina laughed, but Allison's sense of humor was still back in L.A., and so they walked in silence until Allison stopped in front of one of the shacks.

Inside, several women in plain milk-gray dresses sat on the floor cross-stitching threads of red, green, blue, and orange into intricate mosaics on long black dresses.

The women stood up for Dina, each giving her two kisses as Allison introduced her. At first, she assumed the women, their wide eyelids drooping from fatigue, were old like her mother — until they started talking about their infants in broken English, smiling at her with mouths often missing several teeth. With Allison translating, they asked her about her students and why she wasn't married yet, then showed her photos of other dresses they had made, all sold, they bragged, at high prices to wealthy Arabs in America who wore the dresses to fancy banquets. Dina did not tell them she was a wealthy Arab in America, and as far as she could tell, neither had Allison.

"You take dress and help," said one of the women, pointing at the partially embroidered dress on which she was working.

"She wants you to hold it tight for her," Allison explained. "Like me."

Allison sat on the floor, pulling taut a section of the dress so that the woman next to her was better able to stitch on it.

Dina sat on the dusty floor and did the same thing. "I am Sarah," the woman told Dina. Sarah began cross-stitching, her eyes nearly squeezing shut.

"Tell her she needs glasses," Dina said to Allison.

"She knows that," Allison said.

"You know, my grandmother told me that in Palestine all the women in my village could afford dresses like this," Sarah boasted. "To wear to weddings, of course. *Aah Balik, inshallah, habiti.*"

"May you marry next, sweetheart, God willing," Allison translated.

When they took a break for Turkish coffee, the women gathered around Dina, pointing at the pom-poms. Allison reluctantly translated for Dina that their kids came home with the cheers. Sarah picked up the pom-poms and gave an example.

"P . . . p . . . p . . . Palestine," Sarah said, nearly tripping on her dress.

Dina laughed and showed her how it was done with grace. The women tried to imitate her while Allison glared from the side — until Sarah grabbed her hand and made her join, as if it were an old folk dance. Allison never would have made the Kinross squad. The women's bodies, put through many kinds of labor over the years, moved with far less spring than did those of their children. Out of breath, the women soon sat back down to their coffee. Dina inspected a chip on her cup. "Have you ever thought of immigrating to America? Seam-stresses can make pretty decent money there," she asked Sarah, ignoring Allison's warning sign. Too late: Sarah was on her feet.

"I come back soon," Sarah said, leaving the shack. "You wait."

Allison mouthed "just great" to Dina before going back to cross-stitching and motioning Dina to hold another woman's gown taut for her. A few minutes later, Sarah returned, flushed, with a yellowed envelope. "You come, come," she said, motioning to Dina. Then she took a deep breath and pulled out a thin, faded document as if it had been spun from gold.

"It's the deed to her father's house in Palestine," Allison explained. "They like to show these to foreigners because they think no one believes their story. Pretend to read it, why don't you."

Dina held the deed as delicately as Sarah had. Not a stain, not a blemish on the yellowing papers carried around for more than fifty years by Sarah's family.

"I am sorry," Dina said. She couldn't think of what to add to that.

"No, no be sorry," Sarah answered. "I go back one day, *inshallah*."

"*Inshallah*." Dina nodded. Having no other

306

viable answer, she had spoken her first Arabic word.

As Sarah reached for the deed, a ferocious wave of thunder roared through the shack, rocking its walls and forcing the Koranic blessings and maps of Palestine on the walls to sway wildly before crashing down. The women began wailing for their children and knelt down on the floor, covering their heads with their hands.

"Get down," Allison yelled at Dina.

She yanked Dina's arm. Dina obeyed, squatting and covering her head like Allison and the others. She wanted Allison to roll her eyes at her shaking hands and brimming tears, but Allison just grimaced, and Dina could see that she was afraid, too. Then, just as suddenly as it started, the thunder stopped. The women stayed silently in place for a few more moments and then, as if on cue, looked at one another and got up and rushed out the door. Dina stayed put, covering her head until Allison reached out for her hand and led her to the street. The alleys of the camp were filled with people running up and down, screaming, hands flailing in the air. Over the loudspeakers, a voice came on.

Allison pointed at the loudspeaker. "They're saying it was an air raid in retaliation for a mortar attack yesterday on an Israeli naval vessel," she translated. "They fired two rockets at another camp, but we're okay here."

"When was there a mortar attack from here?" Dina asked.

"That doesn't matter in Lebanon," Allison said. "Punishment for and by everyone is often random."

Dina watched as the wailing and hand-wringing subsided and people began picking up signs, bottles, and the squashed produce that had fallen off the carts. The boys with the lottery tickets came back out.

"Don't just stare," Allison said to Dina. "Go help."

Dina hated that all she had done to be perfect and virtuous was nothing compared with Allison, who wasn't even a virgin. As she bent to pick up a rolling tomato, she saw that Sarah's deed was still in her hand. Sarah must have gone looking for her kids. Dina stuck the deed in her backpack and headed toward the school.

"Jamal's going to be even busier now," Allison warned.

"I have to see Sarah," Dina said. Both women knew this was less than half of her motivation.

Jamal's butt was facing her while he faced

the camera, translating as the CNN reporter interviewed people, including Sarah. He took a break when he saw Dina.

"Are you okay?" he asked her.

Dina nodded.

"It's your first air raid," he empathized. "It can be scary."

"I'm glad you're here," she said.

He kissed the top of her head, and they both looked at the residents clamoring for the reporter's attention. Dina waited for Jamal to take over for the camp residents on CNN, but he didn't.

As they left the camp that night, the kids surrounded the Peugeot. Jamal hugged them all.

"Boy, they act like they're never going to see you again," Dina remarked.

"I'm leaving for Gaza tomorrow. The UN is very shorthanded for volunteers there as well," Jamal said. "I told the CNN guys I'd go there with them tomorrow to show them."

"Can I come?" Dina asked.

"To Gaza?" Jamal said.

"It can't be any worse than here."

"You're going to be okay here," he said, as if her motivation were fear. "There won't be another air raid, and Allison will be with you."

"I just thought it would be a chance to spend some more time together," she said, sounding hostile.

Jamal looked her over. "If that's what you really want," he said. "Are you sure?"

Dina nodded with a grimace, trying to maintain some of the hostility that seemed to have turned him on.

Later that night, Dina asked Allison if she would like to join her and Jamal for falafel as it would be their last night with her.

"I need to get some sleep," Allison replied.

Jamal and Dina ate together on a hillside campus bench overlooking the sea. This time, they did see the sunset together.

"The women were so comfortable around Allison," Dina said.

"It isn't nationality that binds us," Jamal said. "It's compassion, and Allison's is pure."

Whereas it was your eyes and butt that inspired me, she thought. "It's all so messed up," she said.

"Someone once said humanity is a concept that is easier to advocate than to bestow," Jamal said. "You'll see that in Gaza, too. Come on, we should get some rest before the trip."

At her dorm, under the carob tree, Jamal took her hands, which were rough and cut.

"You are so beautiful," he said.

"See you tomorrow." Dina smiled.

"Inshallah, habibti," he said, and hugged her.

The next morning God was not willing. Jamal was not downstairs waiting for her, and he wasn't there when Allison came down an hour later.

"I'm sure he explained it all in an e-mail," Allison said. "Come on, let's go."

"I'm not going," Dina decided. "What's the point without Jamal?"

"You are truly sad," Allison said with even more disdain than usual. "Just because a guy loves peace doesn't mean he has to love you or make a good boyfriend." She slammed the Peugeot door shut, and the car sputtered off. Dina couldn't believe that she had contemplated betraying Jake for the last several weeks, Jake who had stood by her even when she insisted on keeping her virginity. She touched up her makeup and called.

"Gosh, D," Jake said. "I didn't think I'd hear from you again."

"So you heard about the air raid on the news, huh?" Dina said. "I should have called earlier. I'm okay."

"Wow, D, be careful."

"How's the chicken case?" Dina asked.

"Can you handle Bud as a father-in-law after working with him?"

"Didn't you read my e-mail, D?"

"Your e-mail?"

"Listen, I got to go," Jake said. "You should read my e-mail."

Dina logged on to her Gmail account right after hanging up.

First she opened Jake's e-mail: *"D., you have changed my life, and that is why I have fallen in love with someone else. Her name is Maria, and she is the migrant worker Bud and I have been working so closely with. You told me over and over again before you left that you needed to be with someone who cared about people. I was so afraid of losing you that I begged Bud to take me on the pro bono case so I could impress you. Then I fell in love, like I didn't know it was possible to fall in love. If it hadn't been for your unselfishness, I would have never met her. And one day I'm sure you'll think this part is funny: She told me that at first she didn't want to go out with me because she thought all I wanted to do was sleep with her, but I told her while I did, I would wait. She'd figured I was going to think she was a freak, but I said how you'd taught me all good women are worth waiting for. I will always love you for that and for leading me to such a generous man as Bud. And to a* lottery ticket. That ticket got us $500 and Maria and I are planning on using it as the first donation to a school we plan to build one day in her mother's name. You are lucky, D., to be filled with so many good things. Call me if you want to discuss further. I love you, Jake."

Dina read the e-mail ten times, numb. Then she hit "delete" and opened Jamal's: "Dearest Dina, by now, you will know that I left without you. It is for the best. My call will always be my work, and I will never live for long in peaceful places. You will tire of that soon. I am not husband material, as an old girlfriend once told me — which is what I assume you are seeking. It is not easy to let go of someone so wonderful. I am sorry I have taken away the innocence that comes from being oblivious, but also hope that you will be another voice for the voiceless. Love always, Jamal."

Patronizing butthead. Dina had underestimated how much control she had over Jake and overestimated how much Jamal cared about her. She wanted to hate them both, but how could you hate people who were nearly saints? Sure, one had fallen in love with his client and the other was in love with the camera, but they were doing good in the world, bestowing humanity, saving people and chickens. Oh, screw all that. She did hate them.

Dina slammed her laptop shut. She went to the bathroom, where a girl was putting on her third coat of mascara. "Where do you get your nails done?" Dina asked her.

"Well, I have a lady who comes to my house," the girl said. "But all the tourists love the spa at the Mövenpick."

Dina wanted to tell her that she wasn't a tourist, that she was Lebanese. But instead she went downstairs and caught a cab.

Dina once more tried to pry her legs off the Mercedes's leather. The cab driver lit another cigarette. "We'll probably be at the Mövenpick in ten minutes."

Perfect. She couldn't wait to massage out Jamal and Jake and unclog her pores from Shatila. She dialed Houston.

"Jake's a two-timing sleaze bucket," Dina said. "Scumbag asshole."

"Your father told me," Randy said. She didn't mention to Dina that she was the one who had busted Jake after seeing him kiss the Mexican girl on TV during a rally for immigration reform. "I told Bud to fire him, but he says Jake is the only person at the office who shares his passion. It's your fault that all they talk about is chicken workers. You started it."

"Mom, I'm coming home," Dina announced.

"Oh, thank God." Randy sighed. "You had me all scared with your talk of Gaza. I just saw on CNN that there is another Orange Alert."

"The Orange Alert means the trouble is your way, not mine," Dina reminded her.

"I'm so tired of watching the news just because you're over there," Randy said. "You'll be back in time for the Neiman Marcus sale. You know how much fun we have there."

"Yep," Dina said.

"Do you want to talk about Jake some more?"

"No."

"Dina?"

"Yeah, Mom?"

"Are the strawberries and figs there really small?" Randy asked. "Tayta Fatima always told me the strawberries and figs were so tiny and sweet that you didn't have to put sugar on them."

All Dina could picture was the fruit in Shatila sweltering on carts with the flies.

The taxi driver drove down a long driveway to the oceanfront, and two valets ran to open the door for her.

"Mom, I got to go," Dina said. She exited

the cab, stickier than if she had jogged there. Who had a Mercedes without air-conditioning? But it was the facade that mattered, and in that way Beirut reminded her of Houston. In Beirut, however, you couldn't completely escape the masses the way you could in the spacious malls her mother practically had raised her in. Two lottery ticket boys tried to come down the driveway, but the valets chased them away. Dina watched the boys run back up to the Corniche. So many lottery tickets but no luck of their own. She opened her backpack to tip the driver. Her wallet had less money in it than she remembered. She dug deeper and pulled out two lottery tickets from the camp — they'd have to do for a tip. The taxi driver looked at her, unhappy, and so she dug into her backpack one more time — and saw Sarah's deed poking out at her.

Her fingers flew across her phone pad. "Allison, I'm sorry about this morning," she said. "Please tell Sarah I'll be there with her deed ASAP."

Dina hung up, hurriedly gave the driver his money, ignored his displeasure at the lottery ticket tip, and walked into the Mövenpick for her massage and pedicure. She'd be quick. She checked her backpack for the deed one more time and went inside.

■ ■ ■ ■

In Houston, Randy wondered why Dina hadn't mentioned the boy with the green eyes. She was sure he had something to do with her tears.

She wanted to tell Fatima that Dina hadn't gone to Gaza. But if she told her that Dina was going to stay in Lebanon, Fatima would continue to ask her if Dina had gone to see that damn house in the mountains yet. But Randy was a little worried about how well Amir was taking care of her mother after seeing his joke about her cutting off her hair.

She walked up and down her house before she found Bud. He was in the kitchen showing Manuela how to make kibbe.

"The key is to get the shell very thin," he explained. "My fingers are a little fat for this, but you get the idea."

"*Sí,*" Manuela said. "Kind of like a tamale, no?"

"Yeah, kind of like a tamale," Bud agreed.

"That's not thin enough," Randy said. She took the shell from Bud and worked it herself. Randy made a perfect kibbe, surprising both herself and Bud.

"I had no idea you knew how to make

kibbe," Bud said. "I just asked the lady over at Drooby's Market what ingredients to buy and thought I'd try my luck."

She handed her kibbe to Bud when she went to answer the phone.

"Mom, I'm not coming home," Dina said on the other end. "When I signed my contract, I committed to staying here the whole summer. I signed a piece of paper, and pieces of paper mean something."

"That's lawyer talk," Randy said.

"I'll bring you back some strawberries," Dina promised.

Randy wiped away her tears after she hung up. She went to make kibbe with her husband and maid. On the way, she picked up the lottery ticket that had fallen out of Manuela's apron and put it on the counter for her.

SCHEHERAZADE

Before leaving Lebanon, Scheherazade returned to the camp, where Sarah had just completed the last stitch on the dress she had been working on before the air raid. Its vertical mosaics were sewn with the richest blues, reds, and blacks, hues that once had indicated family wealth. Scheherazade pulled the dress over her head. Magnificent.

She had taken money from Dina's wallet earlier and laid the cash down where the dress had been left for the night.

Back in Los Angeles, Scheherazade paused at the petrol caravan's back window to marvel at her reflection in the cool linen of the embroidered dress.

The very sight of this exquisite gown would get Fatima out of what was sure to be a disastrous mood after the dinner with the photographer named Tiffany from the Iranian Jew's store.

Scheherazade climbed up the eucalyptus tree, past the fig tree. Before she could peer into the living room window, whispering just below distracted her. She hung upside down from a tree branch and peeked into the petrol caravan. That mortal Sherri Hazad was looking even more severe in her dull blue costume as she reprimanded the man and woman in black. "Look, I appreciate the tip, but you need to stop taking these pictures," she warned them. "It is not warranted."

"It's not?" said the man in black, turning his attention back to the house.

Amir posed menacingly in his jihadist outfit in the living room. A very tall woman with broad shoulders, wearing a *kefia,* the black-and-white Arab head scarf, flashed away with her own camera.

"We know they often take pictures of themselves before a bombing," the woman in black ventured.

"Let's not get carried away," Sherri Hazad cautioned.

Amir then posed with his arms crossed, head covered in the *kefia.*

"He might be looking for just the right outfit for the seventeen virgins in heaven," the man in black said.

"Maybe, but I don't want to see your SUV here anymore," Sherri Hazad said. "I'm going to get a wiretap in place on all the phones billed to that address, and we'll do a little monitoring of his e-mail. That's legal. You being here is not."

Ya Allah, if only these three could feel me slap them, Scheherazade thought. What *afreet* filled them with feverish ideas that young men were willing to die just to deflower virgins? Especially Amir.

She found Fatima oddly jubilant in the kitchen as she ate kibbe, humming to a Frank Sinatra song with a full mouth. Scheherazade touched her on the shoulder. Fatima quit singing and gasped when she saw Scheherazade's new dress.

"Oh, what a dress," Fatima said. She put on her nearby glasses the better to examine the embroidery stretched out across Scheherazade's bosom. "How did you know today would be a special occasion?"

She motioned for Scheherazade to look out at the couple. "This is it, *inshallah,*" she said, seeming to glow. "I went to fry more kibbe — she eats a lot, but *ma'alesh,* it's okay — and I come back to this joy. *Allahu akbar,* look how she is caressing his hand."

A person not living on as much hope and delusion would have seen that Tiffany was rubbing bronzing cream on Amir's hand. Fatima bit into another kibbe. This was the first time Scheherazade had seen Fatima eat the cooking she always bragged about.

"You were too pale before to be threatening," Tiffany said to Amir, dabbing on a final smear of bronzing cream. "Let's go, big boy. The money shot."

Amir pumped his biceps and sneered, and Tiffany started clicking away.

"I'm so glad your grandma got us together," Tiffany said. "This has been really cool. I needed to expand my portfolio."

The two high-fived. "Right on," Amir said. "Do you think we ought to take some pictures of me in, say, a doctor's outfit?"

Tiffany laughed so hard that her cackle turned into snorts. Fatima grabbed Scheherazade's hand. "The girl laughs like the donkeys in Deir Zeitoon, but no one is perfect," she decided. She stepped out of the kitchen and let out a fifteen-second wedding trill from deep in her throat. Her ululating caused Tiffany to lose her balance during a perfectly good shot. Amir turned his terrorist audition glare on Fatima.

"Are you okay, ma'am?" Tiffany asked.

"Would you like some desert, Miss Tiffany?" Fatima said, and gave her a full-denture smile.

Tiffany looked to Amir. "Is that an Arab tradition?" she asked. "Giving a little bit of your desert to guests?"

"Dessert," Amir said. "You want *dessert?"*

"Maybe later," Tiffany said, and started refocusing her camera.

"*Sí,* you don't seem like the kind that would say no." Fatima winked. "My Laila is a bit like that, too. Normal. It's okay with me."

Fatima turned up the volume on "Strangers in the Night" and swayed to it.

"Ignore her," Amir told Tiffany. He gave the camera his "stupid Middle Eastern hot dog cart owner" look, the one he used for sitcom auditions.

Scheherazade paced around Fatima, unable to dance to the dull music.

"If they would only get married in the

next three days, I would wear a dress as fine as yours," Fatima announced. Scheherazade would have basked in Fatima's awe and adoration if Amir's *thowb* had not flown past them as fast as her carpet had brought her back from Lebanon.

Amir was left only in his briefs as he put on Baluchi pants and a plastic saber while Tiffany looked on, camera at the ready.

"He adds rain to the mud with his lewd behavior," Scheherazade said. She reached inside her new dress and got her lace handkerchief for Fatima's tears.

"They're just being friendly," Fatima said. She ignored the handkerchief and forced out optimism. "Let's leave them to get to know each other a little better."

"What's left to know?" Scheherazade asked. "You can't give someone like that a house in Lebanon. In the time of my youth this would be okay, but today the people back home prefer to appear demure and blame the public decadence on America."

Fatima held up her hand and let her cane guide her up the stairs, not even bothering to wish Amir and Tiffany a good night. She sat down at her dresser and dared to look at her purple stubs in the mirror. Scheherazade handed her the hairbrush, but she pushed it away. "I've decided Amir and this girl will behave and be happy," she announced.

Scheherazade tried to brush out Fatima's purple stubs for her and then paused. "Fighting the truth is so much more work than facing it," she hinted. "What we are born is who we are. We can change the outside appearance, we can change where we live, but inside it's the same. I know. I've been shifting between time and space for —"

"For 1,128 years," Fatima finished. "But change is possible. That's why I wanted you to go see Randa."

Scheherazade saw the hope in Fatima's eyes. "I did not have a chance to visit her," she apologized. "But I'm sure she and her family are okay." She did not tell her that she had visited Dina, for she did not want Fatima asking her about the house in Deir Zeitoon she had forgotten to visit.

"Randa is the one child who knows how to take care of herself," Fatima agreed. "*Ya Allah,* she is always telling everyone to come see her house. I tell her my house in Lebanon is much nicer than hers and Dina should go visit, but she doesn't listen. Randa's house is so big that all of Deir Zeitoon could live in it, but it doesn't have any marble and no bidet. She told me it was colonial-style, like the British and French colonization hadn't destroyed the Arabs, like colonization was a good thing."

The pilgrims at Plymouth Rock, no matter how proud she was of Laila's Thanksgivings, didn't figure into Fatima's definition of colonial.

"Randa married very well," she added, ignoring the ringing phone. "She did not marry from a *fellahi* family. They were city people, not peasant."

She looked at the phone. "Amir tells me to never answer it if he is home," Fatima said. "But I think he is too in love to hear it."

She picked it up. "Hello," she said, and waited for a response on the other end.

"Fatima?" Ibrahim said through static and line glitches.

"Ibrahim?" Fatima said, remarkably wordless.

"Do you get my . . ." but Fatima could not make out the words through the interference on the line.

"Get your what?"

"Get my . . . read it . . ." was all Fatima could make out.

"Amir and I read the Koran together every night," she told him. "And you are well?"

"I try again . . ." Ibrahim said through several clicks on the line. "When your phone line better."

He hung up, and Fatima looked at the phone. After a long while waiting for him to call back, she turned to Scheherazade. "How Ibrahim and Randa battled," she recalled, trying to not look back at the phone. "He always calls back."

"This daughter defied her father?" Scheherazade said, her voice laced with disapproval but preferring conversation about Randa to gazing at a phone all night.

"Randa demanded that he be more of an American father," Fatima explained. "By doing 'what he had to make his children typical.' "

"Is that what an American father does?" Scheherazade inquired.

Fatima shrugged. "I didn't have a father, so I didn't know how Ibrahim was supposed to be, just as I hadn't known what Marwan and Ibrahim were supposed to be as husbands, as I never saw my mother with a husband."

Scheherazade sighed. "My father adored my sister Dunyazad and me. He bounced us on his knees, rode with us on horses groomed silky, snuck orange blossom sweets from the king's table into his turban for us.

And the stories he would tell us at night to put us to sleep. The morals in his tales were spun into mine, and my king —"

"Hey, who's telling the stories here?" Fatima interrupted, wishing so much that Scheherazade's tale of her father's adoration was a story any one of her daughters could be telling of their father, but Ibrahim's love couldn't be seen so easily in stories.

"I shall remain quiet, *ya seiti,*" Scheherazade acquiesced.

"Randa was the child from whom Ibrahim and I went from being called Mama and Baba to Mom and Dad. Randa made all the kids follow her, except Laila, who was already too used to Mama and Baba," Fatima said. "She would buy us cigarettes so we could smoke them with our friends, not the *argileh.* But neither Ibrahim nor I could stand the smell. She was furious with Ibrahim for not building a bomb shelter like all our neighbors. Ibrahim said the Russians weren't coming. He didn't get her a hula hoop because he said it was bad enough how cheap Arab girls looked in the movies. Millie told Ibrahim the Arab women weren't cheap but exotic and sexy. No man wants his daughter to be exotic or sexy. Ibrahim would never even say such words in front of his daughters."

"Sexy is not an ugly thing," Scheherazade lamented. "Vulgar, though, is another matter. Why do they have to always make me look so vulgar?"

"Randa was worst in the summer," Fatima said, unwilling to indulge Scheherazade's vanity, especially when talking of one as self-absorbed as Randa. "Every one of her friends at school — and Millie and her kids, too — went to cabins up north on the lakes. But we stayed at home with the fans running on high, eating Popsicles. We were alone on the street and with no homework. If there had been school, the kids would have been doing homework together. Every school night, we made them sit together and do homework for four or five hours even though we couldn't help them much ourselves. But in the summer, there was no homework and the TV did not have things on it all the time like now. Randa would sit in the living room chewing pink gum and making big bubbles."

"Not so bad," Scheherazade said. "Surely, it's not as if Ibrahim beat the girls with a broom like I once saw an aunt do to one of my dear cousins."

"*Ya Allah,* no," Fatima said. "Ibrahim only once raised a hand to one of his daughters.

Randa, of course. It was the time she demanded that she attend camp like all the other children. When he refused, she set up a tent in her bedroom. One day while I was on the porch playing cards with a few women from the Arab Ladies Society, I smelled fire, and it was not the charcoal from the *argileh.* I went upstairs and found Ibrahim standing over Randa with his belt next to the campfire she had built, asking her if she had any idea how many young girls had died in house fires in this country — the houses are made of wood here, you know. I was even angrier with her. But I took the belt from Ibrahim and told him that if he ever so much as pulled a strand of her hair, I was going to kill him, just like I'd heard Millie's husband say to her."

"Never mind the killing," Scheherazade said. "Were you able to repair the house damage?"

Fatima nodded. "But we ended up with one less bedroom, which vexed Randa even more. The Arab Ladies Society never wanted to play cards at my house again, and at least that made Randa a little happy, as she considered our friends almost as embarrassing as ourselves. When everyone came back from camp, Randa focused on getting what she called cheerleading clothes."

Fatima pointed to a picture of a teenage girl in a high ponytail dressed in a cheerleader uniform. "When I told Randa — Ibrahim couldn't do it calmly — that this cheerleading was *aabe,* she said it made her popular."

"But didn't Ibrahim want these girls of his to be known?" Scheherazade said. "To get good husbands early."

"Once when the kids were little, I convinced Ibrahim that we should go on vacation like Millie and her family," Fatima explained. "Randa doesn't remember because she was only three, but one summer, when we had only six kids, he agreed, and we went to meet some Deir Zeitoon cousins who lived in Florida, where they were making an orange grove. The children had a great time with the ocean. On the way back home, we stopped at a little restaurant off the big highway in Georgia. A young man was serving Coca-Cola with peanuts outside the restaurant, which the kids had never seen. So I let them try it. How they giggled. All the Coca-Cola made them have to go to the bathroom. The waitress led me to the ladies' bathrooms. There were two doors. One said 'coloreds,' and one said 'whites.' All the people in the restaurant turned around to see which one we would go in.

Laila said these must be the laundry rooms. The waitress — I think she felt bad for us — said to Laila, 'No, honey, that's how we sort people around here. I wish I could tell just from looking at you all, darling, which one you should use.' I told the girls to wait and went outside and asked Ibrahim what color we were. Ibrahim grabbed my arm so hard it bruised for a week and dragged me into the restaurant. We found the girls were happy as could be eating chocolate ice cream with some men who all looked like nice grandfathers. One of them patted Randa on the head and said, 'You're just about the cutest little mulatto I ever seen.' Ibrahim's face turned into a frightening purple and red I had never seen before, and he yanked the man's hand off Randa. 'You don't touch my kids,' he yelled so loud that the gas attendant looked in. The man stood up and told Ibrahim, 'Here I am trying to be nice to you people, and you go threatening me. You get your family out of here before I call the sheriff.' Standing, he was a very big man, much bigger than Ibrahim, so all Ibrahim could do was tell the girls to go to the car. Then he drove straight back to Detroit without a word. I kept pacing that night we got home because I didn't know what color my children were and why my husband had turned such an awful red and purple in front of such a friendly man. When I asked Ibrahim for the third time, he finally spoke and said it didn't matter because the girls should never leave the house again. He said he'd rather they were unhappy at home than dead outside. Then he sat down on the bed, and his face turned a white I had never seen before. It frightened me as much as the red and purple had, and I wanted it to go away before the girls saw it, and so I begged him to talk."

Life's patterns often came easy to Scheherazade after 1,128 years. "His sisters were killed in Lebanon," she said, not trying to muffle Fatima's tears.

"In Deir Zeitoon, three years before Ibrahim came to America," Fatima whispered. "He was thirteen years old. It was the spring, and Ibrahim's mother was in the neighboring village of Deir al-Bortugal for the birth of her oldest daughter's first child, the daughter whose marriage to the sheepherder Ibrahim had arranged. That afternoon several Druze men came into the village looking for the Abdullah family. They were looking for the Maronite Abdullahs, who they said had murdered their father because they mistakenly believed he had shot one of their uncles twenty years earlier.

They broke down the door to Ibrahim's house while he was doing his homework. They dragged with them two of his sisters, covered in bleeding scratches, guns pointed at their heads. They had taken his sisters from a henna party for one of their friends who was to be married the next day. The men demanded that Ibrahim lead them to the person who had killed their father. Ibrahim told them that they had the wrong Abdullahs. He pointed to the Koran in the house, to the prayer rug, but they were so drunk with vengeance, they would not believe that Ibrahim and his sisters were not of the very same Abdullahs who had supposedly killed their father. Ibrahim had no names to give them, and so the leader cocked his gun at one of the older sisters' temples. Ibrahim begged and pleaded with them to whip him more, but they shot his older sister. Ibrahim screamed out a name in Deir al-Bortugal so they would spare his other sister. One man stayed with Ibrahim and his dead and living sisters, while the rest went to Deir al-Bortugal. When they came back to say there was no such person in Deir al-Bortugal, the leader shot Ibrahim's other sister. Ibrahim waited to be shot himself. 'No, you have let your sisters die, and that shall be yours to relive every day and every night,' the oldest one said to him, as if he were a sage rather than a killer. It was Marwan's sister who helped Ibrahim take their bodies to be prepared for burial and cleaned the house before Ibrahim's mother returned. Ibrahim had hoped that if his mother did not see the blood, it would help her to not lose her mind. But by the next year, she had cried herself to death. From the night Ibrahim told me this story, I did everything to hide any dangerous truths of my children's lives from Ibrahim, although I wasn't very good at it because I often wanted his advice on what to do. But when I could hide the bad, I did. He felt like he couldn't protect his daughters either that day in the peanut and Coke café."

"Do your children not know this of their father?" Scheherazade asked.

"He begged me not to soil their hearts with such a thing," Fatima said. "In time, they would come to know their own sorrows."

"Your husband distrusted all men in the presence of his daughters, just as my husband distrusted all women in the presence of men," Scheherazade said.

"With each daughter that was born, Ibrahim laughed less and less," Fatima concurred. "He stopped being the man who used to tell me jokes in Arabic when I first got here so I could laugh sometimes. I couldn't understand American humor back then, but I loved his old Juha jokes. I can't imagine him telling a joke today."

Scheherazade recalled how Ibrahim had tried some humor — a joke about Fatima — with Laila, and that warmed her memories of Detroit.

Fatima pointed to a photo on the vanity of a teenage Randa and Laila trying to wash a frozen turkey far bigger than the sink.

"Ibrahim should have laughed, Randa was so ridiculous," Fatima said. "She would force Laila to get involved in her schemes to make us typical, although Laila was content to just get through every day without gaining weight. That's all Laila cared about, which actually made her the typical one. Randa would tell Laila to play Elvis Presley and the Beatles and other nonsense really loudly and wait for Ibrahim to lecture them on the sins of the musicians, as their parents' friends did. But we didn't even understand the words, and as long as the girls were in the house safe, he didn't care what they did. Once Randa asked me if I thought it would be okay with Ibrahim for her and her sisters to go to the school dance. I told her *inshallah*. But in private

Ibrahim said, 'Date? Only when a man walks on the moon.' Then I told the girls that, and I meant it just as much as Ibrahim. When President Kennedy started talking about going to the moon, all I could think is *inshallah* not before my girls are married. Mr. Armstrong, God bless him, didn't do it until most of my girls got to college at least. By then, they all sat straight, crossed their legs, didn't laugh loudly, and smiled and nodded politely only at good boys."

"Al-hamdulilah," Scheherazade said.

Fatima's dark mood then gave way to a smile. "Laila has turkey on Thanksgiving, but do you know what Randa has?" Fatima winked. "She has lamb because it turns out Bud Bashar Bitar doesn't like turkey. But that's a small price to pay for love. . . . Ibrahim used to tell her that if she didn't stop blowing bubbles with that ridiculous pink bubble gum of hers, no Arab man would marry her, which of course made her do it even more. So love's joke was on her in the end."

"What did Bud Bashar Bitar want with her?" Scheherazade said.

The incredulity in Scheherazade's voice irked Fatima. "Everything Randa did at home was to make us all more 'outstanding typical people,' as she called it, not just herself," Fatima explained. "She always made her sisters believe they deserved better — and Bud Bashar, too. It is why her two oldest married wealthy American boys — whiter than new Detroit snow, I tell you. Now she is worried because she told me Dina left her betrothed."

"Dina left him?" Scheherazade smirked. "Give the house to Dina. Let Randa's daughter have Lebanon whether Randa likes it or not."

"I would never want her to be so far away from Randa forever," Fatima said. "When Randa moved to Texas, I said that it was an American tradition to come home at Christmas, and she told me that Detroit wasn't home anymore. I said Detroit is where your mother is, so it is home. She asked me why I had never gone to visit my mother in Lebanon, then. It was the meanest thing any of my children ever told me. But she calls me every day, so *maalesh,* it's okay."

"I have heard enough of this daughter," Scheherazade said. "Just leave her your Avon colors to paint on another face."

"Then what will the homeless man with the dimple do for money?" Fatima asked. "I have decided to leave him the Avon to sell, as he can't seem to find another job. No, I will leave Randa Mama's Koran, as she needs faith and her past, and Mama's Koran gives her both. And Randa will want it because it looks expensive."

Tiffany's loud laughter carried up the stairs. Fatima reached to twirl her missing hair.

"I brought you something," Scheherazade said to distract Fatima from the donkey laugh. She spun around in the embroidered dress.

Fatima clapped her hands. "This dress is for me?"

Scheherazade took the gown off and was left standing in a lilac slip of Indian silk. "Let your children see you at least once dressed as we dressed, not as they imagine we dressed," Scheherazade said.

"And I'll leave it to Soraya," Fatima promised. "Then, *inshallah,* you can be proud of her using your name."

Fatima looked at the calendar. "How will it be in three days?" she said. "I have told you much now."

"You have lived eighty-five years without really knowing tomorrow, and now you need to know the next three days." Scheherazade sighed. "Just put the dress on."

Fatima was not satisfied with Scheherazade's answer but could not keep her hands away from the dress. As she held it close, both women heard the door slam down-stairs.

Scheherazade leaped up to her window perch and then chortled. "Come, Fatima," she said, waving. "Look."

"Thanks for everything, Amir," Tiffany called out as she got into her Volkswagen. The girl had left the house fully clothed.

"Al-hamdulilah," Fatima said. "She is dressed and doesn't want to spend the night. She will know how to behave in the village."

"Her laugh is not that of a donkey in Lebanon," Scheherazade noted. "It is that of Soraya."

"Every boy is attracted to someone who reminds him of his mother," Fatima said. "That is why I am sure Ibrahim had a very kind mother because with time he didn't just feel obligated to me but also attracted."

"Attracted?" Scheherazade said, still surprised that Fatima couldn't admit, even to herself, that her husband simply had loved her.

Fatima held the dress close to her.

AMIR

Before Tiffany had pulled out of her parking spot, Amir was uploading the photos she had taken of him. Jesus Christ, this had been the best date Fatima had ever set him up on. Much as he hated going out for the Abu Nidal roles, he made a dashing terrorist through Tiffany's lens. And she had taken the photos for free. All she had asked for in return was that she be allowed to use the photos in her antiwar collage. The evening had been an excellent value: In addition to free photos, he was going to be part of a work of art.

He clicked on a photo that Tiffany had taken of him in his Osama beard. His arm was around Fatima, and she was attempting to hide her purple stubs with her hands. Looking at his grandma's hair in a photo reminded him all the more how much she was falling apart. No one had responded to his last e-mail, nor had Lena said when she would visit. Jesus Christ, maybe Fatima's kids weren't getting the full picture.

```
Dear Family,
    I trust you are all doing
well. The weather here today
was just slightly foggy. But
```

340

the temperature was in the upper 70s. In my last e-mail, I mentioned that Tayta had cut off her hair. I've attached a photo so you can see for yourselves. Another way you can all see the new do is to come visit. She's yakking to herself more than ever, and she might actually enjoy having someone to listen while she's doing it. She's got a house in Lebanon she's willing to give away, if any of you want to come on over and talk to her about it. Great location, tax-free.☺

Peace out, Amir

He looked at the photo one more time.

PS: The guy with the mustache and machine gun is just me. She has not been kidnapped. Still here waiting for your visit.

The only one he did not send it to was Laila, as he figured from hearing Fatima talking to herself that she had enough on her mind.

He flipped through the mail quickly. For the first time since Fatima had moved in, he saw a letter addressed to her that wasn't from Ibrahim. It was from Minneapolis, in the sloping handwriting of teenage girls, sealed with a Hello Kitty sticker. Minneapolis? He placed the letter on Fatima's medication tray.

When Amir walked into Fatima's room, she stopped talking to herself. He set her pill tray down.

"Hi, *habibi*," she said, ignoring the tray. "I think this Tiffany is *noor hayatuk,* the light of your life. Her laugh is very loud, let us say, but the house in Lebanon has very strong walls. The neighbors won't hear."

"I'm sure, but I'm still —" Amir stopped himself when Fatima reached for her hair to twirl and there was none. For the first time in his life, Amir heard his mother's voice as wisdom in his head: You just have to tell her things that will make her think she's happy.

"Tiffany is a regular blast," he enthused.

"*Wallah?* Really?"

Amir winked, and Fatima's dentures opened into a smile so big that it revealed the bluish tops of her gums. "When do you think you and Tiffany might go to Lebanon?" she said. "Get married first, though. No *aabe,* shame. You are the great-grandson

342

of Hashem Riyad Mustapha Abdul Aziz, and you must live up to that."

"Tayta, I've never even been to Paris," replied Amir, who didn't think an ancestry of sheepherders, tobacco field workers, and matchmakers was all that great. "First, I'd like to see Europe. Then there's that yoga retreat in Costa Rica I've always dreamed of."

"What are you talking about?" Fatima asked.

"I'm just saying that there are a lot of other places on my vacationland map I'd like to see, too, if I ever get a vacation," he said.

"Lebanon's no vacation, *ibni*," she said. "It's our home."

"Yes, Tayta," he said by rote. "It has beautiful roses."

He handed her the envelope. "This came for you today," he said. "It says it's from a Decimal Jackson in Minneapolis."

"I don't know anyone in Many Happy Police," Fatima said.

"What about Auntie Hala?" Amir said.

"Her name is not Jackson," Fatima said.

"I'm still going to go ahead and call Auntie Hala," Amir said.

"Hala's a gymnotologist," Fatima said. "What can she do to help? Send us birth control pills? I needed a gymnotologist before she and the others were born, not after. You know what a cardiologist is? It's a heart doctor. Isn't being a heart doctor a better way to help your mother?"

She patted the bed for him to sit next to her on the mattress. "Your grandfather called tonight to see if we were reading the Koran every night. Do you know in Lebanon he —"

"Oh, Jiddo," Amir interrupted. "He called yesterday about —" The teakettle went off downstairs, and he decided to not mention Ibrahim's letter because she would start obsessing about finding someone to read it, and he was too busy to deal with that at the moment.

"I got to go, Tayta," he pleaded. "I have a big audition I can't blow. I'm going to put sage in the tea."

He added the last part because it thrilled Fatima any time he used something from the garden. He put the Minneapolis letter down on the tray. "I'll read it for you tomorrow," he said. "And the Koran. Don't forget to take your pills. Want me to turn on the TV? Maybe the Lions have an opening pitch tonight."

"No, they don't," Fatima said, waving him and his ignorance of sports away.

FATIMA

Paris? Yoga? Costa Rica? Fatima was frightened. Could it be that her favorite grandson, even if he married Tiffany, didn't love Lebanon any more than he cared about the Tigers and the Lions?

Scheherazade handed her the pills on the tray.

"Amir didn't even wait for me to swallow them," Fatima said. She flung the tray into the garbage.

Scheherazade let the pills fall but swooped down to retrieve the letter. "Shall I read it?" she offered.

"I need to focus on the house and Amir," Fatima said, lashing out. "I don't know this person, so how can her letter help with those matters?"

Fatima picked up the phone, but as she dialed, the static and clicks on the phone made her decide to hang up. "Ibrahim is probably asleep, anyway," she said. "*Inshallah,* by tomorrow the phone will be okay again."

"Why don't you tell me another story of Ibrahim," Scheherazade suggested.

"Maybe the phone in Detroit is having problems," Fatima said, distracted. "That makes more sense. Probably he forgot to

345

pay the bill. I'm usually the one who remembers and —"

"Fine, I will read the letter," Scheherazade interrupted, and pulled out her own nearby glasses from her bra. "This will be today's story."

"You can't read English," Fatima said.

"The language of love and anguish is universal," Scheherazade said. "Those are the only letters people still write in their own hand."

Scheherazade opened the letter with the edge of her gilded silver compact. Then she let herself slip into the world of the letter so that she could see it being written and best know how to read it. The writer was as tiny as Fatima, but the bump on her nose was much smaller.

DECIMAL

Decimal sat on her hands to make it harder to scratch the itch on her neck. She hated wearing Shetland wool — even Hello Kitty sweaters — in the summer but didn't want to catch a cold from the medical center's air-conditioning system. She owned barely any summer clothes. It was such a short season in Minneapolis, and she spent so much of it in doctors' waiting rooms, that she didn't have much use for shorts and tees. Maybe air-conditioning was another reason not to start as a premed student next year. Medical school classrooms — especially anatomy ones — were very cold.

According to the *Newsweek* she had read at the eye doctor's last week, she probably would live to be a hundred even with all her allergies. Did she really want to spend the next eighty-three years of her life freezing indoors? She'd most likely work to the bitter end because according to the January issue of *Money* magazine at the dermatologist's office, it would take that long to get a decent portfolio.

Decimal looked at the only person not looking at her, a pale woman reading the greasy, creased May issue of *Good Housekeeping,* from which Decimal had cut out the dairy-free brownie recipe the previous day.

"One-fourth miserable, one-third bored, another one-third mildly hopeful, and the remaining one-twelfth miscellaneous and stuff," Decimal whispered to her mother, Brenda, and discreetly pointed at the *Good Housekeeping* woman.

Mother and daughter were just seventeen years apart, and so they enjoyed many of the same waiting room games. Brenda had invented this game at the ear specialist's when Decimal was five; it was called "Guess Exactly How Happy That Person Is."

"Nah, I'd say two-fifths bored, one-tenth happy, and one-half worried shitless," Brenda figured.

The personality analysis never got much more upbeat. Although Decimal and Brenda felt comfortable in medical plazas, they knew ordinary people didn't come to doctors' offices for the joy of it. They never ever found out which one of them was correct.

"We can't ask them how unhappy they are because we got manners and stuff," Brenda had explained to Decimal when she was six years old. "We're high-class people even though everyone can see clear as day that I screwed up."

Decimal understood that Brenda couldn't hide her screwup, which was Decimal herself, but believed that Brenda could dress a little more like she had class. Brenda was a stunner today with her strong, thick black hair tied in a fuchsia scarf and her cat eyes all done up in black eyeliner. Her long fingers made her zirconium ring look totally elegant. But her jeans sat too low for a mom, and her halter top exposed too much of her natural muscle tone. Brenda belonged somewhere, such as Florida, where it was ordinary to show off so much flesh. Some-place warmer, without a daughter who had to visit medical centers all the time. Decimal felt absolutely sure of this today.

"What do you think about the creep eyeing me up and down over there?" Brenda asked, readjusting her halter top to suit her cleavage better.

"Ninety-nine point five percent pervert," Decimal said, which she said about any man Brenda mentioned. She figured that probably the perverts' mothers liked them, and so she always gave them a half-percentage-point of nonpervert.

Decimal readjusted Brenda's halter to minimize the breast exposure.

"It's my Arab side that got this DD cup," Brenda apologized. "I can't help it."

"They do breast reductions on the sixth floor," Decimal said.

"We already spend enough time with doctors," Brenda retorted.

Decimal pulled a pen and notebook out of her Hello Kitty bag. "I'd better start my homework."

"We've been waiting here for like a hundred hours," Brenda said, jiggling her leg up and down. "How much longer do you think it'll take?"

"It's only been thirty-seven minutes,"

Decimal replied. "You can go home, Mom."

"Are you eighteen yet?" Brenda bit back. "Since I remember when I got my stretch marks, the answer is no, so don't tell me what to do."

"Maybe you should go get some coffee and stuff," Decimal suggested.

"Can I have some money?" Brenda asked.

Decimal reached into her Hello Kitty purse and handed Brenda five dollars.

"That ought to be enough," Decimal warned, and flipped her lopsided black curls over and clipped them with a barrette. "And put on your coat if you're going to go to the gift shop. It's about 25 percent more freezing than here."

"Okay, honey," Brenda said, and bit a nail as she looked at Decimal. She pulled out the barrette and adjusting it to her liking "Want me to pick up your hay fever prescription down at the pharmacy?"

"Nah, we'll do that after," Decimal said. Her eyes rested on the red purse of a woman in equally red sweats with matching red hair. "How about we play What's in Her Purse?"

"Let me get the coffee first," Brenda said. Then she swaggered to the elevator so that the pervert was able to ogle her a little longer.

Decimal jiggled her knee the way Brenda had and looked back at the woman's red purse. "Three lipsticks, two nail files, half a pint of water, seven multivitamins," she mumbled to herself. The game just wasn't any fun without Brenda. Not much ever was. After a little more jiggling, Decimal took a notebook out of her backpack and stuck her iPod in her ear to listen to Prince. She chewed on her pencil, readjusted her glasses, sneezed, and then began to write.

To: Ms. Fatima Abdullah
Detroit, MI?

Dear Mrs. Abdullah,
We've never met, so you might find it strange to hear from me. If you're reading this, it means I got your address from my grandmother (your daughter, Hala). Here goes my first snail mail letter ever. To you. What do you think of that? I'm hoping you'll want to read it as I heard you're really literary and always give your kids books with pretty covers for their birthdays.
First off, my name is Aisha, but everyone calls me Decimal because I'm good at math. My mom (your granddaughter Brenda, who I'll keep calling "Brenda" instead of "Mom" so you don't get

confused) is pretty good at math, too, but most of the counting she does is predicting how long her latest boyfriend will last. I always guess, too. My guesses are closer to one month and hers are always closer to one year, and I'm almost always right. I don't gloat over it because I wish the opposite were true. She's a really good catch for a nice guy. Aside from me, she doesn't have much baggage and I'm supposed to be in college next year. And sometimes, she'll pick on other people behind their backs to make herself feel better, but they're usually people on TV so that's not such a bad habit.

Even if you don't know Brenda that well, you probably know the real problem is that she has terrible taste in men. I wish she didn't. Then she'd have met someone and they probably would have had another kid. It can be pretty lonely being the only child of an only parent who goes out a lot. Especially when I'm too allergic to even have a cat or dog, unless you consider Hello Kitty. My grandparents — Gran (your daughter Hala) and Dr. Wang (Gran's husband, although separated) — said the bad taste started even before Brenda met my father, like five years before that when she had a crush on Prince in the eighth grade and used to sneak into his old club downtown. The one on First Avenue called First Avenue. It was exceptionally logical for him to name it that, seeing as musicians are not very logical if I go by the ones Brenda dates. Brenda's men are losers. Except my dad.

Do you know my dad (Tyrone)? Probably not. Brenda and he didn't have a big wedding and stuff like that because as you know Brenda got pregnant with me their junior year of high school. She had to finish high school by doing a GED, and Tyrone worked at a Mobil owned by a bunch of Arabs. Kind of not so impressive when you think that all four of Brenda and Tyrone's parents worked as doctors at the University of Minnesota, which is also where I was conceived. I'm just guessing that's where I came to be. I don't really want to ask, but having grown up practically on the campus, I know that there are lots of places two people could make a baby. Tyrone's parents were very nice about me being born, but they didn't like Tyrone falling into the cliché of unwed African-American teenage dad. So he married Brenda and was no longer unwedded but still a teenage dad. Gran and Dr. Wang wanted her to have an abortion. I would have been Brenda's second abortion, and I think a second pregnancy really messed up her hormones and made her indecisive so in the end it was too late. Having me was her only option. She was going to put me up for adoption, but then Gran saw something on the news about how black kids never get adopted and get messed up in foster care. That's when she told Brenda that she would deliver me personally and that I would not be given away. And Tyrone's mother convinced Brenda that she would never, ever get over giving me away and stuff. I personally think she would have gotten over it. She's actually much stronger than most people suspect. Anyway, Dr. Wang was major pissed off at Brenda and Gran, even when Gran arranged for me to be born in a hospital far away from the U. hospital.

Brenda thought that at least when she married Tyrone, Dr. Wang would be happy. But he wasn't. They were married such a short time, he probably doesn't remember that she did make that effort. And that's why my last name is not Wang, like Brenda, but Jackson, like Tyrone. I think that must make Dr. Wang happy at least.

Brenda told me once that Jackson is a slave name. I told Tyrone this when he took me and his other kids to Valley Fair one day and I couldn't go on the Power Tower on account of my altitude sickness and then he spent a couple hours talking to me about slavery while his other kids got to go on the Corkscrew and Steel Venom and all the other rides that also make me sick and stuff. I told him white Jacksons must have had a lot of slaves to name because look at how many black Jacksons there are. Michael Jackson, Jesse Jackson, Reggie Jackson, Mahalia Jackson, etc. Tyrone still says that my Jackson Hypothesis made him so proud of how smart I was. He still calls it that so I know he was telling the truth.

Most of the time, Brenda and Tyrone get along pretty well, even better than most undivorced people. They have a lot in common — they're both middle class kids of upwardly mobile minorities who became huge disappointments to their parents at the exact same time. So that — and me — has always bonded them. I have friends who say I'm lucky my parents are divorced and stuff. They have to listen to their parents fight all the time. That would suck. Tyrone and Brenda laugh a lot and like to say "remember when." Now, more than ever, I think about how the best times of their lives — you can tell it from the laughing — all took place in high school. Before I was born. I'm the same age now as they were when the best days of their lives ended.

I can't help calculating things like this out. Not only Brenda and me, but Gran is pretty good at math, too, especially when she's making a numerical list of all the things that Brenda has done wrong with her life. I love Gran, but I'm glad Brenda doesn't make lists like that about me. Anyway, Gran put her math to good use becoming a doctor and stuff. And then she married a doctor, too. Brenda says that marrying a doctor is what every mother wants for her daughter. But Gran says that you didn't like Dr. Wang, even though he was a doctor. If he wasn't any nicer to you than he has been to me, I understand.

Brenda says not to take Dr. Wang not liking me too personally — just like Gran didn't worry about you not liking Dr. Wang or Dr. Wang's parents not liking her. If you didn't already know that Mr. Wang (Dr. Wang's dad, one of my great-grandfathers) didn't like your family, I hope I haven't offended you. I heard you all never met each other, as you and your husband, Mr. Abdullah, didn't come to the wedding.

"Decimal, you're not writing mean things about me in your diary again?" Brenda asked, and jiggled her leg. "That really hurt when I read the last one."

Decimal stopped writing.

"I'm over that phase, Mom," Decimal answered, and jiggled her leg, too. "Ms. Jorgenson says we're supposed to write a letter to a distant relative to get to know them better."

"So I suppose you're writing to Dr. Wang." Brenda laughed.

"No," Decimal said. "I'm writing to my great-grandmother."

"Honey, she's dead," Brenda said. "Don't you remember that weird-ass funeral in San Francisco?"

"Not Dr. Wang's mother," Decimal said. "Gran's mother."

"I got no shortage of other relatives and stuff you've never met that you could write to instead," Brenda suggested.

"I picked her already," Decimal decided. "The letter is due on Monday, so leave me to get it done."

"Do you think you'll be ready to go back to school on Monday?" Brenda said, and jiggled her leg faster.

"Mom, your cell phone." Decimal motioned to Brenda's purse, which was ringing loudly.

"Thanks, baby. What would I do without you?" Brenda said, and reached in for the phone. "Brenda Wang speaking."

Decimal saw two things pop out of Brenda's bag with the cell phone: a Beanie Baby and the five dollars. Damn it.

Brenda stuck out her hand to Decimal, and Decimal gave her mother her pen.

"Yes, yes, great to hear from you," Brenda continued on the phone, teeth clamped on the end of the pen. Her loud voice gave no consideration to the other waiting patients. "Uh huh. Uh huh. Let me run some numbers and different scenarios and get you a quote by tomorrow."

Brenda winked at Decimal, both knowing that Brenda already had figured out the quote and was just playing hard to get in sales, the way she never did in her personal life.

Decimal tuned out her mother and dug out another pen from her Hello Kitty bag.

Brenda's super skills at math — and the fact that she is totally charming — make her a good insurance salesperson. She can do her job and sell polices and stuff anywhere, including waiting in doctor offices.

There are two reasons we spend so much time in doctors' offices. One is that I was born with eye and ear trouble and allergies to lots of stuff — strawberries, dust, pollen, eggs, dairy, wheat, you name it. Oh, and animals (Hello Kitty stuff — which Gran gives me all the time — is the closest I'll ever get to having a pet, which is why I still like her at my age). I kind of blow that theory that I read in Parenting at the allergist's last May that the younger you have your kids the healthier they'll be and stuff. The other reason we come here a lot is that Gran and Dr. Wang are both doctors and so sometimes we go to visit them at work. We live with Gran, but we only ask her for money at work. Brenda says it's harder to say no at work than it is at home or over the phone. Gran is always giving me things anyway, including this Hello Kitty pen I'm writing to you with. Dr. Wang gives us money just so he can see us disappear from the sight of his colleagues, especially all the other Asian doctors with their highly overachieved children. "Practically the entire brown and yellow population of this state worked on this campus when I was a kid," Brenda always tells me. "Now, their kids are even more successful." Brenda says "successful" like it's a dirty word but I think it'd be kind of cool to be successful, don't you?

Now that Brenda and I are older, we don't really need money much from either Gran or Dr. Wang. Brenda does pretty good and stuff at her health insurance sales. But sometimes we still go to Dr. Wang's office and ask. Brenda says she just likes to freak him out, but I think she misses him. Gran says they used to be really close when Brenda was a kid. Brenda was Dr. Wang's favorite until I happened. I kind of think sometimes that he'd like to get to know me better, maybe take me to his chess games, like he used to take Brenda, but I can't be sure because he has never made eye contact with me.

"Check this out, Decimal." Brenda gasped. Decimal stopped writing and took the health insurance application from her mother.

"Greg Sorenson, thirty-eight, divorced, nonsmoker, takes cholesterol medication, no other illnesses or sexually transmitted diseases," Decimal read, jiggling her leg up and down. "Cool."

"He's going with the PPO 1500 plan,"

Brenda added. "Doesn't like HMOs."

"And smart, too," Decimal agreed.

"We're going out to dinner on Friday," Brenda said. "That is, if you're going to be feeling okay to stay home alone."

"I'll be fine, Mom," Decimal assured her.

"Yeah, you're probably right," Brenda said. "I'm hungry."

"Maybe if you'd bought a Snickers with that five dollars, you wouldn't be hungry," Decimal reprimanded her, jiggling her legs faster. "Give them the Beanie Baby back."

"Don't start, missy," Brenda said. "Let's not forget why we are stuck in this building."

Decimal bowed her head. Then she went into the Hello Kitty bag and pulled out a few more dollars. "You need to eat more protein," she said. "With the five dollars, this should be more than enough for a hamburger."

"You need protein, too," Brenda replied. "We'll go to the Dairy Queen afterward."

Even if the only things Decimal could eat were Mr. Mistys because they were the only dairy-free item, she liked Dairy Queen. It was almost impossible for Brenda to shoplift anything at the Dairy Queen.

"Call me if the doctor calls us in," Brenda yelled back as she walked to the elevator.

"And tell my grandma I said hello and stuff. No, wait, better not mention me at all. Just tell her we're having nice Dairy Queen weather."

As Brenda got on the elevator, waiting room focus shifted from Decimal's wool to Brenda's sleek midriff. Decimal put in some eyedrops and went back to writing.

Brenda wanted me to tell you that it was Dairy Queen weather here today. Brenda's really trying to be good but it's slow going, especially with the new shoplifting thing. Don't mention it to Gran because she would probably flip out. I've taken charge of the money, making sure she always asks me for some, so maybe that will help. And Brenda is beginning to date a much higher caliber of men and maybe that will help with her depression. Before, she used to go out with any cute guy she sold a policy to, but now they have to also look good on paper. So that's a big improvement and stuff.

Have you ever thought about how many great-grandparents I have? Eight. And you and Mr. Abdullah are the only ones still alive. That must make you feel pretty good. On the other hand, I'm sorry to hear about your divorce. I doubt yours was as easy as Brenda's and Tyrone's because they didn't have anything to divide except me. And Tyrone let her keep his half of me. As far as divorced teenage dads go, I was pretty lucky. Tyrone eventually bought that gas station where he worked, and he sends me money every month. And I go to see him every now and then, and he calls me once a week so we can talk about my college plans. He'd be pissed off big time if I didn't go to med school. Tyrone says that although he knows Dr. Wang hates him, he cared about education more than anything and that's why he respects him. Brenda says if it weren't for me, she probably would have become a nuclear physicist because that's the least Dr. Wang would have expected. She says she wouldn't have minded because she liked science a lot. Brenda also says Dr. Wang doesn't like me because I'm half black. But the truth is he blames me for Brenda not having the time to become a nuclear physicist. Brenda makes it a racial thing and stuff so I don't take it personally. Tyrone says that Dr. Wang might not be a racist but he's an ass. Dr. Wang and Gran got separated over me 17 years ago. But Brenda and Gran say not to think of it that way. That would be like you, Mrs. Abdullah, not forgiving yourself for Gran and Dr. Wang getting separated the first time, on account of all of the nagging of you and Mr. Abdullah and Dr. Wang's parents, and all the ensuing fighting between Gran and Dr. Wang.

Despite her bad role models, I think Brenda would really like to get married. I mean why else would she be dating so many policyholders? It's not just for sex. Everyone on TV with all their kissy faces and stuff make you think there's nothing better. But I think it's like a drug — a happy feeling that lasts a really short time and then you have to pay for it for the rest of your life. But don't worry, I'm a good girl — I don't do drugs. Even if I wasn't a good girl, I'm sure I'd never do drugs because I'd be allergic to them. Still Gran always gives me a gift certificate to Marshall Field's every Christmas just for not doing drugs.

I tell Brenda that it's not like second chances never work. Tyrone's been married to the same woman since I was two, so that's a pretty long time. She's fat and always lecturing everyone on what they're doing wrong so I call her the Holy Roly Mother. She doesn't like me, and neither do their three kids. Sometimes I try and talk all hip-hop and stuff around them so they'll like me, but I don't do it very well. They don't even bother to laugh at me. But Gran insists I stay in touch with them. She says they're the closest people I have to siblings and you never know when I might need them for an organ donation or something. She's a doctor, so she thinks about these things.

Gran says that you were very proud of her becoming a doctor but didn't like Dr. Wang because he wasn't from your village. I have to say that I don't agree. There are a whole heck of a lot things I don't like about Dr. Wang that have nothing to do with him not being from your village. Like how he abandoned his favorite daughter and how he doesn't like Tyrone. Dr. Wang's parents were FOBs like you but from China, which really isn't that different from your village in Lebanon, if you think about the rice in your families. Both Dr. Wang and Gran told Brenda that a meal almost always had to have rice because that's how they grew up. So they had more in common with each other than regular Americans, who wouldn't have needed rice at every meal, maybe would have even preferred potatoes. And you know what? I prefer rice to potatoes.

We studied Lebanon in school a little. Hopefully, all the bad stuff is exaggerated, in the way that people think everyone in the Midwest is fat and likes to go bowling. Still, I guess it's good you left all that trouble. And if you hadn't come here, Gran would have never met Dr. Wang, and Brenda wouldn't have ever been born and met Tyrone, and then I wouldn't have ever been born. So thanks for coming to America.

Do you ever wonder what the world would be like without all the people that you helped somehow bring into it? From what Gran says it sure seems like a lot of people.

"I'm freezing," Brenda announced as she returned. She opened her compact to wipe away some ketchup. Then she offered it to Decimal, as she always did.

"I can't look at myself today," Decimal said. "And you're freezing because that's what happens when you walk around a hospital without a coat. Eat a breath mint. That will calm you down."

Brenda smirked before she opened her purse so that Decimal could see that she hadn't lifted any breath mints. But now there were two Beanie Babies in one bag.

"They have a psychology department on the second floor," Decimal said, and went back to writing.

I look at myself in the mirror a lot. I guess most teens do. But today . . .

"Decimal, what time is it?" Decimal looked up to find Brenda jiggling her leg and shaking her watch as if she could make it work that way. Decimal grabbed the watch from Brenda.

"It just needs a new battery," Decimal explained. "I'll get one after school tomorrow."

"Tomorrow, honey?" said Brenda. "I don't think —"

"Do you like Mrs. Abdullah?" Decimal interrupted.

"Right, your letter," Brenda said after a final shake of her watch. "We were here in Minneapolis, and she was all the way over in Detroit. Like Dr. Wang would say, when you have so little vacation time, do you really want to spend it in Detroit?"

"Did she knit you sweaters and bake cookies and stuff?" Decimal said, thinking of all the things Gran didn't do.

"She didn't have time for that," Brenda said. "Shit, she was a raising a boy and a girl that weren't much older than me. I would have just died if I had more kids. Do you believe I have an aunt that's only like six years older than me? I got cousins older than my aunt."

"That's far out," Decimal said, trying to sound amazed.

"That aunt, Lena. She lives in NYC, New York," Brenda raved. "She must be almost forty by now, totally single and free and stuff and I bet gets weekly massages and pedicures — how glamorous is that, you know?"

"Well, maybe we could go visit her one day," Decimal suggested.

"That life's not for people who screwed up," Brenda said.

"Gee, thanks, Mom."

"I screwed it up in the best possible way, honey." Brenda smiled. She kissed the top of Decimal's head. "As long as you don't do the same."

Brenda's cell phone rang again. Decimal sneezed and handed her another pen.

"This is a big one, Decimal, a company policy," Brenda practically bubbled when she looked at the incoming number. She handed her phone to Decimal. "Make it sound good."

"Brenda Wang's office," Decimal said very efficiently, deepening her voice a third of an octave and holding her leg down to stop it from jiggling. "Just one moment, please."

"What in the world would I do without you?" Brenda whispered. "Hello, hello," she said to the phone, walking away.

Like I was saying, I look at myself in the mirror a lot. I see sickly and pimply, but I don't see Arab, or Chinese, or Black. I do see someone who could definitely pass for Latino but not a hot one like Shakira or Jennifer Lopez. The good thing about not looking Black, Chinese, or Arab is that I've never been a victim of a hate crime, at least not for what I really am. Once a couple of black kids called me a wetback and a white kid called me a Spic. But since I'm not Latino, I didn't get offended. I bet I could have marked Latino on all those college applications. It would require three less pen checks than marking Asian, Caucasian, African-American, and Other on college applications — or on Match-.com, if I end up trying that out in my lifetime, although Brenda says it's totally not worth it. But marking Latino would be a lie. Then again I love tacos, but I don't know how to eat with chopsticks, don't get turned on by Barry White, and I'm allergic to something in falafel. I used to think I would look weird ice fishing, but once someone thought I was Eskimo, so I guess I could go ice fishing one day if Brenda would ever want to do anything fun. But she says we spend too much time freezing in medical plazas, so there's no need to go freeze our asses off on the lake and stuff.

"Aren't you Dr. Abdullah's granddaughter?" a nurse asked Decimal.

"Is she in today?" Decimal said.

"Isn't she always?" said the nurse. "You have a super day now."

Decimal held an insincere smile until the nurse was gone. Then she went to the attending desk nurse. "How much longer is it going to be?" she inquired.

"Just a few minutes, hon," the nurse answered. That meant at least another fifty-five minutes. Decimal grabbed some extra Kleenex and went to the pervert. "If my sister comes back up, tell her I went downstairs to see our mom for a minute."

Decimal walked across the street to the Boynton Student Health Center, where Hala counseled university girls on birth control and safe sex and did pregnancy and Pap smears for them. A grateful patient had given Hala flowers, and so Decimal's arrival was announced with an allergic sneeze. Hala, the white of the coat highlighting the white in hair that she hadn't had a chance to cover in months, hugged Decimal tightly, as if she hadn't just seen her at breakfast.

"Hi, sweetie." Hala smiled. "What are you doing here?"

"We had an appointment over at Fairview. I thought I'd come up and say hi." Decimal shrugged. "I don't need money or anything."

She sneezed again, and Hala moved the flowers.

"How is your new hay fever prescription working out?" Hala asked.

"I printed out my scholarship applications for Arizona State and Stanford," Decimal said by way of answer. "I'm still counting on a school giving me a 50 percent scholarship."

"That's great, sweetie," Hala said. "But if it doesn't happen, look what I was reading in the *Minnesota Daily.*"

Hala showed Decimal an article she had clipped from the university's newspaper. "See, 73.8 percent of the new freshmen this year were from the top 20 percent of their class," Hala read. "I know you have your heart set on seeing the world, but there are summer internships you could do that would take you to other places."

Hala wanted her to go to the university and keep living with her and Brenda. She also wanted Decimal to go to an Ivy League school to make up for Brenda. Decimal didn't want to set Hala's expectations up for either option, although the percentage of schools that would accept her was very high.

"I guess we'll see who ends up giving me the best scholarship," Decimal said.

"So smart." Hala beamed.

"Could I get Mrs. Abdullah's address from you?" Decimal asked.

"Whose address?"

"Your mother's."

"Why in the world would you want her address?"

Decimal explained her school project. "After our teacher grades it, I really do want to send it to her," Decimal said. "That'd be cool."

"But she doesn't know about —" Hala stopped herself. "Well, she's quite old."

"That's why I'm writing to her."

"Well . . ."

"Well what, Gran?"

Hala looked at her file cabinet, where a black-and-white photo of Fatima in her wedding dress rested.

"She sure was pretty," Decimal said.

"I've never heard anyone say that about her before," Hala remarked. "I have her address at home. I'll give it to you tonight."

"You better put it on your list," Decimal recommended, and Hala pulled out a notebook and wrote "mom's address."

"I got to get going before they call my name and I'm not there," Decimal said, for once sweating in her wool.

Back on the second floor, the pervert told Decimal that her sister had come back up and then gone downstairs. Decimal was sure she had gone to see Dr. Wang. She sat back down and saw another Beanie Baby on the chair. After today, Decimal decided, she'd make stopping the shoplifting her top priority. She jiggled her leg for a few seconds and began writing again.

I just saw your photo in Gran's office. I love your wedding dress. Did you look different before and after you were married? When I look in the mirror sometimes, I wonder what I would look like if I were married. Did you know that Brenda is setting up Gran on a date with a lawyer who took the PPO 250 plan? That's a very low deductible, which is often a sign of wealth and good self-preservation. But I don't think Gran will go for it. She has never actually divorced Dr. Wang. But Brenda thinks Gran should get married again. I do too, but married back to Dr. Wang, even though he doesn't like me. And even though Dr. Wang doesn't like me, I'd like to know more about China. And I'd like to know a little more about being Arab or Lebanese or Muslim and stuff. Maybe if I did, I would understand why people could be so angry that they would hijack planes and kill all those people. I mean I get to feeling pretty bad about my life, waiting in doctors' offices for most of it, but I'd be much more likely to kill myself — but only myself.

Brenda came back and handed Decimal a Toblerone and its receipt.

"Dr. Gupta said I shouldn't eat chocolate, and the Beanie Babies are lame," Decimal said. "You don't even like cute things."

She stuck the Toblerone in Brenda's purse. Then she pulled it back out.

"You know what," Decimal continued. "I'm going to return this and the Beanie Babies myself."

"What are you going to tell them?" Brenda wondered. "You forgot to pay for them?"

"Why don't you go tell them that?"

"I went over to immunology and showed Dr. Wang your SAT scores," Brenda answered as she took the chocolate back. "My baby, my National Merit scholar, can just name any college she wants. You know what he said? 'Well, at least the girl is going to college.' Screw him."

"I'm surprised you've waited this long to throw my scores in his face," Decimal said.

"Oh, I've shown him before. I just wanted to show him again," Brenda boasted. "They're having a charity bazaar downstairs to raise money for the bloodmobiles. They got some cute pot holders."

"You don't even cook."

"But I know people who do. Maybe I could buy Gran something," Brenda said. "I'll be back in five minutes."

"You're going to miss the appointment," Decimal said, worried.

"I have never missed any of our appointments," Brenda reminded her.

"Don't forget your policy folder," Decimal said, holding it up for Brenda. "You never know who you might meet looking for insurance in a place like this."

Brenda sashayed back for the folder. "You're so right. What in the world would I do without you?"

Brenda had come and gone so many times

in the last seventy-four minutes that even the pissed-off pervert had lost interest in watching her jiggle her leg as she waited for the elevator. Decimal rolled up the collar on her sweater and picked up her pen.

Did I tell you that I got a boyfriend? Imagine someone actually liking me. We were both working at the drive thru at McDonald's in Dinkytown because our teachers told us that it looked good on a college application to have tried making money. Paolo can't eat anything with peanut oil, just like me, so I started bringing him lunch and then he'd bring me lunch and then sometimes we'd play Xbox together or go look at the animal dioramas at the Bell Museum and we fool around a little but only with each other. We hold hands and talk and stuff, too. Paolo is from Brazil. He came here with his mother like ten years ago. She's an associate professor of psychology and stuff. Get this, his grandparents went to Brazil from Syria, which is right next to Lebanon. You know how Hala says that you wanted her to marry an Arab? Well, if I were to marry Paolo, that would be coming full circle for you because I'd be marrying an Arab. But I probably won't marry Paolo, for many reasons. One of the important reasons is that I don't want to be hit. Paolo has never hit me, but the reason his mother left his father in Brazil was because he used to hit her and Paolo and give them black eyes and everything, even though he was a professor and stuff just like her. He'd say he was sorry, too, but then he'd do it again. Anyway, boys who grow up around a man like that often become abusers themselves. That's in all the magazines in all the doctor offices. You know physical abuse is not thoroughly covered in insurance policies, which is a shame Brenda says considering how much abuse is around.

Another thing is I don't think Paolo and I are in love. I've taken love quizzes in Cosmo, Self, and Glamour at several doctors' offices, but none came out definite. I think you have to have a comparison point. I'll probably only know if I loved Paolo when I get another boyfriend and can match up their good and bad qualities and see who comes out on top. I don't know what married looks like, but I don't think Paolo and I look married. He's way too handsome to be married to someone like me. He's handsome like if his mom were a supermodel and married a supermodel, not like those supermodels that have kids with old rock stars. And it's not like we're really inseparable, which Brenda says married people are supposed to be. But I'm very grateful to Paolo for liking me.

"Decimal, exactly what are you doing down here?" Hala stood over Decimal minus her white coat. Two nurses waved at her as they passed by.

"Stuff," said Decimal. "Right now, I'm writing to your mother."

"Is Brenda in with the doctor already?" Hala demanded to know.

"No, she went to help with the blood drive," Decimal said. She wished she had a college acceptance letter or another scholarship application to distract her grandmother.

The elevator dinged open, and there was the distraction. Brenda exited the elevator escorted by Bob, a university security guard who had known Brenda and Decimal for years.

Bob looked at Hala and then at Brenda. "I thought you didn't want me to let your mom know you were in the building," he said. "And then you take me right to her."

Brenda stared at the ceiling. Bob shook his head. "Brenda, I can't ban you from the building, given your parents' positions here and how often your daughter needs to be here, but please don't come back to the bazaar until you can look without taking," he cautioned. "It is a charity event, after all. You ladies have a nice day now."

Bob left, and the pervert surveyed the three generations of women as they jiggled their legs and assessed one another.

"Mom, it's a disease," Brenda said. "I can't help it."

"Unlike your brothers, you are not a doctor. So I'll be the one to decide what is a disease and what isn't," Hala said. "Let's just diagnose shoplifting as another one of your screwups and add it to the list."

Decimal sneezed, hoping that would work as a better distraction. Instead of a hug or Kleenex, Hala gave her a frown.

"Why didn't you tell me you were here, Decimal?" Hala said gently. "I went to your allergist, I went to your ophthalmologist, I went to your ENT specialist, and I couldn't find you. Then I thought about you writing that letter to my mother and all the things I didn't want you to tell her about . . . and that's when I knew which floor to go to."

Brenda put her arm around Decimal. "I didn't think there was any reason to worry you about this," she said. "I've got it under control."

"Don't hide behind your daughter," Hala admonished her. "Are you keeping this one or not? Three unwanted pregnancies in one lifetime. I'm a gynecologist, and I have a daughter who is such a complete idiot. Idiot enough to come to the very medical center where her mother became a counselor on birth control education because of her mistakes."

"Fine, Mom," Brenda answered. "Just go and pretend you never knew this happened. Decimal will take care of me."

"No, Decimal is going down to my office," Hala ordered. "I'll stay with you. That's what moms are for, not daughters."

"I don't need you to do that," Brenda said.

"I have to stay," Decimal stated.

Brenda shook her head and motioned Decimal to the elevator.

"You know, in the village my parents came from you would have been shunned for this," Hala said. "You're lazy, you're irresponsible, you're selfish, you're cheap, you're promiscuous, you're . . ."

Decimal hated it when Hala started her Brenda list, the only list she remembered without having to write it down.

"Gran, please stop," she begged. "She didn't do anything wrong. Honest. She really isn't pregnant."

"Decimal, stop defending her," Hala said.

"Yeah, Decimal," Brenda said. "I can handle this myself."

"Decimal, go down to my office, now," Hala ordered again. "Someone half your mother's age would know how to not get pregnant."

"Just go down to Gran's office," Brenda pleaded.

But fifty-five minutes had passed since Decimal had asked the nurse about how long the wait would be. "Decimal Jackson," the nurse called out.

The pervert watched three generations of women glare at one another in confusion and fear.

"What's going on, Decimal?" Hala steeled herself to ask at last.

"Nothing," Brenda interjected. "Nothing."

"But Mom —" Decimal began.

"I said 'nothing,' Decimal," Brenda warned her just as the nurse returned.

"Are you ready, Miss Jackson?" The nurse smiled. "Nice to see you, Dr. Abdullah. We'll take good care of her, don't you worry."

"Decimal?" Hala said, looking at her with the last traces of hope left in her.

"I didn't mean to get pregnant, Gran,"

Decimal told her.

"Oh, God, no," Hala breathed. "Brenda, how could you let this happen to your own daughter?"

"The point is I'm being responsible, Mom," Brenda said. "I brought her here because I told her she was getting a birth control and abortion consultation even before we went to the clinic because I didn't want this happening ever again."

Accusing pairs of eyes shifted around until Hala began to cry softly, followed by Brenda. Decimal reached into her Hello Kitty bag and handed them each a Kleenex. "Let someone else take my place," she told the nurse. "I don't need to see the doctor, after all."

"What are you doing, baby?" Brenda said.

"Look at your mother," Hala warned. "Don't make the same mistake she did."

"I'm not a mistake," Decimal snapped. "You're the one who always says I'm a gift from God. Were you just saying that to make me feel better?"

Hala sat down. "No," she answered, not totally convincingly.

"I've been writing to your mother, Gran, and I've realized a lot of stuff doing that," Decimal continued. "I was thinking about how she raised ten kids and she barely knew

English. Still, she did a pretty good job, and I already got a head start because I speak English. And none of Mrs. Abdullah's kids seem so messed up."

"That's because you don't know them," Hala said. "I don't understand how this happened."

"You're a gyno; you should know," Brenda said.

Brenda put an end to the discussion of how with that. Hala didn't need Paolo and other stuff in her head, just as there was probably so much stuff Hala didn't want Mrs. Abdullah to know. Just as Decimal was going to bond with this person inside her and tell her stuff that she would not want Brenda to know.

"Decimal, having this baby because of an eighty-five-year-old lady from a Podunk village in Lebanon is incredibly stupid," Hala said. "For a highly intelligent teenager."

"Mom, remember when we used to play Who's the Worst Off in the Room?" Decimal ventured. "Well, you never picked you, and neither did I."

"I hid you from all the rough parts," Brenda replied.

"Nah-uh," Decimal said. "In fact, I'm not going to tell my kid even 40 percent of the stuff you've told me you've gone through."

Decimal sat down next to Hala. "Gran, everyone says my mom is a loser for having a kid when she did and stuff. Can you imagine how much more of a loser she'd be without me to keep it together for her? What if I would be lost without this person inside me, you know?"

"What about college, baby?" Brenda asked. She ran her fingers through Decimal's hair and adjusted her hairpin.

"Gran was telling me just today how the U is a perfectly fine place to go to school," Decimal said. "It's not Ivy League, but it's not the crap school you said it was when you decided not to go to college. Maybe we could try a baby-sitting system."

"That didn't work with you," Brenda said. "That's why I decided it was a crap college and quit."

"I'm better at figuring out things than you," Decimal reminded her.

Brenda jiggled her leg. Hala held it down. Then Decimal put a hand on Hala's leg to stop her jiggling.

"I'm only one-third happy about this and the rest just scared poor," Brenda said, readjusting her shirt and bra. "You have no idea what this is doing to me."

"I do," Hala said.

Decimal sneezed, and the other two each

handed her a Kleenex.

Later that night, Decimal took the prenatal vitamins Hala had given her, along with a long list of other things for her allergies and sight and hearing issues. Decimal read through the list one more time and then put on her baggiest flannel pajamas and curled up in bed to finish writing her letter.

The only time in my life I miscounted anything was my menstrual cycle. I calculated it at 28 days, but it really was 26 days. I think that's why I'm pregnant. I'm sure none of this is coming as a shock to you as I'm sure Gran will have called you by now to cry about it, the way Brenda cried in front of Gran. I hope you were nice to her.

When I thought the right thing to do was have an abortion, I thought about not telling Brenda, but then I thought if there was anyone I knew who would understand and stuff, it would be Brenda. She pretty much threw stuff around for two whole days. Then she calmed down and told me she'd kill me if I told anyone about this and that we'd take care of it together. She got extra mad when she thought about how she'd sat down and told me all about sex and how to avoid it and somehow I hadn't listened. I had been listening — it's just that I wasn't thinking about her much when I was with Paolo. Anyway, Brenda said not to tell Tyrone especially because he would flip out if he knew his daughter was sleeping around. I personally don't think having sex three times in your life with the same guy really qualifies as "sleeping around." But I'm not looking forward to telling Tyrone.

The popular girls figure I'm a loser. But you know what, at least I'm not one of those kids hooked on drugs, or with some fatal disease. But what do I know — the parents of those kids are probably going "well, at least my kid's not having a kid." And I can only imagine what the parents who get all worked up about their kids missing tennis practice and stuff would think if they had me for a kid. But really it's not so scandalous — I mean, Paolo and I are the same age, it's not like he was a teacher or something gross like that.

Mrs. Abdullah (I don't want to call you Great-Grandmother Abdullah in case that makes you feel your age), writing to you has really helped me make this decision. And this kid will be one-eighth your genes. That's pretty cool, huh? I'm two months along, so that means I have 210 to 220 days to think about a name, probably closer to 220 days, as I heard first babies come late. I have a lot of pills to take. Gran talked to Dr. Wang to get his input on my extra prenatal care because of my aller- gies. I could hear her crying on the phone when she was talking to him. He's the only person she's ever really been able to open up to in a crisis. Kind of romantic, don't you think? Maybe I've made a mistake so big it will bring them back together.

I felt bad because I heard Gran telling Dr. Wang that because they are doctors people are always asking them questions about how to live well but they wouldn't ask if they could see what a mess their kids were. She said the only questions they could answer for sure were those you could diagnose with the EKG or ultrasound or MRI, and even then you couldn't be totally sure.

You can always visit us. Brenda and I would visit you but whether we went by car, bus, air, we'd barely have enough money and stuff to cover one of us, let alone both of us.

I noticed tonight in the mirror that I had a big, fat zit on the right side of my chin. I can just tell it's juicy inside. Really what I wanted to see is if I looked like a mother in the mirror. I think I do.

Lots of Love,
Aisha "Decimal" Jackson

■ ■ ■ ■

THE 999TH NIGHT

■ ■ ■ ■

SCHEHERAZADE

It was the dawn of the next morning when Scheherazade forced her hand out of Fatima's fortress grip so that she could fold the Hello Kitty letter closed. The more Scheherazade had read, the tighter Fatima's grip had gotten.

"This girl is thanking me for her decisions? *Allah Yustar,*" Fatima screamed. "I talked to Hala three days ago, and all she said was that there was a nice summer breeze. No mention of this child ever in the last seventeen years of weather reports, and this child is now having a child. Even when Hala comes to visit, she never comes with her daughter, sometimes her sons — two doctors, *nushkar rabna,* praise the Lord. I just assumed her Brenda had become a spinster and it caused her too much pain to talk about it, like it does me with Lena."

Unable to find a response that would not offend her further, Scheherazade tried massaging Fatima's shaking hands.

"Speak," Fatima commanded. "I'm sure you want to reprimand me for having another daughter that didn't marry a Muslim. Well, you can't because he converted. It was easy, a meaningless gesture to make us happy."

"It wasn't meaningless if it was to make you happy," Scheherazade pointed out.

"He was still from China," Fatima answered.

"So? Some of the best tales I tell take place in China. Like the ebony horse who made a prince of a man. *Kan ma kan, fi qadim al-zaman,* there was, there was not in the oldness of time —"

"It's not about the Chinese, *ya hamra,*" Fatima interrupted. "They are very smart. If we didn't invent the Arabic numerals first, the Chinese or the Indians would have, but this Chinese boy was not from our village, not even close. Ibrahim knew how hard it was to marry an outsider. We were sure he would leave Hala for a Chinese girl. I did not want her to be sad later. And look at the results — a child like this. I thought Amir would be the death of me."

"Perhaps if you had been more welcoming of Dr. Wang," Scheherazade wondered.

"We were," Fatima said. "All the loans we

took out for Hala's medical school — we refused when Dr. Wang offered it to pay us back when they became wealthy, as if we didn't have pride. But his parents . . . they wanted him to marry a Chinese girl, and so they spoke to Hala in Chinese even though they knew English. That would make her cry."

"Perhaps you spoke to Dr. Wang in Arabic," Scheherazade said.

"No, I did not," Fatima replied. "In fact, I didn't say a word to him at all in any language. And yet they eloped without telling me."

"Oh, child, do not marry a stranger you meet. Our chaff is better than foreign wheat," Scheherazade quoted from one of her own stories.

Fatima nodded. "I told Hala how neither Ibrahim nor Marwan would have dared to treat me badly because then my uncles would have taken care of them — come all the way over from Lebanon to do it — and everyone in the village would have known," she said. "Their whole family would have been shamed. But when a girl marries an outsider, she doesn't have that protection."

"He was not a stranger to her."

"Ha, his parents used to call Hala the white girl like that was bad," Fatima recalled. "But Millie said being white was the best thing you could be. She said her husband wouldn't have minded our kids dating each other if he thought of us as white instead of darkies. I had to remind Millie my daughters didn't date anyone — of any color. They just married."

"And Hala ended up with two boys and one girl and six grandchildren," Scheherazade said. "*Smallah, smallah,* she has more descendants than any of your other children. I would call it a successful marriage."

"Even though she is a gymnologist, I do not think she planned on three children," Fatima said. "She always said that I had five times too many kids, so I think she only wanted two, which is the number of times she separated from Dr. Wang."

"You divorced your husband," Scheherazade countered.

"Only once, and I waited a long time before I did," Fatima said. "I gave it a chance. For sixty-five years, I gave it a chance. She should have tried longer. Perhaps if they had not separated the first time, their daughter wouldn't have become such a bad girl. All but one of my girls were long ago married when I divorced. I could not wait on Lena any longer."

"You and Dr. Wang agree on condemning

Hala's girl," Scheherazade said. "With so much in common with him, it's a shame you were one of the causes of his first separation."

"Do not accuse me of their unhappiness," Fatima seethed. "It takes time to admit that happiness between two people has left forever."

"Where did your happiness go?"

"It wasn't the disappearance of happiness so much as the appearance of sadness." Fatima sighed. "We were too peaceful. Too peaceful. We hardly talked for thirty years."

"Ah, you could no longer trust him with your words," Scheherazade said.

"I still trust him."

"What is love if not trust?" Scheherazade said. "My husband did not behead me because he trusted me to be faithful, unlike his first wife had been with her servant."

"I am not a heroine like you," Fatima said, defending herself. "But my Hala was born in a time of heroes and rationing. There was even a shortage of births. It was the end of the world war. I was one of the few that had a husband too old to go in the military, so I kept on having babies. Hala was the third girl in a row, so I felt Ibrahim's fear even though she was a happy child. . . . She always gave me things, things she made at school, look, even her diploma."

Fatima pointed out a framed photocopy of Hala's diploma from the University of Michigan medical school. Then she flicked Decimal's letter away from her bed.

"Those who give like to get," Scheherazade said. "Give her the house."

"What would people say in the village square about her family?" Fatima shuddered. "*Inshallah,* I have Amir and Tiffany, which makes it much easier for me to die from the shame that will surely get me now."

"But Amir can't —" Scheherazade censored herself as Fatima was too shaken by the letter to take any more bluntness. "Accidents have been happening since before the *jahiiyaa,* the time of ignorance. We do not abandon people for accidents, and I think Hala understands that."

"I did not protect my children well from accidents," Fatima said as heavy tears formed in her eyes.

"Surely you cannot be this tormented merely by babies born out of wedlock, as shameful as that is?" Scheherazade clucked as she gently wiped away Fatima's first tear with the edge of her veil.

Fatima pushed the veil away. "*Khallas.* Enough," she pleaded. Scheherazade thought to inquire a little further. But

Fatima lifted her hand to make her stop talking, and Scheherazade understood that Fatima's thoughts were no longer about Hala.

Then she fell silent for the longest period since Scheherazade had met her. Scheherazade attempted a slightly different approach. "So if you had a daughter that married from the village, she would have been your happiest child?"

"But I do have a daughter who married from the village," Fatima said, slowly looking at Scheherazade again. "Miriam. Ibrahim's first child."

"Ah, the firstborn." Scheherazade smiled, trying to get back to the prideful Fatima. "Always so dear."

"Her face was the plainest of all my daughters," Fatima said. "But it was never easy to see her face because she was always looking at the ground, especially when the children at school began making fun of her. She had a twisted foot when she was born."

"Still, a boy from your village wanted her." Scheherazade beamed. *"Mashallah."*

"All my married daughters were pretty enough to marry on their own at least once," Fatima asserted. "Except Miriam. But *al-hamdillah,* we were able to marry her off. To Joseph Yusef. In New Castle in

Pennsylvania. Joseph Yusef's great-great-grandfather was once one of the biggest landowners in our valley, but he had so many children and they had so many children that eventually no one had a piece of land big enough to make a living from. Joseph Yusef's grandfather left Deir Zeitoon because the American missionaries told many young men in our village that America was the saved place."

"His father became a Christian?" Scheherazade said.

"Don't be silly," Fatima said. "He was saved financially. The missionaries visited Deir Zeitoon once and brought us many Bibles in English and lots of medicine. Mama said not to worry about the Bibles. They only wanted to make the Mount Lebanon Christians their kind of Christians. They gave me a Bible they had translated into Arabic, and Mama told me to thank them and not mention that I couldn't read it in any language."

"Would your grandmother, the great matchmaker, have chosen Joseph Yusef for Miriam if everyone were still back in Deir Zeitoon?" Scheherazade asked.

"What other choices were there, really?" Fatima said. "Ibrahim met Joseph Yusef at a village convention in Lebanon, Pennsylvania, which has no Lebanese people, but the Deir Zeitoonis thought it was a funny name, so they put on their tarbooshes and got together there every year. One day, Ibrahim asked Joseph Yusef, who had driven his grandfather there, if he would like to marry Miriam."

"She and Joseph Yusef agreed so amicably to your arrangement?" Scheherazade wondered.

"I'm sure they would have been happy if Joseph Yusef had lived long enough for the marriage to last more than six months," Fatima said. "But at least she had a child."

"Ya'salam." Scheherazade winked. "She had another miracle baby like Amir."

"No," Fatima corrected. "She got pregnant right before Joseph went to Vietnam. He was one of the last American soldiers to die there . . . finally, something she was able to feel proud about. Which was far more than Ibrahim was expecting her to get from marriage. . . . *Ya Allah,* how can I talk to Ibrahim again? I must call him back to prepare the will for the house in Arabic, but I might blurt out something about this terrible letter girl. I will die of this shame, won't I?"

Fatima bowed her head, her purple stubs staring Scheherazade in the face. It was dawn, and Fatima had not slept all night. Even an old lady counting down time should be spared at least a few hours of conscious mind, especially if it was holding her back from calling the man who loved her. Scheherazade reached into the Ottoman coin belt tied around her waist and pulled out a little satchel filled with chamomile leaves and special herbs. With Fatima's troubled eyes shifted to the letter on the ground, Scheherazade slipped the contents of the satchel in her water glass. She handed Fatima the glass and wiped off one of the pills Fatima had tossed on the floor. She lifted Fatima's head with her hand.

"Take just one of these pills," Scheherazade said. "*Min shan khatri,* for my sake."

"Promise you'll tell me then," Fatima replied.

Scheherazade put her hand to her heart. "I will tell you everything I can tell you. I vow on your mother's mother's grave."

Fatima's hand went to her heart at this most solemn of promises. She swallowed the pill, with Scheherazade guiding the water down her throat until she shoved her away.

"That's enough. I'm not your camel," Fatima said. Her focus was already beginning to fade, and Scheherazade gently brushed her hands across her eyes as she drifted into dreams, surely of the house in Deir Zeitoon.

Scheherazade put the covers over Fatima and lay the dress she had brought from Lebanon on top so that the old lady would have something beautiful to wake up to.

In the meantime, Scheherazade decided, she would pass this new day with Miriam, a daughter whom Fatima had not asked her to go see, as if she were beyond concern, perhaps because she was well taken care of as a martyr's widow.

Scheherazade flew across the mountains and across the widest expanse of wheat fields since the glory days of the Fertile Crescent until she came upon a quiet town of tiny hills dotted with sizable homes, most marred by chipped paint, overgrown lawns, and silence. Not far from there a town for bigger houses identical to one another was being built. That was where Scheherazade found Miriam and the war hero's son. Fatima's bump on his nose was partially hidden from the sun by a hard hat.

ROCK

In Miriam's mind, her marriage had not been that short. In fact, it wasn't until three

401

months after they were married that Miriam's husband died in Vietnam. In the course of their highly sentimentalized marriage — lived mostly apart — Joseph Yusef had managed to leave Miriam with two things: a son still in her womb and a tremendous amount of debt. She had learned to manage both of his legacies, but not without great difficulty. Miriam never spoke to anyone about the sacrifices she had made and vowed to herself that Joe would remain a hero forever — a hero to everyone but Rock, the son she had named after the actor Rock Hudson, one of the many classic film stars she would have preferred to have married.

Rock had known since the fluid drained from his ears as he came out of the birth canal that his father was not a real martyr. His mother was. They were a team, his mother told him, the only family the other had, and so they had to be honest with each other. She had been very honest with him.

"Joe couldn't even live long enough to make me give you his father's first name," she told the six-year-old Rock when his dying namesake was on the cover of *Time* as the first famous closet homosexual to die of AIDS. "We're throwing away all your G.I. Joes. Heaven sakes, no Rock of mine is going to play with dolls, even ones that are war heroes like everyone thinks your father was."

"Good lord, your father gambled away all his money on stupid things," Miriam said when Rock asked for an increase in his allowance to buy new amps for his band. "After Joe died and you were born, I started out at Smith's kneading dough. Slaving at four in the morning. Imagine how hard it was to get a baby-sitter for you at that hour. It took me ten years to work up to head baker and fifteen years to clear his debt. That's why they call money 'dough,' you better believe it."

"For Pete's sake, Joe never ate," Miriam warned Rock when he turned down a second helping of hamburger hot dish. "They almost didn't take him in the army because of his weight. He would have never died a hero then."

"Holy moly, your father dreamed too much," Miriam said when Rock announced that his band might get a gig in Youngstown or Akron. "If he was alive today, he'd have died alone with his fantasies. Did you know he talked about opening a hotel in Florida? I worked to the bone to pay off that swampland he bought. Me, I had no dreams, and I ended up being head baker and then assistant manager at Smith's. That's how life works."

For all Miriam said about Joe, Rock allowed himself to think only one word about his father: *resentment.* He resented his father for leaving him a closet martyr for a mother. Starting with his mother and then his namesake, Rock had dealt with a series of people with closet issues all his life.

After Miriam had taken away all of his G.I. Joes, Rock's head filled up with terrible thoughts he couldn't stop from coming, thoughts about what life would be like if his father had come back, if they had moved to the Florida swampland, what Joe would have done if Miriam had forced him to eat seconds of hamburger hot dish. Rock would always get headaches from those thoughts — until Walt Smith saved him. Walt Smith was Miriam's boss and the owner of Smith's Supermarket. Rock was in third grade when Walt told him about square footage while he was explaining a supermarket remodeling he never went through with.

Ever since then, Rock had gambled nothing in life, dreamed nothing, eaten everything on his plate, and pushed away all terrible thoughts by squaring numbers in his head. He would pick a number and start squaring from there — 3 squared, 9 squared, 81 squared, 6,561. When he'd get in the millions, he'd go backward. Twenty-one years later, Rock built homes for people moving on, subdivisions that cloned small towns into outer-ring suburbs of Pittsburgh and Cleveland. Today Rock was pounding nails into the roof of the last still-uncompleted "Mount Vernon Colonial," the most popular four-bedroom, four-bath model for families planning to move to Sycamore Grove Estates.

"Yo, Rock," Mike called over from the four-bedroom, four-and-a-half-bath Montebello model he was working on. "I bet if you hadn't told the swucking architects to add straps to the roofs, this whole subdivision wouldn't last through one blucking Doppler 10 tornado warning."

"The ratio of square feet to perimeter was off by 0.1," Rock called back. "My grandmother could have figured it out in her sleep."

Rock was feigning modesty, but his spatial and mathematical adeptness, particularly the gift for squaring, was the reason he had gotten a partial scholarship to study engineering at Penn State. But the week of freshman orientation, Miriam had caught a bad cold, and so he had deferred college. She had sniffled that he should go, but her heart hadn't been in the sniffle. A year later, Rock joined the military. Miriam didn't get another cold then. She couldn't have stopped him without looking like an antiwar war hero's wife. He returned to New Castle after eight years because one doesn't abandon a war hero's widow forever.

"Come November, I might take the family down to flippin' Dollywood," Mike yelled over.

Mike looked forward to the off-season, but Rock hated the winter because he had to fill his working time with what he called the New Castle graveyard shift, literally digging graves. It got pretty hectic sometimes.

The money wasn't that good, but Miriam didn't charge him rent. Rock's only expense was Brittney. She was still a little kid, just eight years old, and so there wasn't much to spend on her yet. Her mall days were still a couple of years off. He already had calculated how much to put aside every month for college.

"Wanna grab a brewski after work?" Mike shouted during a lull in hammering. "Sounds like we could pound back a few."

Mike always laughed louder the lamer the joke.

"Don't you got to go to my surprise party, bud?" Rock shouted back.

"Dang, I almost lucking forgot," Mike yelled. "What the heck do you want me to getcha? *Gardner's Mathematical Games?*"

"You bet," Rock hollered. Ever since they had met in first grade, Mike had been getting him the latest *Gardner's Mathematical Games* for his birthday and Christmas. Aside from becoming a born-again Christian and therefore no longer swearing, Mike had changed little since they were kids, when his academic performance destined him to this job as much as Miriam's oppressive love had done the same thing for Rock.

After work, Rock and Mike carpooled back to New Castle in Mike's sky-blue pickup. Rock had driven in the morning, and Mike had to readjust the driver's seat as he had seven inches on Rock. During their morning drive Mike had slept, because he'd been up all night playing *Left Behind: Eternal Forces,* the Christian video game Rock had gotten him for his birthday.

"Don't you ducking wish we could afford to live in the houses we build?" Mike asked as he drove. "Brittney'd like that, I betcha."

"Of course she would," Rock said. "Who wouldn't?"

A person could get lost in the subdivisions' conformity, never having to think about what shade the trim should be or even what door style to get. Rock couldn't pick a door style without overthinking. It would start with "What type of wood should I go with?" move on to "Which style would be too heavy for Brittney to open on her own?" shift to "Would Brittney know what to do if there was a fire in the house and she couldn't open the door?" go on to "Were Brittney's mother and stepfather thinking about her safety?" and end with "Why did my wife leave me for Mike?"

He didn't ask Mike his last question as the pickup passed through the green and concrete highway landscape. He never did.

Near their exit, there was a sign that said, WELCOME TO NEW CASTLE, POPULATION 28,000. Someone had graffitied below "down from 48,000." Mike rolled through stop signs that had become unnecessary years earlier and drove past houses with yellow ribbons on the mailboxes, past boarded-up diners, bakeries, drugstores, and businesses. Smith's Supermarket was one of the few places that remained open, as was Nahla's Restaurant, a Lebanese diner that looked like a pancake house from the outside. "If Joe hadn't brought me to this backward town, you would have grown up eating great Middle Eastern food in Detroit," Miriam told Rock every time they passed Nahla's.

Outside their old high school, two Marine recruiters were talking to a group of boys with hair several inches longer than military regulations. "You hear about Ryan Kapinski?" Mike said. "Sucking dies for their sucking freedom, while his own parents couldn't afford to pay their Penn Power bill last winter. I'd like to show those prucking Johnny Jihads how to be grateful. Ever wish we were still enlisted?"

Mike made a fist and mimed shoving it through the window, as if the window were an Iraqi.

"Life right here is just fine," Rock replied.

"Praise Jesus," Mike said, readjusting the Bible on his dashboard.

Rock had loved the army. The military was the job that paid you to let them do the hard part for you, the thinking part. There wasn't any better gig. Civilian construction workers sometimes had to calculate where to put the nail, but at Fort Bragg construction projects were mapped out very clearly. Combat was unlikely back then, and so there had been no need to think about killing Johnny Jihads or anyone else.

"You coming to Brittney's Bible class graduation next week?" Mike asked.

"I got no other plans," Rock said.

Rock had always hated Sundays the most because everyone was busy with churches, dads, family potlucks — all things that weren't part of his life. Nowhere to go, plenty of time to think. Walt would come over with a chicken from his store about to hit its expiration date. Miriam would roast it with a rice and cinnamon stuffing, and then the three of them would watch a video Walt had chosen from the 99-cent pile at his store. Walt particularly got a kick out of bringing over *Rocky* movies. Still did.

"I'm goin' to put in a new kitchen floor this winter," Mike said. "Carla's thinking we should get them new tiles, Spanish, they call 'em. I'm thinking plain blue, same as the truck."

Rock hated how thinking now crept into mindless conversations with Mike, the one person in life who once had been his buffer to deep thought. Why would you put something as beautiful as Spanish tile in a kitchen where people could walk all over it? How had Carla and Mike gone from adulterers to domesticated Christian tilers? Would Carla have stayed with him if he had taken her to Spain or even to New York, as he'd promised, so that she could audition for a musical? Would Brittney end up with a great

voice, like her mom? Would she waste her
high school years in a band, as Carla had,
thinking she'd be the next Madonna? Had
he and Mike told Brittney enough times
that the military was no place for a girl, even
as a doctor, which he hoped she'd be?

Mike pulled up in front of a yellow Crafts-
man with early-summer daisies and mari-
golds in bloom. It looked like happy people
lived inside.

"Get out so I can pick up your mucking
puzzle book from Smith's," Mike said with
a laugh. As he drove off, he shouted out the
pickup's window: "Too bad God won't let
me look at porn no more. Else I'd get you
some."

Before Rock could head inside, he was
grabbed in a tight hug. Rock knew the hug-
ger before he could see her face: Houda, a
woman who was two-thirds his height and
twice his age and width, was his father's
sister. She wore her hair, which was just a
shade less bright than her red nails, in what
she thought was an elegant bouffant.

"Happy birthday, kiddo," Houda said.

Dawood, standing in the shadow of Houda's hair, stuck out his hand to Rock. He
was some sort of cousin from the family's
village in Lebanon, and he always wanted
to shake hands. Houda had taken him in

411

five months earlier, after he'd lost his fry job at Aladdin's Deli in Queens and ended up owing a lot of people a whole lot more than falafel. Dawood was just another stray for Houda, who had taken in seventeen dogs and three husbands since Rock was born. The dogs and husbands were all gone now. Dawood was the doughnut fryer at Smith's. However, he preferred to be called a sous-chef.

"I checked your mail for you," Houda said, and handed Rock several envelopes. "You got six cards."

Houda opened the mailbox for him every birthday to see if all his other aunts had remembered to send a card. She was the baby-sitter Miriam had found during those 4 A.M. shifts. Although Houda disliked Miriam, she had helped her maintain Joe's heroic image. However, unlike Miriam, she didn't share Joe's flaws with Rock.

"You're just like your father, Rock," she went on. "All the men from our village are so strapping." Rock was only five foot six, and Dawood was even shorter. What little height Rock had, he owed to Miriam, who was the shortest member of her family but taller than Joe had been.

"We'll sneak in so your mom doesn't yell at me for being late for your surprise party,"

Houda continued. She gave Rock another pat on the cheek, scratching the bottom of his chin with her shellacked hair, which smelled like fried cauliflower and eggplant. Houda fried all her vegetables, but only secretly, announcing to the world quite convincingly that she had no idea why she was so fat when she was a vegetarian. "Don't go telling anybody," she used to warn Rock when she'd make him a fried zucchini sandwich topped with fried tomatoes, fried onions, fried potatoes, and fried mint leaves. His aunt, the closet fryer.

"See you soon, *inshallah*," Dawood said. *"Bon soir."* He put out his hand for another handshake and followed Houda's hair to the front entrance of the house.

The first thing Rock or anyone else saw when he walked into Miriam's kitchen was yellow tiled walls with pictures in wooden frames of Joe in his uniform, Rock as a baby, Rock in his uniform, and Miriam in her wedding dress, along with a black-and-white photo of Fatima in her wedding dress. Everyone got to be in photos all by himself in Miriam's house.

"It's my birthday boy," Miriam boasted as she limped over to him. "I was just saying to myself there was some good reason I've been slaving away in the kitchen all day, and here he is."

Miriam went to kiss Rock's cheek. She saw Houda's lipstick on his face. "Your father has such tacky relatives," she said. "Well, happy birthday, son. Can you believe it's been twenty-nine years? But we made it."

She drizzled a platter of raw kibbe with olive oil and sprinkled it with parsley.

"The kibbe looks great, Mom," Rock said before his cell phone rang. Miriam eyed him as he looked at the number until it went to voice mail.

"Jiminy Cricket, you're seeing someone and you don't want me to know about it," Miriam concluded.

"Something like that," Rock agreed. "Come on, we've left people hiding far too long this year." He took the raw kibbe from her, and they went into a wood-paneled living room decorated with thick mustard drapes, old movie posters of famous men and women in love, and coil rugs.

At exactly this time every year, a crowd of twenty jumped up from behind yellow velour furniture that was just a few months older than Rock and began tooting horns. They were led in this endeavor by Carla and Brittney. Walt Smith, bald, fat, and altogether charming, was the first to hug Rock

414

and give him a pudgy man's slug.

Walt had been Miriam's boss since what he referred to as "the tragic death of young Joe," although Walt had been born the same year as Joe. Rock knew that Walt praised Joe only out of respect for Miriam. Joe had borrowed a lot of money from Walt over the years, and Walt had been paid back only for the money borrowed for the swampland in Florida, the only debt Miriam knew about.

Houda, followed by Dawood, popped out from behind a Naugahyde recliner. "Surprise, handsome," she shouted. "It's your birthday."

Dawood shook Rock's hand again.

"Daddy, Daddy, look what I got you," Brittney squealed. Rock took a box clearly wrapped by a little girl — too many ribbons and not enough paper — and unwrapped a G.I. Joe.

Brittney smiled up at him. "Mommy says it's vintage," she said.

Rock hugged his daughter and looked at Carla. Vintage was easy to find in New Castle: You just had to dig into your neighbor's attic. But the G.I. Joe was not a gift for Rock. It was a stab at Miriam.

Carla always let everyone know she was born again, but she was also a closet avenger. Back when he and Carla had been

415

in love, a delusion that had ended completely when Rock had stayed at Fort Bragg and Carla had gone back to New Castle to take care of her ailing mother, Rock had told Carla about Miriam throwing away his G.I. Joe dolls when Rock Hudson died. Although Rock had liked Carla's mother — he'd always liked everything about Carla — Carla hated Miriam. Rock couldn't blame her. Carla's mother, who'd eventually died of Alzheimer's, had had a much more legitimate reason for always forgetting everything Carla said.

Even now, Miriam ignored the G.I. Joe. "Look everyone, I made kibbe," she said. She limped to the dining table and laid the tray down with rare grace. In response, the guests salivated and clapped. This was Miriam's signature dish, made just for Rock's birthdays and Joe's annual memorials, the only two occasions when she entertained. "I don't just make grape leaves like everyone else," she bragged.

"Miriam, you still haven't found me a nice Jewish girl who can make kibbe like you," Walt said. For the twenty-nine years Miriam had been working for Walt, she had promised to find him a nice Jewish girl but had failed. "Even though my great-grandmother was an amazing matchmaker,"

Miriam always told Walt by way of apology, "I guess my family only wanted to give me the family curses, not gifts."

There were no other Jews at the party, practically none in town besides Walt. The other guests were Italian, mostly Carla's relatives — her aunts and uncles, all pushing the seams of their sweats, hair still feathered back mid-1970s style, the last time most of them had felt sexy. That was about the time Carla and Rock were both conceived.

"Just think," Carla said to Miriam. "In four years, Rock will be as old as Jesus when he died. Did you know Jesus was a carpenter, too?"

Carla's relatives, Catholics by birth, shuffled their feet, uncomfortable with religions that weren't simply inherited. But despite her feelings about Rock, Carla wanted Brittney to see some good Christian qualities in her father.

"Say hallelujah," Brittney proclaimed, raising her hands. "My daddy and Jesus do construction."

Who was this adorable, Savior-loving child with teeth in need of braces? She had his nose bump and his perfect scores in math, but he really knew she was his when he caught glimpses of her forehead wrinkling

417

up. He knew she, too, was a closet thinker.

Rock once had promised Carla that after her mom passed, they would move to New York, that they would leave New Castle the way nearly everyone in their high school band had. But Carla got pregnant before her mother died. She said Rock hadn't used a condom because he secretly wanted her not to get a chance to be a singer. By the time his eight years in the army was over, Rock couldn't help thinking that he had disappointed Carla over and over again, just as Joe had done to Miriam from the grave. Mike and Jesus had replaced him easily.

Brittney let go of Rock's hand and pulled off a rubber bracelet way too big for her wrist. "Look what I got for you with my allowance," she said, shoving the bracelet onto Rock's wrist.

"See those letters? They stand for 'What would Jesus do?' WWJD. Get it?" Brittney explained. "The Lord is coming, Daddy, and Mommy says you're going to be saved in time."

"Uh, it's very elastic, honey," he said, catching Carla's eye. All the others not born again looked at Rock sympathetically.

"Come on, big boy, open your other gifts," Walt urged him.

Rock went to the gift table. "Thank you

all for coming," he said. "I'm honored."

Dawood shook Rock's hand again. *"Kul sinni wa inta salem,"* he said. Miriam and Houda shrugged. They had no translation. They could translate single words, but a whole string of them was a little much. Dawood didn't understand that it took only a generation to lose a language.

"Same to you, buddy," Rock said, and shook Dawood's hand again.

"Start with the cards," said Miriam. "My sisters always send the best cards." Miriam bragged loudly about her family. In private, to Rock, she talked about how her family had married her off just to get her out of the house. "I'll never be like that with you, Rock," she would say. "You can stay with me forever."

Rock opened the cards from Miriam's sisters while Brittney danced around him, stopping occasionally to kiss him.

Rock was opening a book from Fatima — the most multicolored version of *A History of the Arab People* she'd given him so far — when his cell phone rang again.

"It's your birthday," Carla said, always sighing at him now the way Miriam did. "Answer it."

"Geez, Louise, go ahead," Miriam chimed in. "There will still be kibbe left when you're done talking to your new phone friend."

Everyone waited for him to answer it. Rock didn't get many calls, and when he did, it was almost always from someone who was already in this room. He let it go to voice mail.

Brittney tugged on Rock's U2 T-shirt. "Oh, Daddy, the Lord is full of surprises," she exclaimed. "Just look."

A pair of chubby hands held a massive cake in the shape of a pastel space shuttle. Miriam gave one of her seldom-heard giggles when Walt poked out his head from behind the cake.

"Remember how you always wanted to be an astronaut?" Walt said. "Well, here ya go. Your very own Rockette. Get it?"

Rock flinched for only a moment when Mike followed in behind the cake, carrying one of the books Walt stocked just for Mike to buy Rock on his birthdays. Mike handed it to Rock and then put his arm around Carla. "Happy birthday, buddy," he said with a smile.

There wasn't a huge dating pool in New Castle for the under-thirty crowd. Carla had had plenty of alone time when Rock was at Fort Bragg. There were no bars for single mothers without child care and no cable at her mother's house. Instead, she had watched evangelist TV and built up resentment toward Rock and a fondness for Mike, who had dabbled in real estate after he got out of the army and helped Carla sell her mother's house, a hard thing to do in New Castle. More people were dying than buying, as Walt always said.

"Dig in, folks," Miriam told the crowd. Everyone homed in on the raw kibbe, ignoring the cheese twists and the seven-layer dip. "Kibbe was Joe's favorite dish." Miriam sighed. "My mother taught me to make it for him when we got engaged."

After everyone had his or her glass filled with Country Time Lemonade, Walt raised his glass in a toast. "Many, many more, kiddo," he said.

Glasses clinked. Houda dinged her glass with her red devil nails. "And to Joe," she cheered.

Rock's cell phone went off when he held his glass up to heaven for Joe.

"Just answer it," Carla snarled.

Rock put down his glass and turned off the cell phone. "She'll call back," he said. Miriam and Carla kept looking at him.

"Get me a beer, buddy," Walter whispered to Rock. "I got a six-pack in the fridge, but I don't want your mom giving me the old lecture about how I need to slow the calories."

Rock found Dawood in the kitchen cutting up the space shuttle cake for the guests. "I'd shake your hand, but me a little sticky," Dawood told him.

"You wanna beer?" Rock asked as he grabbed one for Walt.

"I don't drink," Dawood answered.

"Not much of a drinker myself," Rock replied as he took half the cake's launch pad for himself. No one could make sheet cake like Miriam. Dawood just smiled and watched him eat as if he were a movie, which made Rock uncomfortable. "So, uh, you ever been to Iraq?" Rock asked him.

"Why would I have go to Iraq?" Dawood said, pronouncing the name with the guttural Arabic his grandparents used, as if one couldn't say it without sounding pissed off.

"You're from around there," Rock said. "I thought you might have gone for spring break or something before it all went to hell."

"Have you been to New York?" Dawood asked.

"No," Rock said.

"New York is much closer to this town of yours than Deir Zeitoon is to Baghdad," Dawood said. "But I don't say you're from around New York."

"No, I guess not. . . . A lot of my old buddies have been sent over to Iraq," Rock went on without thinking.

"Haram," Dawood mumbled.

Haram. Sacrilege. One of the few words uttered in Arabic by Miriam when she recalled the suffering in the world, particularly her own. He didn't know if Dawood considered the death of the American soldiers or the invasion of Iraq the sacrilege. Maybe both. He really didn't want to think about it anymore.

Dawood finished cutting the cake just as Brittney came in. Her forehead wrinkled when she saw Rock's face. "What are you thinking, Daddy?"

Rock tickled her stomach. "Want some more cake, baby?"

"I can't, Daddy," Brittney said. "I came to say bye 'cause we've got to go or we're going to be late for service. Don't forget to come to my graduation this Sunday. And don't drink any of Mr. Smith's beer if you can help it. It's the devil's Pepsi." She kissed him goodbye and skipped out.

"God is better than a meth lab, right?" Rock shrugged, not knowing why his thoughts never drifted to any options in between.

Dawood shrugged back and took the cake to the living room. The party was down to the regular old Catholics and Muslims and Jew. Carla's relatives had finished the kibbe and so were obliged to move on to the seven-layer dip, which they did with slightly less enthusiasm. Houda discreetly placed some tortilla chips in her purse. Walt helped Miriam clean up, and she giggled at something he said.

By the time Rock got up at 5 A.M. on Sunday to get ready for Brittney's confirmation, he had finished the math teasers book and had not returned his last six cell phone calls. He would today, he promised himself, and then pushed the thought away. By 6 A.M., Rock was driving on US 422 with Miriam, Houda, Walt, and Dawood, heading to the Cornerstone Church in Youngstown for the eight o'clock service. The Yusefs were New Castle's only Muslim family. Until 9/11, they had been known mostly as a military family. However, for a few weeks after that day, people who had never invited Miriam and Rock over before asked them to Sunday dinner and other neighbors came over with cakes to show that President Bush was right: Arab Americans and Muslim Americans were Americans period. That very support made them aware that they were no longer just Americans.

The Cornerstone Church in Youngstown once had been a supermarket owned by Walt. Now it held two thousand people every Sunday. The band was jamming. The drummer was tight, and Carla's voice rocked out in praise of God's love. Rock watched her on the video screen. Carla had said that this church was a little too liberal for an evangelical church, but it was good to be around God-fearing people, and it gave her a bigger audience for her singing than she'd ever had.

"Amazing what they've done with the place," Walt remarked. "The pulpit is right where the fruits and vegetables used to be." They found seats in the unobtrusive middle, near what had been the cereal aisle.

Up front, Brittney skipped in with several other girls in white ruffle dresses. The video screens showed them up close and giggling. When Carla stopped singing, the boyish blond minister motioned for everyone to sit.

"Let us pray," he said. The two thousand people bowed their heads. Rock could not imagine all the thoughts that must creep into prayers, and so he began squaring 8, in honor of Brittney's age. He tuned out the service, Dawood's uncomfortable shifting, Miriam's sighs, and Walt's comforting hands, one on Miriam's arm and one on Rock's.

But the minister's voice kept coming through the church's powerful speakers.

"The righteous shall flourish like the palm tree: He shall grow like a cedar in Lebanon."

"What he say about a cedar tree in Lebanon?" Rock heard a confused Dawood ask Houda. "Is America going to invade Lebanon?"

Rock looked up at the minister. What had he just said about Lebanon?

"The righteous shall flourish like the palm tree: He shall grow like a cedar in Lebanon," the minister repeated.

Who was righteous?

He looked at the WWJD bracelet Brittney had made him and then couldn't stop thinking about the cedars in Lebanon. Lebanon, whose food he had grown up eating, whose language came out of his mother's and Houda's mouths at unexpected times, where so many Marines had died when he was a little kid. How many Marines had died in Iraq? How many Iraqis had died in Iraq? This religion his daughter loved had always been a New Castle thing to Rock, but its roots were not in a former supermarket. Its principles came from where his grandparents had come from. It had come to New Castle from the Middle East with a stop in Europe, just as his grandparents had. Those thoughts ran through his head until Walt squeezed his hand hard enough to make him hear his ringing phone. This time he was thinking so hard that he answered it so that it would stop disturbing his thoughts.

"Oh, yes, yes, ma'am . . . I've been meaning to call you. Yes, I'll go," Rock whispered. "But I can't talk now. I'm in church. . . . Bless you, too."

Rock hung up and put the cell phone on vibrate. From afar, he saw Carla looking at him. Two people away, he felt Miriam doing the same thing.

"Who's your call girl?" Dawood whispered.

"You don't say 'call girl,' dude," Rock whispered. "You say the girl who called. Big difference, especially in a church. Besides, she wasn't a girly girl."

Houda gave them a warning look, shaking her shellacked 'fro. "*Bien,* what kind of girl was she?" Dawood said in a quieter whisper.

Rock hesitated and then motioned his distant cousin closer. He had to tell someone or he would start thinking about it too much.

"I've got a gig in Iraq," Rock whispered.

"Gig?" Dawood asked.

"Shush," Houda whispered.

"What does 'gig in Iraq' mean?" Dawood whispered to her.

"Gig?" Houda whispered. "Well, it means. . . . Oh, my God. Rock, what gig in Iraq? Are you back in the reserves?"

"What are you talking about?" Miriam said in a hush.

"Dude, I was whispering because it was a secret," Rock groaned.

"When were you going to tell us?" Walt said.

"Iraq, no, no." Miriam stood up, sobbed, and brought all the attention away from the sermon and those about to graduate. "My son cannot be sent to Iraq."

The minister stopped preaching. Miriam's outburst had taken many in the church back to the reality they escaped from at least once a week, surrounded for two hours in faith and hope and the promises of the power of prayer to bring their husbands, sons, brothers, and boyfriends home safely. Miriam no longer was crying alone. A less godly man than the boyish minister might have displayed more irritation at this intrusion on

428

his sermon. "My brother is there, too, ma'am. He's my best friend," he told Miriam quietly, and then spread his arms out to encompass the congregation. "Let us pray for your son and all our soldiers in harm's way."

They all bowed their heads in unison. "You'll just tell them you're your widowed mother's only son," Walt whispered.

"No one is making me go, Mom," Rock told her. "Stop crying and let the minister go on."

"I've already given up so much for this county," Miriam wailed. "But not you. Please, no." The more reserved women of the congregation covered their mouths to hold back their cries, and younger women clasped the hands of the plump older women who were frailer than they were, having known the losses of Vietnam as Miriam had, which had been numerous in this town. Rock wanted to tell them that their sons and brothers in Iraq and Afghanistan were much braver than they could imagine. He didn't think he would be brave enough if he were still in.

Mike walked up the aisle and hugged Rock. "You kick some ass over there, buddy," he said.

"Shut up, Mike," Carla yelled at them

from the stage. As she walked down to Rock, the cameraman followed her, not seeing the minister waving at him not to. Everyone watched on the TV monitors. This was proving to be her biggest performance to date.

"I have prayed every night that you would be called, and here you are in church being called," Carla began. "But this isn't the kind of calling I meant. You have a daughter to think about."

"I'm not going to fight," Rock explained. "I'm going to be building schools over there. Righteous stuff. Someone has to do the righteous stuff."

"You build schools again you bombed," Dawood hissed.

"What do you want America to say? The damage is already done," Rock said. "All we can do now is fix it."

"You can't fix dead people," Dawood snapped.

Rock heard the one cry he couldn't bear to hear. He looked down at Brittney's face, which had crinkled into thinking furrows, thoughts cruising through her head.

"You're why I'm going," Rock said, and picked her up. "I can pay for your college in two years with the money I'll make."

"I can pay for college," Mike said. "Who

430

knows where I'll be in real estate by then."

"I don't want your help, Mike," Rock answered. "She, at least, is still mine."

Brittney's forehead crinkled more as Carla's face reddened.

"Let us pray for peace and freedom for all of God's children," the minister said. Despite his boyish face, the minister's voice made it clear that this was not a matter of choice. Most of the congregation prayed with their eyes open, looking at the Yusefs until the choir leader confiscated the cameraman's equipment. Then the minister pounded his fist on the podium, commanding attention. "One man's decision to go to Iraq reminds us of our own war efforts," he told them. "The clothes drive we're spearheading for Iraqi orphans, the funds being collected to help with college fees for U.S. soldiers' children, in conjunction with the New Castle Widows' Relief Fund." That was an organization Miriam had started, an altruistic effort that forever reminded the community of her tragedy.

Rock did not hear any of this because he saw that the bounce in Brittney's white gown was gone. Mike and Carla each held one of her hands. "This will probably save your dad's soul from damnation," Carla comforted her. Brittney's forehead started uncrinkling.

"Really?" Brittney asked Rock.

"Listen to your mother," Rock said by way of an answer. "Especially while I'm gone."

Carla mouthed "thank you" but did not smile.

Two days later, Rock was at home alone packing. He had made Walt take Miriam to help organize his surprise going-away party at Smith's. He'd gotten most of what he needed in a duffel bag. It would be 120 degrees there. He saw Brittney's WWJD bracelet. He had meant to put it in his duffel bag. For now, he put it on his wrist.

Rock originally had downloaded the job application from an ad in the paper because it had given him somewhere to hide at lunch when Mike would talk about the minutia of his life with Carla with the other guys on the job. It was a long application, and it had forced Rock to do a lot of thinking. They were offering nearly $100,000 a year for contract workers, compared with the $1,500 he took home every month here. He'd even be able to pay back Walt for all of Joe's debts.

The San Diego–based construction company warned him of the bombings, the kidnappings, the deadly spiders, and all the other things that were killing both Iraqis and Americans. He'd heard on CNN the other day that the death toll so far was 100,000 Iraqis and 759 U.S. soldiers. But he was not going to be in theater. He was going to be building a school. Rock figured that despite all the deaths, the majority of men and women were coming back alive and uninjured. He was, in fact, looking forward to being the man — the only man — who took care of his daughter. She would go to college somewhere else, somewhere good.

There were more people in Smith's waiting to tell Rock goodbye than had ever been there as customers in Rock's lifetime. Walt turned the Muzak down, and everyone clapped. Rock made his speech brief. "I wish you all safety and peace," he said. "Now, party on." Rock talked to several people before going to his mother. Miriam's real tears and her crocodile tears had melded together over the years, but today the crocodile was missing.

"You're all I have," Miriam sobbed.

"I'm coming back." Rock hugged her. Whole, he told himself. Dying did not scare him, but he couldn't bear the thought of Miriam having to care for him if he came back incapacitated.

Brittney snuck in between them and clung

to Rock. "I'll pray for you all the time, Daddy," she said. "I always do."

"Thank you, sweetie."

"Did you know that I have heard the cedars of Lebanon mentioned thirty-five different times in the Bible so far?" she told him. "I'm always counting Bible things so I don't fall asleep in church. Even while I'm praying for you, I'll keep counting cedars and tell you how many more there are."

"We're going to go now, Rock," Carla broke in.

"All right." Rock nodded. When he was able to get out of Brittney's hug, he looked at Carla, but he didn't hug her. He couldn't stand to touch her. He still saw her and only her when he masturbated, always had since he was sixteen, when she had replaced the black-and-white movie stars on Miriam's living room wall as his inspiration.

Mike smothered Rock in a hug. "Don't let them puck you around, man," he said. "Or else I'm coming after them — you tell them that." And then they were gone. Rock had planned to take Brittney's bracelet off when she left, but he didn't.

He watched them drive away and then took Miriam's hand. "Mom, you are not alone," he said. "You should marry Walt."

"Where are all these crazy thoughts coming from?" Miriam said. "First Iraq, now Walt."

"Say yes if he asks you is all I'm saying," Rock replied.

"Why would he do that?"

"Because he loves you."

"Fiddlesticks," Miriam said. "Men have never loved me. And now, with all these wrinkles on top of it all."

"So if you were young and beautiful, you'd marry him?" Rock asked.

"What would I want with an old man like that then?" Miriam retorted. "That'd be like marrying my dad. My dad didn't even like having me around that much. Besides, Walt doesn't think of me that way."

"Maybe because you don't let him," Rock said.

"He's just impressed with how I can do the books at the store," Miriam said.

"He could have just bought a calculator," Rock said.

"He's always asking me to fix him up with a nice Jewish girl. He's a Jew," she added just when Rock thought she had run out of excuses. "You know how they are about us."

"Have you ever seen Walt with another girl, Jewish or not, nice or not?" Rock asked. "Maybe if you'd stop talking to everyone in town about how great my dad was, he'd have a chance to ask you."

An hour later, it was time for Rock to leave New Castle.

Miriam was too distraught to drive Rock to the airport, and so Walt gave her a sedative and laid her down to rest on the couch in his office. "I'd better stay with her," Walt said. Rock really hoped Walt would come out of the closet about his feelings for Miriam.

Houda drove Rock's pickup, and Dawood sat next to him as Rock watched New Castle sink into the hills. Dawood shook his hand once and then again.

"Au revoir," he said. "Go and come back in peace, *inshallah."*

"Inshallah," Rock said back.

Houda cried as she hugged him, and he smelled the Fritos she'd snuck out of the supermarket.

From the airplane, Rock watched America shrink into cookie-cutter tracts he had helped build, growing patches where everything, at least on the outside, looked like everything else — where his work was indistinct. They were towns that rarely made it to maps — certainly, he was sure, not the maps of America studied in the Middle East.

Rock turned away from the person next

to him, who looked like she wanted to start a conversation. He was the world's best silent partner. He had never let his mom or his wife or his daughter or his best friend know his thoughts. He barely let himself know them. He was going where people would want only his thoughts on construction. He was going to a place everyone wanted to help, send aid to, invest in, unlike New Castle, which everyone wanted to leave.

He didn't want to think of the people in New Castle, who would not go anywhere until he came back. He began squaring 7 for the number of years he had loved Carla before she had noticed him. Maybe he could keep squaring it until he got to Baghdad.

■ ■ ■ ■

THE 1000TH NIGHT

■ ■ ■ ■

SCHEHERAZADE

As Scheherazade left New Castle, she thought that its first immigrants must have been blessed with a very good sense of humor. Not one castle, old or new. In fact, New Castle reminded her of the quiet that filled the villages back home after a battle had been lost on home soil.

Back in Los Angeles, Scheherazade climbed up the eucalyptus tree and inhaled the scents of hope and life she had lost in Miriam's presence. From there, Fatima appeared most at peace as a result of the satchel of chamomile and special herbs she had given her. The embroidered dress from Lebanon still lay across her lap.

It took Scheherazade only a moment to notice that a new petrol caravan was parked below her tree.

"I checked with this Amir Abdullah's agent," Sherri Hazad said from inside the petrol caravan. "She says he's not scheduled for any auditions tomorrow, so maybe that wasn't just wardrobe he was wearing the other day."

"Hmm," replied a man wearing an identical severe blue costume.

"I'm the new kid on the block," Sherri Hazad told her partner. "I got a tap on the phones, but other than that I'll defer to you on how to proceed."

"First, remember that if there isn't anything here, we can look into the possibility of recruiting him to help us better infiltrate the community," he told her. "So we have to keep it civil. By the way, there is entirely too much interference on the phone tap. When the call came in from Detroit, no one could make out what the guy was saying, so he never got to finish — and Detroit's an Arab hotbed. All we're getting are calls between people not understanding the other, and that's not helping anyone."

Scheherazade refused to let them annoy her further. She climbed from the tree into Fatima's room. Decimal's letter was still on the floor, and she placed it on the night-stand next to Fatima. *Miskinni,* poor thing. It would be unbearable to know that the longest branch on one's family tree had grown so fast because of what Scheherazade used to tell her beloved sister Dunyazad was loose behavior. But loose did not mean unloved.

Fatima's chest moved up and down heavily, and her forehead was coated with a cold mist of sweat. "My potions have always worked exceptionally well, *ya seiti.*" Scheherazade shook her gently. "*Yallah,* wake up."

Fatima gave her an unconscious swat but did not respond beyond that. Scheherazade gently patted her cheeks. Nothing. She picked up the embroidered dress and hung it up by the windowsill. Then she massaged Fatima's swollen pink and purple hands. She gracefully waved her wrists across Fatima's face so that the aroma of eucalyptus would wake her. She whistled gently, letting her breath course between Fatima's purple stubs. Nothing.

Scheherazade snuck away from the old woman to Amir's mosaic bathroom, the one place in the house that justified turning the care of the house in Lebanon over to him. She turned on the water and looked for the rosewater and lavender oil. None of the odors from the many bottles lining the bathtub's edges were familiar to her: lavender shampoo that barely smelled like lavender and lemon soap that smelled of pine, all with price labels higher than coveted frankincense.

This indoor plumbing of today did cut down on the number of servants needed to run a house, but people no longer knew how to bathe. They actually stood up most of the time and let the water fall on them. Where was the comfort in standing under a waterfall that was not real when the world was filled with real ones?

She stepped out to the garden, which was fragrant with jasmine in the dusk breeze. She picked open flower buds, grabbed a handful of mint and tucked it in her silk corset, and plucked some rose petals. She floated the clippings from the garden in the tub and went to wake Fatima.

"I made you a *hammam*," Scheherazade cooed. "*Yallah,* don't waste it."

No response. "Hey, as a mortal princess I never once drew my own bath," Scheherazade said a little less tenderly. "I'm treating you like royalty, as I think every woman should experience that once in her life. Get up, by God, and enjoy it, *ya,* Queen of America. Now. We can even go back to talking of your death if you wish."

With that, Scheherazade shook Fatima until she sat up. "Don't cry, *ya awladi,* my kids, I'm coming," Fatima mumbled. Then she buried her head back in the pillow as if needing to hide in her dreams again.

"You've been sleeping for eighteen and a half hours," Scheherazade announced with a jingle of the gold coins on her belt.

"What?" Fatima said, and shook her head until she was wide awake. "Why did you let me? *Ya Allah,* I only have one day left to get Amir the key. And I still need to call Ibrahim about the papers."

She seemed to have forgotten about the letter, *al-hamdulilah.* Scheherazade followed Fatima and her cane to the bathroom, nearly skipping to keep up with her sudden energy. The aroma rising from the bathtub quickly calmed Fatima. Her hurry drowned in the scent of the water.

"I don't want to get my cane wet," Fatima said. "My grandfather made it —"

"Yes, yes," Scheherazade interrupted, and took the cane from her. She slid the pink robe off Fatima.

"Did Tiffany come again?" Fatima asked.

"I wouldn't know," she said. "I was visiting Miriam."

As she carefully helped Fatima, practically a twisted skeleton of brittle bones, into the bathtub, the old lady turned to her.

"You didn't like her, did you?" she said.

As the warm water quickly enveloped Fatima, her face fell into the same look of

445

paradise she'd seen for the first time on Millie's face when she had bitten into that tube of cookie dough forty-three years ago.

"Without your cane, you have the same limp as your daughter," Scheherazade remarked.

"I didn't ask you to visit her because I knew you wouldn't like her," Fatima complained.

In response, Scheherazade forced open the jasmine buds so that Fatima could breathe them in.

"*Ma'leesh,* it's okay," Fatima said. "No one likes her, but that is my fault."

Scheherazade gently sprinkled the bathwater on Fatima, but Fatima did not relax completely. "When I found out I was pregnant with Miriam, I thought it was the perfect time for Ibrahim to have his first child," she remembered. "Mr. Ford had finally allowed the union to come in after Ibrahim and fifty thousand other workers went on another strike. The strikes were the talk of the town, but Ibrahim was never hurt like Marwan."

"*Al-hamdulilah,*" Scheherazade replied. "Thanks be to God."

"Then Miriam was born two weeks early," Fatima went on. "With the twisted foot. On the day Pearl Harbor was attacked. Her birth was the only thing she ever did prematurely. Everything else, she was last to do."

"Like marrying?" Scheherazade asked.

"Way before that," Fatima replied. "I first noticed it with those silly physical education classes they make the girls take in this country, as if life isn't a physical education. She always insisted on taking part, even though I could have gotten her a doctor's excuse. I told her, 'Why do you want to do something that you already know you will finish last in?' But I think she thought she might not be last. Always with the fantasies, that one. She used to hang up pictures of movie actors on her wall — Cary Grant, Clark Gable, Humphrey Bogart — men old enough to be her father, like she might one day marry a star. But she did not marry until she was thirty-six, and then her time with Joseph Yusef was so short, *Allah yirhamu.*"

"Sometimes a few days of happiness can sustain a lifetime," Scheherazade remarked.

"At least she no longer had to listen to people talk about her not being married," Fatima said.

"How do you know people talked of her?"

"Wouldn't you have?" Fatima said. "I know what Nabila, Hikmat, Aida, and the rest of the Arab Ladies Society, all full of their married daughters, were always saying, I'm glad those gossips, may they all rest in peace, died before they could whisper about Lena."

"They criticized the rose," Scheherazade said, quoting a favorite proverb and reprimanding Fatima by splashing her with water. "They said its cheek was red."

Fatima splashed her back. "Miriam didn't help matters, always frowning," she said. "She started saying the house was too crowded. Lena and Bassam were the only other children still at home, but they were only eleven and fourteen; then Soraya moved in with Amir. Soraya was seven years and seven months younger than Miriam and already had a miracle child. I saw the anguish on Miriam's face. She started talking about moving to an apartment and living alone. A girl living on her own like her parents didn't want her? *Aabe,* shame. Millie said it was okay, but Millie was American, so she didn't understand. I even asked Millie if she knew any American boys, but she said all the young men she knew were either already married or divorced. I told her that divorced was okay, but Millie was Catholic and wanted no part in that. I may have never divorced Ibrahim if she were still alive next door to shun me."

"But Miriam's life turned out so lovely," Scheherazade said a little too effusively.

"Miriam was the first sign that our marriage was to be dark," Fatima remembered. "Ibrahim blamed himself for her being a girl, for her foot, for not being as pretty as Marwan's Laila. I used to tell Miriam not to feel bad about how Ibrahim always looked away from her because he didn't want her to see his pity, especially after we took her to surgeons who only did more damage and she had to be content with their 'We're sorry.' I told her we were just lucky she wasn't born with polio or something like smallpox because the doctors would have probably killed her. And Hala told her it wasn't her fault, and she was going to become a doctor and fix the mess the other doctors made."

"Sometimes just the implication that there is fault to be had makes one feel fault," said Scheherazade, who was beginning to sympathize with Miriam despite herself.

"*Yallah,* she survived." Fatima sighed.

"Survived what?" Scheherazade said.

"Life, which is all I hoped for all my kids after —" Fatima stopped herself.

"After what?" Scheherazade prodded. But Fatima only looked straight ahead.

"Ah, so now you have learned my trick of

stopping at the most tantalizing part," Scheherazade said. "Come now, do not save all the good stories for the last night. After what?"

Scheherazade dipped her hands into the scented bathwater and massaged Fatima's temples and neck to relax her into continuing.

"When I was a mother with Lena, people used to say I was too old to know what was going on with her," Fatima said. "When I was with Laila and Miriam and Hala, everyone said I was too young to know what I was doing. I was not the right mother at any age for any of my children."

Fatima dunked her head under the water and cupped her shriveled breasts.

"Maybe if Miriam had drunk from me." Fatima sighed. "She and Hala are the only ones I did not breast-feed because of the war — I had to work. All the factories were in need of women. But Ibrahim didn't want me doing disrespectful work for a woman. So I started at the White Castle. I was one of the first women ever to work there. I'd make hamburgers, two up and six across."

"Was White Castle nicer than New Castle?" Scheherazade asked.

"There was a man in New Castle willing to marry Miriam, and I think she was grateful for that," Fatima said.

"Gratitude is a huge part of love," Scheherazade agreed.

"I was half Miriam's age when I married the first time, so she was probably doubly grateful," Fatima said. "She wasn't like Lena with a big job to give her status. Just a secretary at Ford. I'm sure people thought she would be able to marry an older man, like I had the first time. But I told Ibrahim whatever man he could get for her, please don't let him be too old. So she married someone ten years younger."

"Smallah, smallah." Scheherazade winked.

"Ibrahim told Joseph Yusef that after he finished with Vietnam he would get him a good job at Ford," Fatima continued, ignoring Scheherazade's wink. "But he didn't live, and Detroit was all strikes and lay-offs in any case. Still, I told her to come home. Amir and Rock were close in age. But she said Joseph Yusef was too important to her to leave the town where he had planned on growing old."

Scheherazade crushed the lavender leaves in her hands to release their oil and then massaged the oil into Fatima's scalp, in between the stubs of purple hair.

"That son of Miriam's is *azeem,* an amazing house fixer," Scheherazade noted. "Perhaps you should give Miriam the house. Her son is a hundred percent of Deir Zeitoon, the only grandchild you have like that."

"A Jewish man really actually does like Miriam, Soraya told me, and *inshallah* Miriam will marry him," Fatima replied.

"Inshallah?" Scheherazade said, massaging Fatima's neck.

"She has spent almost her whole life without a man. Alone is not good," Fatima said. "But she can't go to Lebanon with a Jew for a husband."

"*Y'khsara,* too bad," said Scheherazade, crushing the rose petals to release the last of their aroma. "When my husband was in charge, from even long before the caliphs ruled with faith in God and man, Jews lived among us as *wazirs,* merchants, and bankers, and oh, the poets among them that flourished in Andalusia."

"That was before the European ones took Palestine," Fatima reminded her. "But it was through a Jew that I met Amir's Tiffany. The wrath of Israel is not all that we have received from them. Certainly they did not bring me the worst wrath I have known."

Before Scheherazade could ask what wrath she was speaking of, Fatima closed her eyes and dunked her head under the water, which caused half of it to splash onto the marble floor.

Fatima came out of the water long enough to say, "Don't let my cane get wet. I'm leaving that to Miriam." She plunged back under the water.

AMIR

Amir was rehearsing with his *thowb,* beard, and script when he heard Fatima splashing in the bathtub, apparently having a water fight with herself. At least she was awake. Her long sleep had bothered him. She had even refused to wake up when he had shouted that the Lions were on TV. Maybe he had said the wrong animal. Maybe he should have said the Tigers. She also had missed a whole cycle of pills.

He stepped out to the front lawn to water it and saw Soap Boy's newest SUV. On the upside, he had heard at his own audition today that the soap might be killing off his ex next week. He was a lousy lover, even as an actor.

Before he could give his former lover's wheels the finger, his cell phone rang.

"Yeah, Tiff, tomorrow's the big day-o," Amir shouted into the cell phone over the sound of the hose. "If things go well, I might need you to come over and make my grandmother take her pills and get her all calmed down. She digs you, dude. You're the best beard ever."

Amir put the cell phone away and heard more splashing from inside the house. He began watering the fig tree to drown out the sound of Fatima drowning in insanity. Why were his lavender bushes so picked over? Where had all the rose petals gone?

He looked up at the bathroom window, where Fatima's solo water fight had only gotten louder. Jesus Christ.

"Excuse me," said a little female voice behind him. Startled, Amir turned around and sprayed a very tan, skinny string of a girl. She jumped back as he turned off the water.

"Kid, I'm sorry," Amir said. "You caught me off guard."

The tiny thread of a person started shivering. Amir released the shawl around his neck and wrapped it around her tightly.

"Really sorry, kid," he said. "I almost washed away all that bronzer."

He thought it was funny, but she only sneezed. "That's just my color. It doesn't wash off," she said with an accent Amir couldn't quite place.

"That's cool," Amir said. "Let me get you some dry clothes. You shouldn't talk to strangers, but I'm safe."

"That's a pretty dress you're wearing," the girl said through chattering teeth. "But I'll be fine with these clothes. I'm very near where I have to be, I'm sure. Maybe a tenth of a mile away at the most. In fact, I thought this was the house."

The girl reminded him of someone. "Who are you looking for?" he asked. "I know the neighborhood pretty well."

"Fatima Abdullah," the girl chattered. "She should be pretty old. Let me just look at the address again."

She sneezed and dug into her tiny purse, which Amir noticed had a Hello Kitty sticker. Then he placed the accent: Minnesota. The Hello Kitty envelope from Many Happy Police.

"Dude, you're the girl that sent the letter yesterday," Amir said. "Sorry, we haven't had a chance to read it yet."

"Oh," she said as she looked up at the splashing water. "Well, I suppose she doesn't need to read it anymore since I'm here and stuff."

Amir offered her his hand. "I'm Amir, her grandson."

"I'm Decimal, her great-granddaughter," she explained.

"From who?"

"I'm Brenda's," Decimal said.

It took Amir a couple of seconds to place his cousin Brenda on the family tree. "Oh, yeah," he said. "My mom says she is quite the . . . I'm just glad she and Aunt Hala sent you to visit. I was beginning to think nobody was going to respond to my e-mail."

"Nobody sent me," she said. "This is a 100 percent surprise."

"She could use a pick-me-up," Amir said. "Come on in. I've got a Mickey Mouse sweatshirt to keep you warm. I got it when I played Pluto at Disneyland. Don't say that's not real acting — it was one tough gig. How about some of Fatima's kibbe?"

"Kibbles?" Decimal grimaced. "Isn't that dog food? I'm allergic to dogs, so I don't think I'd do any better with their food. No offense, you know."

Jesus Christ, the girl didn't even know what kibbe was or, more important, that Fatima had been the best kibbe maker in greater Detroit. Amir opened the front door for Decimal, and the girl clutched her Hello Kitty bag a little more tightly as they went inside.

Agent Sherri Hazad

In the new SUV, Sherri Hazad turned to her partner.

"Maybe the girl's an accomplice," she said. "Did you see how he waited for her? He kept watering the fig tree just to give himself an excuse to stay out."

"Could have been a signal to the girl as to where to stop." Sherri Hazad's partner nodded.

"Or he might have been using that loud-ass water hose to make sure no one heard his phone conversation. I caught the words 'the big day tomorrow,' and that syncs up with what the grandmother was saying."

"It's a world we don't really know," Sherri Hazad's partner admitted. "Anything's possible. Good work your first year out."

"Now what?" she asked.

"You tell me," he said. "I want to see how you handle this. And get that phone tap fixed so they can actually talk to each other."

Fatima

Fatima stopped ducking in and out of the water when Scheherazade finally held her still enough to hear Amir's knock on the bathroom door.

"Sounds like she's got company," she heard a muffled female voice say from the other side of the door. "I could come back later."

"No, you're the company," Amir said to the other voice. "You'll make her day."

"Okay," said the female voice.

"Amir, is that Tiffany?" Fatima shouted. She whispered to Scheherazade, "Go get my hearing aid and faraway glasses."

"There isn't enough time," Scheherazade said.

"I said go," Fatima shouted, and shooed her toward the bathroom window.

"We've got company, Tayta," Amir shouted. "You might not want her to go."

"Company?" Fatima yelled. They never had company unless it was someone Fatima had invited to dinner to marry Amir.

"She's family," Amir replied.

Fatima heard a girlish giggle and sat up as straight as her body and the bathtub let her. Of course, if Tiffany agreed to marry Amir, she wouldn't be company. She'd be family. Who knew Tiffany could giggle? Charming giggle, at that.

"I read in *National Geographic* that everyone's like family in Lebanon," the girl outside said. "That's cool." Yes, it was. It meant she understood Deir Zeitoon. She would teach him to love the house and Deir Zeitoon.

Fatima inhaled the scents from the water. She would call Ibrahim tonight and finalize it. It would be the last time she spoke with him before what could at this point only be a quick death, a death she was, *alhamdulilah,* fully prepared for. She hoped he had paid the phone bill so they wouldn't get cut off again.

"What does 'Tayta' mean?" the female voice asked.

"Grandma in Arabic," Amir answered.

"You can call me Tayta, too," Fatima shouted out to them.

"Well, of course she can," Amir shouted back at her. "Now come out."

Fatima put both arms on the tub rails to hoist herself up. It did not work, nor did it on the second and third tries. *"Yukhrub beit el-shetan,"* Fatima swore. "Curses on the devil's house."

She splashed back into the tub.

"Tayta, what's going on?" Amir called out.

"I can't get out of the tub," Fatima shouted back.

"Oh," Amir said. "Well . . . do you want me to come get you out?"

Fatima would rather have eaten Millie's cabbage rolls 101 times over than have her

459

grandson see her naked. But she had no choice. "Okay, but you alone," she said. "She is family, but still . . ."

"What?" Amir said as he tentatively opened the door.

He averted his eyes as he came toward the tub and stretched out his arms to her. She took his hands and then averted her eyes, mainly because she couldn't stand to see him see her naked, especially in that ridiculous beard.

"*Yallah,*" Amir encouraged her. "One, two, three."

Amir pulled her up by the arms, the beard tickling the back of her neck. But she slipped out of his grasp and splashed away.

"Jesus Christ, I don't know what happened," Amir said. He looked away so that she could reposition herself without him seeing anything.

"In all those physics classes you must have studied more than the stars," Fatima said, trying to sit up straighter. "You made a bathtub that has too much gravity to escape."

"It's not your weight," Amir said, eyes still averted. "You're slippery. How much bath oil is in there?"

"It's all from the garden," Fatima replied, knowing that the floral scents were far better than the smell of aging flesh that her friends and husband in Detroit emitted and that she could only assume she also had developed.

If Amir couldn't get her out of this bath tonight, this would be where her flesh would die. And it would be in Amir's arms, as she had wished for the last three years. But if she was going to freeze to death, wouldn't that already have happened in Detroit, where freezing was a more natural cause of death than it was in Los Angeles?

"Try again, *habibi*," Fatima commanded. "Pretend, like you do for your hobby, that you are big and strong."

Amir's eyes opened to a narrow squint, just enough to see through his lashes. He took his place in back of her. "Give me your hands again."

"Get that thing away from me," Fatima said, and flicked the beard away.

"Thanks for reminding me," he said. "I need it to stay fresh." He took off the beard and stuck it outside the door. "Kid, hang on to this for me."

"Okay," the girl said from outside. "Is there anything I can do?"

Fatima vigorously shook her head.

"No, thanks, honey," Amir said, and closed the door. "This water better not make the dye in my *thowb* run. *Yallah. Wahad, tinan, talata.*"

Fatima was excited enough to hear him counting in Arabic that she made her best effort to defy gravity, but she found herself letting go again.

"Okay, Tayta, I'm going to have to look at you so I can get this right," Amir said.

Fatima closed her eyes as he opened his beyond a squint.

"Are you sure you don't need some help?" the girl called out.

"You can't do it alone. She's practically family," Fatima said, giving in. "Let her in. I don't want you looking at me any longer than necessary."

Amir opened the door. Fatima, even without her faraway glasses, could see that this person was much too small to be Tiffany. Amir's beard, which dangled from her hand, was almost half her length.

Fatima instinctively covered her drooping breasts. The girl sneezed and pulled a Kleenex out of her purse. Fatima thought she could make out a cat on the purse.

The girl sneezed again. "I'm sorry," she said, and blew her nose. "I think I'm allergic to all those plants floating in your bathtub." It was such a little girl's voice. The awful letter's cat stationery came back to Fatima. No, please. No.

Fatima slipped out of Amir's grip and into unconsciousness.

"Tayta, Tayta," Amir said. "Stay with me." Amir bent down to get Fatima out, and Decimal came to his side to help.

Amir patted her hand to revive her and waved some of the lavender leaves in front of her nose. Fatima opened her eyes. "I still have one day, and I need it," she said. "So make the girl go away."

"One day? She's your great-granddaughter," Amir said. "Her name is —"

Fatima held up her hand.

"She's not ga—" Amir said.

"Just as worse," Fatima interrupted. "Make her go away."

Amir looked at Decimal. "Go eat some kibbe or something until I come down. Take the beard with you."

The girl bowed her head. "I'm sorry if I've inconvenienced you, Mrs. Abdullah, ma'am," she said, and closed the door behind herself.

Fatima crossed her arms in front of her breasts in defiance as well as modesty. She waited in silence, shivering in the water until he took her hands again. "I had no idea you could be so cold, Tayta," Amir said.

"The water is freezing," she replied, pretending not to understand him.

Amir heaved with all his strength, once again expecting her to slip away. But this time Fatima rose out of the water like magic. Then he found his hand landing on a pile of his best Ralph Lauren Collection. Amir wrapped Fatima in a big blue towel and ran his hands up and down her to warm her.

"I didn't even know I'd brought the good towels up here," he said. "I thought I'd put them in your room."

"Where's my robe?" Fatima asked.

Amir saw the tattered pink threads hooked onto Fatima's cane, which stood in the opposite corner from the bathtub. "It's over there with your cane," he said, looking at the distance between the cane and the bathtub. "Tayta, how did you get in the bathtub?"

Fatima merely gave him her arm so that he could guide her back to the room.

"Make that girl disappear, and that will be the last thing I'll ever ask you to do," she said. "Never look in my underwear drawer and make the girl go away."

"She came all the way from Minneapolis to see you," Amir said.

"You make her go away," Fatima ordered.

"Don't you want to do the last thing I'll ever ask you to do?"

"Fine," he said. "I have a big audition, and I don't have time to argue about this. I'll call Auntie Hala right now."

Amir helped Fatima into her bed and pulled the covers tight around her. "You slept through a couple of doses of these yesterday," he said as he handed her pills.

"I don't need them." She sighed.

"I'll put on *SportsZone* as soon as you take them," Amir promised.

"I don't have time for that," Fatima said.

"What are you so busy with?" he wondered.

"It's a surprise," she replied. "A big one. You'll see sometime tomorrow."

"I don't have time for surprises tomorrow," Amir said.

Fatima took his hand. "I'm sorry if my big surprise tomorrow will interfere with your hobby. Really. I didn't pick the date."

Then she saw Scheherazade perched at the windowsill and the embroidered dress from Lebanon hanging from the curtain railing.

"That's my dress for tomorrow," Fatima told Amir. "Do you like it?"

Amir eyed it floating in the breeze. "I saw it laying on you while you were sleeping," he said. "You'll be the best-dressed lady at whatever funeral you're attending next."

"It's for your mother, too," Fatima added. "Maybe she could wear it when she comes to visit you in Lebanon. You could go see the real cedars. Not those skinny things Americans call cedars."

"And what would I do with a cedar tree, climb one?"

"Just make the girl go away before you kill me, too," Fatima said.

As Amir turned to go out the door, the letter from Decimal floated off the nightstand and landed at his goat fur audition sandals, which Soraya had gotten him at some Renaissance Festival she'd worked. Amir picked the letter up. It was open. He smiled at how Fatima liked to open mail even though she couldn't read it, always waiting for the postman back in Detroit when the only thing she could really understand was the bills.

"Don't you even want to know why she sent you a letter?" he said.

Fatima waved him away.

AMIR

After draining the bathtub and tossing out the wilted remains of half his garden, Amir sat down on the toilet and read Decimal's letter. By the time he flushed, he knew that Fatima somehow had learned its contents.

He found Decimal sitting at the dining room table looking at his new head shots. "I blow-dried your beard for you," she said. She handed it to him very warm. "I took all my allergy pills so I won't bother her with my sneezing."

Amir felt no biological connection to Decimal even though she had Fatima's nose bump, but he felt that they had a vibe thing going, as Soraya would say. They were both far more intelligent than the life choices they had made would indicate, both taking care of people who should have been taking care of them. But even good people, he reasoned, have their limits, and he had reached his.

"Sorry, kid, you have to leave," he told her.

"But I haven't even gotten to talk to Mrs. Abdullah," Decimal protested.

"Consider yourself blessed," Amir advised. "Now, what's your grandma's number?"

"I'll do it myself." Decimal sighed and pulled out her cell phone. "So should I tell Gran I'm staying with my second cousin or my first cousin once removed?"

"I have no idea," Amir said. "Jesus Christ,

I've never even heard of you before."

"They probably called me Aisha," Decimal said, "even though less than 11 or so out of 251 people that I've met in my life so far would know that's my real name. It's African. My dad chose it."

"Aisha is also Mohammad's wife," Amir said.

"Is he a cousin or an uncle?" Decimal asked. "I figured there had to be at least one Mohammad in the family, given that statistically it is the most common name in the world. I read that in *Time* at my dermatologist's office."

"Auntie Laila's oldest is a Mohammad, but he doesn't have a wife. I meant the Prophet Mohammad's wife," Amir said. Fatima had taught him a lot about a book she couldn't even read.

"Interesting," Decimal said, and continued to dial. "Gran kept forgetting to give me the address, so I ended up looking it up in her address book and sent it. I went to cross it off Gran's to-do list, but she already had, and then I thought, Gran's getting old and confused and stuff. But then I heard her talking to Dr. Wang downstairs and saying how Mrs. Abdullah would just die if she ever found out about me. I didn't want to be a cause of death, so I came here in person so she could see that aside from this baby thing, I'm not so bad. First, I thought that because Mrs. Abdullah was alone and old, she might have a lot of cats and I would be allergic, but then I thought I wasn't worth her dying over and I took my allergy pills and the cash my mom is supposed to use but doesn't and came. I'm glad she has you instead of a cat. At least I got a road trip out of it, which my mom says is one of those things that will be hard to do once you have a kid."

Amir lost Decimal's train of thought early on and was glad to hear someone pick up on the other end.

"Hi, Gran," Decimal said on the phone. "I'm fine. I'm in California visiting Mrs. Abdullah . . . you know, your mom. . . . I'm not being funny . . . she seems very nice, Gran, I see where you get it from."

Amir slapped his beard back on and left the room with his script. Let the girl deal with her baggage on her own. He paused at the stairs, listening to Fatima yell at herself about the shame of this girl over a Perry Como record. A minute later, Decimal stood next to him at the stairs listening.

"Gran's coming tomorrow," Decimal told him. "She'll fix everything."

"You know what pisses me off?" Amir

469

said. "In the thousand days and nights she's been living with me, hardly a single one of you came to visit. But you get pregnant and Hala's here on the next plane."

"Nobody cares for the generation before them as much as the one that comes after," Decimal explained. "Like Brenda puts Hala through hell and doesn't even apologize. With me, Brenda at least apologizes and stuff."

"I send out a weekly e-mail to all of Tayta's kids and hardly hear anything from anyone," Amir complained.

"I'm sure it could be a proven fact that 50 percent of people suck," Decimal answered. "You just got a very large number of that 50 percent in your family. You want me to help you write the e-mail tonight? I'm in the top twelfth of my class in English and stuff."

"Well, you do seem to write letters with quite an impact," Amir admitted, and the two went back to the kitchen computer while upstairs the cursing of Decimal's arrival continued.

Amir began typing, and Decimal looked over his shoulder.

Dear Fatima Relations,
    I hope you are doing well.

The weather was slightly
cloudy today, but still warm
and pleasant. We finally had
family visit. Decimal Jackson, who is Auntie Hala's
granddaughter. Nice to know
someone did —

"According to the *O* magazine at Dr. Pa-
tel's office, some things you got to keep to
yourself, like, say, being scared about having a baby, because that'll scare the people
around you," Decimal said. "Other stuff you
got to be honest about."

Decimal shoved Amir out of the computer
chair, hit "delete," and began typing. Amir
proofread over her shoulder.

Dear Family:
  The weather here is fine.
Slightly cloudy but very warm.
So how come none of you come
to visit your own mother/
grandmother? Am I supposed to
take her on 100% just because
I'm so flaming gay? Do you
think homosexuals have the
market cornered on compassion?
Well, gay doesn't mean compassionate, patsy, or dilwad.

Heck, gay people have even been serial killers. Do you know who is the one person that did come to visit Tayta? Decimal Jackson. She is only 17 and three months and she managed to make it on her own. What's your excuse? Sadly, Decimal was the wrong person to come visit because she pretty much nearly caused Tayta to drown herself. I'm sure the arrival of this girl has raised Tayta's chances for a fatal incident and stuff one hundred percent.

Sincerely,
Amir

"Whoa, that last bit is harsh," he said.

"But it's true," Decimal replied. "My mom's in health insurance, and I know how actuaries calculate things."

"Tayta would hate it if she knew I was sending out an e-mail like this," Amir said.

"You can always blame me," Decimal said. "She can't hate me more."

"I'm sorry about that, kid," Amir said. "Tayta's just very methodical about the sequence of things. First comes birth, then lots of homework, followed by massive amounts of education at the best schools possible, then marriage, and then a baby. You skipped a lot of steps, and I'm just listing the vital ones."

"So did your mom and dad do it in the right order?" Decimal asked.

"Sort of," he told her. "I'm one of the original sperm donor babies — direct from the Michigan Sperm Bank, one of the first in the country. My mother sees the future in more ways than one. I was on a couple of medical magazine covers as a zygote and fetus."

"That's way cool," Decimal said. "At least Mrs. Abdullah's very open-minded about sperm and stuff."

"Tayta prefers to think of me as immaculate," he explained. "I'm just lucky that my mother reached menopause without falling in love with a man and having a child with him. I was always worried before then that she'd resent that she'd hadn't waited it out for free sperm."

"My mom's pretty price-conscious, too," Decimal said. "It's her job. But I think you're being way hard on yourself. I was a mistake, so my mom had no choice, but your mom chose you to be here."

"My mom had me because she found out

her ex-husband was having a kid," Amir said, and rummaged in his desk drawer until he pulled out three postcard-size yellowing ultrasounds and handed them to her. "She was very competitive with the new wife, being as they had been best friends. But then she didn't know how to support me — at least that's what she told me — so she dumped me off with Tayta, and that was the best thing for all of us, according to my mom's first therapist. He said going out on the road was how my mom found herself, and without her finding herself, I would have been lost."

Decimal examined the ultrasounds, trying to find Amir in them. "Here I am," he pointed out. "Pretty cute, huh? I was one of the first babies to get take-home photos from the doctors."

"You kind of look like my baby looks," Decimal said. "Except mine doesn't have 'Michigan Sperm Bank' written at the bottom."

"Sometimes I wish that Tayta believed I was a sperm baby so she could accept the gay thing, as she'd have some sperm to blame it on," Amir sighed.

"You got to wonder about the sperm yourself," Decimal said.

"One day, sure." Amir nodded. "I mostly

just bring it up in front of my mother to guilt-trip her, but I don't want to do anything about it while Tayta's here."

"You're a good man," Decimal said, and hugged him.

"You're very comforting, like what I'd imagine a mom would be like," Amir said, patting her head. It had been a long time since he had had someone to dump on. "You're going to do fine, you and your bun in the oven person."

"I think so," Decimal agreed. "So how do you say 'great-grandmother' in Arabic?"

"I don't know," Amir said. "Great-tayta, I guess."

"Not that I'll need to know that," Decimal said. She sneezed and scratched her arms through the Mickey Mouse sweatshirt.

Then the stomping began upstairs, with emanating sounds that were a cross between singing and wailing. "Jesus Christ, I haven't heard that since Detroit," Amir said, staring at the ceiling. "I think she's trying to do the *dabke*."

"The what?" Decimal asked.

"The *dabke*, kid," he said. "Don't you know anything? At every wedding they dance the *dabke* and . . ." He stopped himself. He sounded like the crazy lady upstairs, and besides, this girl wouldn't know anything about weddings, either.

FATIMA

Kick once, step back, and stomp. Repeat. The sight of herself in her new embroidered dress made Fatima want to *dabke,* made her almost forget the girl downstairs. She didn't even notice her hair in the mirror.

"This music is terrible enough without you singing off key to it, too," Scheherazade said as she watched Fatima's old Frank Sinatra record spin on the turntable.

Scheherazade flipped through Fatima's collection: more Perry Como, Peggy Lee, Rosemary Clooney. "You have no real music," she decided. "I will have to sing for you. *Yallah.*"

Then Scheherazade hummed an old village song loudly enough to drown out the girl downstairs, and Fatima found a rhythm in her body she had not felt course through her in seven decades. She waved her head scarf in her hand while Scheherazade circled around her in bare feet, gracefully waving her arms overhead and snapping her fingers, all of which were adorned in intricately woven silver rings.

"I have not worn such a fine dress since the day of my engagement to Marwan,"

476

Fatima remarked. "It was in the garden in Deir Zeitoon. The band played until sunrise; everyone was so happy except me. I had never seen my mother and uncle eat without dividing the food into proportions to see how many days they could make a dish last."

Then she heard Amir laugh outside at something the girl said, and she plopped down on the bed, exhausted.

"What, no more dancing?" Scheherazade inquired, disappointed. "Fine. I've got something else we can do."

Scheherazade stepped out and a few minutes later returned with the Oster sixteen-speed blender box with the Avon samples. She dropped the box in front of Fatima, but Fatima did not even flinch from the dust it emitted.

"Why was I not told of this girl earlier so that such horrible thoughts would not be on my mind at death?" she said.

"You're not dead yet," Scheherazade reminded her. "So no, the shame will not kill you."

Scheherazade dumped out the forty-year-old contents of the box and began arranging the tubes and compacts on the vanity. She opened a perfume bottle called Avon Occur! She grimaced and tossed it back in the box.

She beckoned Fatima to come sit at the vanity.

"Don't you want to look extra-special for our final night tomorrow?" Scheherazade asked.

"It's easy for you to be so casual about death. You're immortal," Fatima said, feeling a flutter in her stomach at the thought of tomorrow. "I only get one chance at it, and I don't need makeup for it. No one in God's name will care what I look like, especially if I failed to leave behind a good family."

Scheherazade barely listened as she opened up tubes. She sniffed and then tossed most of them.

"Hey, don't waste all that," Fatima protested.

"When's the last time you used this?" Scheherazade asked as a caked tube crumbled apart.

Fatima remembered when the colors had been so bright with names such as nude peach, pearl pansy, and ruby royal rouge. "I never used it," she said. "I just sold it, but not very well."

Scheherazade held up two shamrock-shaped glass serving trays. "Those I received as my Avon representative sales award." Fatima beamed. "Even though I couldn't

sell the makeup, everyone in the neighborhood thought I knew what I was doing with
kids because I had so many. So they would
buy the Avon toys from me. Maybe from
Marwan I also learned a little bit about peddling. It's all in the listening, he said. He
told me that when I asked him why he never
talked. When I peddled the Avon, I didn't
feel good in English with the neighbors,
except Millie. So I listened to the women
tell me stories like you listen to me now.
Then they would buy from me, and Avon
gave me a lot of bonus toys to say thank
you."

Scheherazade dug farther into the box and
pulled out a bottle of Avon Charlie Brown
no-tears shampoo, an Avon Peanuts soap
dish, an Avon Volcanic Repeating Pistol, and
several Avon cat cars. Scheherazade pointed
the Avon Volcanic Repeating Pistol at Fatima. "Come sit down and let's put these
cosmetics to use, partner," she said, imitating one of the cowboy roles for which she'd
seen Amir wishfully rehearsing.

Fatima pushed aside the gun. Scheherazade took her hand and forced her to sit
down at the vanity.

"A swish of some kohl and a dash of
cinnamon powder can give a girl cheeks like
rosebuds, lips like jujubes, and a face round

like a full moon," Scheherazade said. She held a couple of powder compacts up against Fatima's cheek for comparison. "Just listen to me on this. I have a lot more experience."

"When you were helping Amir get me out of the tub — I know it was you — did you hear him talk in his head about the house in Lebanon?" Fatima questioned.

"No, sister, I cannot hear words that do not even exist as thoughts," Scheherazade said.

Scheherazade's truth numbed Fatima, and so she was able to apply the face powder without any flinching on Fatima's part. Scheherazade feathered a generous amount of blush onto Fatima's cheeks before Fatima pushed her hand away. "Is the girl still here?" she asked.

"No one is more dear than the child but the grandchild. She is your daughter's grandchild," Scheherazade told her. "How would you feel if one were to spit on Amir?"

Fatima would curse that person's entire line of ancestors. But this was different.

"She is a disgrace," Fatima said. "*Ya Allah,* Mama was the best person in the world, and I have no one worthy of her house, my grandfather's house."

"*Khallas,* stop," Scheherazade said. "You

were a child when you left your mother. You did not know her as an adult to know she was not perfect, as you have not been perfect. What do you really know about her life? She could have had many affairs herself."

Fatima slapped Scheherazade. "I did deserve that," Scheherazade conceded. "But no one should describe her own olive oil as crude. Paradise without people is not worth setting foot in, so leave the house to God and put its key in the underwear drawer and go talk to her instead."

"The key." Fatima remembered. A powerful wave of heat fired by sadness rippled through her body. She still trembled from it when she was finally able to form words again. "The key is still in the guest room. We did not find it yet."

"Maybe it is not here," Scheherazade said.

"*Allah yustur,*" Fatima said. "I know it is here. Do you think I imagined it being here? You think I'm crazy? Because you're the only crazy thing in my life other than my children. *Yallah,* let us go."

"Take that girl with you," Scheherazade said. She dabbed what once had been coral peach lipstick onto Fatima's lips before Fatima flicked her hand away.

"You go with me," Fatima insisted.

"I've never been anyone's servant," Scheherazade reminded her.

"This is of urgency," Fatima said. "Tomorrow is the 1001st night."

"That's your urgency," Scheherazade replied. "I've got forever, so I can't damage my hands with manual labor. You have a girl downstairs who can help you."

"I'll ask Amir," Fatima decided.

"He's going to tell you to wait until tomorrow," Scheherazade said, "with this big audition he keeps talking about."

"He will understand the urgency," Fatima said. But Scheherazade's face told what she already knew: He would not understand. Scheherazade pointed her manicured index finger downstairs.

Fatima shook her head. "I have never allowed anyone to dig through those boxes other than myself, and I will not let her be the exception."

Then she screamed like a woman escaping a fire for her grandson. Amir in his *thowb* and beard was there in thirty seconds.

"Oh, Jesus Christ, Tayta," Amir panted, out of breath. "What happened? Why is your face so flushed? Let me call a doctor."

"It's called beauty," Fatima answered, smiling broadly enough to crease some of the cocoa deluxe foundation.

"Oh," Amir said, examining her more closely. "Huh, I've just never seen you, oh, I don't know, so beautiful."

"I need to go to the guest room," Fatima said. "I have to find the key to the house."

"What house?"

"Stop saying stupid things," Fatima reprimanded him.

"Oh, Lebanon again," Amir said. "We'll do it tomorrow."

Fatima saw Scheherazade enjoying Amir's predicted bad behavior from her perch on the windowsill.

"I have to get the key," Fatima said.

"This is the biggest callback audition of my life," he replied. "What could be so important that it couldn't wait until tomorrow night?"

"I'll be busy then," Fatima insisted.

"Look, we'll do it on the weekend," Amir promised.

It was tragic that he did not know this was his last chance to be good to her.

"Fine," Fatima said. "Send the girl up here."

"Oh, Tayta, I knew you'd come around," he said.

"The girl can still lift things," Fatima said. "She's young, and it's early in her pregnancy. Get her."

A few minutes later, Amir came back up with the girl, who still was clutching her Hello Kitty bag. He edged her toward Fatima.

"Go on, kid," he said. "I'll see you both later."

"Wait, *habibi*," Fatima begged. "Don't come home too late tomorrow. I need you to be here tomorrow night. *Min shan rubna,* it's the last time I'll ask you to do anything for me."

"I'll do my best," Amir said as he left.

There was only one best: that she would die in his arms. When Fatima looked at the windowsill, Scheherazade was not perched there. She had no choice but to look at the girl.

"Both you and Amir have such nice dresses and stuff," Decimal said, looking over her shoulder as if she hoped Amir were still there.

"I can't hear you," Fatima said.

Decimal made her way toward Fatima. "You look very pretty," she said more loudly. "My mom — that's Brenda — she's got your same goddess finesse with makeup."

"God give me strength," Fatima said. She stood up with her cane. "Take me to the guest bedroom. I'm sure that's where the key is."

"What key, Mrs. Abdullah?" Decimal asked.

"*Ya Allah,* you don't know anything, that's obvious, or your belly wouldn't be about to stick out," Fatima answered. "The key to the house in Lebanon. Take my arm and help me out. Turn left at the hallway."

Fatima did her best not to flinch when the girl touched her. To get into the guest room door, Decimal had to shove aside a box filled with facial hair parts: beards and mustaches of various lengths and a few Styrofoam heads modeling long-haired and curly-haired wigs.

"He should have put about 3.5 feet of chrome from the living room in here to help with the lighting in this mess," Decimal said.

Fatima thought that funny but pursed her lips tightly.

"Whereabouts is the key, Mrs. Abdullah, ma'am?" Decimal asked.

"Look for a box of old clothes," Fatima told her. Fatima remembered the last time she had held the key: April 4, 1974.

Decimal clung to her Hello Kitty bag to work her way through clothes racks and boxes overflowing with board games, sports equipment, camping supplies, and *Boys' Life*

485

magazines and books. Decimal stopped in front of the cedar chest, unable to hold back a sneeze. She wiped her spittle off the chest.

"My grandfather built that," Fatima said, and Decimal got her first sighting of Fatima as a proud rather than a defeated woman. "He made it when I was born so my mother would have somewhere to put the things for my wedding."

"What's inside, Mrs. Abdullah?" Decimal asked.

"You can't have the wedding dress," Fatima said. "In Lebanon, all babies are made after weddings."

"How do you know?" Decimal said. "A lot of people are better at covering up things than me and Brenda. That's what Brenda always says."

"What are you talking about?" Fatima said. She was annoyed with the girl's mumbling, although it was she herself who had purposely tried to silence her by lowering the volume on her hearing aid. "Please just look for a pair of blue pants. They are in one of the boxes in a blue backpack. They're made of blue that looks like bad spaghetti."

"You mean corduroy?" Decimal said. "What kind of box would they be in?"

"Yes, cordelias," Fatima agreed. "Now look."

Fatima could not bear to dwell on the Levi's in the backpack. *Yukhrub beit deeni,* curses on my faith, she thought, for giving me no other distraction than talking to this girl. Maybe she could make her moral with a story, the way Scheherazade had taught her sister Dunyazad morality through her stories to her king. But Scheherazade had had 1001 nights. Fatima only had one. Still . . .

"I was pregnant for my second wedding," Fatima ventured. "You can get married without a dress, like I did, and take no pictures."

Decimal scratched her arm. "They say in *Psychology Today* that divorce is almost as inevitable and complicated as sex and stuff," she said. "I'd just rather skip a postdivorce stage because apparently it's one of the most depressing times in a person's life."

Fatima was stuck on a child using the word *sex* so casually in front of her. Then again, this child had "done it," as Fatima used to hear Millie and her kids refer to the bad girls at their school. It had shocked Fatima what Millie talked to her kids about. Now it shocked her what her own kids allowed to happen to their kids.

"Your baby should have a name," Fatima advised her. "A family name."

"It's going to have Paolo's last name, Mrs. Abdullah." Decimal smiled. "Nassar. Remember how I told you Paolo was born in Brazil but his grandparents came from Syria? They were two of six million Arabs who did, you know. Paolo's mother told me that. She was full of interesting facts and figures before I got pregnant and she started hating me and stuff. And I got some other facts that will make you even happier. Did you know if Paolo's Syrian and I'm one-quarter Lebanese, my baby's going to be three-eighths more Arab than me and just three-eighths less Arab than you?"

Fatima had no problems following Decimal's math. It just didn't make her happy to see how it characterized her family. Avon mascara flaked off of Fatima's eyelashes and onto her cheeks as she held her tongue because she wanted the girl to keep working.

The girl opened a box before Fatima could tell her to ask first. She dug in and pulled out book after book with covers with Arabic calligraphy. She sneezed from the dust.

"You can't sneeze on those," Fatima shouted. *"Allah yustur."*

Decimal opened a dark blue book. "Have you read all of these?" she asked. "I'm a big reader, too."

"Too bad you can't read Arabic," Fatima said, as though she herself could. "Then I could give them to you."

"Are they mostly fiction or nonfiction?" Decimal said.

"They're all Korans," Fatima said. "You shouldn't touch them if you haven't washed your hands."

"Sorry, I didn't mean to offend you." Decimal bowed her head.

"It's not me you are offending," Fatima said. The Korans were gifts from friends in Detroit who had come back from the *Hajj* to Mecca. Fatima had never opened any of them, as her mother's Koran was all she had needed in her life, but had given them their own storage box. She wished her children, their children, the Mexican ladies on the bus, the homeless guy with the dimple on his cheek, Amir's handsome neighbor boy — any of those people — could read Arabic so that she could disperse the Korans among them.

"The green ones are my favorite," Fatima said.

"I didn't know the Koran came in colors," Decimal replied.

"Green was my mother's favorite color because she said a green field meant a good harvest," Fatima said.

"I like green, too," Decimal said. "I knew we'd have a lot in common. Besides just getting pregnant as teenagers and not having husbands."

"I had a husband," Fatima said. "And I married another one before my baby was born. And I was nineteen, not seventeen."

"Nineteen years old is less than 20 percent more of my entire life span so far," Decimal pointed out.

"How long were you with the father before . . . you know?" Fatima said, biting into the Coral Satin Sheen on her lip.

"That time, it was twelve minutes," Decimal said. "Paolo likes me, so he doesn't go super fast and stuff, like he says he could. But the baby part only takes a nanosecond. It's not that I miscalculated, if I think about it. It just that for a few seconds it felt so good, I couldn't stop. But it kind of hurt, too, like three times as much as a hay fever shot. Brenda says giving birth is seven hundred more times painful than that. But I guess with having ten children and stuff, you must know a lot about the feel-good parts and the feel-bad parts and all."

Fatima rubbed her eyes, as if that would make the girl and the forty-year-old makeup go away. But they were both still there irritating her.

"How do you say 'key' in Arabic?" Decimal asked.

"Muftah," Fatima said.

"Mufta," Decimal said.

"No, *muftah,*" Fatima said.

"Muftahy," Decimal repeated.

"No, that means 'my key,' " Fatima said.

"I'm no good." Decimal sighed. "Here I was thinking you could teach me Arabic and then I could teach my kid and stuff."

It had taken Fatima's family three generations in America to birth someone who wanted to learn Arabic from her instead of despite her. And now she had so little time to teach the girl anything. Nor could she teach her Arabic if she put her on the street. "The first words you should learn are from the Koran," Fatima told her.

"Well, we have plenty of those to choose from," Decimal said. She headed toward the box marked "Lebanon."

"As soon as we find the key, we will start," Fatima agreed. The girl began looking in even greater earnest, an earnestness none of her children had had when Fatima had tried to teach them anything.

"I was born in the very house whose key we're looking for," Fatima said. She didn't care if the girl listened, but she did not want to dwell on the key itself as the girl looked for it. "My grandmother, who was Deir Zeitoon's midwife and matchmaker, brought me into this world, and then the whole village knew it in fifteen minutes. My grandfather had prepared *kunafi* for all the neighbors to celebrate."

"See all that we have in common," Decimal said. "Your grandmother birthed you, and my grandmother is going to birth my baby."

"My mother rested in bed for forty days and was given the best food and strong chicken broth so that I would drink the healthiest milk when I sucked from her breast," Fatima countered. "When Ibrahim wrote to my mother to tell her that I had had my first baby, I made sure he let her think the people in Detroit did the same thing."

"They don't do that in Minnesota," Decimal said.

"Nor Detroit, *ya bint,*" Fatima replied. "I did not rest at all. In America, even if I had had a son, no one would have cared. Even when a son gets his first tooth, they do not have a party here. I was alone with my first baby all day. Except when Millie started coming over with her baby. We did not know each other. We used to watch one another in our yards between the hanging laundry, walking with our babies in our arms to get them to stop crying. One day, she just came over. Even though I didn't speak enough English to have a conversation back then, we would sit and exchange crying babies. She'd walk with mine, and I'd walk with hers. So we felt someone was helping us out with our babies. I told Millie she and I should have had our babies in Deir Zeitoon."

"What exactly is Deir Zeitoon?" Decimal ventured.

Fatima reached to twirl her hair at Decimal's pronunciation of her beloved village. "It's where I grew up," she explained. "My great-grandfather built our house himself with the help of his brother. They used limestone brick and cedar and olive wood trim."

Fatima paused and waited for Decimal to yawn or interrupt her, as she had come to expect from her family at the mention of this house. But Decimal didn't.

"I'm not giving it to you when I die," Fatima told her. "So stop asking about it and just look for its key."

"I'm sorry," Decimal said. "I didn't mean that I want it."

"Oh, so now you think you're better than

493

my house," Fatima scoffed. "*Aabe.* Shame. You should be so lucky to have been born there."

"I'll stay quiet," Decimal promised. "But if you want to tell me more, I'll listen."

The girl was careful as she continued to look through the boxes, and soon she pulled out a key hanging on a Detroit Tigers lanyard.

"I got it," Decimal exclaimed.

Fatima took the key from her and warmed it in her hand. A simple box key. An American key. Not a skeleton key in a pair of blue cordelias.

"This is the key to the house in Detroit," Fatima said. "That house went to my husband in the divorce."

"Who's he going to leave his house to?" Decimal asked.

Fatima had never once thought about that, and she was sure Ibrahim had not, either. Although they had stopped having long discussions years before the divorce, Fatima still knew most of Ibrahim's thoughts, as well as most of the things he did not think about.

"I bet the kids will all fight for that one, the way Gran talks about how great Detroit was," Decimal said.

"My children couldn't leave Detroit fast

enough," Fatima corrected her.

She wove the Detroit key under a mosaic of embroidery on her dress to keep it in place. Fatima would mark the key for Ibrahim in case he lost his spare. She wanted to leave him something besides the children and their problems.

"Gran said they couldn't stay in Detroit on account of Dr. Wang getting such a good offer in Minnesota," Decimal told her. "But she sure goes on about how she and her sisters used to build tents indoors in the summer to pretend they were camping and went on field trips to the River Rouge plant, which half the kids' dads worked at. And Mr. Abdullah and you took them all to Florida for your first family vacation, and they had peanuts and Coke in Georgia. She's pretty nostalgic in her old age."

Fatima had never heard one of her children referred to as being in "her old age," nor had she ever thought about her children having a lifetime of memories, stories they told over and over. She knew that her children had left not only because of the factories closing. They had left in part to escape their parents' darkness. "Just look for the right key," she said, spitting out a crust of lipstick that had fallen into her mouth.

Decimal opened another box, this one filled with yellowed, musty textbooks on American history, algebra, and English grammar.

"Wow, these calc books are ancient," Decimal said, and sneezed. "Printed in 1971. Cool. Could I borrow these?"

"No," Fatima snapped.

"Sorry." The girl was at least polite. Why had Hala not taught her daughter and her daughter's daughter right from wrong? Perhaps God had not debilitated her yet so that she herself could teach the girl right from wrong. Instilling morality had been postponed too long with this girl.

"Go downstairs and get Randa and my mother's Koran from my underwear drawer," Fatima said. "That is the one we'll use. Make sure you wash your hands before you touch it."

"You're going to teach me to read Arabic and stuff?" Decimal smiled.

"Wait," Fatima commanded. She took the Detroit key out of the embroidery. "Put this in the underwear drawer. But don't look at anything else in there."

Even though Fatima didn't like this girl, unlike Amir, she obeyed her well, and so she would not look. Perhaps if I had been giving her the orders from the beginning,

Fatima thought, there would be less shame today.

Decimal took the key, excited as she bounced down the stairs.

Her bounce, although from such a small person, knocked a blue pouch out of one of the boxes. Fatima reached for it, but before she could open it, Scheherazade appeared at her side. Fatima placed the pouch on her lap, covering it with her hand.

"Is she not charming?" Scheherazade commented. She blew the dust from the boxes out of Fatima's purple stubs and wiped the flaking mascara off her cheeks.

"She's a most terrible shame. *Aabe al-shoom,*" Fatima said. "That is why I must teach her as much Koran as possible while there is time."

"Perhaps you should find her a husband, too," Scheherazade said.

"She is not my responsibility," Fatima declared.

"She's your granddaughter," Scheherazade said, watching Amir rehearse in the garden from the window.

"She is not my granddaughter," Fatima told her. "She is my great-granddaughter."

"Yes, she is your great-granddaughter," Scheherazade said, and applauded Fatima's admission.

"Stop clapping," Fatima shouted. "Your joy is giving me a headache."

"At least offer her Zade's services," Scheherazade suggested.

Fatima shook her head and rubbed the pouch in her hands.

"I rarely asked Zade for help," Fatima said. "Nadia's boy and girl are the hardest grandchildren for me to talk to."

Fatima drifted off to a place Scheherazade couldn't picture.

"Twins succeed doubly in half the time," Fatima finally said quietly.

Scheherazade bent down to catch a hovering tear in Fatima's eye, but it stayed put. "*Inshallah,* we will find this key quickly. Do not waste our remaining time on more tears. I will move fast."

As Scheherazade opened the boxes, all that she uncovered were alien objects to her: two baseball bats, two baseball gloves, a basketball, a game called Battleship, Rolling Stones records, and a calculator bigger than China's finest abacus.

Fatima turned away from the boxes and rolled the blue pouch in her hands.

"Amazingly, eighty-five years of life and all you dragged with you was a wedding dress and some nonsense," Scheherazade remarked, looking over what she was sure were Amir's toys. "So many girls, and you never kept any of their things."

"The girls outgrew them or took them with them when they left," Fatima said. "Millie and I had a big garage sale the year the last big civil war in Lebanon ended and got rid of most of the old stuff. That way Amir was able to have his own room with just his things, and Millie was able to die with everything in order for her kids. She was gone a few months later with the lung cancer."

"To whom did Millie leave her house?" Scheherazade asked.

"She didn't. I learned from her mistake," Fatima said. "All her kids had moved to Florida, and they didn't know what to do with a house split four ways — she only had four kids — and so they had to sell it. Now they don't have a home in Detroit, and it's like Millie was never there. I don't want to put my kids through that."

"Did I ever tell you the story about the cucumber peddler in Kabul who thought everyone wanted his bags of cucumbers when they were all content with their bags of apples?" Scheherazade said.

Fatima gripped the blue pouch tighter. "You don't tell the stories," she answered. "I do."

Scheherazade shrugged and dug into one of the boxes. She held up two identical baseball gloves. "These are both for the same hand," Scheherazade said. "How is that going to keep you warm in the winter?"

"They're not for the cold," Fatima explained. "They're for baseball. It's an American game where you catch the ball with the hand with the glove and you throw with the hand with no glove. All the kids play it in Detroit in the summer."

Scheherazade stuck her fist into the glove. "It must be a small ball."

Fatima hesitated before opening the blue pouch on her lap and pulling out an autographed baseball. "This one was signed by the great Detroit Tiger Al Kaline," she explained.

Scheherazade reached for the ball just as Fatima pulled it away.

"So a boy only needs one glove," Scheherazade said, reaching for the ball again. "But you spoiled Amir and gave him two?"

Fatima put the ball back in the pouch and went silent. Scheherazade looked at the two gloves in her hand.

"Twins succeed doubly in half the time," Scheherazade said, repeating Fatima's words about Zade and his sister. Scheherazade walked through the boxes. Two of everything, exactly the same, sticking out of most of the boxes.

"Bassam with the dimple, Lena with no husband, Laila, Randa, Hala, Miriam, Soraya, and Nadia," Scheherazade said. "That is eight children. You said you had ten children."

"I do," Fatima said after a long while of silence in which she caressed the baseball. "Laith and Riyad would have wanted the house."

"When did your boys leave you?" Scheherazade said. She did not use their names as she could tell that Fatima had not said them out loud in some time.

"It was on April 4, 1974," Fatima told her. "They had just graduated from Ann Arbor the year before. There was a terror of tornadoes in the Midwest that day, but I only know about the one that my boys went away in."

"Allah yerhamhum," Scheherazade whispered, and folded her arms around Fatima. She kissed the top of the old lady's head. "Two sorrows can erase thousands of days of happiness."

"Especially when you caused the sorrow," Fatima murmured, falling into Scheherazade's embrace, "like Ibrahim and I did."

"You do not have the power to make a

tornado," Scheherazade told her.

Fatima had heard many people say this to her in the last thirty years, but her self-imposed torture helped her make peace out of something with no human *rahma,* no mercy. "But we put the boys in its path," she said. "They were born the day the Korean War ended. *Inshallah,* we thought, they will not fight wars. America is now finished with wars."

She held up an MVP trophy and from inside pulled out a photo of two redheaded teen boys in University of Michigan uniforms. "They wanted to be Tigers," Fatima said. "But Ibrahim and I hoped they would be engineers one day even though we barely had bank loans available to send more children to university. Luckily, even though the boys weren't, to be honest, as good as their sisters in math, they got into college because they could play baseball well. And we did not have to pay anything."

"So after university, did they play with your Tigers?" Scheherazade asked.

"Laith was told he was not good enough, and Riyad damaged his knee the last year in college," Fatima went on. "But they were more than good considering they played a game their father didn't even understand, as much as I tried to get Ibrahim interested in it. They talked about going to Lebanon for the summer after school. But then the Yom Kippur War came, and we did not want them to go there. We begged them to get more degrees so they would not go to Vietnam. They were both barely accepted into the University of Illinois to study more biology, *mashallah,* but we had such a party to celebrate. Ibrahim even barbecued hamburgers, like Randa had always wanted. We were selfish. We wanted to save them from being Arab and from being American. I gave Laith the key to the house then and told them that on Mama's soul, as soon as things got better around Deir Zeitoon and they finished their degrees, they could go back home to see the house. They went on a bike trip that April for spring break because I didn't want them taking a plane to Florida with their friends, like they wished, with all the hijackings back then. When Ibrahim and Ghazi and Elias brought Riyad and Laith back to Detroit, the key was in Laith's pants pocket. We gave them a Muslim farewell. Everyone walked in their funeral, but I could not leave them in unmarked graves. God forgive me, I made them gravestones of marble."

"That happens back home sometimes, too," Scheherazade said, and held her hand.

Fatima kissed the photo of the boys twice and put it back in the trophy.

"I heard the Greek lady saying to Millie that it was irony, that we had literally loved them to death, but Millie never repeated it to me, even though her sons went to Vietnam and came back okay," Fatima said. "I threw away the clothes I wore to their funeral although they were in perfect condition, for I refused to believe there was anything to come for which I would wear them again. That is why my children do not tell me of Laila's cancer. Or anything but the weather."

"Nor to Ibrahim," Scheherazade said.

"He moved away even more from his girls." Fatima nodded. "He was shamed in front of their kindness after he had showed them so little. Both of us would have mourned the loss of any of our children just as long. I know that to be true. But the rest of the world saw how Riyad and Laith were favored, and so they pitied us so much, like Millie, like my grown-up daughters, that there was no getting out of the misery. Ibrahim had married me out of duty, but I did not want him to feel obligated to my sorrow when he had so much of his own. I stopped talking of all problems with him, even small matters like weeding the garden. None of my daughters who married after had big weddings as there was no time when it seemed appropriate for us not to be in mourning, even as tragedies far greater than our own changed the outside world."

"You can't compare sadness to sadness," Scheherazade said.

"At least my boys did not know sadness. Their faces did not remind Ibrahim of his sisters, and so for the first time he enjoyed his children," Fatima said. "We sent them to camp. They got everything Randa and my other girls had not had. The bomb shelter had passed out of fashion, but they got swings, Boy Scout camp, and permission to date. The rules that applied to the girls didn't apply to the boys, and yet they were always watching out for their sisters before the girls married — and even after — and helping Millie with the yard work after her husband passed. . . . Riyad was in love with Millie's daughter Lisa. They called them high school sweethearts. Until the day of Millie's funeral, when I had no choice, I did not look at Lisa again, not at the man she married, not at the three children she had with him. God forgive me, never seeing that girl again was the only good thing that came of Millie's death."

"But then Amir filled the house again,"

Scheherazade said.

"No one ever filled it again. But when the boys had been gone a year, Soraya came with Amir to live with us," Fatima told her. "Her laughter made Ibrahim freeze — she was the closest in age to the boys and their favorite sister — so she would leave Amir with us for longer and longer periods of time. She hated to see her father hate to see her laugh. Zade and his twin sister were born the next year. The world had new twins, and life went on, except for us."

Scheherazade caught the mascara-blackened tear as it finally spilled out of Fatima's right eye. "The first thing I had Mr. Kim write in my funeral instructions was that I be buried next to them," Fatima said. "My boys were the only ones who asked about the house."

"The keys have never left Laith's pants?" Scheherazade said.

"Two years after the funeral, Ibrahim retired," Fatima said. "He couldn't stand being at home with nothing to do but watch news about Jimmy Hoffa's disappearance — he was a man who was a big leader in the union Marwan helped start. So Ibrahim said he would go back to Deir Zeitoon to fix the house. We were sure after all these years it would need many repairs. It was only supposed to be for two weeks. But he got trapped in Deir Zeitoon for three months because that was when the civil war started in Beirut, and the roads to the airport were closed. So he spent his time repairing the house before he put the Mansour family in charge of taking care of it. Deir Zeitoon, *subhan Allah,* was spared the worst of the civil war. He put the key back in Laith's pants when he returned, like somehow Laith still needed to know where the key was."

"Lena and Bassam with his dimple must have been children then," Scheherazade said after a while. "Surely you found light in them being home. God left you one son."

Fatima, still clutching the Al Kaline baseball, stood up and pulled out a rusty *Adam-12* lunch box. She undid the latch and watched several pictures and folded papers fall at Scheherazade's feet, pictures of a serious-faced young boy holding up awards and trophies. Scheherazade opened one of the pieces of paper. It was a tattered certificate that Fatima must have folded and unfolded hundreds of time: "Young Scientist of the Year." Scheherazade opened one certificate after another: "Rocket Scientist of the Future," "Tomorrow's Pioneer in Medicine," and so on.

"My Bassam was born the year John Kennedy became president and a woman in Florida caught a 680-pound sea bass," Fatima said. "The year Laila got engaged. It was a year of big things and great hope."

Scheherazade flipped through the photos of the boy genius. "How happy you must have been taking these pictures," she said.

"I don't remember." Fatima shrugged.

"How could you not?" Scheherazade said. "So is this boy operating trips to the moon now or running this Microsoft place everyone talks about so much?"

Fatima reached to twirl her missing hair. "He's a drunk in Las Vegas," she said when she couldn't find a strand to twist.

The light from the hallway filtered into the room as Decimal opened the doorway, clutching the mother-of-pearl Koran and a photo album, the scent of the lemon soap from her scrubbed hands practically overpowering the cedar chest's aroma.

Fatima covered her eyes, "Shut the door, girl." As Decimal did so, Fatima put the Al Kaline baseball back on her lap, letting her new dress cover it.

"I'm sorry I took a while, but I had to go throw up a little first," Decimal said. She carefully handed Fatima the mother-of-pearl Koran and a photo album. "Then I washed my hands and stuff doubly good, Mrs. Abdullah, before I touched anything. I saw this photo album on your dresser, but I didn't look at anything in the underwear drawer. I thought you might be able to show me a picture of Gran in Detroit."

Fatima willed herself not to look at Scheherazade. "I'm divorced, so stop calling me Mrs. Abdullah," Fatima said to Decimal. "You can call me Tayta, but not too often."

"Okay," Decimal agreed.

Fatima motioned for the girl to sit next to her on the cedar chest and took the album from her, careful not to dislodge the pouch from her lap. Fatima turned to a picture of three little girls and two boys dressed in Arabic folkloric clothes. "Hala is from the time when my children dreamed of prescribing drugs, not taking them. That's Hala — your Gran, as you say — and her sister Nadia outside the mosque on Joy Road. The girl with the bowed head and shiny shoes is Miriam. These two here are my boys, Laith and Riyad. Detroit built the mosque the year after Nadia was born, and they even brought a sheikh from Lebanon. We prayed there once a year."

"How come you only went once a year? I thought you were supposed to pray five times a day," Decimal asked. Fatima ignored

Scheherazade's laughter from the other side.

"Do you pray five times a day?" Fatima inquired.

"I'm only one-fourth Muslim," Decimal said. "I'm 50 percent Christian and 25 percent Taoist. My mom says I can pick whatever one I want or become a Hindu because they don't eat beef, which I don't digest so well. All I know is I can't be all of them 'cause I'd be so busy praying, I wouldn't have time to do anything else — five times a day and stuff for the Muslims, trekking to church every Sunday and all the saint holidays for Christians, and going back to China to my ancestors' shrine every time I did something bad or needed a little luck and stuff."

After listening to yet another story with too many words, Fatima decided it would be best to cut the girl off and get right to her schooling. She motioned to the girl to open the Koran to the first page.

"Bismillah al Rahman al Rahem," Fatima began. "In the name of God the most merciful."

SCHEHERAZADE

From under the fig tree, Scheherazade saw Fatima turn her head to the window for the second time. When she did not see Scheherazade, her face softened, almost as if she were relieved to have no choice but to look at the girl.

Scheherazade left, flying over a desert pitted with cactus and big petrol caravans and even bigger signs with men in cowboy hats and women in nearly nothing at all until suddenly a city rose out of the vast desert. It had more blinking lights than there seemed to be stars in the universe and colorful machines that clanged more than a troupe of court jesters dancing in their wooden shoes. There was no sun or moon to see from inside these palaces and monuments once glimpsed in Paris, Venice, and Luxor but never in such perfect condition. She had been born more than a thousand years after Ramses II ruled the real Luxor, and she was happy to see this new one before it, too, disappeared into history, as had so many wonders in her lifetime.

She floated in and out of green velvet tables with bright red chips, moving statues, and musical fountains. Finally, she reached a spot with little flashy adornment — aside from a long table for drinking and one of those televisions with Fatima's ESPN playing. Next to the cash register at the drinking circle, Scheherazade saw a photo she easily recognized: Fatima in her wedding dress. At the long table in front of the photo, Bassam let out another burp as he took a gulp from his glass.

Before sitting down next to Bassam, Scheherazade opened her gilded silver compact and checked her kohl in the mirror. In her rear view, she observed that even though he barely smiled, there was no mistaking the beauty of Bassam's dimple.

Bassam and Lena

I'm a fucking piece of shit. I fucking hate my fucking life. Fucking asshole. I'm all fucked up.

Having silently completed these daily affirmations that uncountable years at AA meetings had not changed, Bassam finished what was in his glass and then motioned to Candy, the blond bartender, for another round. Candy had been working there every night for as long as he had been a customer, which he calculated to be a fucking long time.

"We're like an old married couple, you and me," Bassam said to Candy.

"What do you know about couples?" Candy muttered, as she usually did when he said this.

512

"Hey, I was good to all my wives," Bassam replied, and that was mostly true. He'd married the first one at nineteen and the last one at thirty-nine, but he was almost forty-four now and single. "Tonight it's just you and me, babe."

It wasn't even an attempt at flirting, and Candy knew it. "At least I get paid to be here," she said, leaning in with her silicone implants to borrow a cigarette out of his shirt pocket. "What's your frickin' excuse, Sam?"

He'd run out of excuses long before. He tugged at Candy's blond perm, her cue to bring him his second drink of the night. Her hair wasn't her real hair, and he was pretty sure Candy wasn't her real name. If it were, he thought, that would mean that every fourth time people fucked in Vegas and had a baby, the result would be a girl named Candy. That's how many fucking Candys he knew here.

Just as he didn't know Candy's real name, she didn't know his. Bassam's name tag on the limo company's suit uniform said "Sam." So did the name tags of most of the other drivers who worked for the company. I am Sam, he thought, like half the fucking Arabs in America. The Samihs, the Samers, the Samirs, the Wissams, the Osamas —

screwed over the most — almost all became Sams in America. However, the other Sams had accents.

Vegas was a long way to come just to be a dumb-ass driver. Maybe that was why nearly every other Sam always found it so damn necessary to inform passengers how he'd been a "man of medicine" or an engineer back in Morocco or Egypt or Pakistan.

For his part, Bassam never told his passengers how Fatima and Ibrahim had paid for his rehab and taken out loans to supplement his undergraduate and graduate degrees at Ann Arbor and Harvard, finding new false hope with every scholarship he was awarded. What the hell — maybe he wasn't designing Fords and Lincolns like his high school buddies back in Detroit, but he was driving them. Ibrahim, who had lectured him on driving foreign cars, could at least be proud of that. And if Fatima ever came to visit, she could see that he wore a suit to work, as she had always dreamed he would.

Candy came back with Bassam's club soda and apple juice. Bassam gave her a thank-you tug to her perm and took a sip. Fatima was right about him being on a bar stool in Las Vegas, but he wasn't drunk. He'd been sober for a thousand nights, ever since September 11, 2001, when he had realized it was too fucking dangerous to be both drunk and Arab in America. That was when he became a driver. Before that, he'd done dumb-ass jobs in which it was easy to stay drunk; that accounted for just about half the fucking jobs in Vegas. However, Bassam had never driven under the influence. Just as when he was a child his only wish had been to disappear so that he could not cause his parents any more grief, he did not fear his own death but feared causing someone else's.

Bassam's eye caught an extra-large couple holding hands and waddling into the bar. They pointed to the black-and-white photos of long-dead celebrities who once had gotten hammered here. Shit, Bassam thought, the couple fancied themselves slumming it off the Strip, getting to see the fucked-up natives in their fucked-up environment, as their fucking travel book probably suggested. Candy gave them a pretty smile, and they ordered some cheese fries with their beers. Fat Midwesterners — the Vegas cliché, he thought, the snobbery of an Ivy League education making a rare appearance. Then he remembered that for far longer than this couple could have been married, he, too, had been a Vegas cliché: a guy with a drinking problem sitting at a bar while his miserable wife was out crying shit-faced to her friends about him at another bar. But he didn't drink anymore and had set his last wife free in a reasonably pleasant divorce. He had switched his addiction to gambling. Candy put down a picked-over bowl of peanuts from a table she'd just cleared. "Eat something before you piss off."

"I'll grab something on my way to the tables," Bassam answered. "Just waiting on the fucking tourists." He looked at his watch; it would be another hour before they ate all they could eat at the buffets.

"Why don't you go play with the big boys tonight?" Candy suggested.

Because, he answered silently, I could end up a big-ass winner. Over his lifetime he had gotten used to being a loser, and as a sober man, he didn't want to go out of his comfort zone. Kicking tourists' asses was still living in Loserville.

Candy's bar was Bassam's favorite, as familiar as shuffling an old yellowing deck of cards. Although he had been a cheap-ass customer for the last thousand days, he had spent several years here as a functioning drunk and a few more years as a nonfunctioning drunk. Hell, Candy even kept his framed black-and-white photo of Fatima above the cash register for him. The bar owner, who was somehow related to Candy, appreciated Bassam's business over the years, and Candy said she didn't mind having one more photo to dust. Ibrahim had told him as a teenager — or, more accurately, juvenile delinquent — to honor his mother even if he couldn't respect his father. Keeping Fatima's photo in the place where he spent the most time was his way of doing that, although he didn't look at the picture too often. He wanted to stay sober.

But Fatima was with him even at the gambling table. Just as she could juggle the entire price list for all the varieties of olives at all the Arab *ducans* in Detroit, Bassam could memorize every card laid down at a game; he had a photographic memory for up to five decks of cards. Altogether, that was only 260 things to remember.

His fucking sci-fi-freak friends in high school thought that with such gifts, he would be a brilliant fucking mathematician one day. But while they had stayed home and watched *Star Trek,* Bassam had met a girl. She had told him that if he really wanted to take a trip into outer space, it would be better to smoke grass with her than watch *Star Wars* at the mall for the twenty-second time. Her boobs had been damn convincing. When he had come home that night with the high worn off, the quiet — aside from that giggling kid Amir — of his parents' home had become even more unbearable. Before going to bed he took a few shots of his father's *araq*. Fatima had said it was for special occasions, but with Laith and Riyad gone there never would be special occasions in the house again, and no one missed it.

Candy handed Bassam the bar phone. "Sam #2 said to call him when you settled in," she said.

He pushed the phone away. "I don't feel like calling the fucking butthead back," he answered.

"I thought you'd say that, *ya hamar.*" Bassam turned to find Sam #2, né Hossam Akawi, standing behind him, wearing a Utah Jazz cap.

"Baseball caps and Arabs don't fucking go together," Bassam said, and reached to take the cap off.

Sam #2 put the cap back on. "Neither do Utah and jazz, so it's all good."

Bassam shrugged. Immigrant philosophy beat anything he'd studied at Harvard.

The two drove the same Town Car, with Sam #2 usually taking the night shift and Bassam the day shift. It didn't really matter to Bassam, but Sam #2 had a family and liked to spend daylight with them.

Sam #2 motioned to the club soda. "God keep the evil away," he said in Arabic, holding up the mother-of-pearl cross around his neck to Bassam's face. Bassam didn't speak Arabic but understood it well enough to know that Sam #2 disapproved of him in all languages. He couldn't tell Sam #2 that he needed this sober view of drunks to disgust him into staying sober. That, he believed, would make him sound like a fucking pansy wuss.

"I'm not drinking, pal. This is just home," Bassam explained. "Everyone needs a fucking home."

"A fucking home, asshole?" Sam #2 ranted. "What do you fucking know about not having no home, jerkoff? Let me tell you about not having no fucking home."

Then Sam #2 went off on his own personal Lebanese tragedy. It was the only rant in which this devout Greek Orthodox used the word *fuck* and all its derivatives. The fucking war in fuck-all Lebanon when he was a fucked-up child. Then he became a fucked-over man without a fucking home because it was occupied by displaced squatters the one fucking night he and his beloved mother had gone to visit his father in the fucking hospital where a UN doctor was trying to amputate his leg again, which had been badly amputated the first go-around by a fucking overworked doctor. Finally, he fucking fled alone to Syria in a fucking van one night as his mother fucking sobbed. Then there were all the fucking long years of fucking struggle in Jordan to get a visa to fucking Las Vegas while he got a fucking Ph.D. in law from the fucking University of Jordan.

What the fuck was a Ph.D. in law? But Bassam was shamed silent, as he was when the other Sam cabbies one-upped one another's geopolitical sob stories, shaking their fists at the television news while they argued with the words coming out the anchors' mouths.

"Okay, okay, fine," Bassam said. "I've got a home, dude, but why go there when I've got all this fucking sunshine here?"

Sam #2 looked at Bassam's pasty face through the glare of his twenty-four-hour neon life.

"Yeah, that's some tan you got going on, buddy boy," said Sam #2, all fucked out.

"It's all in the sunny outlook, my friend," Bassam explained. "You get to be unlucky here. In other places, they'd call bad luck being a loser."

"Luck, schmuck, listen good," Sam #2 said. "There's a belly-dancing convention at the Luxor. I got Sergei's car. I convinced him to take the day off. I'll drive that, and you drive ours. That crazy Russian has no idea what he gave up."

Sam #2 wasn't excited about half-naked women. He once had told Candy that his wife, whom he had met while getting that Ph.D. in law at the University of Jordan, would have been Miss Palestine if there still were a Palestine. Candy had been so moved by this that she had punched Bassam, who was sitting at his usual stool, in the shoulder, as if it were his fault someone didn't love her that much.

What Sam #2 was excited about was the Saudis. They were in town and would be all over these belly-dancing girls, drunk and horny. The tips promised to be huge.

"You don't need me," Bassam said.

"I hooked us a two-limo family, *habibi.* Take the limo I drove over in," said Sam #2. "I'll go get the other one and meet you at the Luxor in an hour. Don't be late, *compadre.*"

"Arabs speaking Spanish bugs the shit out of me," Bassam called out after him.

Candy put down another club soda, his third tonight. For variety, she had added

521

cranberry juice. She handed him the phone. "Take this call," Candy said. "I'm not your goddamn secretary."

"I'll be there, shithead," Bassam said into the phone. "Don't fucking check up on me every fucking minute."

"Hello?" Laila said on the other line. "May I speak to Bassam?"

Shit. His sisters usually called the bar earlier "just to say hi" in case he was hanging his head in a toilet puking and/or dead. He used to try to explain that he wasn't suicidal, just self-destructive. Still they called.

"Hi, sweetheart," Bassam said cheerily.

"I'm fine, same as usual," Laila replied, always acting as if he had had the common courtesy to ask after her. "How are you?"

"Super," he said, as usual.

"Super," Laila said as they lapsed into silence.

"Well, I'd better get going, Sis," Bassam said.

"Sure, I just wanted to say hi . . . and let you know that Lena is in Las Vegas . . . for a convention."

"Half the people in Las Vegas are here for some convention or another," he told her.

"She's staying at the Venetian," Laila added. "Maybe you could drive her somewhere or something."

That concluded Laila's big attempt at interfering.

"New wife?" Candy asked as she took away the phone.

Bassam shook his head. "You got any brothers or sisters, Candy?" he asked.

"Not really." She shrugged. "But I got a couple of half ones."

"I got nine . . . or seven," he said.

"Very funny," she said, helping herself to another cigarette. "Sam #2's waiting."

His sisters had all come out to help him over the years. Even Laila had gotten on an airplane to bring him books on taking it one day at time. There might have been a Koran in the book bag. The books all had colorful covers, and so he knew that his mother had helped Laila pick them out. He had taken Laila to see Wayne Newton, this chubby housewife whose oldest son was nearly his age, who was being eaten up by a cancer he was afraid to ask about. She had begged him to have faith in a dream.

But Bassam hadn't spent enough time sober to have any concrete dreams. There was his early plan to be the next David Bowie. That had been in the mid-1970s, when he had worked at Amo Zaki's falafel shop to make the money for an electric bass.

But the nights in those clubs had led him to become a pioneer in a new wave of cocaine addiction. When the principal had called to tell Fatima that Bassam had been caught with coke, she was furious. "How could he use Coke?" she had said. "Coke is on the Arab boycott list of companies doing business with Israel. Shame, *aabe*. Pepsi. Pepsi is okay. I am not raising Zionists." That was how far Bassam and his choice of drugs had stepped away from his parents' immigrant bubble.

At Ann Arbor during college, when his parents were less naive about him, he had met Carol. She somehow had gotten pregnant — while they were high, they assumed, as they didn't remember having sex that month. As they were boyfriend and girlfriend, they also assumed the baby was probably his and got married. His parents did not attend that wedding — or any of the others. They weren't really weddings, just civil ceremonies. Bassam had decided to follow Arab tradition as the only son and named his baby Ibrahim, but the boy was stillborn.

Bassam had married four times since Carol. Most good first dates ended in marriage followed by divorce. Part of his generally addictive personality. The women shared his addictions, particularly the alcohol.

"You're the reason the Koran recommends not drinking," Ibrahim yelled after Bassam's second marriage ended. "Look at you — a hobo."

"The word is 'alcoholic,'" Bassam had replied, as if medical terminology gave it dignity.

Bassam couldn't do anything in less than extremes: He couldn't go on a date without getting married, he couldn't drink without becoming an alcoholic, and he couldn't get an education without getting a Ph.D. He couldn't be a success without being a complete success or a loser without being a complete loser, and the latter came more naturally.

Candy motioned to the clock. "Sam #2's waiting," she reminded him.

Bassam drove straight past the Venetian, past crowds of conventioneers, any of which could have contained his sister. Lena was the closest to him in age, just three years younger. Lena's many accomplishments — National Spelling Bee finalist, Mini-UN delegate, and today an M.B.A. with a high-powered job in television — had always been overshadowed by the crisis of Bassam.

As Bassam entered the Luxor, guilt over

Lena was swept away by girls — well, *hardened* women despite their best efforts at trying to look cute in pigtail extensions. They wove through the lobby in pastel scarves twisted into bikini tops, diaphanous slit skirts, and bras with tinsel fringes, all bedazzled with blinding quantities of rhinestones. He followed the women through the slot machines to the belly-dancing convention, or the "casbah," as the casino signs read. The badly recorded Arabic pop music, with its heavy emphasis on the keyboard, sounded no better than the shit Sam #2 listened to in the Town Car.

On the walls of the casbah were life-size posters of American belly-dancing queens in heavy kohl with names like "the legendary Jamila," "the glamorous Jasmine," "the visionary Aziza," and of course "the scintillating Scheherazade."

Several drunken Saudis were gathered around the smoky stage, clapping and hooting to semiclad dancing women. Even though the Saudis no longer wore their *thowbs* and headdresses in the States, especially since 9/11, there was no mistaking these ones, tall and doughy with Indian subcontinent faces set off by wiry hair. Bassam picked up the faint odor of frankincense and sandalwood that always surrounded them, that lingered in the Town Car long after they had gone home.

Three of the Saudis clapped and danced in a circle, shouting *"Yallah, ya banat Arab."* Arab girls? Fuck no, Bassam thought. The Saudis knew that these weren't Arab women. That was why they were having such a kick-ass good time. The women were a fantasy. Women who looked as cheap and easy to them as McDonald's. Women who didn't think of them as the faces of terror. For the women, the Saudis were a fantasy, too: rich, handsome, interested, really rich.

Bassam pushed aside a dancer's veil that swirled into his face but didn't leap into high-speed subservient mode like the other Sams who had leeched on to this gig. Devout Muslims for the most part, they couldn't bring enough drinks over fast enough for the Saudis.

"We could use a little cash to improve the minaret at our mosque," Sam #17, aka Wissam, said in Arabic to a Saudi who looked to be about nineteen.

"God is great," the Saudi replied, handing Sam #17 a stack of twenties and taking the Amaretto and Coke from his hands. "If this is not enough money, let me know how much you need to make it the most beautiful minaret in America."

Sam #17 bowed, smiling as he flipped through the money on the way back to the bar, where Bassam joined him. Sam #17, along with many of the other Sam cabbies, thought Bassam, like them, didn't drink because he was a Muslim.

"Jerkoffs. Maybe I can get them to pay for some new prayer rugs," Sam #17 said. "My boy Ahmed said the mosque really needs some. A good boy. He's going be a doctor one day, just like I was in Algeria."

In Sam #17's enthusiasm over his oldest child's future, Bassam heard Fatima's once-high hopes. Too fucking dark of a place to go, so Bassam looked for a quick distraction and settled on a belly dancer with a green rhinestone-studded bra and black hair with dishwater-blond roots. He held her eyes for his habitual six seconds and smiled. Shit. Force of habit. Big fucking mistake, he thought as she responded with a huge grin. It was too late to take back his smile, and so he kept it on his face as she sashayed over to him.

"You look familiar," the woman said, her voice a surprisingly demure contrast to her heavy makeup. "Were you at the convention in Richmond?"

"Nope," Bassam replied.

"My name is Candy," she said. "What's yours?"

He couldn't offer to buy her a fucking drink. It would lead to marriage. It always did.

"Tell her you don't have a name and walk away," Sam # 2 whispered, magically there for him. "*Amigo,* there's good money to be made tonight. I'm taking my half now. I've told the others to come get you when they're ready."

He slapped Bassam on the back — extra hard — and left.

"What'd your friend say?" this Candy asked.

"What would you like to drink?" Bassam replied.

"I like green apple martinis," she said. A hip drink — five years ago. But not bad for someone who probably had been a prom queen runner-up two and half decades ago.

"I'll get you one," he said, smiling, "but then, honey, I'm going to have to skedaddle back to work."

When Bassam came back with her drink, Candy looked a little hurt, as if his whole work thing were an excuse. But it was honest, which was more than most of what was said in this town.

"Here's my card, if you want to give me a

call. The convention finale isn't for another three days," Candy told him. Her card said she was a masseuse. "I've got a number coming up: the Dance of the Seven Veils. Maybe you could stay and watch. My belly-dancing name is Fatima."

As she pronounced his mother's name the American way, with the stress on the second syllable instead of the first, Bassam knew it was no longer possible for this woman, masseuse or not, to give him a hard-on. He would not marry her.

"Girls are still determined to save you," a cheery voice said as Candy left to shimmy with the other women from her North Carolina troupe. Bassam turned to face Lena. His only younger sister was right on the cusp of turning forty but with a face so babyish that she could still wear pigtails if she wanted. Not that she would want to. Fuck, Bassam could see that she still had pimples, and she didn't do anything to hide them. She lived among the pretensions of Manhattan's elite, surrounded by reasonably convincing cosmetic surgery, and she didn't even put on any fucking lip gloss. It was like she had given up on love or sex — or whatever the fuck people called it — before she'd even tried it.

"What are you doing here?" Bassam said,

enveloping her in hug that should have been a little more enthusiastic.

"I heard there was a belly-dance convention," she said, shrugging.

She was swaying her hips to the music now. She would be horrified if she realized that she was doing that, and so Bassam didn't tell her.

"I meant what are you doing in Vegas?"

"NATPE," she said. "It's a television industry convention."

"I drove a bunch of them around today," he remembered.

"Lucky you," she said.

"They were fuckin' assholes," he replied.

"That's why I told them I couldn't go with them to Cirque du Soleil tonight." Lena smiled. "I told them I had to see my brother."

"You should have told me you were coming," Bassam said.

"I left a message with Candy at the bar a week ago."

Yes, yes, you did, he told her silently. "Candy can be a blond ditz," he said aloud. "She must have stuck the message in her fucking hairdo and lost it."

"How come you have your name tag on?" Lena asked. "I thought you worked the day shift."

She sniffed loudly. Bassam knew that she couldn't tell if the alcohol smell was from him or from the drinks in the other cabbies' hands. He didn't lean in any closer to help. He was tired of having to prove himself to the worriers, which he knew from AA was completely selfish. But he wanted his sisters to believe for themselves that he was sober.

"I can make extra money doing two shifts," he answered, sounding uncharacteristically ambitious. "How's your job?"

"I love it," Lena lied.

Lena was successful despite herself. With her knack for numbers, she had soared in finance, with the network moving her up, always as an example of female promotion. So timid, she wasn't the natural choice. However, the more natural choices had been more aggressive in everything, including getting husbands and having children, which inadvertently put them out of the running.

And she was a good sister. Even though she had never even taken a puff of Millie's Virginia Slims, she had never given him away to their parents. When Fatima had identified the smell of pot in the house as mold, she had made Lena spend most of 1976 cleaning under cabinets and shelves for hours, scouring for the source. Meanwhile, Bassam would leave the house to continue his high at the park, telling Fatima that he was rehearsing his clarinet solo with the junior high school marching band for the bicentennial fireworks celebration.

"Two hundred years," Fatima had scoffed as he hummed John Philip Sousa music while walking out the door. "We have vendettas in Lebanon twice as old as that."

Lena stuck out her tongue at Bassam as he left, which made Amir, toddling behind her, giggle. But as much as she had fought with him about the pot when it was just the two of them, she did not tell Fatima that the school didn't have a marching band anymore. She hadn't wanted to add to the sadness in the house.

She was laughing as Candy and her troupe twirled blanket-size silk scarves around their heads.

"It looks like a fucking sheikh's harem rebelling," Bassam joked.

Lena began chuckling, which involved some snorting. Still, her beauty lay in how easy it was to make her laugh. They had to leave the room as women in reinforced rhinestone bras turned to look at them.

"We're mean," Lena said, finally getting control of herself.

"Oh, come on, you're ten times better,"

Bassam told her. "Hell, I am."

He swiveled his hips in a pivot, wanting to hear her chuckle more.

"No, I'm about as ridiculous as them," she concluded. "But I know I'm not sexy. They don't."

"You could have any guy you wanted," Bassam told her.

"That's pretty lame for a pep talk." She held up her hand, just as Fatima always did. "It's okay. I've done okay in other areas. We each have our strengths."

Bassam had very few strengths. "Whatever happened to . . . ah . . . what's his name?" he asked. "The personal trainer."

"The guy I went out with for five years? That what's his name?" said Lena, trying to make light of a man who had cheated on her as often as the opportunity arose.

"He wasn't a drunk, was he?" Bassam said.

She shook her head. "Men without paddles," she mumbled.

"What?" Bassam repeated.

"Men without paddles. It's something I heard my assistant Lucienne say the other day," Lena explained. "Men who just float aimlessly from spot to spot forever, like most of the men in New York. Like Tony. That was his name. Like —"

"Like me," Bassam finished for her.

Bassam watched reruns of *Sex and the City* sometimes when Candy had it on in the bar. Lena needed to get out of Manhattan. It was too bad she was successful there. It would be hard to leave success, he imagined. He wanted to tell her that in any other city men would appreciate her, but those were not comfortable things for a failed brother to tell a smart sister.

But maybe a sober brother could do more for her. He was that now. What would a sober brother do for his little sister? Then it came to him.

"You should come visit more often," he said. He was going to find her someone. Yes, that was what he, as a sober man, would do. He would not rest until he did. After all, it was in the blood. Fatima always said his great-grandmother was some amazing matchmaker in Lebanon, and his father had found Miriam a husband.

Sam #17 tapped Bassam on the shoulder. Standing behind him were four red-eyed, weaving Saudis.

"Here's your driver," Sam #17 said to the Saudis.

"I'll bring the car around," Bassam told them. "Where is it you gentlemen would like to go?"

"The Bunny Ranch," one slurred.

"The Moonlight Bunny Ranch," another corrected.

"It's near Reno," Bassam said. "You want to go all the way to Reno?"

"Yes, the Moonlight Bunny Ranch," they said, nodding.

Bassam bowed as he, his sister, and Sam #17 watched the Saudis totter outside. "Why defy your stereotype when you can afford not to?" he said.

"Gross," Lena mumbled.

Sam #17 looked at her with appreciation. "Finally I see you with a nice girl," he whispered to Bassam.

"Dude, this is my sister," Bassam told him. "Lena."

"*Bint Arab,* an Arab girl." Sam #17 bowed with flourish. "I am Wissam. *Ahlan wa sahlan,* welcome, welcome, most welcome."

Lena shuffled her feet, uncomfortable around friendly men. Bassam thought it was too bad that Sam #17 was married. And no longer a doctor.

Sam #17 motioned to Bassam that they should get going.

"I'll walk you to your car," Lena said.

"How are you going to get back to your hotel?" Bassam asked. He wanted to give her a ride but didn't want her to be in his car with this evening's customers.

"I'll take a cab," Lena said. "Maybe I'll go back and watch the dancing for a little while longer."

"Why take a cab when your brother drives a limo? I'll send someone over to get you in about an hour," he said. "Just meet him outside."

"I don't want to get you in trouble," she said, as though his job were important.

"I won't tell the driver that you're my sister, so you won't have to make small talk with him," he promised. "I'll just say you're a regular that I can't pick up tonight."

He hugged her goodbye, this time tightly. He knew she would stand in place until he drove out of sight.

"So is your sister married?" Sam #17 asked Bassam as they walked to their respective limos. The first question asked of a *bint Arab*. Bassam shook his head, surprised at how sad that made him.

"I'm going to find her someone," Sam #17 vowed. "A nice Arab guy. Or a good Muslim."

"That sounds like a fucking good plan, *affendi*," Bassam said, and gave Sam #17 a high five and got into his Town Car. The four Saudis were coming down from their dancing and drinking.

"Sir," said a Saudi. "Do you think it is better that we still tell the women at the ranch that we are Indian maharajahs?"

"Are there still maharajahs in India?" Bassam asked. He wondered exactly what he had learned at Harvard. Bassam offered the Saudis cigarettes and then took one himself.

"Italian is probably your safest choice," Bassam shrugged. "Be Italian."

"Inshallah," they said, and after finishing their cigarettes were soon snoring.

Good. Bassam enjoyed driving in silence. He lit one of the Saudis' cigarettes and turned on Lucky 98 FM and hummed to classic rock that had seemed so much more meaningful when he was a high high schooler. He drove along the Strip past a troupe of freaky-ass clowns, a Swiss Heritage Brotherhood gathering with lederhosen on, and a posse of giddy senior citizen women in matching red hats followed by their less giddy gray husbands. He turned his head to look back at a group of hotties in tight shorts and cowboy hats. One girl flashed him a grin, but before he could grin back, another hottie gesticulated and pointed ahead, and he turned back around just in time to avoid slamming into the car in front of him. The Saudis woke up with several groans, jolted by his sudden braking, but they fell asleep again quickly, except for one.

"Do you have any hip-hop music?" the Saudi asked.

"I'm not so hip, and I can't remember the last time I had any hop," Bassam replied. The guy was much younger than Bassam originally had thought. "You should sleep. It's about another ten hours and ten minutes until we get there."

"Ah, so you go often," the Saudi said.

"Everyone thinks the ranch is in Vegas, so they fly here instead of Reno," he said.

This was the tenth time Bassam had done this boring-ass desert drive in the last year. The owner of the Moonlight Bunny Ranch had turned out to be a real patriot. Last June, he had offered the first fifty returning Iraqi servicemen to visit the ranch free sex and 50 percent off for the next fifty days for all other returning military.

"Does your wife know you go here?" the Saudi asked.

"I'm not married at the moment," Bassam said. "How about you?"

"Next year, *inshallah*," he answered. "It will be hard for you to find a good woman. Women don't marry here. Just sleep around."

"I fucking wish, my friend," Bassam said.

The Saudi handed him a business card. "This woman, she doesn't even know my name and she gave me her phone number," he said. It was Candy Fatima the masseuse's card. At least she had gotten over him.

"She's not cheap," Bassam said. "She's lonely. There's a difference."

"There are more moral ways to be lonely," the Saudi said.

"Like going to a whorehouse?" Bassam asked.

"I am not going in," the Saudi said.

"Your friends are," Bassam said.

"One of them is the older brother of the girl I am marrying next year, so I must be polite and ride in the car," the Saudi explained. "The other two are only indulging in the drinking. But he will be upset if we spoil his fun, and it is our duty to allow him fun."

"Nothing like a free people." Bassam smirked.

"That's our way," the Saudi countered. "We have family obligations, and he is ours as his company employs half our families. You know how family is."

"Not really," Bassam said.

"Do you know what my wife to be told me about coming here?" the Saudi said. "She said that she would not marry a man who defies Islam by gambling, drinking, and whoring like her brother."

"Sounds like a good woman," Bassam said.

"She is," the Saudi agreed. "*Deep in the mine the gold dust is merely dust. . . . Gold, when extracted, grows much in demand, and when exported as aloe fetches gold.* That is nine-hundred-year-old Arabian poetry, my brother, before we even knew we had what you Americans call the black gold. Whores and alcohol or severe Islam allows us to hide from the truth — which is that we let people with more money than us take our religion backward, that we made a deal with the devil for easy money in return for our silence."

All the talk of silence reminded Bassam of his sister. He exhaled and dialed Sam #2 on the car phone.

"Listen, dude, where are you?" Bassam said to Sam #2.

Sam #2 told him that he had just left his Saudis at the MGM for a little blackjack.

"Perfect," Bassam said. "I need you to pick up a girl at the Luxor and take her to the Venetian. After you pick her up, I'm going to call your cell phone and you pretend that I'm some other Sam and say in Arabic how hot you think she is."

"*Compadre,* you cannot get married to-night," Sam #2 warned.

"Her name is Lena. She's my baby sister," Bassam told him. "She's visiting from New York."

"*Bint Arab, mashallah,*" said Sam #2. "Is she married?"

"Not yet," said Bassam.

"Man, why not, homie?" said Sam #2. "How about Nassim for her?"

Nassim was Sam #6, a pretty cool guy from Tunisia.

"He's just a fucking driver," Bassam said.

"Right," Sam #2 agreed. "But homes, he has an engineering degree from Morocco."

"Just call me when she gets in the car but don't say anything about me being on the line."

Bassam hung up. The Saudi was looking at him in the rearview mirror. Damn, he still wasn't sleeping.

"Why isn't your sister married?" the Saudi asked.

"We kind of have a messed-up family," Bassam replied.

"That happens in America." The Saudi sighed.

"It happens everywhere, dude," Bassam said. "We just talk about it. All the time. To

542

our friends, on the radio, on TV, in chat rooms."

"It doesn't seem to help," the Saudi said.

No, it doesn't, Bassam thought. It's all fucked up. I'm fucked up.

A few minutes later Sam #2 was looking at Lena in the rearview mirror. She did not see him because she was watching a family outside Circus Circus celebrating the birthday of a boy who was sitting on his father's shoulders, blowing a whistle. The boy's hair was black and frizzed out by the Vegas steam, like hers.

"People keep their kids out here too late, you know," Sam #2 remarked.

Lena nodded. The truth was that if Lena had had kids, she would have carried them on her shoulders any time of the night. In fact, every one of her birthdays for the last five years had been marked by tears for the children she had not given birth to, children who lived only in her imagination.

Lena pulled out her Palm Pilot. She wanted to be a woman with a schedule that had ballet lessons, play dates, and soccer practice rather than back-to-back meetings with the sales team leaders on the coasts. There was just one more call scheduled for today: the toughest sales call of all. Lena dialed it.

"Hi, Mom," Lena said. "I hope I didn't wake you."

"Oh, *habibti*," Fatima gushed on the other end of the line, as she always did no matter how late it was. Lena wished her mother didn't get so excited every time she called. "It's pretty humid here, Mom," Lena replied. She found a few other adjectives to describe a June night in Vegas: hot, sticky, damp, balmy. That filled up another minute.

"Everyone needs a witness to her life," Fatima segued, not asking after Bassam. "You and your husband don't have to love each other too much, but someone to know you are here on this earth. Someone who knows what you sounded like yesterday and will be there to hear how you sound tomorrow, even if he has nothing to say."

"Inshallah," Lena whispered into the phone so that the driver with the same "Sam" name tag as her brother wouldn't hear.

"Try harder, *min shan Allah*," Fatima pleaded.

"I heard it was a little foggy in Los Angeles today," Lena answered.

She saw Sam #2 looking at her from the rearview mirror, witnessing her barely holding her happiness together for her mother.

"How's your health?" Lena continued on

544

the phone. "Great. I was just going to e-mail Amir today to say that I was thinking of coming next weekend. . . . No point? Why?"

Sam #2's cell phone rang. "Listen, I need you to say in Arabic that she's really pretty," Bassam said on the other end. "Don't let her know I'm telling you to say it. Did you flirt with her?"

"She's talking to your mom," Sam #2 whispered. "She's your sister. What's your problem?"

"Oh, some friend," Bassam replied. "You think all those other women you flirt with aren't somebody's sister?"

"I'll talk about her being pretty, but that's it," Sam #2 said.

"Well, just do it before you get to the Venetian," Bassam said.

Lena was still on the phone. "No, Mom, New York hasn't been too hot yet. Sunny but nothing to complain about. I'll tell you more about it when I visit next week. What do you mean, don't visit? I want to. I insist."

Sam #2 slammed on the brakes in front of the Bellagio. They screeched loudly enough that Fatima screamed into Lena's cell phone.

"No, Mom, everything is super," Lena said. "I'll call you later."

Lena hung up as Sam #2 pulled away

from the curb. "*Affendi,* I almost ran off the road," he shouted in Arabic to his cell phone. "I got this real beauty in the car. She's something — best-looking tourist this week."

In the back, Lena blushed. The driver would be embarrassed, she thought, if he knew she understood Arabic. She didn't hear Bassam telling Sam #2 not to overdo it.

"Oh, gorgeous," Sam #2 said. "A little heavy in the hips, nice chest, small waist, big eyes."

Heavy hips? She'd have to go to the gym more.

"What?" Sam #2 said, trying to follow Bassam's words on the other end. "Heavy hips? No, I meant honey hips. New York girls, man."

Lena stopped pinching her stomach fat. New York? So she looked like she was from New York, not Detroit. Good. Any further praise was cut off by her cell phone again. She expected it to be Lucienne with her meeting schedule for the next day.

"Mom cut off her hair," Randa burst out. "Soraya saw with her own eyes."

"I just got off the phone with her," Lena said. "She sounded fine. Totally strong. She even told me she didn't need me to visit.

546

Oh, God . . .”

Fatima would no more tell her not to visit than she would cut off her hair.

“See, I told you,” Randa said, and hung up to spread the word elsewhere.

At the Venetian, Sam #2 opened the door for Lena.

“The driver who told me to pick you up took care of everything,” he told her. “Including tip.”

“Really?” Lena said. Bassam hadn’t forgotten. Sam #2 watched Lena walk away with her thoughts, which were now on Fatima’s hair.

When Bassam arrived back at Candy’s bar, he walked past several belly dancers who had found their way there for a drink. Candy handed him a club soda, this time with a little grenadine syrup for variety. Pomegranate. Just what his mom put in the sauce for her grape leaves and stuffed eggplant.

“What are you staring at the glass for?” Candy asked. He took a twirl of her perm into his hand. There was only one Candy for him.

He would take it slow for once. “Candy, would you like to meet my mom?”

Fatima wouldn’t like Candy, but she’d like

to meet someone before he married her, for a change.

"Why would I want to do that?" Candy said, looking at the picture of Fatima by the cash register.

"Candy, I don't even know your last name," Bassam said to this woman who had been his truest friend.

"Cane."

"Candy Cane," he said. "I like it. It's sweet."

Like she hadn't heard that one before.

"And what's your last name?"

"My real name is Bassam, you know."

"Buy some what?" said Candy, and waited for the punch line.

"It's Bassam," Bassam said. "It means 'smile' in Arabic."

"That's not very funny."

"That's because it's true," Bassam replied.

He motioned to her to help herself to a cigarette from his pocket.

"A girl called Lena phoned here for you like six times," Candy said. "Said something about you guys needing to go to L.A."

"I'll call her in a few," Bassam said. "Another sister."

"Whatever you want to call her, boy." Candy shrugged.

"So, Candy Cane, where did you go to

school?"

"Lincoln High," she said. "You went to Kennedy, I bet."

"Harvard."

"You're a regular fucking riot tonight."

"Candy, I believe you are my fucking paddle," Bassam told her. Hope in a bottle blonde instead of just a bottle. He had no idea what she would want with an asshole like him, but for now she — no, she and he together — was an obsession worth exploring.

■ ■ ■ ■

THE 1001ST NIGHT

■ ■ ■ ■

SCHEHERAZADE

When Scheherazade landed in Los Angeles for her 1001st visit to Fatima, the first person she saw on the sidewalk was the homeless man with Bassam's dimple. There was no mistaking the resemblance, even beyond the dimple.

She would not be in Los Angeles tomorrow, even though she felt as if she were an established citizen, even more so than were the mortals she had whirled through today. In the unfiltered Pacific sun, the homeless men, aside from the one with Bassam's dimple, had all changed in the last 1001 nights; the homosexuals and underweight beauties of her first few days had been exchanged for younger and thinner ones. The people on the bus and the shiny polished petrol caravans had increased steadily every day so that the bus was harder to get on and the traffic had even more petrol caravan blockages. It hadn't even been three years, yet many buildings had risen up quickly since and just as many had disappeared. Not much seemed to be allowed to grow old here.

She wondered about the soldier she had followed to Los Angeles. Had he gone back to Iraq after his father's funeral? Had he come back again and gone again? Perhaps she would look for him tomorrow, either here or there.

Outside Amir's home, standing next to the petrol caravan, Scheherazade heard Fatima reciting loudly from the Koran and Decimal repeating after her in Arabic more accented than Nadia's, more accented than Agent Sherri Hazad's.

Scheherazade climbed up the eucalyptus tree. Fatima still was clutching the Al Kaline baseball in her hand, but it was as clear as a perfect diamond that great-grandmother and great-granddaughter had been up all night. She would give them more time together before the last day. Then Amir interrupted her quiet generosity.

AMIR

"Hallelujah, hallelujah," Amir shouted as he turned off the engine, keeping time to the gospel music coming out of his Honda.

He looked at the SUV parked in front of the fig tree and gave it the finger. "I'm the man," Amir sang out. "Screw you and your SUV, buddy; the soap's going to kill you off tomorrow. Slowly and painfully. Hallelujah. Halle—"

"Bismillah al-Rahman al-Raheem," came Fatima's surprisingly powerful voice from inside the house. It competed for attention with the cheap car radio. He turned off the gospel music.

His soon-to-be-dead-on-TV ex-lover and the whole neighborhood surely could hear Fatima. However, he was feeling too blessed today to care. He covered his ears when he heard Decimal repeat the Koran after Fatima in Arabic.

"It's *bismillah,* kid, *bismillah,* in the name of God. It is all you have to remember," Amir mumbled. Whatever. They hadn't even noticed him disappear for his audition. He turned on the hose so that the garden would continue to flourish like that of a successful person, which, after landing the part today, he was.

When he turned to water the rosebushes, something light green with a tiny pink streak caught the edge of his right eye. He turned to find that the pink was on the fig tree. Could it be? He moved in closer. Yes, it was a fig. Today had been filled with two enormous hallelujah moments. First, the director was off his all-protein diet and high on carbs during the audition, and now this. The fig tree had fruited.

SCHEHERAZADE

When Amir went inside, Scheherazade came down from the eucalyptus tree to look at the fig. How had she missed this miracle? A tree that had not fruited in sixty-seven years finally had found a home in America.

Scheherazade climbed back up the eucalyptus tree so that she could see Fatima's reaction when Amir showed her. This time, she was distracted by the closer voices below in the petrol caravan.

"He knows we're here," Sherri Hazad said from inside. "Talking about poisoning us with soap . . . the grandmother showed me some 'expensive soap' in the kitchen. I used it. I should get myself checked."

"It might just be soap," Sherri Hazad's partner cautioned.

"What about the cousin taking a job in Iraq?" Sherri Hazad pointed out.

"Thousands of guys have," Sherri Hazad's partner reminded her. "I checked out the construction company. He's already saved

556

the taxpayers thousands of dollars by re-working the original blueprints. No time to think out a plot with insurgents."

"And the guy driving the Saudis all around the Nevada desert?" Sherri Hazad asked. "There are weapon-testing sites out there."

"Perhaps we should question Amir Abdul-lah sooner than later," Sherri Hazad's partner conceded.

Fatima's Koran recitation filtered into the petrol caravan. "Maybe he's got the old lady indoctrinating for him," Sherri Hazad said.

"Remember not to jump too far ahead," he said. "But true, no one should ever underestimate the influence someone has over someone else, intentionally or uninten-tionally."

Scheherazade believed this to be the only thing she had ever heard anyone in a petrol caravan say that made any sense.

FATIMA

Fatima had not slept all night. After she had spoken so much about her sons earlier, there was no way she could. After today, she would have her entire afterlife to sleep. With the Al Kaline baseball clutched in her hand, she had spent the night sitting on her grandfather's cedar chest doing what she was sure would be described at her funeral as her final worthy act: teaching this awful girl the miracle of the Koran. They took only occasional breaks, during which time she instructed the girl to look for the cordelia pants with the key.

Soon she would dismiss the girl to call Ibrahim. He would be the last earthly person she would speak to besides Amir.

"Let us do one more thing," Fatima said. "Open the Koran to *Ayat al-Kursi.*"

"What, ma'am Tayta?" Decimal said.

"Ayat al-Kursi." Fatima sighed. "The most important verse in the Koran. It's very simple."

"What's it about?" Decimal asked.

"Learn it first," Fatima said. "Then, if we have time, I'll tell you what it means."

Decimal opened the book backward, at least to Fatima's Arab eyes.

"What page is it on?" Decimal said.

The book had gotten very heavy for Fatima in the last couple of days, and so she left it on Decimal's lap as she delicately turned the pages to the right one.

"Bismillah el-rahman el-raheem," Fatima passionately intoned, pointing with her index finger at the flowery calligraphy as if she were actually reading it.

"Don't you want to put on your glasses?"

Decimal asked.

"I don't need glasses to read the Koran," Fatima said. "You don't worry about my reading. Just repeat."

Fatima lowered her hearing aid to minimize the girl's frightening accent. Still, she found comfort in the *Ayat al-Kursi*. But at the line about God owning everything on heaven and earth, she suddenly pictured the house in Lebanon in chrome and dropped the ball. The girl started to chase it, but Fatima put up her hand. *"Lahu ma fi semawati wa ma fil'ardi,"* she continued, and motioned for the girl to keep reciting after her while she hobbled to retrieve the ball.

When Fatima bent down for it, Decimal, who was focused on the book as though she, too, were really reading it, looked up just as the tremble in Fatima's worried hand made her drop it again.

Decimal caught it before it rolled out the room and handed it to Fatima

Fatima held it close. "Let us look for the key again."

"You don't want to read any more Koran?" Decimal said, disappointed.

One could not discourage a sinner from reading the Koran. She had just taught the girl how God never sleeps on his duties, and neither would she. The key would have to wait. Maybe the girl could be rescued, her newfound virtue a final gift to a dying woman. *Inshallah.*

"If Zade, my matchmaking grandson, can get you married off, you could have a fresh start, have even more kids — legitimately," Fatima said. "He's not so good at his job as I am, but I don't have his time."

"Who would marry a pregnant girl?" Decimal said.

"You're right," Fatima agreed, recalling the circumstances of her own marriage. "It would have to someone duty-bound. Well, then, perhaps Zade himself might be a forgiving husband. He's a little old for you, but cousins are good. My grandparents were very happy cousins. No in-law problems, you know."

"Cousins?" Decimal said, and began dry heaving in big gulps as she ran out.

Fatima marveled at how every woman's morning sickness came for no reason. But the baseball signed by Al Kaline just for her boys stared back at her. Too cruel to leave it to Ibrahim, but who else was her sons' heir?

She turned to put it in the cedar chest and found Scheherazade lying on the box. She sat up and helped Fatima sit next to her, rubbing her fingers along Fatima's face to smooth out the Avon creases. "I'm going to have to freshen you up," she said. She blew dust off Fatima's new dress and began combing out her purple stubs.

"You smell like old beer." Fatima grimaced and held her nose.

"That's because I just came back from Las Vegas," Scheherazade announced.

Fatima let go of her nose but did not ask after her son. She did not want to hear anything bad on her last day.

"He's fine," Scheherazade answered.

Fatima remembered how she always told Ibrahim the same lie. "People his age are presidents of countries," she said as her fingers tapped the ball on her lap.

"Let Bassam take the house," Scheherazade suggested. "Maybe he'll meet a nice Arab girl and start over."

"What would a nice Arab girl want with Bassam?" Fatima asked. "A middle-aged man with no money. . . . Besides, the Azar family makes the best wine in the valley, in all the world, some say. Their vineyard is not far from the house. Even the bad things we do best. I can't put milk in front of the cat."

"Back home, the house would be his," Scheherazade said. "As your only living son."

Fatima shuddered. Since Bassam had

turned fourteen, Fatima had stayed up until dawn thinking of all the things that could happen: Bassam could hurt himself in an accident, be killed in a drug deal, get liver cancer, not get into Harvard, or, worst of all, kill someone. "After my boys died, I became afraid for all my children and stopped enjoying them except in my dreams," Fatima recalled. "Then Bassam turned me into a night owl, so I hardly dreamed."

Fatima wiped away a tear that had spilled onto the Koran.

"Let us not talk of tearful things," Scheherazade said. "Don't you want to look nice today?"

"Does it have to be today?"

"Today always has to be today, just as yesterday was yesterday and tomorrow will be tomorrow," Scheherazade explained. "You're mortal. That's how it goes. Sun up, then sun down, then sun up. And so on. Since time began."

"I'm not ready," Fatima fretted. "I still have to find the key. And call Ibrahim. How many hours do I have left?"

"With me?" Scheherazade said. "A few."

"Then what happens?" Fatima asked.

Scheherazade shrugged again and went for the Avon.

"You promised you would tell me," Fatima admonished her. "The time has come, and you still haven't told me. *Aabe alacki,* shame on you."

"You're the storyteller this time, not me," Scheherazade pointed out.

"How would I know?" Fatima countered. "I'm not God."

"Neither am I," Scheherazade reminded her.

"If you don't know how, then how do you know it is going to be tonight?"

Instead of answering, Scheherazade picked up the Koran and carefully turned to a certain page. She placed it on Fatima's lap. "Oh, would that I had prepared for my life," she read aloud.

"When would I have had the time to do that?" Fatima demanded.

"You've had the last 1001 days."

"I was preparing for a funeral!" Fatima replied.

"I didn't tell you to do that." Scheherazade shrugged. "You did."

Fatima's eyes flashed frustration, just as Scheherazade's did when Fatima began a story of Deir Zeitoon. She raised her cane as if she were going to beat Scheherazade with it.

"I had to plan out every detail of my

funeral so that my children would be spared the anguish of doing that," Fatima said, her voice shrill. "Not like I was with their brothers."

"Was the funeral the part of your boys' lives you really remember the most?" Scheherazade asked.

"No." Fatima sighed. "But it seemed like taking care of my funeral was the only thing I could do for my kids, especially since I couldn't give them all the house. Let us be honest, I could not even marry them all off. And now I am going."

"Going where?" Scheherazade said.

"To heaven, of course," Fatima replied.

Scheherazade pondered that. "If you say so."

"I'm not going to hell on Judgment Day," Fatima vowed.

"I wouldn't think so," Scheherazade agreed. "What shall we choose to do today to celebrate our last day together?"

"Dying's not a party," Fatima said, but Scheherazade pointed again to the book.

"Oh, would that I had prepared for my life," Fatima recited for her again.

Scheherazade grinned, which Fatima did not like. "What are you saying?"

Scheherazade clamped her lips together tightly, holding her breath. She did, however, indicate the line in the Koran again.

"Oh, would that I had prepared for my life," Fatima repeated once more. Scheherazade's grin took up even more of her face, which wasn't easy as she hadn't let go of her breath. Fatima really did not like that grin. She circled Scheherazade, cane ready for attack.

"What is it that you're trying to not tell me?" Fatima demanded. Scheherazade put her hands on her hips, frustrated. She let go of her breath. "What more do I . . ." Fatima began. But the sun had risen high enough that its rays spilled into the room. In the sunlight, the answer came to Fatima. "*Ya Allah,* I'm not dying today?"

Scheherazade threw her hands up in the air. "As I said, I'm not God any more than you were with your sons," she cried out. "But I shall assume that you probably wouldn't have the strength to hold that cane up so high if you were about to leave the mortal world within hours."

Fatima lowered the cane slowly. "So I'm not dying?"

"How should I know?" Scheherazade said.

Fatima pushed Scheherazade away as she approached her with a brush coated in old blush. "To know you have 1001 nights to tell your stories is a gift and a curse. But when our tales are over, so are our lives," Fatima quoted Scheherazade from their first night together.

"There is not just one way to hear a sentence." Scheherazade sighed. "All I meant was that life is in the end a collection of stories that are connected through us. Stories keep us entertained and enlightened, and if we don't know the ending, all the better. Look, I'm the one who kept our stories going by not telling you the ending, as I don't really know it. You already thought you knew the ending, but you didn't. Indeed, those are my favorite endings. Surprise."

Scheherazade let out a roll of laughter that rattled her bangles more ferociously than ever before in Fatima's presence, and Fatima sat down, placing the Al Kaline ball back on her lap. "No, no, no," she declared with three taps of her cane. "I can't keep on living forever. That is impossible." The sudden prospect of more life was more overwhelming than what she had thought had been a death sentence from Scheherazade 1001 nights ago.

"You won't," Scheherazade promised. "Eventually, you will die, and then you will be given your answer as to how. It will happen, but you cannot know yet. God is always with the patient. That is written in your Koran, too." She picked up a compact to apply more Avon to Fatima's already sufficiently inflamed cheeks. "Death is written for us no matter what, but living your life so that it is filled with stories is the best way to wait for it. Like your boys did, and like you did before they were gone."

Fatima rolled the Al Kaline baseball between her hands. "Perhaps now I have more time to take care of everything for my children," she finally said, hope resurfacing.

"There is never enough time for that," Scheherazade bemoaned with another flourish of blush.

"You perfected yours," Fatima said.

"Only in my stories." Scheherazade sighed. "My babies are long gone. But immortality lasts and lasts. For the first couple of hundred years the power is exhilarating, but then it gets very lonely. There are too many ghosts to haunt my evenings. Why do you think I came to you? I always need someone to keep me company for 1001 days. To deal with one's stories alone would be too much for any soul — my children, my husband, my court, my sister and father are just stories now. But 1001 stories from another person are exactly enough. No more. And no less. One thousand is a boring number. And 1002 is just too much, no offense. Whether you count in English or Arabic, 1001 stories are perfect."

Fatima bowed her head. "Leave me alone with my life. Go."

"Not yet," Scheherazade said. "One more day, one more story. Stop pouting. So death is just another thing in your life you have no choice in determining. Ten children and two husbands and you still thought you could control fate. *Smallah.*"

"Go," Fatima repeated. She stood up tall and raised her cane again, bearing hip pain to threaten Scheherazade with it. As she did so, the Al Kaline baseball dropped out of her lap. Fatima quickly put down the cane to follow Scheherazade when she chased it. Neither the mortal woman nor the immortal woman could reach it before it rolled to the door. It was picked up by a hand Fatima recognized very well: Amir's.

"Al Kaline," he read, attempting breezy conversation. "The Tigers never had anyone like him."

Fatima knew Amir had no idea how great Al Kaline had been but had heard enough of her shouting about death and life from the other side of the door to be disturbed.

From behind him, the girl sneezed. "Look what I found downstairs," she said. "Amir says it's the key to your old Ford Mercury in Detroit. Maybe you could leave that to your son Uncle Bassam."

Fatima pretended not to see Amir nudge Decimal quiet. "Let us continue with *Ayat al-Kursi,* child," she said, feeling cursed that this girl must have heard her speak of Bassam to Scheherazade. Or worse, Amir had been gossiping about the family. "And we must find the key, and I must call Ibrahim before I . . ."

Fatima stopped. There would be no dying tonight. Amir handed her his cane.

"First, look outside the window," Amir told her.

"Later, *habibi,*" Fatima promised. "I'm so tired."

He was always seeking excuses to leave her, and she had just given him one. But he did not take it. Instead, he took her hand and led her to the window. He pointed over the SUV at the fig tree.

"Without your faraway glasses, you probably can't see it," Amir said. "But there's a fig on the tree."

"I'm not in the mood for your acting nonsense," Fatima reprimanded him.

Scheherazade leaned down from the eucalyptus tree and cupped the tiny green and pink fruit in her hand for Fatima to see better. Fatima's hand went to her heart.

"Ibrahim said he was sure it could bloom one day in America," Fatima said, almost breathless. "No one back home — I mean in Detroit — believed him."

Their Lebanese friends had told Ibrahim that he would have to go to California if he wanted the tree to flourish, but he had said that California was even farther away than Detroit from real figs. Fatima reached her hand out the window as if to grab the fig, and the sun on her arms warmed her spirits. Then she reached for the phone. Ibrahim would not believe this. But the static on the line was too much. She hung up and started to dial again when a beat-up Honda Civic covered in bumper stickers sputtered to a halt in front of the house.

"Jesus Christ, please let that sad thing move on," Amir groaned.

It did not. Instead, Soraya emerged from it, beads and bangles jangling like Scheherazade's. She looked up at them and blew kisses.

"I'm here." Soraya waved. "I love you, Mom."

"God, I hate it when she says that for no reason," Fatima said, and hung up the phone. "It makes me feel like I'm going to die." Then she remembered that she wasn't.

The Abdullahs

Soraya waved as the Honda Civic sputtered off.

"The least you could do in your life is drive American to make her happy," Amir said as he emerged from the house.

"Don't talk about Rob's car in that tone of voice unless I break up with him." Soraya laughed, but all Amir could muster in response was half a smile. She purposefully frowned as she pointed at Fatima's window. "Yes, we should be serious. How is she doing?"

"You were just here four days ago and didn't even want to see her."

"Well, that was before I was sure," Soraya said. "You know, about —"

Mother and son were distracted by a blue Ford Taurus that stopped in front of them, moved ahead, and then paused and reversed. A fifty-something head peeked out.

"Soraya?" Hala said.

"Hala?" Soraya replied after a closer inspection.

Hala parked next to the SUV. The two sisters were embracing when two other sisters pulled up: Nadia in a new Ford Focus and Randa in a black Cadillac.

Falling in line behind the Cadillac was a

Dodge pickup with Pennsylvania plates. Miriam got out of the truck with the assistance of a rotund man. As she limped toward Amir and Soraya with her brave martyr's smile, she nearly was hit in the center of the street when a Lincoln Town Car braked hard in front of her.

Bassam leaped out of the driver's seat. "Sorry about that, ma'am," he said to Miriam.

He opened the passenger door for Lena. "Oh, it's you, Miriam," Lena said. "Look, Bassam, it's Miriam."

Bassam took a few seconds to recognize these middle-aged women as his sisters. "Huh, what do you know?" he said. "Just like in life, Lena and I are always the last to arrive."

Fatima's two youngest were surrounded by their older sisters, all hugging and sniffing for alcohol.

Amir watched these people he had come to know through Fatima's nightly stories to herself. As an only child, Amir had never had a chance to experience sibling rivalry, but he witnessed it now as the sisters pulled apart to examine how much each had aged since the last time they had seen one another, who had lost her figure, and who looked like she worried about money the least.

Amir was not standing alone in observing the family.

"Nice to see them all together like that," the rotund man commented. "Miriam's always talking about how much she's suffered without them. Hello, I'm Walt Smith."

"Right on," Amir said. "Yoo-hoo, ladies and gent. I'm Amir. *Ahlan wa Sahlan.* Welcome."

He waved as he heard "e-mail" and "thank you" come at him.

"And I'm Miriam's —" Walt began.

"Boss." Miriam sighed. "Walt, this is my brother Bassam, and these are my sisters, Hala, Soraya, Lena, Nadia, Randa — wait a minute. One of us is missing."

They all began counting out their birth order to figure out who was not there. It took only a second. The oldest.

"Laila," Lena said.

They all bowed their heads.

"I left her a message about a 'living with cancer' project we're doing at the U," Hala said. "It has a great list of ideas."

"I flew through Detroit today," Randa jumped in. "I thought about calling her."

"I got the answering machine this morning," Lena told her.

573

"Me, too." Nadia nodded.

"This was the first time I'd ever flown to Detroit," said Miriam, who had never even driven back since her marriage to Joseph Yusef. "I should have called Laila. My foot hurt, though."

They all murmured in sympathy, and Miriam heaved one more sigh.

"I didn't call, either," Soraya said. "I mean, I just couldn't tell Laila."

"Tell Laila what?" Amir said.

"About Mom," Bassam answered. "Thanks for letting us know, kid."

"Know what?" Amir demanded.

"That last e-mail sounded so angry," Randa explained. "So I went back to the e-mail with the attachment and opened it. Usually, I don't like to open attachments. Viruses, y'all."

The others shuffled and nodded. "I e-mailed your mother that you were playing some sick joke with Photoshop, making it look like Mom had cut off her hair," Randa continued. "But Soraya said she'd had a vision of Mom just like that."

"Decimal confirmed it," Hala added. "We knew she wouldn't cut her hair off unless . . ."

"My son's in Iraq, my sister's in remission, and my mother's dying," Miriam

574

sobbed as Walt put an arm around her.

"You're all here because she cut her hair and now you think she's dying? You couldn't come to visit her because she was alive?" Amir asked. The siblings shuffled their feet. "Jesus Christ, you guys suck. Sorry to have wasted your time, but she's just going crazy."

"She'd have to be the dying kind of crazy to cut off her hair," Nadia said.

As Amir prepared his reply, he could find supporting evidence only for Nadia's claim: talk of the underwear drawer, Mr. Kim's funeral instructions, blabber about quickly marrying him off and burial plots, her secret walks at night, the cheap makeup fit for a wake, even though Muslims didn't do wakes. Maybe the Arab funeral circuit hadn't just been to have a social life.

"Y'all, I sent Dina to go check on that house in that village just so Mom could relax before . . . you know." Randa breathed deeply.

"The house? Is Tayta right?" Amir said. "You all came here because you want her to give you that house before she goes?"

"Not me," Soraya protested. "I envision several gigs over the next few years."

"I'm a loser, so count me out," Bassam said.

The others were preparing equally valid reasons when a black Mercedes double-parked in front of the SUV. Darcy Dagrout, a woman made attractive by her designer clothes, jumped out, forehead furrowed in a way capable of destroying any Botox treatment.

"You Judas," she screamed at Amir.

"Jesus Christ!" Amir said. "Not Judas."

"When were you going to tell me?" Darcy said.

"Tell you?" Amir said. "Jesus Christ is the role of a lifetime, and you didn't even call me for it."

"Why didn't you tell me that's who you saw yourself as?" Darcy said.

"I take in my sick grandmother who thinks I have no earthly father. I'm single with lots of male friends. I drive a Honda Civic in West Hollywood. How's that for humility?" Amir shouted. "Yet you didn't think I could do Jesus."

"I looked at all that as humiliating, not humility," Darcy shouted back.

"There are a whole a lot of other disciple roles I've missed out on," Amir snapped, "because *you* didn't see the big upswing in churchgoing. Everyone's doing it since 9/11. Jesus Christ, it's all over the news."

"My granddaughter graduated from her

third Bible study," Miriam confirmed.

"If you thought you could pull off Jesus, you should have thrown a hissy fit or something so that I would have listened to you," Darcy said. "Why did I have to find out that you wanted to be Jesus from the FBI?"

"The FBI?" the Abdullahs said in unison, each unconsciously taking a step away from Darcy.

"Yes, some Little Miss Agent came asking me yesterday what 'role' you were rehearsing at the moment. She seemed a little concerned when I said I didn't see myself getting any big 10 percent from you anytime soon," Darcy said. "That's when I conducted my own investigation. But another G-man type got to the director first and scared him shitless, so the director informed me that he was going to rework the casting. If you'd gone through me, I'd have diverted the FBI to another audition."

"The role's not mine anymore?" Amir said. The presence of all these people here for his dying grandmother was the only reason he did not lunge at Darcy, although his insides rattled.

"That's what happens when you try to save 10 percent," Darcy said.

Then a voice from above spoke. "Who wouldn't try to save 10 percent?" Fatima demanded from her bedroom window, angered by the sorrow she had heard when this woman had told Amir he had lost his hobby.

The Abdullah brood on the lawn looked up at Fatima, who was leaning out the window with a scrawny girl at her side. Fatima's children took a step back from the house as they saw her purple stubs. They crashed into one another until they were clinging together, the live view of her missing hair being even more disturbing than Amir's photo attachment.

"Tayta, please," Amir groaned. "I can't take —"

Fatima held up her hand. She took in the people hovering near the fig tree. Could this be? All here? There was Bassam's dimple. She counted her daughters as they stared at her. "Randa? Lena? Hala? Nadia?" she said. "Miriam? Oh, you are almost all here."

She looked up at the eucalyptus tree, where Scheherazade smiled at her. "*Ya Allah,* my children."

Fatima saw all of those people on Amir's lawn as the chubby-cheeked babies she had bathed in the laundry sink in Detroit, babies who now had been adults decades longer than they had been her responsibility. She did not dwell on the one who was not present. Since she herself was going to live, she would ask Laila to come visit later.

"Are they not beautiful?" she asked Scheherazade.

"Why is she talking to the tree?" Randa fretted.

"At least she's not talking to herself," Amir replied. "The tree's an improvement."

"Who are those people coming out of the handsome neighbor boy's new jumbo car?" Fatima asked.

All turned to follow Fatima's gaze as Sherri Hazad and her partner put their hands on their holsters, using their free hands to hold up their badges.

"Hello, Mrs. Abdullah," Sherri Hazad said. Fatima looked from Scheherazade in the tree to Sherri Hazad and gasped. *Ya Allah.* This was the one she had spoken to of making love to her husbands? *Ya Allah, ya Allah.* How, even without her faraway glasses, had she confused them? Preparing for her funeral had cost her too much common sense. "Amir Abdullah, I'm Agent Hazad, and this is my partner, Agent Ramsey. We'd just like to ask you a couple of questions. Standard procedure."

"That's her," Darcy whispered. "The FBI agent. At first, I thought her badge was a prop, but it's not."

579

"Jesus Christ," Amir fumed. "Jesus Christ, he was my big break. I lost it because of these guys?"

"As Karl Marx said, 'For the bureaucrat, the world is a mere object to be manipulated by him,' " Nadia muttered.

"Professor Abdullah, I'm sorry you feel that way," Sherri Hazad said to Nadia. "Your classes were so invaluable to my training. If it weren't for you, I probably wouldn't be where I am today. Do you remember me from your honors Modern Arabic Colloquial Dialects? Class of '97."

Nadia took another step back.

"Can my granddaughter come down, please?" Hala said.

"Hala, the girl is getting more innocent," Fatima said, putting her arm around Decimal. "Recite the Koran. *Yallah*."

"*Bismillah el-Rahman el Raheem,*" Decimal began.

"I have friends high up in the ACLU," Nadia interrupted. "I'm sure this is an invasion of civil rights."

"Professor Abdullah, you have all my respect, but let's not mention your son Zade," Sherri Hazad said. "A dating service and yet he's dateless? And he goes international when he has such a large client base to work from right here with his family."

The siblings looked at one another, searching for a logical explanation for the four generations of bad luck in love gathered before the FBI.

"How can this be legal?" Randa said by way of an answer.

"It's called the Patriot Act, and it's as legal as, say, changing your name from Bashar to Bud," Sherri Hazad said. "The Patriot Act gives us the right to question and conduct sneak and peek searches. Even if all we find is undocumented domestic help, Mrs. Bitar."

"God, Randa, this is your elitist fault," Nadia said. "Clean your own bathroom."

"Bathrooms," Randa corrected. "I have six because I'm a hardworking American."

"We had a report of suspicious behavior from this residence, some speculative information on a young Arab male," Sherri Hazad explained. "The source said they had seen comings and goings at strange times by Mr. Abdullah in various disguises and of a Fatima Abdullah, sometimes wearing a scarf, sometimes not, talking in the garden to an unidentifiable individual, possibly under the influence of cocaine and other unidentified narcotics. That's something we need to be looking into in this day of terrorism, you understand."

Amir looked over at his spurned lover, who waved and smiled from his porch. It had taken him three years, but he'd gotten him good. However, nothing Amir had ever done to him deserved taking away the one dream he worked so hard for, the chance to actually have a starring role, to be somebody besides the unemployed guy who lived with his grandmother in the house his weird mother had bought him.

"So why were you investigating my son and me?" Nadia said.

"Just as part of Mr. Abdullah's family," Sherri Hazad explained.

"We barely even know him," Hala protested.

"I do," Soraya corrected.

"My husband died for this country," Miriam wailed.

"Funny, then, that you have a dartboard with his picture on it," Sherri Hazad replied. "Anyone could see you throwing darts at it if they peeked in at the right time of night."

"Miriam," Walt exclaimed, expressing everyone's surprise.

"You don't know what he was like," Miriam said. "You just care that he was a war hero."

"He willingly married you, Miriam," Soraya reminded her.

"Don't be so hard on her, Ms. Abdullah," Sherri Hazad said. "It's really no different than you going for gigs in places like Tijuana so you can experiment with and sell antiaging creams that are not FDA approved here. Or like the professor trolling the high-end jewelry websites from her son's office — and after everything you told us about the abuse of diamond workers in South Africa. And it's no worse than your brother purposely losing at cards, which is half-assed, backward illegal. Or poor Lena here who ends up lending her last boyfriend money for a pyramid scheme that lands him in jail. At least all of you had your family to support you through that. Me, I'm an only child."

Sherri Hazad didn't see that Fatima's children might as well have been raised as only children for all they knew about one another. Questions punctuated with hurt floated among them.

"Lena, I could have been there for you," Bassam said. But Lena shook her head.

"You could have relocated to Minneapolis, Miriam," Hala said. "I would have helped you."

"But then you would have known," Miriam answered. The others nodded, for indeed pride and the facades they had put

583

up for Fatima had extended to one another.

"Mr. Abdullah, we'd like to take you to the field office for some questioning," Sherri Hazad said.

"Jesus Christ," Amir mumbled, as unaware of his aunts and uncle all looking away from one another as he was of Fatima looking from one of her children to the others and then back again with a heart that suddenly weighed too much. "Jesus Christ."

"I'm . . . I'm . . . dying tonight," Fatima announced, lying about something that she had thought for the last 1001 days was a truth she was hiding. She suddenly didn't want Amir to leave her alone with her children and their secrets, these strangers of her flesh. "I want to die in Amir's arms. It's the last thing I'll ever ask him to do, and do you want him to not do the last thing his grandmother will ever ask him to do?"

Bassam turned to Sherri Hazad's partner. "My mother's impending death is fucking setting me a little on edge," he began. Fatima lowered her hearing aid and covered Decimal's ears until Bassam was done. "Don't take my goddamn sobriety away from me. I can still fucking blame others, and I will blame you. Do you want it on your head if she dies without the one person she wants near her? The rest of us are just fucking filler."

"*Ya ibni,* stop," Fatima begged. She looked at Scheherazade in the tree again to apologize for what she called Bassam's fucking language. But Scheherazade was gone.

"You can't know that she's dying," Sherri Hazad said. She turned to Amir. "Or can you?"

"Agent Hazad," her partner cautioned her as he reemerged from the SUV. "I just got off the phone with D.C. We've got a little bureaucratic snafu here."

"See," Fatima said to Darcy. "Go get Amir back his hobby."

"Tayta, please," Amir began, but could not continue. What if this really was the end of Fatima annoying him at least seven times a day? Grandson was the only role he played as second nature, a role that had filled up his life. As much as he fantasized about being free of Fatima, she was the only person who had never left him, like it or not.

"You have been destined to be Jesus since before you were born, and it should be yours," Fatima said. "No Sheikh Sabeer in tights. Go get it for him, miss."

"I would if I could." Darcy sighed. "But all this FBI talk got the film a lot of buzz. The whole A-list wants to do the part for scale now."

"I'm afraid there's not much we can do about Jesus," Sherri Hazad's partner apologized while reading his BlackBerry. "But on the upside, it looks like we don't need to question you any further due to that snafu I mentioned."

"You better question the hell out of me after costing me that part," Amir said.

"Sorry, but there's not much need to," Sherri Hazad's partner said. "Just got word that we already had all of you checked out a couple of years ago when a Mrs. Randy Bitar offered to assist us with interviewing the Arab-American community in Houston. Guess you didn't notice us that time."

Sherri Hazad turned as red as the stripes of the American flag to which her grandfather the peddler had pledged his citizenship. "I do apologize for any inconvenience to your phones due to an unforeseen glitch we're having with the phone company involved," she murmured. "Let's just let the illegal creams, diamonds, gambling, and what have you go. So you all go inside and have a great little reunion until . . . well, best of luck to you, Mrs. Abdullah, whatever you decide to do tonight. Good day."

The FBI agents and Darcy watched as seven of Fatima's children — and Walt — shuffled into the house, trying to avert their eyes from one another, particularly Randa.

"I wasn't really going to go to work for them," Randa explained to them. "I just didn't want anyone thinking Bud and I were terrorists, but then I realized by offering to help them I would let the neighbors find out that we were Arabs, and that just was worse than offering to be patriotic."

Fatima shook her head and looked at her other children. It had taken her impending funeral to bring them together. But there would be no funeral. She hoped they would not be disappointed. She was flattered that they all had wanted to come. But mostly she was sad that they had so many secrets from her — and from one another.

FATIMA

With her children surrounding her, Fatima propped herself on an embroidered pillow, ostensibly to die. Fatima wished they'd all stop looking at what was no longer there: her hair. She reached up to twirl a strand, momentarily forgetting its absence herself, and that was when she decided that she would not tell her children right away that she wasn't dying. Why spoil the moment by confusing them, especially when their own lives were more confusing than any mother should have to hear about?

"Stop staring, all of you," she demanded. "I put my hair away for Laila."

She smiled at her children and kept smiling, which undoubtedly was disturbing to them all. Decimal fluffed Fatima's pillows for her, just as Scheherazade always did.

"Your dress is very pretty, Mom," Soraya said. "It's nice to see you in something other than that dreadful robe."

"It's yours when I'm gone," Fatima told her. Her children shifted uncomfortably, able neither to deny nor to accept her reference to her death.

"It's from Lebanon," Nadia finally commented. "I recognize the embroidery."

"I work with a lot of drivers born all over the Middle East," Bassam offered. "We all have the same name. How's that for Arab unity, Nadia?"

"We've done some amazing surgeries on injured Iraqi children at the hospital," Hala threw in.

"Rock is in Iraq building schools and bridges," Miriam reminded her.

"I worked with Tony Shalhoub on a TV show at the network a couple of years back," Lena reported.

"If I could almost be Jesus, I could almost be the next Omar Sharif," Amir said with distinctly false hope.

"Dina sent me pillows like your dress," Randa added as her siblings took one more step away from her. "I arranged them around the papier-mâché longhorn she made in fifth grade."

Yes, Fatima thought, Ibrahim and I raised children who only tell us things that make us happy. Her children treated her the way she had treated Ibrahim after the boys had gone, with silence that was supposed to be comforting — supposed to. But as parents, she and Ibrahim had not gone out of their way to make the children happy, as Millie had with her kids. Millie once had said that her children's happiness was more important than anything else, even more important than their becoming doctors or lawyers. Fatima had not seen the difference.

"It's only sixty-seven degrees outside, and it's June," Hala broke into the dead air.

"I can't believe Minneapolis is warmer than L.A. right now," Lena ventured.

"When we left New Castle today, the mosquitoes were out in full force," Miriam added. "They say it might hit a record high this summer."

"Texas is about the same but humid," Randa said just as her cell phone rang. "Hello . . . Dina . . . Dina . . . hello . . .

dang it . . . I lost her. See, I'm the one —
yes, me — trying to get through to Lebanon.
I'm the one willing to make a phone call to
the Middle East on my tapped phone."

Randa went to the hallway in search of
reception — and in search of redeeming
herself.

"The same thing happened when your dad
tried to call today," Fatima told the others.
"I tried calling him twice yesterday, but the
line kept cutting out."

"Oh crap. Jiddo," Amir remembered.
"Wait a minute."

As Amir ran downstairs, Fatima waited
for the others to tell her that they had talked
to Ibrahim, but they stared out the window
instead at the FBI's SUV. Fatima looked for
Scheherazade at the windowsill or in the
eucalyptus tree, but all she saw was the little
fig on the fig tree.

"Vegas had a nice breeze going today,"
Bassam said, and Lena nodded.

Fatima's children began to fidget, devoid
of weather reports, *alhamdulilah.* "The
weather in Deir Zeitoon is perfect," Fatima
informed them. "And I'm sure you all want
to know who I'm going to leave the house
in Lebanon to."

They all mumbled "no" and did not look
her in the eye. "Oh, I wish I could give the

house to all of you. But I don't want you to fight when I'm gone," Fatima said. "A house cannot be divided eight ways. I want you to become friends forever. You are supposed to be friends; you're supposed to tell each other things. That is why it would be easier for me to give the house to just one of you. Blame me rather than each other for any unfairness. I'll already be dead."

"I'd probably be gunned down with my husband." Nadia sighed. "So you should give the house to someone else."

"I know, *habibti,*" Fatima said. "But I am leaving you Mama's letters instead. Maybe you can read one for us today."

"Sure, and Zade is getting a bride for Amir very, very soon," Nadia added.

"There is no need," Fatima said.

"Because I love Tiffany," Amir told them as he came back in carrying the envelope from Ibrahim.

"And I love Candy," Bassam told Fatima. "But look, Mom, I'm not marrying her. Haven't even asked. Just going to try the dating thing for a change."

"Don't take too long about it," Fatima advised. "Otherwise, people are going to think you're gay."

Fatima could not take back the word, having spoken it loudly enough that it had shocked her children nearly as much as her purple stubs had.

"Tayta, you said . . ." Amir smiled.

Fatima held up her hand. "Amir, you cannot have Tiffany or the house," she said. Those chosen to play a divine prophet do not inherit earthly possessions. Nor do they marry. He belonged to the world, not just one woman. "*Ya Allah,* what has become of my world?"

Her children had no answer to that question. Aside from nice weather reports and Arabic heritage platitudes, none of them had much experience comforting her. They had left that job to Ibrahim and Millie and later Amir, completely skipping their generation. They looked at her purple stubs until Randa returned, ear still pressed to the cell phone.

"Mom, Dina is in Deir Zeitoon," she announced. "She has a woman with her that was born in the village. Can I tell her where to take Dina?"

"Take her where?" Nadia said, the others not quite trusting Randa, either.

"Tell her she's looking for the house with the terra-cotta roof, wood-burning stove, the cedar closets, and the four marble steps that lead to the top," Decimal said. "And the garden with lavender and jasmine and the fig trees all with figs."

This latecomer in Fatima's life knew more about the house than her own children did, which made them all bow their heads.

"Yes, the house is three houses down from the blacksmith's," Fatima said.

"Mom, he may have gone out of business in the last seventy years," Randa pointed out.

"No," Fatima said. "Otherwise, who would sharpen the plow blades and make the pots and pans for the new brides' homes?"

"Fine," Randa said. Everyone watched what Fatima thought was the ritual of mother-daughter banter that her girls had not known with her. In reality, Dina was telling Randa that Deir Zeitoon was congested with Internet cafés and beeping cars.

"It sounds so charming." Randa smiled into the phone.

"Did she find the blacksmith?" Fatima said, anxious.

Randa began to repeat as much of the truth as she could. "The blacksmith closed his shop fifty years ago, when all his sons went to America," she reported. "They own a hot dog shop in Cleveland."

"Tell Dina to go to any Abdul Aziz home," Fatima suggested. "There's one just past the *ducan:* the vegetable seller's, opposite the tailor's place."

"The lady with her says there aren't any Abdul Aziz in the village," Randa relayed.

"What is this woman's name?" Fatima asked. "Is she the Mansour lady?"

"Reema Jawad," Randa said.

"There are no Jawads in our village," Fatima replied. "Is Dina sure she's in the right village? Can she see the fountain in the town center?"

Randa nodded. It was no longer the town center and no longer had water anyone would dare drink, but Dina had seen it.

"My cousin Jamila Abdullah lives two blocks toward the mountains from the fountain," Fatima said. "Jamila means 'pretty' in Arabic, but she was ugly. She had a black mole on the back of her neck."

Randa shook her head as she listened to Dina. "I'm sorry," she said. "There is no Jamila Abdullah there. She remembers an old lady with a wart on her nose who moved away fifteen years ago. Could that be who you're thinking of?"

Fatima shook her head. "That must have been Aida Dumani," she said. "Whatever happened to her? And her sister Dalal. I wonder if she ever married. She was jilted by a boy who left her for America."

"Dina says Aida died at her son's house in

Beirut five years ago," Randa reported after hanging up with her daughter. "And her sister Dalal finally married a man who worked in Sierra Leone and moved to Africa. Dina needs to go back to Beirut. She has work tomorrow."

"She'll find the house next time," Fatima said. "Remember when they put in the Fairlane Mall and your father got lost in the snowstorm because the new bus routes blocked off his usual roads? Well, it's like that. Oh, my poor Aida. She was such a nice girl. Like Millie, but without the cigarettes and English."

The only person who laughed was Walt. "You must be the Jewish man," Fatima said, and turned to Miriam. "Marry him and be happy for just once in your life."

"I would never never marry someone Jewish, as long as you live," Miriam promised. "I wouldn't do that to you."

"Miriam, stop making me tired. You think I have to be dead for you to be honest — and happy? Is that your excuse?" Fatima said, and looked to her other children, who all looked at the floor.

"The weather here is so darn sunny, even if it is colder than Minnesota," Hala offered.

"No mosquitoes," said Miriam. "Cool and . . ."

Miriam tried to find more weather words and looked to Walt for assistance. "Did you tell her about how low the pollen count was this spring?" he suggested.

"*Ya Allah,* who will you keep abreast of the weather when I am gone?" Fatima asked her somber children. "And when I'm gone, will you ever laugh when you think of me?"

"We never laugh at you, Mom," Soraya vowed.

"I meant laugh in a good way," Fatima said. "Like before. Do you remember before?"

She did not have to tell them that she meant before the boys died. She reached for a purple stub as she waited for one of her children to speak. At last, one did.

"Remember, Bassam, how we took Amir with us to the zoo and pretended he was our kid so we could get in on the parents and kids free day but we told Mom we were going to the library?" Lena said.

"Hala and I used to do that all the time with you and Bassam," Nadia said.

"Or remember when Laila used to use my limp to get people's sympathy to let you into places for free?" Miriam sighed.

"How about the time Millie told Mom that she was taking us all to the drive-in, but she actually took us to the school dance so that I could slow dance with Jack Kelly?" Randa laughed.

That Millie, Fatima thought. I'm going to kill her when I do get to heaven.

"Remember how Dad used to buy Mom a new pink robe every few years and then switch it out when she wasn't looking? When she'd figure it out, she'd tell him that we weren't the Rockefellers and want him to take it back." Nadia smiled. "He'd tell her we might not be Rockefellers but she didn't have to dress like their laundry woman."

"Randa, remember how we would be pretending to write sonnets for homework, but we were actually writing love letters to Mr. Johnson, that dreamy drama coach?" Nadia giggled.

"The best was when we stole Mom's Avon samples," Randa said, and bent down to wipe the flaking makeup off Fatima. "Then we'd put the makeup on at school."

"And Mom told us that if we kissed a boy, we'd get pregnant." Nadia smirked. "So we all vowed that if we accidentally kissed a boy, we would marry him."

This sent them all into laughter until they remembered that Fatima still believed this of them.

"Remember when Laith and Riyad pooled

their money together with the Greek kids down the block and got the old Mercedes to impress the chicks?" Randa said, imitating teenage boys. "Dad got all union on them about how German cars were destroying American jobs."

They all laughed until they recalled Fatima was in the room while they had spoken of the twins.

"Remember when Laila made us turkey for Thanksgiving?" Bassam blurted out. "It was so dry, but we all kept chewing it because that's what Randa told us real Americans do."

Her children laughed again, extra hard to compensate for having mentioned the boys. But Fatima did not mind hearing her boys' names. She was glad that these living children seemed to have gotten away with some happiness and that today they could recall that it had been with one another. Bassam's laughter echoed Ibrahim's rolling chuckles, which barely had been heard in decades. Fatima pictured Ibrahim sneaking in the pink robes, the way he always warned her that Millie was working against them, and the way he had gnawed his way through Laila's turkey.

Fatima joined her children in laughing and couldn't stop. It had been too many years since they had let the worst day of their lives separate them. This would be as good a time as any to tell them that she wasn't going to die today, that they had more time together.

"That's it, kids, I'm leaving it up to your father to decide which one of you trouble-makers to leave the house to," Fatima began. "But —"

"Tayta, Jiddo told me to make sure you read this," Amir interrupted and handed her Ibrahim's letter. "I think it's why he kept calling. It's all in Arabic. So I think he wanted to tell you what it said over the phone, but the FBI jacked his line in Detroit so badly, we couldn't hear him well enough."

"Why didn't you fax it to me?" Nadia said. "I would have read it."

"Why didn't you come visit?" Amir answered.

Nadia snatched the letter and opened it. She bit her lip harder and harder as she read. Then she looked at her mother.

"He just wanted to say hi and tell you that he found an old letter from your friend Aida, the one Dina said had died," Nadia explained. "It doesn't matter, though, since she's already gone."

"Read me Aida's letter with all the words," Fatima ordered. "That must be her handwriting, because it is not Ibrahim's, and it says more than hi."

Nadia shook her head. "How about I read you one of your mom's letters?"

"Read it to me," Fatima insisted. "Show me the education you could have gotten from your father for free. *Yallah*, let's go. Read."

Nadia shook her head again. "Do you prefer your FBI student to read it for me?" Fatima demanded.

Nadia breathed deeply and began. It took Fatima a moment to get around the sound of such perfect yet accented classical Arabic coming from her own child.

"April 4, 1989. Bismillah al-Rahman al-Raheem, *In the name of God the most merciful. Dear Sister Fatima. I hope God keeps you and your family safe in America. I am writing to you to tell you that I am moving to Beirut. The war was very bad again this year, after a few years of some calm, and my arthritis is also bad. I will go to Beirut to live with my son, who is now a plastic surgery doctor. I think of you every day, my sister, and hope that your daughters and the son that remains with you are in good health. I am sorry you did not see the house again. When Ibrahim came here after your sons died, I had just lost my arm in the bomb blast at the Rashid*

600

bakery. Do you remember it, the one across from the old tailor's shop? It was hard for me to get around then, but now I am used to it. My son tells me of fake arms I could get, but I was lucky enough compared to those who lost two. It was so terrible when Ibrahim came here and found that everyone in both your families had either died or fled. As you know, Ibrahim came in the worst year. He was here just as it was all destroyed, and I'm sure it must have broken your heart more than it already was when he told you Deir Zeitoon was one of the first villages ravaged by the war. But things are better, al-hamdulilah. I passed where your house used to be the other day. They plan to build a hotel there. People say that if the war stops, Lebanon will be a tourist place again, especially for the rich Persian Gulf people. They'll buy beach and mountain villas, like they used to after you left but before the troubles began. Below is my address in Beirut and my telephone number. When you come back home, please call me and I will talk about the happy days and our departed mothers and sisters. With God's blessings, I am your faithful sister, Aida."

Fatima's blood chilled across her body. She stared at nothing as Nadia translated for the others. When Nadia finished, Fatima turned her head away from her children and looked out the window, where Scheherazade still had not returned to the eucalyptus tree.

Ibrahim had come back from Lebanon thirty years ago, after going there to escape the death of their sons. He had told Fatima that Deir Zeitoon and the house were unharmed in the civil war. She had remarked then that if the whole family had gone back to Lebanon as they once had promised one another, their boys would have lived. He had told her not to be silly. It was the first time he had insulted her like that. From then on, she had felt that his duty to her — and to Marwan's memory — should be over. The boys had looked just like her. It was her turn to oblige him for all he had done for her by removing a painful reminder, namely, herself. She had just not known how to end the marriage because he was the only person who was part of her past, present, and future, who could laugh with her about the Sadeq family's overrun rabbit farm in Deir Zeitoon or commiserate with her about Millie's husband. She had told herself to stay until Bassam, Lena, and Amir were grown so that they would have a father around. For all those years, Ibrahim had known that all of them — not just the boys — would have perished if they had returned to Lebanon.

His obligation to her had always been love, something she had never acknowledged, perhaps out respect for Marwan, perhaps because words of love were not things Ibrahim spoke and she hadn't dared presume that the words nonetheless existed inside this man who had rescued her from being a pregnant widow in a country whose language she still did not speak. But most likely he did not say anything because he had not known that she wasn't just grateful to him. After all, she hadn't told him otherwise. Still, he had loved her beyond all other truths, so much so that he had built a whole story about the care of a house long gone. She would not mention the letter when she talked with him next. She would tell him of the fig tree fruiting, no matter how many times the telephone cut out.

Her children had always given her somewhere to focus away from Ibrahim, as they did at this moment. For when Fatima looked up, Laila stood at the doorway.

"Oh, my Laila," Fatima breathed.

Laila slowly absorbed that she was the last of her siblings to walk into this room in Los Angeles. "You are all here?" she said.

Randa not so subtly mouthed, "Mom's very, very sick."

"Don't listen to them, Laila," Fatima said. "You just take care of yourself. How's Detroit? Your boys? Anyone getting married?"

Laila shook her head, and Fatima knew that for all her children would tell her, all of Laila's sons could have gotten divorced last week. Bassam grabbed a chair for Laila and Amir led her to it, but Laila chose to sit on the bed. She took Fatima's hand, which was nearly as sinewy as Ibrahim's had been when she had held it in her hand a week before.

"Mama," Laila said. "Baba has been visiting me almost every other day for the past week."

"Oh," Fatima said. She was glad he was making an effort to visit his one daughter still in Detroit. "Does he know about your . . . you know . . ."

"No, Mama," Laila said. "I'm fine. Really. So fine that he even encouraged me just the other day to come visit you."

"Oh," Fatima said.

"Anyway, every Wednesday and Friday afternoon, Baba takes a nap and then goes to the airport," Laila continued.

"Yes, I know," Fatima said. "To see the passengers from Lebanon."

"Last night he did not come to our house

for dinner on the 8:22 bus as he said he would," Laila told her. "I called him at home, but he did not answer. I drove to the house and could not find him. I waited and waited until a bus driver named Dwayne came to my house and told me that Baba had fallen asleep on the bus and never gotten up."

Fatima's children's eyes welled with hers, but no one let out loud sobs, not even Miriam. Just as Ibrahim had not made many waves in their lives when he was living, he had passed out of them like a calm storm, easy to avoid but still powerful. His children's sadness was as deep as if he had been close to them, as if he had been Randa's typical American dad fantasy. Her husband had been loved by so many children yet left alone on a bus at the end, a bus that took him twice a week to a place where he once imagined his children would have stayed near him, even lived next door, if not in the same house. For 1001 days and nights she, too, had left him alone.

"Remember how Baba called Mr. Ford a VIP? That's what Ghazi is at the mosque," Laila said. "Ghazi wants to bury him the Muslim way."

Fatima nodded. "You must bury him tomorrow."

"Okay," Laila said. "Ghazi will do it right. Next to the boys."

"Al hamdulilah," Fatima said.

Fatima looked at Amir's chrome clock. It read 11:05 P.M. In less than an hour, 1001 nights would have come and gone and her pulse felt stronger than ever. When she had thought that it was she whose days were literally numbered, she had felt strongly that she should not go back to Detroit, not force Ibrahim to take care of her as she died. But she had let him die alone. Why had she never even told herself that she felt more than gratitude for Ibrahim? It hadn't happened in one moment, but she had begun loving him a long, long time ago, of that she was sure.

"I will come home with you," Fatima decided. "I got this dress for his burial."

"I found this in his pocket," Laila said. She held up a rusty skeleton key.

"The key to my house," Fatima said, finally allowing herself to cry. She took it from Laila and slowly rubbed the cold metal in her hand, as if shining it. Some of the rust stuck to her hand, almost burning her palm. She stopped stroking it and held it still in her open palm. Her children looked at it with her. But the key did not do anything: It did not jump, it did not speak, it did not cry with her. It was warmed by her hand, and she felt all the power it had held over her. But it did not compare to these people she had nursed and fed.

She closed her fist around it. She knew that it was indeed her house that had been lost in Deir Zeitoon, not her children's, not even Ibrahim's. Her life as far as they were all concerned had begun in Detroit, just as theirs had. That was where she would let it end. It was where her funeral instructions had said she was to be buried all along.

Her children whispered to one another, all saying how they were going to go to Detroit the next day. Ibrahim must have wondered, as she had of her own postponed death, if any of their children would walk in his funeral in light of how little of their lives he had walked with them. She heard them making flight arrangements through the crackling phones. Yes, she and Ibrahim had been mostly lucky with their children. Luckier, she thought, than their children had been with their parents. Or maybe not. Who knew how they would have fared with different parents?

"Mama, one more thing," Laila said. "The other day Baba and I were eating grape leaves, and he told me that if anything happened, his will gives everything to you,

607

including the house in Detroit, and it would be your choice what to do with it when your time came."

FATIMA AND SCHEHERAZADE

With her children downstairs eating kibbe, Fatima hobbled to the dresser and opened the underwear drawer. She put the key to the house in Deir Zeitoon in with her hair for Laila, Mama's Koran for Randa, the key to the Mercury for Bassam, and Mama's letters for Nadia. Before they all left for Detroit, she would give them their inheritances. Lena also could take her wedding dress. Miriam would have to wait for her grandfather's cane until she was dead. Until then, she could use Ibrahim's. After Ibrahim's funeral, she would put on her pink robe again and give Soraya the dress.

If she eventually died in her robe, that would be fine, but she would not wear it or her usual funeral clothes to the farewell for her husband. She rarely had dressed up for him in this life, but she would now.

Fatima went to her underwear drawer and pulled out the only other house key whose grooves she could re-create without a locksmith.

"To whom will you leave this house in

Detroit?" Scheherazade asked, perched on the windowsill for the 1001st time. "How about —"

Fatima held up her hand. "Someone," she said. "Anyone."

"Inshallah," Scheherazade said.

"I thought he was best left with strangers' faces on the bus rather than endure my death — or presence," Fatima explained. "My face reminded of him of things he lost."

"And things he loved," Scheherazade said.

"Like me," Fatima said.

"I waited 1001 nights to hear you say that." Scheherazade smiled. "Sometimes love becomes an obligation, and at its best an obligation becomes love. Even to a house. But immortality — and what is immortality if not the continuation of our stories? — does not live in a house. People move on, and neighborhoods move with them. They don't exist without us. If we do bloom elsewhere, what stays behind is not home after so many years have passed."

"Why didn't you go to him for your stories?" Fatima said. "At least I had Amir's company. But he did not have me by his side, as he should have."

"Some people are storytellers, and some people, like Ibrahim, are story keepers," Scheherazade answered. "What would he and I have talked about all this time?"

Scheherazade heard attractive laughter outside and stuck her head out the window. She beckoned Fatima to join her. The homeless man with the dimple was dragging a garbage bag clanking with glass bottles as he talked and walked by himself past the house. Tomorrow, with her Avon, he could peddle something besides loneliness. She would leave the Avon at the MTA #4 bus stop for him in the morning.

Fatima looked across the fig tree at her children's parked cars. "They all came in American cars," she noted. "Ibrahim would have liked that."

"I wanted you to look at the laughter," Scheherazade said, and shifted Fatima's focus to Decimal as she watered the yard while Amir pruned the fig tree. Decimal squirted Sherri Hazad's SUV as it finally drove off.

"I would have spoken to Ibrahim again if it wasn't for that woman," Fatima said. "*Ya Allah,* at least someone protects this country."

Across the way, the ex–soap star slammed his door shut. "Kid, never screw over your neighbor," Amir advised Decimal. "It's just not nice."

"I wouldn't screw you over if we were

neighbors," Decimal promised. "Gosh, I hope when I get back Dr. Wang's not going to be hanging around too much on account of Gran crying on his shoulders about me."

"You know how you feel about Dr. Wang, that he doesn't like you? Well, that's how I felt about my grandfather, but I wouldn't be tough enough for Hollywood if it weren't for him because he just knew how to be tough about life," Amir told her. "Maybe your gramps is teaching you things, too, but you just don't know it yet. Not that my grandfather would have been proud of me today."

"I bet Jesus will come back to you," Decimal said. "You just got to have faith. And maybe your grandfather was proud of you. You don't know."

"That's the problem with dead people," Amir agreed. "It's too late to ask them. But kid, if you ever need to get away from your grandpa, just come hang out here with me for a few days. Bring the munchkin with you when it gets here."

"So who should I tell my kid we're visiting?" Decimal asked. "My first cousin once removed or my second cousin?"

"Beats me." He shrugged. "Amir will do. You know, kid, give me some time and I bet I could find you a really great guy."

Fatima shut the window. "*Inshallah,* they will stay friends, and she will come over sometimes for glassy mole, and they will talk and eat."

"Family lines are not as straight as they could be, but they are continuous," Scheherazade said. "Eventually enough generations pass through life and death that everyone's story begins *kan ma kan,* once upon time. When your story starts with that, your life becomes a fable to those with only a trace of your blood."

Scheherazade stood up and took Fatima's hands. She reached up for a moment to remove a smudge of Avon. She looked into her eyes long enough for Fatima to understand that it would be the last time. Then she kissed Fatima gently on both cheeks.

"You have revealed to me a story that is not the world's greatest story," Scheherazade said. "It was your collection of your greatest stories. May I share them with others?"

"*Inshallah,*" Fatima said.

"*Inshallah,*" Scheherazade replied.

Then, as suddenly as she had come into Fatima's life, Scheherazade departed from it. She tossed her maroon veil around her shoulders and disappeared out the window she had entered 1001 nights before. For the

612

last time, she flew over the blossoming fig tree, her eyes and hair still as rich and deep as those of a virgin bride, her bangles clanging, her rings shining, her smile sometimes wavering, her heart eternally beating.

ACKNOWLEDGMENTS

While Fatima was spellbound by Scheherazade, I will always be grateful for the enthusiasm and magic of my editor, Kate Kennedy, and the miracle of my wonderful agent, Jennifer Carlson. I am also indebted to the whole team at Shaye Areheart Books for their commitment to *The Night Counter.*

As I wrote this book, I was blessed with friends and family who offered invaluable feedback and support, particularly Cheryl Cain, Elizabeth Cullen, Natasha Ghoneim, Michelle Goodman, Barbara Hadden, Qevin Oji, Hisun Rim, Phaidra Speirs, Lan Tran, Mimi Younes, and Rachael Yunis. A huge shout-out to my Squaw Valley Girls — Myfanwy Collins, Emily Wiser, and Patricia Dunn — for plowing through the first draft and more. And Pat, thank you for the wisdom. I also thank Sangjin Lee for the heart he gave both me and the book.

I wish to acknowledge the research into

Arab American history done by Greg Orfalea, Michael Suleiman, and Evelyn Shakir, all authors of fine books and journal articles on the topic. I thank attorney Nawar Shora at ADC for the legal fact-checking on the Patriot Act and other matters.

There are many translations of *The Arabian Nights;* my quotes were taken from Husain Haddaway's *The Arabian Nights* (W. W. Norton, 1990).

This book began as a short story published in *MIZNA.* I was privileged to work on this novel at two of my favorite places on earth: Hedgebrook in Washington and the Mac-Namara Foundation in Maine. Finally, thank you PEN USA for all you do to open the world to writers who would otherwise be voiceless.

ABOUT THE AUTHOR

Born in Chicago, **Alia Yunis** grew up in the Midwest and the Middle East, particularly the Twin Cities and Beirut during its civil war. She is the recipient of a PEN Emerging Voices Fellowship and has worked as a filmmaker, and journalist in several countries. Her work has been published in a variety of anthologies and magazines. She splits her time between Los Angeles and Abu Dhabi, where she teaches at Zayed University.